BLUEGRASS IS MY SECOND LANGUAGE

A Year In The Life Of An Accidental Bluegrass Musician

John Santa

John Santa

Jostens

2505 Empire Drive

Winston-Salem, NC 27103

FIRST EDITION

Designed by JJ Love
Front cover and interior photographs, graphics by JJ Love
Back cover photograph by Ken Hackney
Map by Catherine Hackette

Printed on acid-free paper

Library of Congress Number 2007900661

Santa, John
Bluegrass is my Second Language: A Year in the Life of an
Accidental Bluegrass Musician / John Santa

ISBN 0-9779638-0-2

Printed in the United States of America by Jostens

Bluegrass is my Second Language

For John Santa and June Carpenter

Who became Mr. and Mrs. John Santa

And then became Mom and Dad

My sister and I could not have been more lucky

LEGAL STATEMENT

My lawyer says that since I have used real names in my story, I have to put a disclaimer in it.

So I am.

This is a work of fiction, any resemblance to any persons, living or dead, is purely coincidental.

But since this is a work of fiction, it's OK if I lie so I'm telling you that every single thing I wrote in this book happened and it happened just the way I told it and to the people who are named within.

John Santa

BLUEGRASS IS MY SECOND LANGUAGE

BOOK ONE

BOOK ONE

PROLOGUE

I am desperately trying to get my mandolin in tune.

This is no easy task, as there are about ten or twelve of us crammed in here, this tiny rectangle of a room. If I could manage to stretch my arms straight out to my sides without putting someone's eye out, I could just about reach the rough cut boards that act as high shelves on the plywood sheets that pass for walls. A cold rain is thrumming a steady rhythm on the corrugated tin roof and somewhere a space heater is pouring out heat, which is crazy because even though it's freezing outside, the sardines in this can are about to boil. And as if that isn't problem enough, there's another mandolin player about four guys in front of me, and HE'S trying to get in tune and he's WAY out of tune, not even in the neighborhood.

There's maybe three guys behind me and five or six stacked in front which makes the room a little less than fifteen, sixteen feet long with a claustrophobic low sloping ceiling, and we're all packed in about three or four across, barely enough room to cram ourselves in here, let alone the instruments we carry. The air is thick with a very odd mixture of sweat, a humid wet dog smell and a minimum of three different varieties of aftershave, Old Spice being the front-runner, at least to my olfactory assessment. Banjos are plinking, guitars are strumming and there's the low moan of a fiddle. It is a cacophony of random Bluegrass runs and fills as everyone is frantically trying to get in tune, to stabilize instruments still chilled from the ride and the load-in to this cramped little room. I am clutching my mandolin and an over night case that houses my harmonicas and extra strings. I feel pretty foolish. I literally don't know where we are, or who most of these people are, or what's going to happen next. All I know is that it's taken me almost 20 years to get here, and even though I feel like I stick out like a sore thumb, I am going to get in tune cause that's what the guitar player told me to do and that's what everyone else is doing. Finally the fiddle player (who has been plucking an 'A' string with his thumb for the past ten minutes) prevails and we get the hint and begin to tune to him. I'm almost there when the guitar player grins at me and says "Ready?" and before I can say "For what?" or "No!" a door to my left bursts open and we are all pushed through.

To my horror, I find myself standing on a stage.

Dear God, I can't be on stage: don't these people know Bluegrass is my second language???

This is all my lawyers fault.

Seriously.

She would call me up periodically and say, "My brother's going to be in town tonight or tomorrow or this weekend or whatever and you HAVE to get together. He does a lot of different music, but mostly he's a Bluegrass player and I think you guys would really enjoy playing together."

Now most musicians know when people say stuff like that, ninety-nine percent of the time these little get-togethers are about as successful as being set up for a blind date, which is to say they NEVER work. No matter how well intentioned, you walk away thinking who do these people think I am???? How could they think I could possibly be interested in that (fill in the blank here) person. And the same goes for musicians. But finally she cornered me and tempted me with the promise of a home cooked meal. That's the double whammy: plays to my bachelor AND musician sides.

Will Play For Food.

It was true when the cavemen beat on logs for a little Tyrannosaurus steak and it's still true to this day of pig pickin's and church suppers.

So I loaded up my gear and headed over to her house. I've been playing music since I was thirteen or fourteen, and I have been lucky enough to make a living from it. I started playing in bands like everyone else, but then I branched out into music for industrial videos and then film and commercials and TV shows. Along the way I acquired a lot of instruments and found myself to be the living embodiment of the old saying 'Jack of all trades, master of none.' That's generally meant as a derogatory remark, but in my case it has served me well. I play a bunch of instruments, some better than others, most fairly well, or at least well enough. You see, in my line of work, I don't have to be able to REALLY write classical music. If the scene demands a classical sounding score, I have to only SUGGEST it to be successful. So over the years I have written and played everything from harpsichords to jazz to Gregorian chants to Bluegrass. None of it was GREAT, but it didn't have to be. It only had to set the mood of the scene and time.

Luckily, I love music and listen to just about everything. If I don't know a type of music, I go to the library or the store, stock up on a bunch of scores and CD's and settle in to give my self a brief education. AND I get paid for it.

Bluegrass is my Second Language

Is this a great country or what?

Often in my work and musical travels I have needed to score or play some Bluegrass music. My bible for what Bluegrass music should sound and feel like has always been the "Will The Circle Be Unbroken" album by the Nitty Gritty Dirt Band. This collection of (at the time) old Bluegrass legends (and legends to be) and new hippie pickers (and legends to be) has, to me, always been the consummate example of how Bluegrass should be played and recorded.

I had another reason for liking this album as well: the harmonica playing on it is FANTASTIC. It exemplifies EXACTLY what Bluegrass harmonica should be in tone, color, phrasing and timing. Having been first bitten by the musical bug upon hearing Leadbelly, the famous blues guitarist and singer, it was not long before that infatuation led me to acts like Sonny Terry where I fell in love with his amazingly expressive harmonica. The origins and structures of blues and bluegrass are much closer than one might think on first sight, and my quest for more high quality harmonica players eventually lead me to Charley McCoy, a premier Nashville session player, and eventually to the "Circle" album.

So when I say Bluegrass is my second language, I mean that in the sense that it is not my first, my native tongue. While I have always had some affection and appreciation for Bluegrass, even a degree of affinity, it was not a language that flowed through my heart to my hands, but rather a syntax I struggled to speak with stammer and stutter.

All this is to say, I had some knowledge of Bluegrass, some familiarity with the form and thus, on that fateful evening, packed up my D35 Martin guitar, my mandolin, my Deering banjo, and of course, my harmonica kit which I kept in an old light blue over night bag (also sometimes called a train case) I stole from my mom years ago. And then for some reason, I put my cello in the car as well.

Figured what the heck....

The great thing about a cello is that it'll make ANYTHING sound good.

So I set out on the short drive around Chapel Hill to Jan's where she and her husband Carlie (he's a gourmet cook--she's nobody's fool) had prepared a little spread. To be honest with you, I don't remember what we ate or when. (I do remember it was good, VERY good: like I said, she ain't stoopid.) Since it was late spring of 2001 and the temperature was pretty mild and the humidity hadn't set in yet, I wasn't concerned about leaving my instruments in the car, so I took my guitar in with me to fulfill my contractual obligations and thus earn my supper, leaving the "just in case this turns out good" stuff outside.

I don't remember the meal or much of anything we talked about that evening.

Bluegrass is my Second Language

But I do remember that Jan's brother could flat out PLAY. There's obviously some music floatin in the Yarborough gene pool, and her brother Billy had spent a fair amount of time splashin around in it.

We sat across from each other there in the living room, each taking quiet stock of the other while we tuned up. Billy asked if I knew this one and he started to strum and one song followed the other as we fell in together and began our musical hike, finding our own rhythm as we ambled into an easy duet.

He had a kinda reedy tenor and was doing a bunch of old time songs and it wasn't long before I was saying, OK, OK, hold up on that one and then I would run out to my car and bring in the mandolin and play mandolin on whatever he was playing. And then I went out for the harmonicas and played mandolin and harmonica and then guitar and harmonica on a couple of songs. And then (because he's a good Southern boy) Billy made me play a tune or two of mine and so I did a blues tune my friend Shepp and I wrote and he joined in and it was FINE. And then he started another one and I was running out to get the banjo, and then finally the cello.

Now in general, when I bring in the cello folks get a little tiny bit suspicious, or maybe dubious is a better word. Certainly Billy was. But he had started some depression era song, and it was just screaming for a cello part. See, that's kinda what I do. People ask me all the time: "How do you score a movie?" and

I always answer them the same way: you just watch it and watch it and listen until it tells you what to do, what to play. So after awhile, you just get good at LISTENING and hearing what things "need." This song would sound great with a little lead guitar and some harmonica fills, this one a banjo pushing it along, that one a mandolin. And of course, the cello.

So really, this is all my lawyer's fault 'cause I went out and got the cello and Billy started the song again and I listened and waited and the song told me what it needed and I started to play and Jan's eyes welled up with tears and Carlie came in from the kitchen and it was just like the movies where everyone gets quiet cause Elvis is gonna sing only this was because dear God was this song ever BEAUTIFUL and then Billy stopped right in the middle of it and said:

"Son, these here depression era songs are so sad they make you wanna cry."

And I, thinking I had done something terribly, horribly wrong to make him stop in the middle of such a tragically beautiful tune, could only stare and nod dumbly and stammer out a "yessir..." and he said:

"But man, you put a cello behind it and it'll plumb make you wanna commit suicide."

I of course began to apologize profusely for ruining his song, but he just laughed and said no, no, it's a good thing, not a bad one, and he picked up where he left off and when we finished Jan and Carlie began to clap and Jan had to hug us both and say, "See? I TOLD you you two should get together!

And thus a great friendship was born.

A friendship that would literally change my musical life forever.

1

A STRANGER IN A STRANGE LAND

It was a couple of months after Billy Yarborough and I played together that I got the phone call.

Billy it seems worked for the Ag Commission and newly elected commissioner Meg Scott Phipps wanted to have a little get together at her dad's place in Burlington to meet the folks she was going to be working with. She asked Billy, a very well connected

Bluegrass musician in the Asheville area, if he knew some fellers who might be willing to pick a little at the party. Billy allowed as how he was sure he could provide the music, but as the day got closer and closer, cooler heads prevailed. And by that I mean the wives of course. And to be honest, it didn't really make a lot of sense for these guys to pack up and leave Asheville and drive three and a half hours to go and play a gig that wasn't offering any more pay than the previously discussed Tyrannosaurs steak, and then pack it all back up and drive back another three and a half hours all to play a two hour gig. So one by one the guys canceled.

In a panic, Billy called Bob Stanfield, an acoustic ("doghouse") bass player in Burlington. Could Bob play and by the way, would he track down a couple of pickers Billy knew in the Burlington area and see if they could play the job as well? Billy knew these fellas, had picked with them before and felt good about putting them together in front of a crowd. Sure Bob said, he could do that. Problem was, come to find out none of the fellas Billy knew were available that day, so when Bob called back, he had a list of names all right, but Billy didn't know a single one of 'em.

And that's why I got the phone call.

Billy got a little worried the closer it got to game day, so he was talking to his sister and saying how concerned he was about playing this party with a bunch of folks he didn't know. She said call John, call John. And so he did. He actually called me and said, "Listen we got this here party for Meg, and well, I just don't know any of these fellers, and I'm worried that they might not be any good. So here's what I'm thinking: you come with me to the party, join in with the group, we'll all go up and play a few, if they're good, we'll stick and if they're no good, we'll shoo 'em off the stage and you and I'll play. That way I know it'll be good, whatever happens."

Well, needless to say, I was flattered beyond belief! That he would call and ask me to play with him, I just couldn't believe it! I warned him once again that Bluegrass was indeed my second language and I was a little worried about how folks who really know and live this music would react to my feeble attempts at playing and interpreting it. He kinda waved all that off and assured me we'd be fine, just bring all those instruments and don't forget the cello. We exchanged email addresses and he promised to send info and directions soon.

When you're bald you don't really have a lot of choices when it comes to hairstyles. For me it's always sorta been an all or nothing type thing. Guess that's kind of a life philosophy too, I reckon. In general I'm a pretty open and trusting guy. (Some would say oblivious.) All this is by way of saying, on that fateful Saturday as I strode across the lush green grass of former Governor Scott's back yard, guitar case in one hand, cello in the other, mandolin under one arm, my mom's over night bag under the other, it wasn't till I was about halfway to the back porch we were using as a stage that it hit me:

I don't really look like anyone else here.

Hmmmm..........

As I struggle through the crowd I keep seeing men in long pants (most in long sleeves too, despite the heat) and work or cowboy boots. Not TOO many of 'em are wearing sandals, a loud Hawaiian print shirt (hey, it's summer time!) and shorts.

In fact none of 'em are.

Except the girls.

A couple of them have shorts on.

Aw jeez....

And then there's that whole completely shaved bald head and the goatee thing. My friend Missy says I'm like a big bear. I like that image a whole lot better than saying here I am, a big, fat, bald headed musician from Chapel Hill making my way through a somewhat stunned crowd of complete total strangers.

As I approach the side of the house where Billy said we would meet, I see one middle aged fella with wire rimmed glasses tuning up a mandolin (seems like someone is always tuning up a mandolin), another guy in his late thirties with a mustache picking a banjo, a rather distinguished looking gentleman with his arm around an acoustic bass, Billy with his Martin guitar,

19

and an older fella (in his late sixties?) in a baseball cap sawing away on a fiddle.

And I do mean sawing.

Since I play cello and a little violin, I am aware of a bowing problem called skating. It's when, as you move the bow up or down over the strings, you also impart a sideways motion. This invariably causes a harmonic overtone which dogs about three counties over will begin to harmonize with right before their ear drums burst from the pain.

And this guy is skating all over the place.

Oh man, I think, it's gonna go down just like Billy said: we'll play two or three songs with these guys and then it'll be him and me, and I'll be improvising on a whole bunch of tunes I don't know in front of people who listen to Bluegrass all the time.

I look to the right and scan the crowd. There must be two or three hundred people here.

The first beads of sweat begin to appear, and it has nothing to do with the late August humidity.

Later (almost a year later) I found out that as I was making my way across the yard, one of the players said something along the lines of "Well now, who is this Nazi skinhead summbitch?" and Fred, the fiddle player was quoted as saying, "I didn't know Goldberg played git-tar."

Goldberg apparently was a famous wrestler.

Must still be: seems like I get that all the time.

Needless to say, Billy's the only one who seems

happy to see me. He runs over and makes some
introductions I promptly forget. Turns out we need
to go on and play (even though I am here a half hour
before the stated start time) and he is moving through
the names quickly. We all smile and nod, then it's
down to business. We need to go on. And oh, by the
way, there are five hundred (FIVE HUNDRED!!)
people here today.

Isn't that great?

Now as I have said, I know some Bluegrass and
have some degree of familiarity with the music. But
Billy is naming songs the guys can play and as a group
we either veto or OK them and if we okay them, we
decide on what key to play them in. My problem is, I
know some of these titles ("Orange Blossom Special,"
"Tennessee Stud," "Remington Ride," etc.) but if you
put a gun to my head and said hum this song or I'll
shoot, I'd have to say, "Well, shoot."

So I am just sorta standing there listening
and nodding and praying that once these boys start
playing maybe I'll recognize a melody enough to
participate a little.

The guys decide we need to go on with a bang,
so they run five or six titles down of some fast tunes
and settle on an order for them. That's how we'll go
on: with five tunes we know we're gonna do and the
rest will be made up later. We head up to the big back
porch and begin to jockey for position. Billy, as lead
singer, takes center stage with Jeff, the banjo player

21

and Keith on mandolin to his left. Bob, the bass player, sets up directly behind Billy with Fred in back on fiddle to his right.

Discretion being the better part of valor, I did not do too much jockeying myself other than to make sure I was dead last going on stage where I promptly hid myself to the right behind a big stack of speakers. (There may be tomatoes on the buffet line. It's harder to hit a target you can't see.) I positioned myself not facing out towards the crowd (there are in fact five hundred people here, I can see that clearly now) but facing across the stage in the vain hope that I might be able to read Billy's hands and thus have some vague concept of what chords we are playing in each song. I peek out once more at the gathering crowd. Definitely AT LEAST five hundred people here. From behind the safety of the speaker bank, I follow the line of our mic cables through the lush green grass back to the sound booth. Billy's daughter is going to be running sound for us. My heart sinks.

She is all of fourteen years old.

We check mics, get set up and comfortable. I risk being seen by the multitudes long enough to lean over to remind Billy to remember to cheat his strumming hand my way so I can read his chords, then duck back into my hideout. I have my guitar, cello, dobro, and mandolin laid out around me, tuned up, ready to go. I am the only one who brought guitar stands or plays more then one instrument. We finally get things set after Billy confers with his daughter, and he takes a deep breath and counts off the first song, and it's a fast one and off we go.

We get about, I dunno, ten, twenty bars in, ten maybe fifteen seconds before I think to myself:

Dear God these guys are INCREDIBLE.

THEY ARE BRILLIANT PLAYERS.

AMAZING.

In fact, these guys are so good, I can't possibly play mandolin with them. I'm not good enough. And the way Billy's grinning, I can tell he and I will not be playing slow songs on guitar and cello in ten minutes, so the cello's out. In fact I quickly realize the only instrument I can play that can possibly add to the music or keep up with these guys is the harmonica. I begin nudging the other instruments back into the shadows with my foot. I reach into my mom's overnight bag and pull out a C harmonica. We're playing in G so I play in C, a blues style called cross harp, and I am barely making it, hanging on by my fingertips, no, fingerNAILS these guys are so astonishingly good. We finish the first song (I have no idea what it was) and they IMMEDIATELY launch into the next one and the count off is even faster than the first one, and we're off like race horses sprinting for the triple crown.

Omigod are these guys good!

I'm a pretty good guitar player but it doesn't take long to know there is no way I can keep up with these guys, even on my main instrument, let alone dobro, an instrument I've only been playing a few months.

It's harmonica or go home at this point.

Hiding behind the speaker stack, I play it safe (literally) by just chucking along with the chord changes, don't try to do anything fancy, just stay in the game. Billy is in heaven, his assembled players exactly what he hoped for, kindred spirits all, and so he has completely forgotten his promise to play so I can read his chords as he leans in to the mic and belts out another song I never heard before.

And then a couple of really interesting things happen.

First, since I play banjo, I realize I can read the banjo players' hands and between that and the occasional glimpses of Billy's hands as he rocks back and forth at the mic, I actually feel like I have some idea of the structure of what we're playing. Amid the relief of that plus the sheer joy of how good these guys are, I actually begin to enjoy myself. I mean, what have I got to lose? I'm on stage (sorta) with a bunch of great players; all I gotta do is lay back and not screw them up.

What's not to enjoy?

But then the second thing happened.

Fred-- the fiddle player I was so worried about?

Seems I sorta underestimated him.

A lot.

Bluegrass is my Second Language

For one thing, every time he bows a note a cloud of rosin puffs up like a snowstorm outa Montreal. In fact his fiddle is nearly covered in frosted rosin, so even if he DOES skate, that bow is flat GLUED to the string! And for another thing, it seems that whole skating thing may be more important in classical music than Bluegrass, cause this guy sounds amazing. And now that I look at him and he's warmed up and going (playing with his eyes closed, rosin clouds everywhere) he's not really skating much at all. In fact his technique is impeccable. Almost as impeccable as the notes that pour out of his soul and into our hearts. The guy is WONDERFUL.

And he's playing such delicious parts! Adding the perfect long note, the best slide or bend to emphasize the lyric or mood of the song. He's one of the most tasteful musicians I've ever heard!! And that ain't all: the bass is rock solid, the banjo player is practically playing JAZZ he is comping chords and backing Billy's guitar so well and the mandolin is laying down a line of soaring silver melody that just adds to the over all perfection of what these guys play and who they are.

Now I don't know if there's any corollary to this in your life. There are a few in mine. I've seen so-so actors who, when paired with really really good actors, step up and act beyond their ability, or at least what we though was their ability. I've seen singers who, while OK to good separately, were just terrific together. So I guess there's some precedent for this, but it had never happened to me to this extent in my musical life before.

I just couldn't help myself.

I mean, Fred would play something wonderful and before I could think or stop myself (remember: my goal here is to lay low and not be noticed) I would take his phrase and play it back to him with a little twist on it. And the thing that was really wild was that I WAS PLAYING STUFF I DIDN'T KNOW HOW TO PLAY!

Fred would play a lick and, in spite of myself, I would answer his phrase. But he was playing REALLY cool phrases, musical passages that I had never played before on harmonica--or ANY instrument for that matter. These were parts that I couldn't even IMAGINE myself playing, but here I was playing them!

I would answer a part and then sort of cringe as I thought oh God he's gonna HATE that which was followed immediately by a how the heck did I DO that???? kinda thought. At first when I glanced over at Fred, there was no reaction. From behind the snowstorm of rosin, his face was impassive, eyes closed, bow moving up and down, fiddle notes flying everywhere. But then I would respond, and his eyebrow would arch or his brow would furrow and I would think oh God don't piss him off just play

simple parts, play chords, don't make a scene. But
I just couldn't help myself. Those guys were just so
damn GOOD, and he was playing such great lines that
before long I'd do it again.

Doh!!

Don't DO that.

And then another phrase would leap unbidden
from God knows where and there it would be, out of
my harmonica and there for everyone to hear. We
finish the second song and launch into the third, still
faster than the last. Something has gone seriously
wrong with my mouth and I cannot seem to be able
to control the breath that passes from me to my
harmonica. It weaves and dances around Fred's ornate
fiddle parts like some crazy gypsy dancer as if it's got
nothing to do with me, a life of it's own.

Fred glances over at me and winks.

God in heaven, a sixty five year old man just
winked at me.

I am not sure what that means.

It sets me back a bit, but before long the
gypsy harmonica takes over and speaks even though
I am somewhat reluctant. I notice the other players
grinning at me.

We finish the third song. In the brief pause
between tunes, Fred wags his bow at me as if to say I
hear what you're doing over there you whippersnapper
you.

Can't tell whether he means keep it up or cut

it out, but it doesn't matter cause I can't help myself. My harmonica is possessed. Music literally pours out and I am STUNNED thinking how did I DO that??? I don't know how to PLAY that.

By the time we hit the fifth song, we are all drenched in sweat. I am gasping like a racehorse in the final stretch, the fast paced songs killing my breathing as I inhale and exhale through the harmonica. I'm still behind the speaker so I can't tell how the crowd is reacting. I do know WE'RE having a ball!! The music has lifted all of us and we are all enjoying the ride as each song is faster, more energetic, more fervent than the last. Billy's daughter is a dream: the mix, both on stage and off, is PERFECT. I can't believe that kid!

Seems music runs in the family.

At last we approach the end of the final song in our opening list. I feel like I've been playing up here for three days. I feel like I've been playing up here for three seconds. We're going about a hundred and ninety miles an hour and I'm about to pass out from hyperventilating or lack of oxygen or both.

Now what I'm about to tell you is going to sound like something right out of a movie: too good to be true, but I swear to God it happened EXACTLY the way I'm going to tell it, cause it did.

We all pull the last riff of the song off and come crashing down on the last chord and the song is over, the run is over. Five (or maybe six, I can't remember) really fast songs in a row. One faster than the other, each better than the other as the band coalesced. Six guys who never played together before got up in front of five hundred people and ripped through a bunch of tunes and played like we had been playing together all our lives. It was a truly exhilarating, humbling experience.

We hadn't realized, or intended it, but in doing one song after another, with barely a breath in between, we had not given the audience a chance to respond to us at all. And so in the seconds that followed that last climatic chord, as that last G rang and hung in the air, there was silence.

And in that silence, Bob leaned back from his dark brown bass, wiped the sweat from his brow and nodded around at us approvingly.

"Welp," he said, "We all finished together and nobody got hurt."

He considered for a moment and then added:

"I reckon we're a success."

I had been standing with my harmonica to my mouth, feathering a soft vibrato from the last chord. I brought the harmonica down to my side.

"If........ I'm gonna keep...... playing with you guys," I panted, trying desperately to catch my breath, " I'm gonna..... have to start......running again."

And in that instant, five hundred people

erupted into applause.

Seems like there ought to be a moral to this
story, and if there is one I reckon it's this: music is
the great common denominator.

After we had ourselves a good laugh, we
picked another song and a bunch more after that
and entertained the hell out of those folks that day.
At some point Meg came up and allowed as how we
ought to take a break as folks were ready for supper.
She asked the folks to give us a big hand, and then
someone led a blessing of the food. And as five
hundred hungry people converged on that buffet line,
Meg did a pretty neat thing. She got on the mic and
asked that everyone hold up just a second cause it
seemed to her these here pickers had been working
mighty hard to entertain everyone and the least folks
could do would be let the boys eat first. And damned
if that crowd didn't part like the great Red Sea and
we passed unhampered if not into the land of milk
and honey, then at least into the land of fried chicken
and banana pudding.

Made me proud to be a musician that day as we
walked through that crowd and people said the nicest
things and clapped and patted us on the back.

Like I said: exhilarating and humbling.

Music is a great, powerful thing.

We ate pretty quick cause we couldn't wait to
get back up there and play some more. I was pleased

to find the other guys felt the energy and magic of the day the same way I did and delighted they felt the gypsy harmonica had added to that magic. Six guys who never played together before came together and played and five hundred people clapped and danced and hummed and shouted out requests and by God we did 'em. I eventually got so comfortable I even moved my mic out from behind the speakers so folks could actually see me! And the boys got on me till I strapped on my guitar and took center stage and did a cowboy song and a blues tune. Didn't get much applause (abrupt paradigm shift I reckon) but Governor Scott himself complimented me after the show on my singing and harp playing. AND a pretty young lady allowed as how she liked that cowboy song I sang yes indeed. So things were looking up.

When we finished up for the day, after playing for a couple of three hours for all those folks, Fred came up to me and said, "I don't know who the heck you are, but I sure 'nuff want to play with you again" and hugged me. In fact there were hugs and back slaps all around. I found out Fred was somewhere in his seventies and none of these guys played professionally.

Like I said: amazing.

So the moral of the story ought to be that if you play from the heart, and open yourself to the music and just TELL THE TRUTH, the music will just flat LIFT YOU UP. Cause music doesn't care what you look like, how old you are, what you do for a living, how you dress, how rich or how poor you are, what religion you are, none of that.

All music cares about is if you tell the truth.

And while the truth may not necessarily set you free, it'll let you have a right fine time on a Saturday afternoon if you let it.

2

THE GOOD OLD BOYS

or

The Long Ride Home

Well now when this all gets made into a movie, they'll cut from us playing on the back porch in Burlington to some club or pig pickin' where we'll all be smiling and strumming and there'll be a HUGE crowd (of mostly pretty girls) and it'll seem like we just moved from one gig to the next and everything was hunky dory.

This being real life, and especially this being MY life, that is not at all how things turned out. After we had packed up our gear, we all traded numbers and shook hands and grinned a lot and talked about getting together real soon.

Then we all went home and I didn't hear from anyone for about a month.

Finally bit the bullet, made the call knowing full well someone would eventually tell me the truth on the phone.

"Listen John," they'd say, "there's no easy way to put this. We just don't think you, um, fit in."

While part of me (most of me) believed that, I just couldn't stop thinking about how incredible it had been to play music with those guys, how great they were. I was pretty sure I was going to get the let down speech (why else hadn't anyone called??) but I just had to try.

Instead, when I finally got hold of Fred Minor on the phone he seemed genuinely pleased to hear from me. He'd had some medical problems that had laid him low and Jeff and some of the others had been pulling some long shifts at work, so he hadn't really seen the guys much lately or played much either for that matter but by God wasn't that a good day that afternoon in Burlington? He recommended I give the banjo player, Jeff Wiseman, a call and I did. Jeff promptly invited me to a little get together up at his house in Reidsville this coming Saturday. Keith Carrol was going to be there. Keith the mandolin player? Jeff just laughed. Naw, Keith don't really play mandolin, he's really a bass player. (So much for my being the only multi-instrumentalist in the group.) Well if he's not a mandolin player and really is a bass player, I can't wait to hear him. Well c'mon up to the house then. My buddy Greg Eldred is coming and he's a real fine guitar player, y'all'll have plenty talk about.

I got some directions and said I'll see you Saturday evening about eight.

I suppose it'll come to no surprise to those of you still reading this but I am kind of a city boy. Like most city folks these days, if I can't get to the movie, the supermarket, the party, whatever, in fifteen or twenty minutes, well it's just too far to drive thank you very much. So it goes without saying that when I talked to a buddy of mine about the best way to get to Reidsville and he casually mentioned it would take me over an hour to get there I was not pleased.

Not pleased at all.

Let's see: leave Chapel Hill at seven-ish get up there at eight-ish (MAN!!) play a while, head out at midnight get home a little after one......

What the heck, I'll do it.

That night was a really good night.

Musta been, cause I didn't get home till a little after four in the morning! Once again, I don't really remember what we played, at that point these were all just Bluegrass songs, some vaguely familiar, most completely unknown to me, but I just kept reacting to what I heard and it seemed to go well, cause I kept getting invited back. Over the weeks I got to play with a bunch of good pickers and just plain real nice folks. I don't think Keith made it up to Jeff's that first night, but eventually I got to hear him play the bass and he could flat out spank that bad boy. Likewise Greg didn't make it either. It was a while before I got to play with these boys, but it was definitely worth the wait. Kinda just added to the mystique I reckon.

In fact, turns out (what I then thought of as) the long drive home came in handy. Got to play back a lot of music in my head, learn and remember licks and ideas and think about what I had seen and heard and about the players themselves.

Jeff Wiseman is simply a phenomenal musician. As I mentioned earlier, I had been playing banjo a little before I met up with him at that Burlington gig. I didn't touch that banjo for about a month after I played with him. Now Jeff hates it when I say that, but it's true. He was so good that it just didn't seem polite for me to play the banjo in the same state he lived in. Felt like I needed to slip over into Virginia or South Carolina just to practice the dang thing! I eventually got over it, but I have to this day not gotten over what a great player he is and can say, with complete honesty and accuracy, that he has ruined me playing with another banjo player, likely for the rest of my life. He has such an impeccable sense of timing and phrasing, his liquid mercury banjo lines lacing with such fierce determination yet utter delicacy through the tune, whether fast or slow, that he is unlike any other banjo player I have ever heard. And here's the part that most Bluegrass players won't believe: he is one of the most dynamic banjo players I've ever had the pleasure to see or pick with. It's not just that his playing and stage presence is dynamic, (it is) but I'm talking about dynamics in the most basic musical sense of the word.

VOLUME.

Ask any bluegrass player about banjo pickers, and you'll get a groan and then a roll of the eyes and then the kind of "you can't live with em, ya can't live without 'em" kinda shrug. For you non-players, let me give you a more visceral example.

In most pickin' parlors if you look around a little, sooner or later you'll come across a brick. Now if the perpetrator really has his/her act together, that brick will have a Martin guitar logo stenciled on it. And the brick will be labeled. And the label will read as follows:

BANJO MUTE

Sometimes in small print, the Banjo Mute will come with instructions:

When the banjo player gets too loud (or when he or she starts playing, whichever comes first) Simply throw banjo mute at banjo player. Repeat as often as necessary.

Now I actually saw a bunch of these things places I started going and had to ask Greg what they meant because the only banjo player I'd ever played with was Jeff so the thing didn't make any sense to me. The banjo by nature and design is a LOUD instrument and rare indeed is the picker who can (or will) control or use that volume and dynamic in their performance of the music. Jeff is such a player. Frankly, I was appalled at most of the banjo players I played with when I started playing out a little more on my own. They played at an earsplitting volume, and most were not all that good. (Heck, first thing I did when I started playing banjo was say to myself, ´

lessee...... these here finger picks have GOT to go, cause this thing is so deafening I can barely hear myself think. I STILL don't use finger picks and STILL think I'm too loud sometimes. How these other guys do it is beyond me.) But Jeff has a complete mastery and control of the instrument, the strings and the volume that makes him a pure pleasure to pick with. What can I say?

That boy puts the "U" in purty.

Turns out that ol' Keith was indeed a master of the doghouse bass. He has incredible timing and a remarkable zest for music that manifests itself in his seemingly uncontrollable desire to dance with, around and under (seriously) his bass when the music gets cooking. Whether we're playing in a room with just four players or a crowd of four hundred, he is always able to channel the soaring spirit of the music in his crazy, zany antics while still holding down a solid bass line that compliments and supports the music totally. Again, for you non-players, let me try to explain.

See, no matter how good everybody you play with is, unless you have a REALLY good bass player (or drummer, or BOTH, ---now THAT is pure heaven!!!) there's always one part of your brain that's constantly looking for the beat, always keeping track of where the downbeat or "one" is. When you have a bass player, well the way I've always described it is that it's like wading in warm water that comes up to just below your knees. The bass puts out this low frequency wave that creates a soft carpet in the room. Adds SO MUCH to the other tones in the room, whether they be guitars, voices, mandolins, whatever. And when you have a REALLY REALLY REALLY good bass player, that little part of your brain that is always looking for the down beat, says, hey we don't have to look for 'One' anymore, the bass player's got it and he or she is telling you with every note where it is. Now until you get to relax that part of your brain, you are never fully aware that it's been working there all this time. But when you finally CAN relax, it is incredibly liberating. For the first time, one hundred percent of your musical soul is being IN the music and not looking after the downbeat.

Keith Carroll is one of those players. Playing with him is incredibly freeing, a Zen treat.

I've already talked about Fred Minor, the fiddle player. Let me just add one thing:

In Bluegrass, the fiddle plays a lot; it's constantly moving and churning. I've played with Fred for about two years now, so I figure I've heard him play a couple of billion notes.

In all that time and all those notes, I never heard him play a bad one.

Not a single bad note in two years.

Nothin left to say.

I'm gettin a little ahead of myself here, but

when I did finally get to play with him, Jeff's friend Greg Eldred ended up being a complete surprise and delight. Many is the night I stand or sit beside this talented songwriter/guitarist and watch his fingers fly over the fretboard in utter amazement because I have no idea on God's green earth how he does what he does on the guitar. He plays so fast and so hard that his picks are constantly being ripped from his fingers and flying across the stage or living room. His fingers are usually just a blur and the musical phrases come so fast and are so accurate that it seems impossible sometimes. He's got a great soulful voice and can tear up a song, on vocals or instrumentally. He is also a skilled and artful songwriter and it has been my great pleasure to play on a bunch of songs that he has written. He seems to be able to write pretty much anything: fast, slow, happy or sad with equal craft and grace.

Again, for you non-players, what a really solid rhythm guitar player adds to the mix is the creation of structure. To use a building analogy, the bass and/ or drum lays the literal bottom or foundation of what you play. The rhythm guitar roughs out the shape of the structure, as does the backbeat of the mandolin. Without that solid foundation, you've got a house of cards. Won't stand up to much. But when you're in the groove, man, it's pure heaven, and a good solid strummer will get you there quick! And if he or she can pick out a lead, well that's all the better. What's truly astonishing about Greg is that I've seen him, when he's really cranking, play lead AND rhythm at the same time. (Don't ask me how. I don't know.)

(And yes, I've asked, and no, he doesn't know either. Says it just happens. Music's weird/great like that sometimes.)

My one regret about my introduction to Bluegrass music that Saturday afternoon in Burlington was that Greg wasn't there to join us. What a force of nature we woulda been then! I have tried unsuccessfully to get the original boys I played that gig with back together with the addition of Greg, but haven't been able to make it work thus far.

One of these days....

Now there are certainly other folks I played with back in the beginning, and you'll get to meet some of 'em along the way, but these were the guys who had the most impact on me, who directed and influenced me and my playing and who very graciously opened up doors that let me experience stuff I didn't know existed right here in own my back yard. Besides, I've already over-used words like amazing and incredible and my thesaurus is burnt up from me thumbing through the pages trying to find words powerful enough to describe what these boys sound like. My hope is, if this ever gets published, to have a CD that goes along with it so y'all can hear for yourselves.

We'll see....

Bluegrass is my Second Language

One night Jeff invited me up to his place and
I took my friend Martin Brown with me, which was a
good thing because now I have a witness. Otherwise
no one would believe what a night of music we
experienced that Saturday evening in November.

Seems Jeff had gathered a bunch of real old
time fellas up to the house to pick and grin. We got
there a little before eight and when we came in the
front door it certainly looked to be an odd scene. Jeff
had taken out all the furniture in the living room
so the whole room was open and bare in the center.
Sitting around the periphery of the room in straight-
backed chairs were a bunch of older gentlemen.
Generally, Jeff gathers a pretty young crowd of
players but these gents were a bit more, shall we say,
distinguished than who we normally pick with. Like
eighties or nineties lookin fellers. Needless to say they
were likely as shocked to see me there as I was to see
them as we stormed in the door with guitars and cello
and of course my mom's powder blue over night bag.

(I never think about how I look until it's WAY
too late....)

Kinda said hi and then immediately beat a
path for the bedroom to unpack instruments and stow
cases, but really it was just to get outa that room.
It was weird. It was like a funeral or something. All
these old guys sitting around the sides of the room,
weathered faces with big thick glasses, no one talking,

just sitting, hands folded in laps. Very odd, and of course I felt distinctly uncomfortable sticking out like a sore thumb. At least Martin looked "normal" so I stuck close to him when we went back out and took a seat. No one was to my right, but a fella named Jimmy Johnson introduced himself to Martin on my/our left. We began to tune up.

Jeff and I think it was Keith or maybe Bob Stanfield the bass player from Burlington who stood in the middle of the room along with Fred Minor on fiddle and cranked up a tune. Martin had listened to Bluegrass as a kid and played banjo a bit so he jumped right in with his D35. I listened for a while till the song told me what it needed and waded in with some mandolin, though I was still pretty shy about my mandolin playing at that point. Safety in numbers though....

Ol' Jimmy Johnson was thumping out a pretty solid rhythm and he and Martin got a bit of a party going there and we churned out a couple of tunes. I marveled at Jimmy's hands dancing over the strings: this was no slim fingered virtuoso who had learned to play while he was in college or in music school somewhere. He was obviously a working man with big ham hock hands and thick, callused working man's fingers. But his touch was light and deft and his fingers flew across the fretboard. Looking around, I saw the same thing was true for almost all the older folks in the room. They were all working men, men who made their living from their hands and the labor of their backs. Every once in a while one of those old timers would stand up and sing a song or play a break on guitar or mandolin and we were going along right well. By about nine thirty I noticed those old timers looked to be about sixty five or sixty six and Jeff and the other young players were pulling less and less of the singing chores. By ten thirty, those fellers were well into their forties and by midnight every single damn one of 'em was all of sixteen and playin like Yo-Yo Ma and singing like they were on stage at the Grand Ole Opry!

Now I'm young and stupid, but it didn't take me long to realize what an honor it was to play with these boys. They were a direct link back to the days when, if you wanted to get together and pick on a Saturday night, you stood up in church the Sunday before and said y'all come to my place next Saturday, and people would head out across the fields on foot or horse back or buckboard and come pick. The timbre and tone of their voices harkened back to the old days when there was no satellite TV or eight zillion radio stations to influence the way you sang a song. If you had a radio, what you heard on it sounded exactly like what you were doing in your parlor or church. There was purity in their delivery that was clean and intense and timeless. It was a true honor just to be in the room with these gentlemen, let alone to be playing with them.

By one or two in the morning those boys were in their full glory and as free as a bird on a windy day and all us young puppies were hanging on for all we were worth and enjoying the ride.

A couple of years later Martin, who also works in film, and I would be driving to a job up in Virginia when he put a Chet Atkins CD we had never heard before in the player and we banged on the dash board and nearly drove off the road it was so good and music is just that powerful.

That Saturday night after I had the extreme honor of adding my sweet cello to those voices and instruments as those wonderful old timers sang "Amazing Grace" for the last song of the night, we packed up our stuff and headed to the car. We got in and I cranked up the engine and Martin said Oh My God and I said Yeah and we rode in silence for quite a while until it could digest a bit and we couldn't help ourselves and began to talk about how great those boys were and what a dream of a lifetime it had been to play with them.

But mostly we rode in silence while our memories danced.

3

HABIB

This period of time was particularly rough for me. 2001 had been a pretty rough year. At the end of March that year, my best friend Shepp Wasdell, died of cancer. He was like my brother and we wrote the lyrics for all my songs together. His death hit me so hard I kinda fell off the planet for about a month after that and then the entertainment community, which always feels the effects of the economy first, moved out of the ten year period of growth and into recession. Then came September 11th, and the whole country was reeling from shock and pain. In October my dad, who had been living quite well with his Parkinson's Disease, began a significant regression. My mother was awaiting double hip replacement surgery and as my father became more and more feeble, she could do less and less to help him get around. In October I moved home to Durham to help tend my parents full time. I stayed day and night during the week and my sister would take over the weekend shifts.

While it was an honor to be able to repay my parents for all they have given me, it was still tough. When you're "on duty" you never fully go to sleep lest they call for you in the middle of the night. It wasn't my bed I was sleeping in, they liked the house warmer than I keep mine, all those little tiny things that make it tough to fully rest begin to build up after a while.

During this time I would leave Durham when my sister arrived on Friday evening and drive back to my house in Chapel Hill, walk in the door and head straight for bed. Exhausted, I would cram a weeks worth of sleep into one long night and leave as soon as I woke up on Saturday afternoon to go play whatever music I could find, wherever people were gathering. This was my outlet, my light at the end of the tunnel, my connection to "normal" life and the thing that helped keep me sane.

Most weekends I drove up to Reidsville to play
with Jeff and whatever aggregation of players he
could put together, which wasn't as tough as it sounds
cause Jeff's house was ALWAYS full of music and
joy. If there aren't pickers over there making noise,
well between him and his sons, there's still plenty of
music happening. I will always be grateful to Jeff and
his friends for the hours and hours of therapy they
unknowingly gave me. Music was the best medicine
and I took every drop of it I could find.

After September 11, 2001, a bunch of terrible
things began happening around where I live in the
Triangle area in North Carolina. Most folks were
pretty cool, but some folks felt the need to spit on,
mock or intimidate those they perceived as different.
After reading a few of these stories in the paper, I
determined to do something about it if I could. I hit
upon the idea of gathering some players from each of
the musical styles I played with and putting on a big
concert. I have always had a love for different music
and cultures, instilled I am sure, by my loving parents.
On any given Saturday night, if I went west from
Chapel Hill I was playing pretty traditional Bluegrass
music. If I went east to Raleigh, I was playing blues
and jazz and pop stuff with a bunch of players in
that area. And on some occasions I would meet in
Durham with some Middle Eastern players and we
would play "world" music. I had an interest in sitar

and Indian music since the days of the Beatles and finally had one sent over from India so I could learn to play. I began to talk to some of these folks about putting together the concert. The idea was to show how these different musical styles and cultures could peacefully and joyfully interact. It was somewhere in those discussions that Habib's name first came up. He was apparently a great player of many instruments and someone who would resonate with my plan. I tracked him down by phone and explained what I wanted to do. He was very excited about this and so we met. Come to find out that along with the Middle Eastern instruments Habib played (oud, flutes, drum) he had been studying cello here in the States as well. We got along pretty well and began playing together trying to flesh out what we might be able to do with the concert. One night while I was over at his apartment in Durham, during a break in our playing, I mentioned I wanted to bring in some Bluegrass players I knew.

Well the guy just about jumped out of his skin. Turns out (and y'all thought I was going all this way and there wasn't gonna BE a point, didn't ya?) that Bluegrass is HUGE in Lebanon. (Who knew??) And as a Christian, he was particularly taken with some of the hymns and religious music of Bluegrass. But mostly he and his friends were flat out NUTS about Bluegrass music. He asked me to recommend some records he might send back to his friends in Lebanon and for advice about which local and national Bluegrass acts I thought were "the real deal" and might steer him towards.

Well hell, if it's the real deal you want, I said, why don't you come up to Reidsville with me and experience the REAL real deal for yourself: a bunch of great players sitting around in a living room and pickin and grinnin.

Habib about went crazy and ran to his computer to email his friends back home of his amazing good fortune: he was going to a real Bluegrass jam.

I called Jeff and told him I had this picker I wanted to bring on up and Jeff cleared it with his wife Amy and we got set up for a Saturday night.

Now I apologize for jumping around a little bit in the sequence of things, but I need to mention one of the reasons I was so excited about this evening of music (aside from Habib's infectious enthusiasm) was because Jeff informed me that, at long last, I was going to get to meet and play music with Greg Eldred! We had continually missed each other and at long last it seemed I was going to get to make some music with this "famous" picker I'd been hearing so much about AND Keith was going to come up and play bass! Jeff reckoned he'd keep it manageable, as we also wanted to play some of Habib's tunes if we could, so we kept it to a small gathering.

I met Habib about six thirty over in Durham

and we set off on our way up to Reidsville. Picking him up added some travel time, and though I had warned him it was a long ride, he began to get a bit antsy as we drove further and further into the countryside. It was winter and the sun went down quick and we soon passed all the glitter of the city lights to drive up NC 87 as the fields and occasional farmhouse flew by outside the window. At about forty five minutes Habib allowed as how he didn't want to insult me or anything, but he now had no idea where we were, it was pitch black out and he was beginning to remember that he didn't know me very well and there were a lot of mean things happening to people from his part of the world. I did the best I could to reassure him, that I was his friend and he would be equally well met by these folks I was taking him to and promised him he would thank me for this when it was done. A slightly less restless but still wary Habib sank back in his chair and watched the darkness fly by. It's terrible times that would make a man feel like that. I cranked up some music on the CD player and pressed down on the accelerator, the better to get him there as quick as I could.

He must've been relieved when we arrived at Jeff's and were met by everyone helping to bring in instruments and cases. We set up in Jeff's living room that I had become so comfortable in over the weeks of Saturday nights and began to play. I remember at first Habib only wanted to listen and watch and I recall the way his face lit up and he shot a look over at me every time Jeff took a break or the "new" guy (at least for me) took one of his super fast guitar solos.

Habib was in hog heaven. He listened for awhile and between us brow beating him into playing and his natural musician's instinct, he eventually joined in with us, playing a variety of instruments from flute to oud to an incredibly rhythmic tambourine (that worked GREAT on bluegrass numbers) to the cello.

We were cranking, just flat percolating along: Jeff, standing over by a seated Habib, Keith slapping that bass and dancing around the living room and Greg, swaying back and forth in his chair, completely captivated by the music and me on harmonica and mandolin, just unbelievably happy to be part of this.

We were tossing around breaks as Habib played oud, a mandolin like instrument, with a big ol' grin on his face, his fingers dancing over the strings in a strange and wonderful mix of the music of his homeland and our own beloved Bluegrass.

And thus it was that Jeff spoke the following words that were said for the first time in the history of bluegrass music.

As the music reached a fiery pitch, ol' Jeff leaned over Habib and shouted out:

"Take it Habib!"

And he did.

4

THE QUEEN OF BLUEGRASS

By now y'all are probably used to me starting off by saying, "I'm not really sure, but I think..." and I apologize for that, but see, nobody was takin notes when all this was happenin. At the time all this is going on (by now we're in December of 2001 or maybe early January 2002) I had no idea that I was ever gonna try to write this stuff down and tell my story. I certainly woulda been more careful about documenting things if I HAD known.

So SOMEWHERE in this timeline I got to meet Pammy Davis, the Queen Of Bluegrass. Among Pammy's many distinctions is that she is the founder and CEO (just kidding) of a Bluegrass society called High Lonesome Strings. These folks are pickers who get together on a Sunday afternoon once a month and listen to one of their own bands who are members or just a Bluegrass band that wants to play for the society and then they break off into smaller groups and pick till they're done or they get kicked out, whichever comes first.

After a while of pickin and grinnin up at Jeff's I mentioned a desire to get to know more music, and asked for CD recommendations etc. Instead, Greg and Jeff said, you need to come to an HLS meeting. So that is how I first became aware of these folks and first got invited.

They met at two PM at a community college in Greensboro, and I once again made the hour long drive, by now not thinking much of it. (The city boy's learnin, y'all.) After making just enough wrong turns to get me there a good forty five minutes late (all my friends will verify that I am directionally impaired), I found the right spot, parked in the lot with a BUNCH of other cars, vans and pickup trucks and headed on up to the building.

My other job in the film biz is as a soundman,

meaning that I record the dialogue and sounds that happen on location for a film or commercial or video, whatever. So I am by nature acutely aware of environmental sound, whether that environment is natural (outdoors), or the hum of neon lights or the grind of an air conditioner in the next room. That's my job: to notice and minimize any sound that might interfere with quality of the scene being shot.

Thus, I can barely describe the mellifluous cacophony that tickled my professional little eardrums as I opened those big glass doors and strode down the hallway. Not being sure what was going on or whether the guys would even be there, I left my gear in the car, so I was able to stroll about freely wherever my delighted ears would take me and enjoy this rush of sound. The High Lonesome String members had already divided off into groups and all over the first floor of the modern neon and glass building, the warm, wooden, traditional tones of fiddle and bass and guitar were floating and mixing and converging as what appeared to me to be well over two hundred pickers played their hearts out. It was a wonderful way to meet High Lonesome Strings and I resolved to become a member right then and there. I wandered around, peeking shyly in doorways and glimpsing different aggregations of people and players, different skill and ability levels, different approaches to the songs, but all of them--EVERY SINGLE ONE OF EM--with a BIG smile on their faces.

Bluegrass is my Second Language

My kind of people, my kind of music.

Eventually I ran into Greg and Jeff in one of the groups. After they chastised me and sent me back out to my car (what a wonderland of sound to skate back through!!) to get my instruments, I settled in to listen and play. By now, even though there were other people joining in with us, I was comfortable enough picking with Jeff and the famous Greg to not be intimidated and so jump on in.

I'm fortunate in that there aren't many harmonica players in most groups, so folks are usually pretty intrigued when I start to play. (Once they get past my mom's powder blue over night bag, of course. Gotta do something about that one of these days.....) Also it helps some that, while you often see guitar players who play guitar and harp at the same time (for you non-players, harmonica is often called a harp-- from mouth harp I reckon), it's not every day that you see a MANDOLIN player who plays harp at the same time. PLUS I guess it's time I fess up and admit that I'm left handed so I play everything backwards to the way most players pick, PLUS the whole bald headed thing and well, I reckon I'm just gonna get noticed.

What I'm getting at is, it didn't take too long till we had gathered quite a little crowd around us. Now my natural inclination is to blame Jeff and Greg, both exceptional players, and the other good folks they had gathered around them, but I suppose I can take some little piece of credit as well. We were standing in the cafeteria of this community college and there were sixty-fourth notes flyin EVERYWHERE. It was great. Had a couple of guys on guitar, a fiddle player wandered by, musta heard somethin he liked and joined in, and a rather demure looking older lady in a long dress and pearls played the dog house bass.

You know, rock 'n' roll has been making a big deal of late about the Women of Rock. Well I am here to tell you, the Women of Bluegrass have been rockin the house for DECADES. This was my first experience with the equal footing women pull with men in the world of Bluegrass and I gotta tell ya, I flat LOVED it! Gimmie a woman who can play any day! It's great!

So we picked and grinned (yeah we actually do that) and there was a natural ebb and flow to those who listened and played and came and went and after a while we took a break and Greg walked me around to show me some folks and let me hear a bunch of different music while Jeff, one of the finest banjo players in the Piedmont, got corralled into another room and another storm of notes.

I am constantly amazed at the egalitarian nature of Bluegrass Music: all ages, abilities, sexes, shapes and sizes are welcome. It's pretty cool. Granted, you don't see many people of color, but when I have, everyone has been treated very well, nothin but good old Southern hospitality. (Think Habib.) Particularly if you're a great picker or singer.

Then you get treated REAL well, cause it's all about the music, and nothin else.

Greg walked me around, pointing out this fella as a great player, that gal (sorry, but this is Bluegrass and they call the women gals in Bluegrass) as a great singer, harmonizer, bass player, whatever. A lot of chicks play acoustic bass in Bluegrass. (VERY sexy.) Then we went around the corner and there was this group of about ten folks pickin and most of em were women. Greg said half of these ladies are in a group called Steel Magnolias, an all female Bluegrass band and that gal there on dobro is Pammy Davis, the president of High Lonesome Strings and the Queen Of Bluegrass.

Pammy is a real treat to hear: she's got a great resonator guitar and just makes it sing. She's about as tall as me and at any given moment generally has a minimum of fourteen pieces of jewelry in the shape of a guitar on her person, whether that be ear rings, necklaces, pins, bracelets...you get the idea. Has a real love and zest for music in general and Bluegrass in particular (why else start a Bluegrass society and help it grow to over five hundred members??) and it shows in the way she plays and the things she says with her music.

Course, I didn't know all this at the time. I was just standing there watching a bunch of folks play some pretty darn good music. All the rest came later. During a break, Greg introduced me and we chatted awhile and then they went to playing and we wandered off to explore some more and then ended up over with Jeff where we got back to pickin too.

Round about six thirty the place had more or less emptied out, except for a few diehards and by that of course I mean us and a few of the HLS folks who were cleaning up. We pitched in (our mamas raised us up good) and then were sitting around talking when the Queen of Bluegrass strolled up.

Hey thanks for helping out she said. I'm glad you guys stuck around, I was hoping we'd get a chance to play together. Why'n't you pull those things out. She nodded toward our cases.

So that is pretty much how the security guard found us an hour or so later: Greg, Jeff, me and the Queen of Bluegrass sitting in the college cafeteria wailin on song after song til he finally put us out.

I am pleased to report that my mom's double hip replacement surgery was a resounding success and my father battled back from the brink and Christmas and New Years were a real celebration at my parent's house in Durham. Also meant I was in fine spirits, when, a couple of weeks after the HLS meeting, Jeff invited me to come to Reidsville for a jam. There were to be some other people there, and I feel bad and know it's rude of me, but I don't remember who cause the real draw was that Greg was coming as well as Pammy, who wanted to jam with me/us again.

Bluegrass is my Second Language

I made the by now familiar drive up to Jeff's (see? not even mentioning the time factor) and loaded into the house. Pammy's eyes lit up when she saw the baby bass--my cello. See, it turns out she was relatively new to the dobro (coulda fooled me) and ACTUALLY was/is a bass player. (Yeah, yeah that whole multi-instrumentalist thing again.....look, it's a recurring theme, OK? Just figure it this way: they ALL play everything. I'm just the only one who makes a big deal of it....)

ANYway, we get to playing and Pammy wants to hear the cello so we do a slow song and she's very effusive with her praise. (Like I said, EVERYTHING sounds good with a cello on it....) So we play on. We start at seven thirty, eight, and by ten thirty or so we are charging right along: me on harp and mandolin, Jeff on his sparkling banjo, Greg strumming a blizzard of notes, when Pammy puts down her dobro and grabs my cello out of its stand and says we need a bass on this, we need a bass. I try to explain to her (all the while we're playing) that the cello is tuned differently from a bass so it likely won't work for her. She listens, considers for a sec and then begins tentatively to feel her way around. About thirty seconds later, she's wanging away on my cello so hard that one of the guys says Pammy fer Godssake, it ain't a BASS, you're gonna BREAK it! And she is flat wompin on that thang slappin out walking bass lines and just layin it down. We finish the song and

the Queen of Bluegrass says wow that was fun I gotta
get me one of those things and I'm thinkin damn, my
cello won't even want to TALK to me let alone PLAY
for me after what she did to it!

(The reader will be pleased to know, I'm sure,
that my cello and I have reconciled and are back
on speaking terms. But she DOES always ask when
Pammy's coming back over.......)

We played till late and then split up with lots of
hugs and promises of doing it again real soon.

And that's one of the things I'm proudest of:
on any given weekend, Pammy Davis is such a great
player and so well thought of and so well connected
in the Bluegrass scene that she probably has invites
to at least fifty great music sessions. I am very
flattered to say that Pammy has made it a point on
many occasions since that Saturday night to drive up
from Greensboro to join us in Chapel Hill (or even
Raleigh--longer drive, but we don't talk about that)
to spend an evening playing music with me and my
RDU player pals. And of course I have joined up
with her many times since (though not enough times,
never enough times) when I have driven west to the
Bluegrass jams.

You just can't help but feel special, play a little
better, sit up a little straighter when the Queen Of
Bluegrass comes to pick with you.

I am always honored.

5

BROWN'S AND A BIG SURPRISE

So the time goes by and there are many a weekend of music and laughter and wonderful, wonderful people. Hard to tell which I love more sometimes: playin all this great music or meeting all these warm, gracious people. Southern hospitality lives.

THRIVES.

Many of the folks I met were very generous
with their friendship, time and tutelage. Fred Minor,
the fiddle player, and I play together quite a bit
and I have to say I wouldn't be nearly as good on
the mandolin if it weren't for Fred and his generous
encouragement and kind criticisms, always given
with a compliment following so I won't lose heart.
Greg, Jeff and Keith were and continue to be terrific
sounding boards for honest feedback on my playing
(harmonica, guitar and cello) and my songwriting. On
many occasions the Queen of Bluegrass has coerced
me into pulling out my banjo and joining in a song,
something I would not normally do in a Bluegrass
crowd, at least until I get a whole lot better.

Not only had I lucked into meeting some of the
finest and most respected players in the Piedmont,
they were also the nicest folks in the world.

For a guy who carries his harmonicas in his
mom's overnight bag, I am one lucky sonuvagun.

Suddenly I began to hear names (Haleyland,
Jimmy's Shop, Brown's) that the players I respected
most talked about with an affection that made these
places seem as much a character, a personality, as
the people I was meeting. Each pickin parlor had
its own vibration, own set of rules, its own set of
expectations, own kind of musical experience. And
the players talked about them with genuine respect
and admiration.

Bluegrass is my Second Language

One chilly night in February we're packing up
to go home and talking about meeting next week,
when Jeff says, What'd'y'all think? Think we should
take ol Big John down to Brown's yet? Is he ready?
And the other guys hem and haw but finally agree
that yeah I'm ready. So the plan is set: I'm going to
Brown's next Saturday.

I have been hearing about Brown's since I was
in high school. Brown's was practically mythical:
there is an old tobacco barn in the middle of
nowhere, and every Friday and Saturday night people
come from all over to play there. Back then I heard
that a lot of famous people had played there. On
their way through Greensboro and Raleigh, folks like
Willie Nelson and Jerry Jeff Walker would pull on
over to Brown's and play a set or two. And of course,
local boys like Tony Rice would come down and pick
before they got famous. But aside from that, what we
had all heard was that the folks who played there were
REALLY good. They weren't professionals necessarily,
but they'd come from Danville, Virginia and Winston
Salem and Eden and they all came prepared to stand
and deliver. We were all of fifteen, sixteen years
old and we played rock n roll and listened to Jimi
Hendrix, but that was enough. Great players, great
music: we HAD to find this place.

Problem was, we didn't know where the heck
it was. Best we could do was that it was somewhere
north and east of Greensboro out in the country. I

remember my high school drummer and I heading out on a summer Saturday night (he was old enough to drive) looking for this place, driving aimlessly on the back roads, music cranked up loud, pulling over to ask some poor unsuspecting farmer if they knew where Brown's was. Looking back I reckon we were pretty naive to think we would find this place by dumb luck or that the poor startled farm hands would tell us anything when we pulled over and turned down our screaming rock music to ask directions.

It was a different time then, and though a lot of the folks who play at Brown's now have long hair, folks back then weren't likely to give us long haired hippie types the keys to the city.

(Yeah, even I had hair back then....)

I expect a few of those farmers had a laugh or two at our expense as they set us off down the road in search of a place that was likely in the other direction.

Or maybe not.

Music is a powerful thing. I like to think they were trying to help and just didn't really know where it was exactly. Point is, we never did find that place though over the years we tried again and again. I never knew much more about it than: sometimes famous people played there but most nights the unknown pickers were better than any famous person you could name. Other than that, nothing.

It was Keith I think who told me the full name

for the first time: Brown's Old Opry.

Greg who told me where it was: McLeansville, NC. (Although to this day when people ask me where it is I always tell them to go out to the middle of nowhere and make a right. It's up the road a piece on the left. But then again, as I mentioned before, I'm geographically challenged....)

Thus it was, that on a raw, rainy February night I set out on I 40 West to meet up with Greg at a gas station at the McLeansville exit.

I made good time that night. I was pretty excited.

He splashed up in his station wagon into the lot of the closed convenience store, rolled down the window, and motioned for me to follow him and we pulled out down the dark highway through puddles of water and into the rain.

Down into McLeansville (don't blink.)

Over the railroad tracks, down we go.

Make a right (in the middle of nowhere.)

Go down the road.

Farmland, a few houses.

Fewer houses, more farm land.

Beginning to understand how Habib felt...

Pavement gives out.

Look to the left...

And there are the Port-O-Lets.

Welcome to Brown's.

We go past the big shack that's really an old tobacco barn, turn left just past the Port-O-Lets (have I mentioned them? City boy, remember???) and pull into the parking lot (really just another field.) I start to park but then follow Greg on past and around to the back where there's a smaller building adjoining the main one and some cement steps leading up to a door and a sign that says

MUSICIANS ONLY

I am so in awe that I am sure that statement excludes, and was written exclusively for, me.

Time to go home.

Greg sees me standing there dumb. C'mon man git yer stuff let's get in there and git to pickin. I grab my mandolin and my mom's you-know-what and mount the steps as Greg pushes open the old wooden door painted a repulsive color of green, worn and chipped and weathered....

In we go.

I am desperately trying to get my mandolin in tune.

Bluegrass is my Second Language

This is no easy task, as there are about ten or twelve of us crammed in here, this tiny rectangle of a room. If I could manage to stretch my arms straight out to my sides without putting someone's eye out, I could just about reach the rough cut boards that act as high shelves on ply wood sheets that pass for walls. A cold rain is thrumming a steady rhythm on the corrugated tin roof and somewhere a space heater is pouring out heat, which is crazy because even though it's freezing outside, the sardines in this can are about to boil. And as if that isn't problem enough, there's another mandolin player about four guys in front of me, and HE'S trying to get in tune and he's WAY out of tune, not even in the neighborhood.

There's maybe three guys behind me, and five or six stacked in front, which makes the room a little less than fifteen, sixteen feet long with a claustrophobic low sloping ceiling. We're packed in about three or four across, barely enough room to cram ourselves in here, let alone the instruments we carry. The air is thick with a very odd mixture of sweat, a humid wet dog smell and a minimum of three different varieties of aftershave, Old Spice being the frontrunner, at least to my olfactory assessment. Banjos are plinking, guitars are strumming and there's the low moan of a fiddle. It is a cacophony of random Bluegrass runs and fills as everyone is frantically trying to get in tune, to stabilize instruments still chilled from the ride and the load in to this cramped little room. I nod a terrified hello to Jeff as he tunes his banjo. He smiles a greeting. I am clutching my mandolin and an over night case that houses my harmonicas and extra strings. I feel pretty foolish. I literally don't know where we are, or who most of these people are, or what's going to happen next. All I know is that it's taken me almost 20 years to get here, and even though I feel like I stick out like a sore thumb, I am going to get in tune cause that's what Greg told me to do and that's what everyone else is doing. Finally Fred (who has been plucking an 'A' string with his thumb for what feels like the past ten minutes) prevails and we get the hint and begin to tune to him. I'm almost there when Greg grins at me and says "Ready?" and before I can say "For what?". or "No!" a door to my left bursts open and we are all pushed through.

To my horror, I find myself standing on a stage.

Dear God, I can't be on stage: don't these people know Bluegrass is my second language???

Now in my time I have performed on many a stage. I once played solo, just me and my guitar, for about ten thousand people. AND I got called back for an encore, so I am no stranger to the stage.

But I need to be READY.

Rehearsed.

Prepared.

No one ever told me there was a STAGE at

Brown's. I always assumed we just sat around in a
circle like we do at my house and at Jeff's.

On top of that, this is BROWN'S. These people
know good Bluegrass music, they've heard the best
of the best here. In two notes they're gonna know
the college boy from Chapel Hill is a Pretender and
those tomatoes that have been waiting for me since
Burlington are finally going to be put to the use God
intended.

It's called hubris, folks.

My heart sinks.

There is a worn baby puke green carpet on
the floor that must have been laid down forty years
ago. (It was.) A forest of shiny chrome microphone
stands loom along the lip of the stage. No exit there.
Blocked. Too many players behind me pushing me
forward to go back. Old photographs of old people
on the walls, signs: Royal Crown, Bull Durham. A
long rectangle of a room, bare metal walls, tin sheets,
wooden framework showing. A high ceiling. Twenty
feet high?

The snare drum rain rattles on tin from up
above....

Down in front of the stage a curious anomaly:
a square of hardwood floor, exceedingly fine
craftsmanship standing in stark contrast to the
roughness of the rest of the interior.

Of course....

A dance floor.

No compromising on the dance floor. That HAS to be good: solid, level, seamless, smooth.

Dear God they're gonna wanna DANCE.

Nowhere to go. I slide as inconspicuously (yeah, right) as possible over to the far side of the stage and try to plant myself in a corner.

Maybe no one'll notice....

Greg comes over and grabs my sleeve and leads me to the center of the stage (DEAR GOD!) and starts setting up a mic for me. I retreat stage left over to an old upright piano and lean against it. Put my mom's overnight bag on the keys, my mandolin on top. Greg tries to pull me back. No, no, I need to be here where I can set my stuff out. He walks away. Good. Closer to the door here.

Halfway through the first song, I'm outa here.

He comes back with a mic. Places it in front of me, adjusts it as I finish tuning my mandolin. As soon as he turns his back I reach up and turn it off.

Heh heh heh.

One song, I'm gone.

Everybody saddles up. They all look happy. I wonder if I look like I feel. Deer in the headlights. Someone counts off a song. Good song. Fred fiddles, Greg strums and leans into the mic and begins to croon away. That mandolin player finally got in tune. Sounds reasonably good, I put mine down. Look at Greg's hands, read the chords, pull out a D harp. I try not to look left, out at the expectant faces wondering who the heck the new guy is. Song is really pretty good. Some good players up here. Well, that's what I always heard.

Gotta get outa here before I make a fool of myself and embarrass my new friends. It's one thing to play in a living room and try stuff out but a whole new deal altogether to be on stage in front of a real live audience and a real live well educated audience: these folks don't just LISTEN to Bluegrass, they LIVE it.

I feather in a few long, high notes lacing around and embellishing a few of Fred's sweet lines.

God he's good.

Jeff grins at me.

Well, so far so good.

What the heck.

I push the stand back a few feet and turn on the mic. Can't hurt if I back off....

Sweet Jesus Greg just tossed me the break.

Right across from me is a guitar player, chunkin away.

Hey, it's Jimmy Johnson, from the other night, all those old timers! He smiles, nods a hello. I start to play. Greg reaches over and moves the mic closer. I close my eyes and right on cue the gypsy shows up and starts playing things I never heard, thought of, or played before in my whole life.

Good to see ya gypsy.

We come up on the end of the verse and head to the chorus, I play the last few notes of my break and

The crowd applauds.

Now to be fair, it's a rainy, turrible night in mid February.

Ya gotta be nuts to come out on a night like this, I know I am.

And it's not like there's a ton of people out there, or even twenty for that matter.

But they CLAPPED.

I'm playing at Brown's and people are clapping.

Holy s**t.

We play about forty-five minutes then Greg says we're gonna do one more then the other band is gonna come on and play awhile. I vaguely remember hearing some noise (music?) coming from that little room off to the side in back when we came in and as we were trying to tune in what I now know is backstage. We finish our set and this band comes through. They're all dressed alike in fringed shirts, cowboy hats and stuff. As I slide out the door one of the guys says hey man that is some great harmonica you were playin. I am so stunned I just walk by before it registers. We go down the cement steps out into the cold and then up some ragged wooden stairs into a small, square twelve by twelve room with a few chairs scattered around. Every single one of em has only three legs and is held stable by some jury-rigged contraption or other, whether it's a book, a cinder block, a stack of boards, somethin. A few over turned buckets serve as chairs as well.

What the heck.

Most Bluegrass players stand when they play anyway.

(I still sit. Like to be true to my blues roots.)

There is an oversized space heater that is being paid time and a half to try and keep this room warm and it is earning every penny. It flashes through my mind that we're all going to die in the ensuing inferno. Fred bows out the first five notes of a song and one by one we straggle in.

Now THIS is what I came for. We're sitting in a circle, no pressure, no audience and we are PLAYIN some damn hot music. Five minutes later one of the guys from that band opens the door and says we're gonna do one more then it's all yours.

Dang.

They sure played a short set. What's up with that?

I look at my watch.

It's been right at an hour since we left the stage.

Time flies when you're having fun.

The uniform band starts threading in and I'm

dreading going back out there, I'm nervous about the audience, though not as much as before. We were just having such a good time back here though....

Another guy from the band stops me as I head out the door (I'm last out, as usual.) Hey man, he says, y'all are great. What's the name of your band?

Band?? I laugh incredulously, we're not a BAND, we're just a bunch of guys who pick together. Hell, I don't even know some of these guys, never met 'em before.

Soon as it was outa my mouth I knew it was a wrong, stupid thing to say. His face fell. It was obvious these boys had sunk a lot of time and money and effort into their music only to be smoked by a pick-up band. I hated myself for saying that, and even for thinking it. Music is not a competition, not a contest. It's a team sport and a unifying force and I had disgraced that belief. It was written all over the poor guys face though: Lord help us, these guys aren't even a band and they sound better than we do.

I took a chance, based on what I knew from the short time I had spent playing Bluegrass music with the guys and, even though I had no right to say it, I said, why don't you boys come on out and join us and pick a while. He smiled and said thanks man, but I reckon we'll head on back. Looks like we got some practicin to do.

I nodded, and started to make my way out.

Hey buddy, he called after me.

I turned.

You play that harmonica just like Charlie McCoy.

I about burst into tears. Here I just insulted the guy and he paid me the highest compliment you could give a Bluegrass harmonica player.

Thanks partner, I said, smiling, I really appreciate that. Y'all come out and pick a while.

He said, maybe we'll do that.

I never saw those boys again.

Second set I was a bunch more comfortable with the concept of there BEING a stage, let alone being ON one, and we picked up a storm that night at Brown's. I honestly don't remember much as the whole night went by in a blur. At one point I do remember Greg (much to my dismay) asking everybody to give a big hand to the boy from Chapel Hill and hearing a nice round of applause as I finished up my harmonica break. Felt good.

Seemed like we were just getting started when Greg said well, we'll do one more and then it'll be time to head on home. I looked at my watch: it was just a hair before eleven.

We normally play all night long. Something is weird here.....

We played the song, and Greg went to take off

his guitar, was saying thank you, good night when a raspy voice rang out from somewhere toward the back of the room.

Y'all boys play a couple more.

Ooookay....

Seems odd, but sure......nobody else seems to think this is a little strange or anything, in fact most of the guys seem right pleased.

Hmmmmm.....

So we all saddled up again and did another couple songs, the crowd claps, we start to head off and again from the back of the room that old voice rings out:

"Y'all boys do another one. Do one more."

So, once again, we file back out, strap on the guitars, mandolins, banjos and play ANOTHER one. This one though is Amazing Grace and it's slow and stately and pretty and it is definitely the last song of the night, and then we finish and take our bows and start to pack up our gear.

EXCEPT:

My engine is revving about ten thousand rpm, we're only just getting in the groove, just hitting our stride and we're QUITTING.

Musicus Interruptus.

Man..... I HATE when that happens....

I'm about to scream!

Instead, I lean over to Greg and say Greg, what's the deal? We're really in the pocket, why in

God's name are we stopping?? Greg looks up from the guitar he's putting in his case and smiles. "Funny you should put it that way," he says.

I blink.

"I don't get it."

"Look around," he says, "It's Saturday night. Why do you THINK these fine folks want to get home early on a Saturday night?"

I consider a second.

Ohhhh, I nod, the light bulb coming on, you quit at eleven on Saturday night so you can get up early and go to church on SUNday.

And he smiles as if to say, EXACTLY.

Mollified, I turn back to my own gear and began stowing my mandolin in its case when I hear a soft, almost reverential conversation. It's Jeff, I think, behind me.

Something in the tone of his voice strikes me.... not alarming.... just.... different....

I hear "yessir" then a short pause and "well, yessir" and then "yesSIR" and then "well, thank you" and it hits me that Jeff sounds a bit like a tow headed boy in short pants talking to the preacher after church on Sunday morning. I shake my head as I think to myself: Lots of very odd behavior at this place...... glad to be here and all, but some very odd behavior at this place.....

I glance over to see him shaking hands and nodding with two older gentlemen in overalls and ball caps, except these ball caps bear the logos of machines and feed, not mascots and teams. The men are old and bent, weathered and rough with faces that have stories written between the lines. I kinda shrug and turn back to my harmonicas. A few minutes later I hear Jeff close behind me saying, uh, John, I got some folks here'd like to meetcha.

And then I turn into a towheaded boy in short pants talking to the preacher on Sunday morning as Jeff introduces me to our hosts for the evening and for the past forty years: the Brown Brothers, John and Daniel. Dressed in identical faded blue bib overalls, they are ancient and beaten, but regal and strong. They have a very stately, dignified presence about them.

I, like Jeff before me, proceed to say really intelligent things like, "Yessir!" and then shake hands and add wittily, "No, no, thank YOU!" and "yessir." and "yesSIR."

Oh, I'm tellin ya I was on FIRE that night!

But then came the best part:

John Brown leaned in close and said in that same raspy voice I heard calling for one more from the back of that old tobacco barn, he said:

"You play that harmonica real good, Chapel Hill. You got to come back and play with us some more." and his brother Daniel nodded gravely in agreement and I tell you what, I felt about like I had won an Emmy and an Oscar and the Nobel Peace

Prize and a couple of Grammys, all presented by Mother Theresa (for goodness) and Elle McPherson (for, well, you know, for Elle McPherson)!

After all the time it took me to get here, the Brown Brothers were asking me to come back to play again.

It just don't get much better than this......

Course the fact that they had no idea what my name was, was of little to no importance. The point is they wanted me to come back. I was (and believe me folks, this rarely happens) speechless as Daniel said, "Chapel Hill, you play that harmonica just like that Charlie McCoy fella. Adds a lot, people like that sound. You got to promise me you'll come back."

And I said, as solemnly as I could, cause God knows I meant it:

"Yessir," I said.

"Yes sir, I promise."

"I will come back."

6

JIMMY'S SHOP

We were out back in the lot, putting cases and stands in the cars, when the boys gathered round.

We're thinkin bout goin up to Jimmy's Shop to finish playin. You wanna come?

I musta looked pleased cause they all started laughin and Greg said Wow! Brown's and Jimmy's Shop all in one night--think he can handle it? And they all slapped my back and with hands shoved in our pockets against the cold we trudged off through the waterlogged field, feet slapping in the grass, towards our cars. The rain had stopped somewhere in the last set, and the clouds parted to reveal a moon and stars and the night was crisp and biting and clear and cold, but other than my natural musicians instinct to keep my hands warm, I didn't feel a thing.

Jimmy's Shop!

Don't know ANYTHING about this place, the guys wouldn't give me details just a "yeah, we left there and went over to Jimmy's Shop and played some. Had a bite to eat, played some more, got home about three...."

I envisioned a club or bar, maybe a diner of some kind. There's a restaurant in Durham called George's Garage, maybe it was like that.

Greg hollered out a "Follow me!" and once again I drove off into the darkness.

And so we drove.

And drove.

For a while I didn't hardly notice, I was so high about being asked to come back to Brown's and playing back the evening's music in my head.

But we just kept....

on....

driving......

I began to think maybe this is some kind of hazing thing they do to the new guy: first time you play at Brown's: all the players drive you (farther out) into the middle of nowhere, they all pull over at a six point intersection, jump outa their cars and bang on the hood of yer car saying nice pickin rookie, see ya next time and then all take off in six different directions and when you finally get home at five thirty in the morning after driving all night, there's a message on your machine with everybody laughing.

But no, we just drove on.

And on....

Further...

Just about the time I was starting to understand EXACTLY how Habib felt, the first car put on a right turn signal and one by one the line of cars lit up the night with a bank of blinking red lights. We pulled into a driveway by some big red wagon wheels. The first pick up truck pulled up, stopped and Jimmy's wife hopped out, waved to the line of cars, and headed toward the big wood house lit up in my headlights because I had started to pull over cause I though we were gonna park. But no, apparently we need to drive some more down this dirt road past the house, a barn, another barn, our headlights slicing big arcs of white light out of the dark night.

Finally we pull up by this rather large structure. It's too dark, I can't tell exactly how big or what it's made of, there's just this looming shape, but it seems big enough, and then I see the guys getting their instruments out as I cut my engine and kill my lights.

I gather my stuff up and, as I was the last car in line, I'm the last guy in. I slowly make my way, instruments in both hands and tucked under both arms, staggering towards the slash of light where the guys had gone, trying not to drop anything and I use the nose of my guitar case to nudge open the door and push my way in.

Looking down, I carefully maneuver my instrument cases through the doorway and manage, with a minimum of bumps and scrapes, to get all of them inside and finally, I slowly gaze up and have to catch myself before I drop every precious instrument I own.

Cause there, directly across from me, bigger and redder than life is

A tractor.

Stunned, I look around.
It seems Jimmy's Shop is exactly that:
Jimmy's shop.

If you're ever in your life gonna play real honest to God, down home, old time Bluegrass music, I think to myself, it will have to be while you're sittin beside a honkin big red ass tractor.

Well, I mutter, THIS'll be interesting....

By the time I got all my stuff in and set up
and in tune, Jimmy had fired up the big wood stove
over by the tractor (of course) and the whole shop
had a pleasant warm glow to it. Towards the front
of the shop, right by the heavy metal door where we
came in, a huge rectangular carpet was laid out: the
designated pickin' area of the shop. Otherwise the
room was a large concrete slab, big enough to park
about six or eight cars in, the shop end being toward
the back by the double doors that let the tractor (and
God knows what else) in and out. There are the usual
tools and such, but, at least to my mind, the shop is
dominated by the pickin area: mic stands, old chairs,
mic cables strewn about, a small PA amp/mixer on
the work bench, its little red light glowing signaling
its readiness to make some music.

The guys were milling around, talking, laughing
and trying to pick out a song to play to get that mood
and groove we had going at Brown's back again. Most
all Bluegrass players stand when they play. Being a
Blues player and basically lazy as a teenage boy at
heart, I pulled up a chair, settling in and enjoying
the odd mix of aromas: the comforting burning wood
smoke and the acrid smell of oiled tools and kerosene.

Greg said pull one a them mics up near ya John
so we can hear ya and I reached out and grabbed a
stand and heaved and about fell over.

Seems Jimmy didn't see the logic of BUYIN mic
stands if he could MAKE em, so why bother? The

mic stand that had nearly yanked my arm out of its socket was, upon closer inspection, actually a couple of pieces of pipe welded at forty-five degree angles to each other. That stand and arm were then welded to a huge circular base that must weigh six or seven thousand pounds. Needless to say, the new guy about falling out his chair trying to move a mic stand was just the hilarity the gathering called for and no one was shy about laughing out loud at my predicament (and I am quite sure they were laughing AT me, not with me.) You know what that base is made of Chapel Hill one of the guys asked over the genial laughter. I allowed as how, No sir, I pretty much had no idea what the heck that was except that it sure was heavy and I didn't reckon any one would run off with that mic stand any time soon. Yeah Greg said, Jimmy didn't want anyone to steal em so that's why he spray painted em gold.

And of course he was right: the entire cockamamie contraption was spray painted a garish gold.

Yep, no mistakin one of Jimmy's mic stands, but that disc at the bottom, you know what that is? He didn't wait for an answer. (City boy, of course he don't know.) That there is a harrow....one a THEM, and he turned halfway and pointed to the back end of the omnipresent tractor in the corner. Attached to the back was a series of discs that spread and turned the ground for planting.

When you drive by and see one from your car, they don't look that big and heavy.

Trust me: up close, they are.

Well, I said, it's nice that Jimmy recycles.

No one laughs.

Not a sound.

Tough crowd.

I hauled the mic stand closer and sat down in front of it. Fred started ladling out some big spoonfuls of sweet fiddle and we all joined in and made some fine music. We reclaimed the energy and drive we'd had at Brown's and then some. Had the pleasure of playing with Bob Stanfield, the bass player from the first Burlington gig. I enjoy his playing a lot but for some reason our paths don't cross as often as I would like. Obviously, his playing has got a special place in my heart as he was among the original players who got me onto this whole mess to begin with. So it was Bob and Fred and Greg and Jeff and of course Jimmy Johnson and most all the fellas from Brown's and a few who musta just heard we were coming or just showed up.

I hate to keep saying this, cause I know y'all get tired of me repeating myself, but I really don't know what we played that night. Just a buncha Bluegrass songs. But what Bluegrass songs....

Those boys could pick and we wailed away till late in the night and early in the morning began to wrestle with each other for top billing.

Bluegrass is my Second Language

I do know with a certainty that it was three AM when we quit cause I remember looking at my watch and groaning thinking it would be five in the morning when I got home (assuming I could find my way out of here. And that was a BIG assumption.) Fred was over by the door, opening his case to put up his bow when somebody saw him sneak a look at his watch, and they all began laughing and teasing him. What's all that about, I asked Jeff. Oh, that's just ol' Fred, lookin at his watch trying to figure out if he can make it on down the road to the next pickin place before they close up. Sheeesh I mutter, guy's in his seventies and plays better and longer than me, then runs off to play some more when all I wanna do is go home to bed. I know, Jeff grinned, shaking his head in disbelief, I know.

I think I wanna be Fred when I grow up, I said to nobody in particular.

Well, I know y'all don't believe me, but I really don't think I noticed that Jimmy had a bunch of Playboy pin ups on the walls, least not that first night.

I get pretty focused on the music when I play and often don't notice which folks are there, who comes, who goes, and sometimes, when the music is really good, I don't even notice the girls, sad to say. But at some point on one of my subsequent Friday night visits to Jimmy's shop, I DID notice them gals up there all over the wall above the work bench and

I began telling the same joke I tell every time I visit Jimmy Johnson's shop.

Somewhere in the evening's festivities, during a pause in the music and a lull in the conversation, I'll say in a loud clear voice, "Y'know, Jimmy, I am a single man....."

And the boys will kinda groan and laugh all at the same time, cause they know what's comin....

"And I sure would like to meet one a your daughters up there....."

Hooting and jeering from the boys.

"...I mean, you got TWELVE of 'em, seems only neighborly you'd be willing to introduce me to at least one of em....."

Always cracks me up.

7

THE BLUEGRASS WIDOWS AND THE APRIL FOOLS

One thing that always bothered me every time
I was up at Jeff's in Reidsville or over at Jimmy's shop
in Brown's Summit, was the fact that, in spite of what
I had seen at the High Lonesome String meetings,
there were never any women singing or playing with
the group.

Now I may have mentioned once or twice that I am a single kinda fella and I will admit that upon occasion I enjoy the company of those of the female persuasion.

(Don't pretend to understand em, but definitely appreciate em. My buddy Martin says women build consensus and men build decks. Not sure what relevance that has to the proceedings but I feel there is some wisdom there that needs to be shared with the world.)

When we play at Jeff's all the women gather in the back room, a sorta TV room off the kitchen and talk or whatever. Every once in a while I would hear em singin along: a high harmony would filter in from around the bend, through the kitchen and across the room. Or sometimes when we would get to pickin something particularly hot or pretty, they would come gather by the kitchen door and poke their heads out and nod and grin and then wander back off to the den. Kinda like they would call a time out, come out on the field, give us all a little pat on the butt and then traipse on back to the bull pen and get on the phone or do stats and we'd go back to playin ball.

At Jimmy's, the ladies all gather at a long table in back by the tractor and play cards or talk, always careful to clap after every song and holler out some encouragement or acknowledge a particularly well sung or well played part.

The point is, I don't know a player on the

planet who don't sit up a little straighter, sing a little louder, pick a little harder when there's a woman in the room. Heck, I'd notice it when one of them gals would sashay on through the living room at Jeff's on their way to the bathroom and every single damn one of them fellers would perk up a bit and as soon as that bathroom door closed they'd all slump back down, let their guts sag back out like we just finished Thanksgiving turkey and then BAM! as soon as that door opened back up and she headed toward the den they'd all be sittin as tall and handsome as a how-do-you-damn-do.

Same thing at Jimmy's. And age, shape, size, color, none of it made a damn difference. If it was a female type human what walked on by, they'd respond to her and not a one of em probably knew they were even doin it.

Now when we get together and play with my RDU crowd, we got a bunch of women who come sing with us and every night there's a tussle or two while we boys all try to get as close to them as possible. And yeah, OK, some of it's that boy stuff cause they are right fun to look at and they sure smell good, but most of it is just a pure love of hearing that high sweep of harmony or a crystal vocal line flyin up there like some kinda strange, sweet magic.

So one night I asked Jeff what the deal was. He and Greg just laughed and allowed as how them ladies were pretty much bored with the music they'd heard it so much and so the gals just came along to socialize a bit and keep an eye on their boys. The ladies, Jeff said, sorta commiserate with each other: after all, they're the Bluegrass widows.

Now I am an old school kinda feller, and when I hear something that sets my writer's ear off, a little bell rings in my head and it sounds exactly like the carriage return ding on an old Royale typewriter. I expect there are some who are reading this who have no idea what that sound is, or what a typewriter is for that matter, but suffice it to say that I literally hear a DING when something happens that I recognize is a writing opportunity. Mostly I have been able over the years to ignore this intrusion into my more or less normal life, but every once in a while, the Ding is just so pervasive and persuasive that I can't help myself. (Thus this book.)

So as the echoes of that damned troublesome Ding faded away, I waited a moment or two, looking from Jeff to Greg, Greg to Jeff, waiting for one of them to grab that line. I mean, both of them boys are fine songwriters and there was this song title just sitting there, this golden fruit waiting to be plucked, the song waiting to write itself, it was so obvious....

But they just looked at me like what the heck is troublin this boy now and I finally said well if you guys aren't gonna claim this song, I am sure gonna write it. And they said what song? And I said, Bluegrass Widows. It's a great song title. And Jeff laughed and said, "Well it's original, it's mine and I reckon you can have it if you want it cause I don't see it!" So I went home and wrote a song about the Bluegrass Widows who sit in the other room and tap their feet in time.

They also serve who sit and wait, I reckon.

It took me awhile to write "Bluegrass Widows."

For the first time in my musical life, I was trying to write Bluegrass music that wasn't an exercise or just a matter of scoring some music for a film or commercial project. Something had happened. Something had changed. It was very important to me to get this song right: it was about my friends, our experience and a music I had really come to love and a culture that had welcomed me with, well, maybe a skeptical look on their faces, but really with open arms. I wasn't feeling so much like a guest or a visitor any more, I was feeling at home, and I needed to get the song right.

Doris Betts, my friend and writing teacher at Carolina always said, "Write what you know." I've amended that with a "...and tell the truth," and it seems to work out OK, but y'all will have to be the judge of that, you're the ones who decide to keep reading or not. But I have to say, in general, a good way to go is to tell the truth when you write or play music, so I just talked about driving west up NC Highway 87 to Reidsville to play some music and have some fun on a Saturday night and then just described what I saw when I got there.

I reckon I did all right by it cause when I played it one night up at Jimmy's shop the guys gave it a big round of applause and Fred came over and said how much he liked it. I told Amy, Jeff's wife, that it was really about her and her friends and she bugs me all the time to sing it, so I guess I done good.

One of the things I most wanted in the world as we approached spring of 2002 was to sit outside and play some music. I drive everybody nuts cause even when it's four hundred degrees in July I STILL want to sit outside and play. We're all sitting there sweatin buckets and swattin at the skeeters and I am just all smiles and saying man isn't this great. I don't know why, but I have always liked to play outdoors. Maybe the connection is this: I think there are two things that human beings do that embody the most noble, most ambitious aspects of the human species.

Oddly enough, it's when we imitate the birds.

I think I can say with a high degree of certainty that there are VERY few people who don't, in his or her heart of hearts, really believe that there is just no way airplanes fly. I mean it seriously shouldn't work. That with tons of metal and screeching engines we somehow emulate the grace and beauty of a soaring hawk or humble sparrow is just plain foolishness. And yet we do.

Bluegrass is my Second Language

And yet we do, and we do it magnificently.
And when we don't fly, we sing.

Like the birds, when we set our feet on the ground, we open our mouths and we sing back to the heavens. We take our hands and shape our tools and till the earth and plant and work and then at the end of the day, we take our tools up once again in weary hands and shape our woods and metals and we make tools for those who can't sing so well so that they may have the beauty of flight in the power of a cello line, a riffle of banjo notes, or a strum of a chord on an old wooden guitar

So as we ended up March and headed toward spring and the anniversary of Shepp's death, I thought there would be no better way to honor that date than to gather and play some music and greet the spring and the warm weather.

We'd pick and grin a little for the birds; let em know we're still here, pluggin away.

I had also been trying for months to get the Greensboro Bluegrass players together with my RDU Blues/Pop players, but no matter how hard, or what I tried, it never worked out. So finally I hit on the idea of playing the first Saturday in April and set about announcing it way in advance everywhere I went and trying to get both groups excited about it. I think, in fact there was a fair amount of interest on both sides, as I talked about the Bluegrass Boys to the RDU crowd and vice versa. And clearly the RDU

Players could see some changes in me: my mandolin playing was getting better, my harmonica was playing stuff they (and I) had never heard before and I was singing songs from one group back to the other, so I think both sides were intrigued, but it was a logistical nightmare.

Basically I was trying to organize a party for about seventy or eighty people.

Now if you're a woman, you just let out a low groan cause somehow women get some sorta gene that enables them to see the difficulties involved in planning and doing this kinda thing. (I hold these truths to be self-evident: that all are NOT created equal. When the gene for Planning and Realizing What A Nightmare The Plan Will Be was passed out, we men somehow were in another line trying to get change for the car wash or reading the sports section.)

Being a boy, I had no idea what a HUGE pain in the posterior this endeavor was going to be, and if I had, I never would have pursued it, that's for sure.

And what's worse, being new to Bluegrass, I made the cardinal mistake of the newbie: I made the party a pig pickin.

See, if you play Bluegrass music, there is one thing you can be guaranteed: in any given summer season lasting say, one hundred twenty days, you will play at and eat at a pig pickin at least seven hundred and sixty two times. Being new, I hadn't gotten that yet, I was still enjoying the grub thinkin wow this is great. And I shoulda known better: in the film biz it's pizza. If you're ever having someone over for dinner who works in film fer Godssakes don't order or make pizza. It's the last refuge of the unprepared: the new producer runs short on time or forgets the crew has to actually eat once in a while and grabs the phone and orders eleven pizzas and thinks there that's that. We HATE that. Shows a lack of respect and poor planning.

And God bless em, those Bluegrass boys must've felt EXACTLY the same way, but come Saturday, April 1, 2002 at two PM, there were sixty five people on my front lawn eatin pig and chicken and slaw and hush puppies. About twenty of em were friends and music lovers I knew would appreciate what was coming. Forty-five of em were pickers: Keith was there on bass, Jimmy Johnson sang "I'm So Lonesome I Could Cry" and sounded like he meant it. I had the great pleasure of introducing Fred Minor and Jimmy and the boys to my dad. Greg sang and played, and Jeff rang out on that Deering banjo of his.

On the RDU side, Jen DeMik, who has got one of the most amazing voices you've ever heard, came and sang and blew everybody away. Gina Norman and Megan Day sang harmonies and back up and the occasional lead as well and proved my point about women adding to the mix (as if the Bluegrass boys needed convincing....) Ray St. Clair, my friend for over twenty years came and added his perfect guitar timing and phrasing to the assembled group. Frank Gordon sang some John Prine songs that knocked everybody out and Harry Teuting picked some licks on his Taylor guitar that were icing on the cake. And my good buddy Martin Brown scored the coup of the day by situating himself EXACTLY in the middle of all the Very Best Players. Don't know how he did it, but everybody still hates him to this day cause he had the best seat in the house. (And wouldn't get up. Ever. All damn day....)

Had the rare opportunity to enjoy two dobro players with two very distinct yet very complimentary styles. My RDU buddy Donnie Evans came and brought his 1929 Dobro and his old Martin guitar and Pammy Davis (yeah the Queen Of Bluegrass was at the party too) came and played her resophonic dobro. That was truly amazing. Donnie's dobro style is like the orange yellow sparks of a steel welder. He flashes and slashes and rolls his lead lines around and into the song in a powerful yet respectful way. He plays with honor. Pammy's dobro is more of the blue white of an arc welder: her lines are delicate yet strong, her phrasing a little more open but just as forceful and compelling. It was one of those rare wonderful moments when two great players meet and compliment each other perfectly. They could play a solo, one after the other, and where other dobro players would sound more or less the same, these two players were creating little dobro symphonies for our edification and enjoyment.

And that was happening all over the place.

Guys were just sittin and lookin at each other with a whoa that guy is GOOD look on their faces, grinnin and jumpin back in. I knew these folks would like each other and "get" each other as players but it was gratifying to see that they also liked and respected each other as people too. There were conversations and introductions everywhere. A bunch of folks had brought wives/girlfriends/husbands/boyfriends and kids, which is always a pleasure for me. I love to play for the little kids, see the incredibly pure enjoyment and understanding of the music, the sheer joy it creates in them. Very humbling to sit and watch all this happen and think well I did a good thing here today.

Very nice indeed....

There were other folks who came and played and sang and added to the day, but at some point these are just names to y'all, and unfortunately I can't recreate the music we made as we sat in a huge circle in my front yard that glorious Saturday afternoon in April.

And froze our asses off.

And moved to stay in the sun.

And then moved again twenty minutes later.

And froze our asses off.

Cause this being MY life, and even though the weather forecasters had promised at least a seventy-

degree day, we were lucky to make it to fifty. So sixty
five of us shuffled our chairs and followed the sun
around the yard and tried to be brave, and blew on
our hands to warm our fingers and Martin and some
folks brought their grills and we put the food on the
grills to keep it warm and mostly it was pretty OK.
Certainly colder than I would've liked, but pretty
much OK. Only bummer was that due to the cold, a
bunch of folks left earlier than planned (as soon as
the sun went down) and most of the kids went with
them. But we finally got to the point where we were
a small enough group and we were so cold we could
crowd in my little living room and sing and play in
relative comfort. I had some of my students over and
we gave them a bunch of food to take home (them
being young and poor students and hungry and all.)
My dogs Blue and Seven had a big time. Blue is a
German Shepherd/Labrador Retriever mix and Seven
was a big, handsome purebred English Setter. He
found the big bag of food the students had left outside
and decided we had given them a little too much take
home so while we played inside, he just pulled that
bag off the table and helped himself to some of their
stash in order to even things out. So HE had a great
night. Blue snuggled up with me in the house and
listened to some truly inspired and inspiring music.
She's always had a good ear for the tunes.

At eleven o'clock that morning, as the food got
screwed up and chairs got canceled and tents got lost,

Bluegrass is my Second Language

I swore on a stack of bibles I would NEVER EVER do anything like this EVER again.

At eleven in the evening as Greg and I sat slumped in the living room, trash and broken strings, picks and chairs everywhere, the last two remaining members of the party, I looked at him and said man that was GREAT. Let's do that again next week.

And he said,

I'm in.

8

BLUE AND SEVEN

What kinda book about Bluegrass would this book be if there weren't any dogs in the story? Well rest assured and be relieved: there are dogs mixed up in this waggin tale.

My buddy Mac Monroe says I don't have pets, I have roommates who happen to be animals. That being the case, it wasn't long before I wanted to have my roommates meet my new human friends.

Just seemed like every place I went there was wide-open country and yeah, if you're playing Bluegrass there oughta be dogs layin around scratchin and howlin at the moon with the boys. Lots of times the boys I played with didn't seem to have any dogs around, so I began to bring my own.

It was only later that I started to take the dogs down to Brown's, but pretty quick I'd bring em on up to Jimmy's or over to Greg's when we were a pickin. My dogs had been around music all their lives. One of em, the female named Blue, was actually given to me in a recording studio by a group I was producing called Out Of The Blue when she was just three months old. (Thus the name, get it?) She has been in recording sessions and video editing sessions ever since and has heard a lot of good music as she napped under the consoles with her head on my right foot. Lot a times when I show up places the dogs get the lion's share of attention and it's only later that people'd get around to saying hello to me. She looks just like a German Shepherd, only smaller: she's black with tan and white markings and weighs about fifty pounds. Got one little ear (the right) that's always bent over so she looks like one a them dogs in the movies, sorta perpetually cute. I've had Blue about thirteen years now.

Like I said earlier, that 2001 was a rough damn year. Seven was a pure bred English Setter and I'd

had him about ten years and to say that he and Blue
and I were tight is a real understatement. Those dogs
were some of my best friends and I count myself lucky
that they chose to be with me, and I learned a lot
from them. Seven (also named for Out Of The Blue,
but it's a long story) was a big boy about seventy-five
pounds with a white coat and mottled orange spots.
He came from a line of show dogs and he could put
on the handsome when he wanted to. You don't see
many English Setters around for some reason, and
folks were always stopping and asking about him and
petting on him. As a breed, they're real friendly, easy
going dogs and great with kids. Like Blue, he always
enjoyed the extra attention.

Blue tends to stay pretty close to me, but
Seven liked to wander so he and Jake, Jimmy's big ol
chocolate Lab up at the shop, would run around and
sniff up a storm and then come back to the shop and
nose around for a little pettin and some scraps of
biscuits or what have you. (The Bluegrass Widows up
at Jimmy's always bring food and stuff to drink, God
bless em.)

Them dogs'd settle on in, Jake in the back by
the tractor where Jimmy's wife Martha and some non-
musician types (civilians, I call em) would play cards
or chat while we played, and Sevvie would stretch
out somewhere behind me just off the carpet so that
cement slab would be nice and cool on his belly. He
was never a music fan like Blue, I think he just came

along with us cause he knew we liked it.... so he tagged along.

But Blue, man she loves herself some good music and is particularly fond of bass. Many is the evening at Jimmy's that she would come in, go around to say howdy to the folks she knew and then lay down right in front of Bob while he played his bass. Would just sit there and look up at him like there ya go Bob, that's the ticket, ya got it now, just lookin up at him, her ears up with a smile on her face.

For some reason when Keith plays, she likes to sit in back of him if she can. She'll go and say hi to everyone and then trot around in back and circle around (mat down the grass), pace a bit trying to find the best spot for sonic clarity and then lay down and stay there for as long as we play. That girl loves her some good bass pickin I reckon. Over the years she has developed a real fondness for Keith and his bass playin, stays right by him and listens all night long. One time we were playin up at Brown's and Keith couldn't make it so we had another quite capable feller on bass name a Dub Jordan. Once I got all in tune and set up Blue would come in, circle around and then plant herself in front of the bass for a night of great music. After a minute or two she'd get up and head out the stage door and wander out back. Then she would come back in, circle, then sit. Then out again. Then back. Over and over we all just sat there pickin and singin and watchin ol Blue go back and forth, back and forth. Finally Dub, said, Man I swear that dog is lookin for Keith and everybody started laughin and sayin yeah, that's what I been thinkin too and Dub bent down and nuzzled little Blue with his hand and said Blue I am sorry. I am playin the best I can, but I ain't no Keith! Blue kinda looked at him like, Well, I appreciate your efforts Dub, and then put her head down out in front of her on her paws and let out a long sigh like But boy I wish ol Keith was here tonight, I was really lookin forward to hearin him spank that big fat doghouse bass.

The boys liked having the dogs around I think. Dogs are good for everything in my opinion. When I taught a film course up at the community college, I used to take my dogs in whenever I gave mid terms or finals. Everybody did better when they could break the tension by reachin down and pettin the dogs. Same thing when you're playing too I think.

A wet nose works wonders sometimes.

If you have and love a dog, I won't need to explain much to you and if you don't, well, no amount of explanation will help you understand the relationship a Human can have with a Canine.

After Seven died, I was pretty lonely and upset and Blue was flat out miserable she missed him so much, just pined for him. Back in the beginning, when I went to Brown's I would mostly leave the pups at home, and if I did take them they stayed outside and ran around but now that there was no one to keep Blue company, I decided to bring her with me. So the first Saturday after Seven died, I loaded all the instruments up and put a bowl of water and some food in the car, the sign of a doggie road trip and little Blue lit up for the first time in about a week. We were grieving pretty badly, and I knew I needed some therapy, some healing music and good people and figured Blue could use some too. Plus I just wanted to spend time with her, spend time with my good friend.

As I drove down the dirt road to Browns, I could see there was a big crowd. Often in summer John and Daniel Brown will open the side doors of the barn and folks will sit in lawn chairs and enjoy the evening and music outside.

It was summer, and it was odd to be driving down that sandy road in daylight, but the days were long and evenings balmy and it looked to be exactly what we both needed. I pulled on past the ever-present Port-O-Lets (everyone I know hits the bathroom at Wendy's down at the McLeansville exit, but you never know....) and turned into the lot and went around back to the musicians' entrance. I hopped out and opened the side door of the Caravan for Blue and she jumped down and started nosing around. She immediately was drawn to bunch of young uns fooling around while their parents sat inside, waiting for the music to start. Kids and dogs are a natural mix and Blue is always happy to oblige. She's got this strut she does when she's happy: head held high, big smile, tail straight up and she sort of very regally trots around inspecting things and okaying the proceedings. She went off to play with the kids who began oohing and awing over her. (Apparently, she is able to make it quite clear that she is completely unloved and unattended at home and thus solely dependent upon, and starved for, affection from random strangers and passerbys.) I popped the hatch in back and pulled out some gear, tuned up my mandolin, then my guitar, it being a real pretty evening and quieter out here than inside. I could hear the guys inside over the microphones, talking and laughin and strummin and tuning up, but they hadn't started playing yet, I was fairly early. After a bit, little Blue pranced back my way, having gotten enough loving to make up for the deficit she lacked at home. I went around the side of the car and set out her water bowl and she started to lap up a drink or two.

Just then, the boys inside hit a chord and cranked up a song. Her head jerked up outa that water bowl and she shot a look over to the left where the barn was and her ears went to movin around like only a dog can do as she zeroed in on that pickin. Without so much a glance back at me or a see ya later, she just waltzed directly over to the back door, her tail straight up in the air in her I'm happy/I'm the Queen mode, went right up those four steps and past that "Musician's Only" sign and down the little backstage hallway, and turned left.

At that point, I lost sight of her.

But then I heard the applause.

Seems she had walked through that stage door and right out to the front of the stage (remember: she's never been inside before) and when everyone saw her, they all just spontaneously burst into applause. And she apparently just drank it right on up. Stood there at the edge of the stage, thank you, thank you, good to see y'all, hey how ya doin, just stood, ears and tail up, grinnin and looking out at the audience from face to face sayin howdy. The boys kept on playing and she turned around, wandered over, went up to Greg, looked up at him, waited, and when he didn't give her a pat, she just sat down and looked up at him, expectantly. Eventually, he got the point, and stopped strummin long enough to reach down and give her a little pat and so she went to Keith where she repeated this process until she had greeted everyone she knew and they had officially acknowledged her as well, folks laughin and clappin as she made her rounds, gettin her ears scratched and lickin the hands of a few of her favorites. Then she went over by the piano where I always set up, circled a few times and sat down to wait till I came out.

Now the guys told me all this later. All I heard was laughter and applause as I brought my stuff backstage. When the boys finished the song, I heard

Jimmy Johnson say, well now Blue are ya here by
yourself or did ya bring John with you too?

That got a laugh.

Not that it matters, he added, it's just that we're
curious....

Driving home that night was the first time since
Seven died that Blue seemed even remotely like her
old happy, struttin self. It really tore me up how much
Blue and I missed him. Ten years is a long time. Blue
has always been a point dog, by that I mean, she
always stayed nearby me, always close when I played
or ran or went out somewhere. Seven was always a
perimeter dog, I reckon that's a function of the breed
cause every English Setter I've had has been like that.
When we would play outside in the warm weather,
Blue would curl up beside me or under my cello while
I played (those bass notes again) and Seven would
always be out in yard, working the perimeter, scouting
for us, making sure we were safe.

Kept us safe and made us happy for ten too
short years.

I hope I did the same for him.

I know Blue did.

One time Keith, Greg and Jeff came over and
we recorded some tunes onto a rehearsal CD outside
on the carport, as it was a warm early summer
evening. As usual Blue sat with me as we played. We'd

do a song through once and work out some parts and then I'd hit record and we'd lay the track down. Later I would burn some CD's for all of us to listen and play to. During one of the songs, some car had the temerity to drive down the road I live on. This always sent the pups into shock as they had left pee-mails all along the road clearly indicating that we lived here and everyone else, Canine, Human or Other, were to stay the hell away. So as we sang and played and picked, the dogs chased that car down the road and all that commotion went down to tape and later got transferred to CD as well.

I've told you all a lot how much I admire and enjoy these players and their work so I don't feel egotistical or anything about saying one time I was driving up to McLeansville and I decided I wanted to hear Jeff and Greg and Keith pick a little, to get me in the mood and psyched to play. So I just popped that rehearsal CD in the player and hit go. I was boppin down the interstate, CD cranked up high, little Blue curled up in the passenger seat sawing some logs when we came up on that section of the song where she and Seven had chased that car. Soon as Seven started barkin, she jerked awake and looked around frantically and began to whine and my heart just broke. I turned it off quick as I could, but she was pretty shaken up, just crazed lookin for her lost brother, jumpin in the back seat and then into the front, lookin, lookin. I hated myself it was such a stupid, mean thing to do. I pulled off the highway and finally got her calmed down.

I never play that CD when she's around now, but I gotta tell you, every once in a while when I'm in the car by myself, I put that CD in and let it slide on up to that song naturally and just let it take me by surprise and I take some comfort in hearin my boy barkin and knowin he's still got my back.

9

HALEYLAND

Somewhere shortly after all this, Jeff and Greg
invited me up to Bob Haley's place in Reidsville.
This was another one of those legendary places
like Jimmy's Shop I had been hearing about for
the last nine months or so, and I was excited when
Jeff gave me directions so I could get up there. No
one ever tried to describe Haleyland (as they often

called it) they would just shake their heads and say, man you just gotta SEE it. So I tried not to have any expectations keepin in mind I thought Jimmy's shop was Jimmy's Shop, a nightclub or somethin. (Whenever I do stupid things like that, Mac always tells me it's important for creative people to have a rich fantasy life. I take comfort in that, I really do.)

Nobody remembers how we came to decide it was time to hit Haleyland, and I don't remember why I invited Martin Brown along (after all, he hogged the best seat at the April 1st jam) but I did.

So I made the drive up to Reidsville once again, me and Blue and Martin and a load of instruments, not knowing what to expect other than an enjoyable evening of music. Met over at Jeff's place and he and Greg drove together and we followed.

Went up 87, turned left at the Huddle House (breakfast twenty four hours a day--my kinda place) and then turned onto, I swear to God, Penny Lane.

How to do this place justice? Well I reckon I will do my best to show, not tell and y'all'll have to just trust me that I'm tellin the truth. I will try my hardest, but I know I can never get it right, make you really FEEL this crazy place.

OK, start at the beginning. Haley's is down a simple suburban, normal looking neighborhood street. You would never in a million years suspect that if you go just a few blocks down Penny Lane (although the name oughta tip you off a little) that such a musical place and experience awaits you.

There were about eight zillion cars parked all along the street and in a sorta parking lot in front of what I assumed to be Bob Haley's house, or else a VERY understanding neighbor (being so close to the noise, cars and commotion and all.) Having gotten spoiled from years of playing at places and being in the movie biz, Martin and I naturally ignored the crowded parking lot and just pulled on in figuring we would drop our stuff off at the door at the least or more likely there would be parking for the pickers up close. I found (sorta just made) a space right up front and nosed on in as Blue woke up and looked around with a where in the world are we kinda look on her face.

Directly in front of us is a big grassy yard that is the back of the house on the street. That house looks like a normal every day suburban house built, I dunno, maybe in the 60's or 70's. To my left is Haley's or at least that is what I am led to believe by the huge white sign with black letters surrounded by blinking Christmas tree lights that says

WELCOME TO HALEYLAND

The fact that it's July never bothered Bob Haley, no siree, no time like the present for Christmas tree lights. (I couldn't agree more.)

So the building is the very definition of ramshackle: its rough and weathered boards sorta all tagged together in a haphazard way. To be honest, I didn't really see that much detail that first night: we got there about eight thirty or nine, the sun was well down by then, and I couldn't really see the place much beyond the lit up areas. Blue jumped out and took off over the grass to go tell strangers her tragic tail of neglect and abuse (again) and I pulled my guitar, mandolin and ever present over night case from the back and started toward the door. Greg and Jeff were almost to the entrance and Martin, traveling light with only one instrument (lucky stiff) was on up with the boys, about to head in.

Now there are many distractions between my car and the door: an out house (seems to be a recurring theme at these places), a school bus painted purple and yellow and orange, road signs, everything sorta lit in a random and yet ingenious way, sort of lighting director's idea of a Zen garden. As I push on up the stairs, Blue runs up to join me and I open the screen door into what I assume is a sort of mud room, since once inside the little room, I am confronted by yet another door.

And on that door is a life size poster of country singer Alan Jackson in a cowboy hat and a long gray duster and he's pointing straight at me, and he looks sorta pissed off about somethin. This naturally makes me pause a bit and I take a moment to kinda get my bearings and look down and see there are a couple of chairs in this little ante room, but of course the chairs are the bucket seats from tractors set on legs. (Literally the seats from tractors: Haley is another guy, like Jimmy Johnson, apparently into recycling.) There are beer signs and bumper stickers on the walls too. The beer signs are odd, as most bluegrass places I have been are pretty uniformly no alcohol, no drugs kinda places. Well this'll be new I think. There is the muted din of fifty conversations all going at once and ten banjos and mandolins strumming different chords coming from inside and I take a deep breath and, working the door with my guitar, manage to push on inside.

I see Greg almost immediately and sorta nod to him (my hands are full) as Blue goes into mopey/unloved mode (sometimes I think she does it just to make me jealous) and begins to gather up pats and scratches from the assembled folks. And there are a BUNCH of em. The place is packed and there is a blue haze of cigarette smoke that refracts the cones of dim yellow light as I slowly look around trying to take it all in.

OK, this is where it's gonna get tricky, so bear with me. There is a glass counter, like the kind in a jewelry store, to my left. On top of the counter is a big goldfish bowl. There is a sign laying on the clear glass top in front of the bowl that says:

WELCOME TO HALEYLAND!

five dollar donation appreciated but not necessary

This is the first place that I've been that has ever talked remotely about money, and there are a few fives in the bowl but before I can do anything, Greg is beside me going hey man this is gonna be cool, there's some good players here tonight, me and Jeff are over there, and he nods to the other room where the players have gathered. And then a thin, wiry guy with a wispy, sandy colored beard and mustache, about six foot something, and a cigarette dangling from his mouth appears and introduces himself. John, he says (apparently Greg has warned him I am coming), I'm Bob Haley and this, he says with a glance to the diminutive woman to his right, is my wife Linda. Welcome to Haleyland. And he offers his hand and I shake it.

OK, now I gotta stop, even though I want to get the flow going here, cause somehow I gotta get you to see all these pictures, and try to get you the feel of all of this coming at you at once. See, Bob, God bless em, pretty much looks like a Hell's Angel with his red bandanna tied back on his head and what I learned later was a perpetual one inch ash hanging from his cigarette. So he's a little, um, intimidating, or maybe different is a better word, cause this is not the type or look that I have grown accustomed to in the world of Bluegrass. But he is incredibly earnest and welcoming, warm and friendly all at the same time.

To say that, for once, I feel right at home and actually fit in is an understatement. (Well, except for my mom's powder blue overnight case....that still got some funny looks. But I digress.)

Now I used the word diminutive to describe Linda and I kinda want to take that back because you might read that to mean she is a small person, and physically, she's a tiny thing, but she has a huge, great presence around her. Linda is one a those people you meet and just like right away. She's got a big, warm, welcoming smile. She is a short but curvy woman if ya know what I mean with short brown hair and that killer smile. She sticks her hand out and says we're so glad to have ya and by God you flat believe her, and feel damn good about it too!

So work with me and start to build this picture: biker boy and sweet, round wife, a background roar of music and talking and laughing, the clinking of beer bottles, cigarette smoke haze and now add this to it:

If you move about twelve feet in any direction, you have to step up or down about an inch or two. Seems Bob started having pickers over and the place where I'm standing is the original Haleyland, but it wasn't long before they had to add on cause of the crowd, so they did. And then the crowd grew some

more, so they added another room and yet another.
Thus the step up/down. (Bob told me later: We don't
worry too much about the stepping up an inch or
down an inch difference between the rooms. After all,
we're git-tar players, not carpenters.) So there's about
six different rooms all added on as an afterthought.

And there are records, old 45's and LP's, glued
to the ceiling. That's right: the ceiling. There are
photos, dolls, streamers, you name it: a multitude
of completely random objects, all hanging from, or
nailed to, the ceiling.

There are tinsel and long strings of Christmas
tree lights only with chilies or guitars and banjos
draped in arcs, blinking, flashing and of course beer
bottles hanging down from up there too. (They took
the screw off caps on the big bottles, tagged em into
the ceiling with a nail and then screwed the bottles
back in: instant high fashion honky tonk decor.
Brilliant.)

Directly behind Bob and Linda is a box about
three by three and nine foot high, which I learn
about a year later is the phone booth. Would never've
guessed as the phone is hidden under yards of
glistening metallic strands and illuminated by a black
light in the box top ceiling right next to the small
revolving mirrored disco ball.

I am NOT making this up.

But are you getting the picture?

There is STUFF everywhere: big stuff, little

stuff. The walls are wooden with the cross braces acting as shelves in places. This was the first time I saw the fabled banjo mute brick. There are tiny statues of guitar players, dolls, whatever. Road signs, street signs, bumper stickers ("When I die, bury me at Wal Mart. That way my husband'll come see me." is one of my personal favorites.) The place is a riot of noise, people and STUFF.

In the midst of this, sweet Linda says, let me show you around and thus begins our tour. Greg sticks with Martin and me (apparently a room or two has been added since last he was here) but Jeff (who's more of a regular living here in town) wanders off to go get in tune and meet and greet.

Each room is (conveniently) labeled. I found this out when I was up one Friday about six months later and was told Jeff was in the Lounge. Uh, where's that I asked. Everyone looked embarrassed for me. Linda saved me by pointing up to the sign hanging from the ceiling. It clearly said "Kitchen."

Each room is labeled honey, she smiled.

I shuffled on out, stepped up an inch into the "BAR."

Yeah like you can actually SEE those signs with all that riot of color and distractions up there hanging from the ceiling....

Course, she was right. The rooms ARE labeled. You just have to know where to look....

Continuing our tour, she took us to the

"KITCHEN." Haleyland has electricity (heat in the winter, air conditioning in the summer) but no indoor plumbing. (Seems odd to me too, but I can never bring myself to ask.) The ladies bring food: crock pots full of simmering pinto beans, black iron skillets of cornbread, and if you're lucky somebody up there makes a killer strawberry shortcake. There are tables (picnic and old restaurant) where the Bluegrass widows gather and talk and pass the time while the men play. Periodically one of the ladies will wander out, hoist up the doghouse bass or strap on a mandolin and pick a tune or five, and then they'll head on back to the kitchen to talk to the other widows.

I love Bluegrass.

Martin and I are standing stunned in the kitchen, dazzled by the random mix of colors and styles and posters on the walls, and he looks up and says in a dazed, low voice, "Wow, 'Twenty Five Or Six To Four.' That's one of my favorite Chicago albums." And he kinda shrugs and shakes his head a little, trying to get it all to settle in, a mixture of amusement and disbelief. He takes a beat, looks around and then he elbows me and says look look. And I'm looking but I don't see anything. I mean I'm seeing PLENTY, but what in this jumble of extraordinary things to look at is he trying to get me to see in particular and besides, I'm an audio guy, I'm HEARING plenty, it's his job to capture visuals, not mine. He elbows me again and nods up to the corner ceiling over the heads of the ladies sitting around the tables talking and munching away on the good Southern food.

Seems the next thing he noticed after the Chicago album in the ceiling was the fact that the ladies keep their eyes on the men folk in the "PICKING PARLOR" (clearly labeled) via a closed circuit color TV up in the left corner of the kitchen. I asked the assembled ladies why they had the closed circuit TV and they said, well ya got ta keep an eye on some a them gals what play bass, they git a little frisky sometimes.....

Well, I reckon so.

No indoor plumbing, but a closed circuit color TV.

Like I said, seems odd to me too, but I can just never bring myself to ask.

Linda efficiently moves us along, follow me boys she says and she opens a door and we head down a narrow corridor. About half way down, she stops and turns, her hands out to her sides on the knobs of the doors on either side of her, looking for all the world like the stewardess (sorry, flight attendant) on an airplane showing us the emergency exits.

And these, she says with a smile and a flourish, are our indoor portajohns for the ladies.

And with that she opens the doors.

Well what can I say?

We were so impressed.

I mean what could be better than indoor Port-O-Lets?

We must have LOOKED pleased too, because she nods vigorously and says, yes, we're very happy the ladies don't have to go out in the inclement weather as she lets go of the doorknobs and they mercifully swung shut. Of course, she throws back over her shoulder as she continues down the hall, you gentlemen can use them too if you, you know, need to, but otherwise you should go outside.

Greg follows her through the doorway at the end of the hall.

I shoot a look at Martin who just smiles ruefully and shakes his head.

Indoor portajohns, I say as if proving a point.

You always take me to the best places, he says with a wink.

We go through the door and off onto the LOUNGE (clearly labeled) but really, it's just more of the same and by now I am overdosed on the visuals of the place as compelling and fascinating as they are. If you look to the left you see that half the wall is cut away at waist level so that you have a clear view of the PICKIN PARLOR (clearly labeled). Along with

the view comes the simmering stew of infectious down
home bass thumpin banjo pickin git-tar strummin
heart grabbin toe tappin Bluegrass Music that just
cannot be denied or contained in that small area.
The music flows over me like the warm ocean tide
at Emerald Isle and I cannot, I feel, be blamed for
choosing to stop SEEING and start PLAYING cause
that's all I wanted to do at that point: gimmee my
guitar, lets git goin, I want IN on some a that sweet
stuff right there. Sometimes the ringin of a melody is
just as intoxicating and just as hypnotic as a beautiful
woman. In fact, I have been known on occasion to
walk right past a beautiful woman (or two or, God
help me, three or four) without ever even seeing em if
the music is goin good enough. There's somethin just
plumb tragic about that, if you ask me, but I swear I
just can't help it. (It's plain pathetic, really.) It's no
coincidence the Greeks had the Siren's call be one of
song. I reckon the most powerful thing on the planet
is a good lookin woman who can sing, but really,
that's neither here nor there....

So I leave the tour and beeline on over to where
the locals have gathered around a small circular table
and, facing each other, crank out song after great
song. There's a big feller playing the banjo and a
mandolin player with his fingers sprinting over his
silver strings, and guitars and a fiddle player over
there, oh wait, that's just a mannequin HOLDING a
fiddle.

Sorry.

Don't mean to go all visual on ya, but man, is this a great place or what??

That's a MANNEQUIN holding a fiddle.

Jeez Louise.

!

There's a ring of folks around this central table, all the regulars sitting in their happy circle of music just flat bustin out the tunes. Around that first circle is an outer one of folks I take to be either latecomers or, like me, newcomers. Jeff is already in the group, but I notice he is on the outskirts of the circle, just hovering on the edges, plucking softly at his Deering. Greg joins him and, as I am directly across from them, I follow their lead and saddle up with my mandolin, strap on my harmonica holder and load in an E harp.

I have to admit, I was somewhat perplexed why players of Jeff and Greg's caliber would be relegated to the outskirts of any music jam. They are both clearly well known here and pretty much uniformly acknowledged to be great pickers.

Thing is, they are both gentlemen. It would NEVER occur to Jeff to just muscle on in on a jam he came upon. Same with Greg. In fact, I have seen Jeff leave pickin parties rather than even give the impression that he was steppin on somebody's toes. Thus, as I followed their lead, we stayed on the outskirts of the jam and I laid low and played soft and easy for, I dunno, musta been a half an hour or more. At one point I heard a riffle of Jeff's banjo shimmer through, and after a bit somebody threw a guitar break out to Greg and as their playing began to cut through a little more, I began to work in and around their parts with my harmonica and it wasn't too long before some of those regulars were lookin back over their shoulders at me and grinnin the same way they did with Jeff and Greg.

After about an hour and a half or so, during a lull between songs, the banjo player said to the players, y'all boys pull back a little bit, let's make this circle a little bit bigger, get these boys in here with us, and that was all it took.

After that, we were literally IN.

Now as I have said, I have learned a lot from the boys about music but they taught me a great thing that night at Haleyland: they taught me respect and Bluegrass etiquette. They came into a house that was not their own, and into a group with established players and participants. As good as they are, they didn't mind paying their dues on the edge of town gently inserting themselves and their style into the flow of the music and waiting to be asked to officially come on in and join the circle.

In the film biz we call folks like that a class act. I hope I have learned my lessons well and will do them boys proud as I continue on in my Bluegrass playing life.

At some point I remember looking over and seeing Martin with a big smile on his face scratchin away on his 35 and having a big ol time. Some of the regulars would come and go, but if it's one thing I learnt up real good playin with Jeff and the boys, it was stamina. So we just kept on pickin and grinnin and singin and strummin and while all those folks came and went, we just held our ground. Some of the Bluegrass widows came outa the kitchen and snatched up the bass and plucked a few and Bill Haley hovered around smilin and makin everyone feel welcome and thumpin the bass or pickin a guitar or chunkin on a mandolin now and then. Linda took pity on me and brought me a Pepsi at some point, bless her Southern hospitality heart.

Haleyland is a real interesting study in music just from the pure fact that the players don't really face or acknowledge the audience much at all. The concept seems to be that the musicians are there to play, and play tight, and if there happens to be some folks around to partake of that music, well that's just fine, but it don't change a thing: they came to play. Now every player likes to hear applause and there is that whole sittin up straight for the wimmen thing, I don't deny ANY of that. But really, they just kinda keep to their circle and play to each other and it's all about bustin each other out and playin a good one, one more time. It's pretty intense, pretty wild cause the whole place is thrumming with the energy of these sweaty players and the jam packed party goers who cheer and clap and are packed in and dart around the fringes of this energetic charge of music that spirals out from the central table till it fills the multi-level rooms of Haleyland and bursts through the doors and spills outside into the cool evening air and washes down the street like a steamy summer rain.

I can only imagine what the neighbors think.

10

WHAT'S IN A NAME?

It is a strange part of human nature that, given we don't know the answer to a particular question, we will naturally (or unnaturally) just make something up. I expect if there's women involved it's just guys tryin to look big and important and a know it all to some pretty gal who's turned his head around is all.

Bluegrass is my Second Language

This is by way of explaining (or trying to explain) how I came to be known at Brown's and Haleyland. Now some of this makes sense in a sorta twisted way, but it was still pretty funny when I finally heard this nonsense to my face.

We'll start with the easy stuff first. Not sure when it started, but it probably went down something like this: one night the door to Jimmy Johnson's shop burst open and I pushed my way in, big ol bald head down, instrument cases clutched in my hands and stuffed under my arms, my mom's overnight bag held by a finger or two, just barrelin on in as quick as can be before I drop everything, the dogs trailin in after me.

And ol Jimmy looks up from his guitar as I struggle my way into the shop and grins a toothy grin and says, "Well, lookie who's here boys, it's ol Onion Head! It's good to see ya Onion Head. Glad ya could make it, c'mon on in here and pick a while. Hello Blue! Git on in here and bring ol Onion Head with you!'"

And so that stuck for a while: Onion Head. Remember your visual now: me with my brightly shining dome, hunched over my guitar, sweatin and pickin furiously, destined to go down in shop history as ol Onion Head. Coulda been worse I guess. Just stirrin the pot a little, nothing more. Maybe he just got fed up with me askin about meetin his twelve beautiful daughters. Little revenge there I reckon.

(Although that is a totally legitimate request in my opinion, me being a single kinda feller and all.) So that went on for a few months until one night at Brown's when I walked on stage ol Jimmy announced, "Well, hey there Vidalia." That's Vidalia as in v-eye-DALia. (It's important that you get the pronunciation down right. After all, this is a book about music, and he doesn't just SAY Vidalia, he stretches it out, he about SINGS it: v-iiiiiii-DALE- yaa. Brings him great joy.)

Even so, I still ask about meeting his daughters, and he still calls me Vidalia.

It all evens out I reckon.

Seems the boys down at Brown's had been worried about me for a while now, since I first showed up really to hear them tell it, you know, what with the cancer and all.

Yeah, well if you're shocked, imagine how I felt.

Seems the Brown Brothers just couldn't conceive that a man would chose to look this way, start his day by shaving his head and looking in the mirror and saying, Yep I am ready to meet the world. Let's face it, they come from a time and a generation where no one shaved their heads unless the lice was pretty bad. And they are of the age where if they see somebody who's completely bald headed, their instincts don't jump to fashion, but more likely to chemotherapy.

Thus I became the afflicted down at Brown's.

Now Jeff and Greg and the boys would try to dissuade the Brown Brothers of their notion, but to no avail. Week after week, I would play at Brown's Old Opry and afterwards the Brown Brothers would solemnly shake my hand and say, y'all come back now, you now, if ya can. You know, if you feel up to it and all....

I never knew what they were talkin about I'd just be all oh, I'll be back, you can bet on that till Jeff happened to be standing there one Saturday night and blurted out, "Mr. Brown, he's all right, I swear!!" and spilled the beans.

Try as we all may to convince them I was fine (you tellin me he gets up in the morning and MAKES hisself look that way??? Naw....that boys got the cancer....) it took a right long time before those boys backed down. To be honest with you, I suspect to this day that they're just bein polite is all. Respectin my right to privacy or something. Sorta, well you know he doesn't wanna talk about it, and we respect that, so we'll just leave it alone.

Oh well.....

If you ever see the Brown Brothers, y'all tell I'm all right would ya?

I love to play up at Haleyland.

It's big and loud and brassy and the people are revved up and crazy. We play long and loud and for all we're worth and folks mill around and chant and sing and yell and carouse. If there was ever a place that the word carouse was perfect for, it's Bob and Linda Haley's.

One night about two thirty in the morning I was slumped over my guitar at that center circular table, bottles everywhere, the crowd thinned out and mellow. Ruth Dishman was with me. She is a sweet Southern lady who would kick my butt if I mentioned her age, but let's just say she is a little older than most, a little younger than some, with a winsome wisdom that comes with years. She's got a pretty, pretty first alto voice and sings with the boys up at Haleyland right regular. We kinda fell into the habit of closing the place down, largely cause it turns out she loves her some blues and we found that if we waited till the majority of folks were too exhausted, too romantically involved or just plain gone (both literally and metaphorically), we could commandeer the LOUNGE (clearly marked) for a little late night blues/jazz number or two.

So we were just sitting there in the late night

early morning afterglow of a raucous evening of
Bluegrass followed by a few smoky blues numbers,
with me on guitar and harmonica and Ruth's high
pure voice floating through the gray haze giving
everyone a little peck on the cheek or a nudge toward
the door as needed for a perfect end to the evening.

We were sitting there between songs, wondering
if we were done, waiting to see if the Muse would
have us sing another one or pack it up and head on
home when she looks over at me and says, "Do you
mind if I ask you a personal question?"

I allow as how that would be just fine, she can
fire away, I might not answer, but no harm in asking.

"How long were you in prison?" she innocently
asks.

That sorta filters in through the haze and
(remember what I said about how we make up
answers) I blithely said,

"Four solid years."

She nodded gravely.

"Orange County?"

"Nope." I said, "Chapel Hill and proud damn
of it."

She looked confused.

And then it dawned on me:

She wasn't kidding.

Good Gawdalmighty......

"Uh, Ruth," I said talking fast, "I thought you
were kidding, I was making a joke: you know, four

years, went to Carolina for four years, school, prison, four years, joke....get it?"

"So you never been to prison?"

"GOD no! Where in the world did you get THAT idea???"

"Some of us were talkin about you few weeks ago, wonderin where you learned to play harmonica like that. One of the boys said he's heard you did a stretch in prison and that's where you learned to play so good."

"Well, I will try to take that as a compliment but let me tell you there is absolutely no truth to that story AT ALL!"

We sat there a few seconds, while I randomly strummed a few 9th chords on my D 35, sorta trying to fill the awkward silence, until I had a thought.

"Say, Ruth, uh, do me a favor will ya?"

She nods agreeably, takes a sip of her soda.

"I think it suits me just fine if the folks up here think I learned to play in prison. Don't y'all girls kinda go for that whole bad boy thing? You know, Folsom Prison, all a that?"

"Well I guess..."

"See. I'm thinkin I have never been very good at the whole dangerous guy thing, and this might just be my only chance, so let's just let that rumor fly, whaddaya think?"

She grinned at me.

"Yer secret is safe with me, ex-con." she laughs.

I kinda nod slowly to myself, savoring the concept.

I just let it wash over me, sinkin in...

Then I ruin it:

"You know, down at Brown's they think I have cancer."

"Where in the world did THAT come from????" she asks, incredulous.

She won't believe I have cancer but she WILL believe I went to prison.

Women.

God bless em.

"It's a long story," I say.

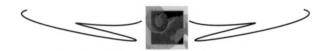

Just about every Sunday, unless I get in too late from playing music all night, I go to brunch with Mac and his dad. (His dad's name is Mac too. I tell people all the time I'm having brunch with the Macs. I think that's funny.)

Mac Jr. is tall and lean, very intelligent with a fast, sardonic humor. Doesn't say much, but when he does it's either so full of wisdom that you about fall over or so damn funny that you're already on the floor. Sometimes he achieves a true Zen state where it's both amazingly true and wise and funny

as hell. He gets that a lot actually. He comes by it
naturally. His dad is in his eighties and is a wizened
ol leprechaun of a guy with a twinkle in his eye and a
story that'll have you in stitches in a minute and ten
seconds.

I had a girlfriend once who asked me as I
prepared for a long road trip for business who I
wouldn't mind spending eight hours with in a car. I
know now that this was/is a trick question, along
the lines of "Do I look fat in this?" But at the time,
I was stoopid. Mac Jr. was the first name outa my
mouth, followed by Martin Brown and Mac's dad. I
reckon you can see why I am still a single kinda feller,
although I assure you, however true the statement
was/is, I won't make that mistake again. (I am that
rarest of commodities: a trainable male.)

Point is, I talked so much over breakfast about
Haleyland that first time up there that Mac Sr.
allowed as how he felt the need to come on up and see
and experience this place for himself. So the following
Friday evening he met up with me at my house and we
packed up Blue and my gear and off we went, once
again making the once long, now welcome ride up to
Reidsville. (Up to the Huddle House, turn left.)

It was fun watching Mac take in the sight that
is Haleyland. We walked past ol Alan Jackson (still
looking pissed.... I wonder what's eating that boy?)
and went on in. He looked around and shook his head
chuckling.

"Well I thought you were exaggerating a little bit about this place, but really you didn't do it justice at all," he says.

About that time lanky Bob Haley, bandanna tied up on his head, cigarette in his mouth, big smile on his face, comes on up and sticks out his hand.

"Good to see ya John, welcome back, glad ya could make it." And turning to Mac he says, "And who's this young fella?"

And I looked that Bob Haley right in the eye and without missing a beat, I said:

"Bob, I would like you to meet my parole officer."

And he shook Mac Sr.'s hand and considered him up and down for a moment and looked at me with a twinkle in HIS eye and said, "Well I hope to God he's retired."

Mac laughed about that one all the way home.

Still, if you see me playing up at Haleyland, don't mess with me or my dogs cause I am a wanted man.

Not sure by who, but somebody somewhere must want me for something I reckon.

And I do have a record.

Actually I've got two or three of em and their album covers are hanging up on the walls of my house.

Like I said, I'm not real good at this whole

dangerous thing. But I'm trying, and, at least in Reidsville, I've got a pretty good start.

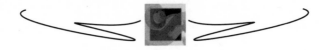

I don't think I've mentioned how this book got started. Originally I was so taken with the experience, the people and the incredible places I had been that I wanted to make a documentary about em and put everybody on TV. (Still do.) This was about the time that the "Oh Brother Where Art Thou?" thing was goin on and I just couldn't believe people were payin fifty bucks a head and driving halfway across the state to go see this "roots" music show (as good as it was) when there was the ROOTS to the roots music right in their own back yard, no more than an hour away and free for the taking and loving. It breaks my heart sometimes down at Brown's to be up there playing and look out into the audience and see all the white hair out there and I just think how wonderful it would be to fill some of those seats with young folks who could plug into this whole experience and carry it forward.

Anyway, I was working with Martin on this documentary thing and he said well write up a treatment and get it to me and we'll get to work. Now a treatment in the film biz is sometimes called a One Page, cause that's what it is: a one page summary of

what you're trying to do. (Martin's favorite example
of a One Page is for Star Wars: Luke Seeks His
Destiny. Yup, that about says it all.) So I set out to
write up my One Page and handed over three pages
to him. He carefully explained the concept to me
(again--as if I didn't know) "Remember: ONE page."
and sent me off to try again. So I came back with
five pages. So he said HE'D write the One Page, why
don't I try a story outline and I did and then the story
outline became this book and then I started writing
and I couldn't stop. I'd be watching Letterman and
the book would be calling John..... John...... from
he other room where the computer was and I'd be
all NO! Leave me alone I'm watching Letterman!
And it would calling, cooing, and I would have to go
in and write which sometimes is cool but is mostly
a pain in the ass if you must know. I will be glad
when this thing is done and I can get my life back,
frankly. Writers, I have found, don't like to talk about
this. Kinda blows the mystique, but it is really quite
annoying.

So I'm up there with Bob Haley and we're
sitting in one of the booths (rolled and pleated
naugahyde--no idea on God's green earth where or
how he acquired this but there ya go) and I am plumb
goin off on this documentary I wanna do and the
power and nobility of the people I have met and their
generosity of spirit and love of the music. So I am
going on and on and waxing philosophical and get

so swept up in my own enthusiasm that I look over at Bob and say very earnestly:

Bob y'all are the modern day patrons of the arts! You spend your time and money and pour your resources into this music and this culture, why you're just like the patrons throughout history! (I'm really in it now) You're like the French salons! You're like the folks from the Renaissance, why, you're like, like...the MEDICI'S--that's you EXACTLY, you're just like the Medici family!

Bob just sits there, solemnly considering, his head slowly bobbin up and down with the infectious rhythm of my tirade, the smoke from his cigarette making his right eye squint a little bit, his wispy beard holding the slow rising blue haze, the perpetual one inch ash just hanging there, waiting, waiting....

And he looks me straight in the eye and says

"Well now John, I don't know these here Medici boys you're speakin of, but if you think they'd fit in, you just invite em on up to come pick with us."

To this day I don't know whether he was pulling my leg or not. I mean, he mighta been serious, he mighta been kiddin.

It's a coin toss.

All I know is, he just gave me a wink and a nod and, noting the perplexed, stunned look on my face, slid outa that booth with a laugh and went off to take care of his fellow music lovers, leaving me sitting there wondering if I had just been had.

I expect so.

I don't do so well in winter. Like I told you before, I like to be outside, love to send some music up to the heavens, make a joyful noise. February is always rough for me. The shortest days, miserable weather (even here in beautiful North Carolina), and yeah, we're in the home stretch for spring, but not for a while yet. Seems like every February, I get depressed. I lock the doors, draw the shades (I actually don't have any shades, but you know what I mean) and either put my Leonard Cohen CD's on random play or just sit in the dark and strum an E minor for, oh, a week, maybe a week and a half. Don't shave, don't shower. Just simmer in the foul, juicy miserableness of my misery. Don't want no company, just me and Leonard and an E minor chord is all.

Somehow in the midst of all this, I managed to stir my psychotic manic depressive butt into the shower, took a razor to my face (and onion head), put on some clean clothes, loaded Blue and some instruments into the car and set off for Brown's.

Got there late to find the stage packed with

players and more in the ready room off to the side. Hands in my pockets against the icy air, I went around front, paid my respects to the Brown Brothers and went out back grumbling at the cold and dark and went on in the square ramshackle cabin of what serves as their "green room." I plopped down on an uneven chair and Blue went over to check out the bass player. We played a while, and as always, music was the salve that soothed the savage beast. Soon I was happy and light and the music carried me away. After a bit we took a little break and the boys were talkin and once again I began to wax eloquent on life and the cruel tricks it can play. Yeah, I allowed, I have been SOOOO depressed: the dark, the long nights, the cold, the snow, the DARK. I boarded myself up in my house for the past ten days, the cold and the absence of light will do that to you, you know... Yeah, I been thinkin I might get me one a them lamps what have them special bulbs or go to a tanning salon, y'know there's a psychological syndrome for this, they've identified it and...

Well, you get the idea. Just goin on and on. Just lovin the sound of my own voice, pontificatin and testifyin to the fullest extent of my medically and psychologically approved maladjustment and those poor boys, God bless em, each and every one just listenin and bein so polite and solemnly noddin every time I made my point for the hundredth time and finally −FINALLY− I stopped to come up for air and one of them old fellers just looked me right in the eye and said

"So....ya got cabin fever do ya?"

And I stopped and looked at him and blinked and I thought to myself well now once again these here boys are tryin to teach me the difference between book smart and life stupid. Here I am moanin and groanin and makin everything all polysyllabic and complicated when really, all ya got here is a simple case of cabin fever and I numbly shook my head and said:

Yeah, I reckon I do, and I looked around at them boys with a genuine fondness and sense of gratitude and smiled and said

Thanks boys. I preciate it.

And that spell was broken and as men will often do when we actually have managed (mostly by accident) to communicate on some deeper level, we all sorta shuffled around a bit and checked our pockets and the time and muttered to ourselves and then Fred started up a tune and we all jumped in, thankful to him for saving us from further embarrassment.

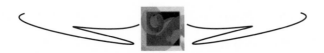

You know, speakin of Fred, that brings up one more story I wanna tell under the rubric of What's In A Name? This likely won't make sense but I promise I

will tie it all up for ya in the end.

Y'all bear with me.

Yes it was yet another Saturday night down at Brown's (and I am proud to say there have been a lot of em) and we were playin toward the end of the evening. It was back in early fall I believe, cause I seem to remember folks in light jackets and such in the audience. Anyway, there was just me and Keith and Greg and Jimmy on stage that night and of course ol Fred Minor, in jeans and a stripped, long sleeve shirt with his ever present baseball cap on, sawin away on his fiddle that I reckon was his best friend the way Blue and Seven were mine.

There was a clutch of younger folks in the audience and after every song, there would be a little stir, some murmurs and giggling from the group until finally somebody hollered out that one of the ladies there was learnin fiddle and had brought hers along and could she come up and play one with the band? Well of course the crowd clapped and cheered, though to be fair, there weren't many folks there that night, not even twenty I don't think. But they made some noise for her and so did we to welcome and encourage her and her friends pushed a clearly mortified and humiliated young lady out of her seat and into the aisle. She was filled with trepidation as she slowly got her fiddle and bow out of her shiny new case and made her way across the smooth wooden dance floor and towards the stage.

Bluegrass is my Second Language

I don't know many instrumentals or fiddle tunes, and I wanted the focus to be on her and her fiddle, not on my harmonica (Jeff and the boys had taught me well) so I just kinda backed up and sat down over by the piano and leaned on back and decided to mostly sit this one out and watch the show.

She awkwardly came on stage and shook Greg and Fred's hands and nodded at the rest of us and Greg set her up in front of the dreaded microphone. She bowed a long note or two to check her tuning and the ever vigilant, ever helpful Fred bowed some notes back at her and she got tuned up and then she took her fiddle down and began to talk to the boys until they settled on a tune she felt comfortable with, and she turned to face the audience and took a deep breath as she looked down on the bow and fiddle she held in shaking hands in front of her. It was a smooth glossy brown, not a mark on it as opposed to Fred's two hundred year old battle scarred veteran violin with stories and scratches on it like the laugh lines around a beautiful woman's eyes. She was nervous, but seemed determined to give that fiddle a story to tell tonight.

She was about thirty years old or so, sorta medium to medium-thin build wearing dark blue jeans and a Carolina blue long sleeved sweater that clung to her pretty nice. She was a good lookin woman.

Then she settled herself, got ready to play.

Kinda cocked her left leg out to the side, shifted

her center of gravity back into her hips and low. She set her shoulders and tossed her brown hair back away from her face and brought the violin up to her chin and....

I was smitten.

Right then and there as I watched, just drinking in the line of her body, the turn out of her leg as she steeled herself to play, I watched her become a truly stunning woman. I could tell she was scared out of her mind, and I truly admired her courage and strength to come up here and play with us. I remembered my own terror the first time out on this stage and was even more impressed. Right then and there I began writing a song in my head about a mandolin player and a pretty girl who comes on stage and plays such a brave, beautiful fiddle that he falls in love with her.

But she leaves after her one song and he never sees her again.

Girl hasn't even played a note yet and she's already inspiring songs.

Now that is some kinda damn woman.

And then the bow made its hesitant first contact with the string and the quavering note came out and I saw her cringe and turn bright red and roll her eyes up to heaven for help or inspiration or maybe the blessed relief of death, I don't know which. But she played on, into the next note and the next after that and Greg strummed and everybody held their breath for that one tragic instant and I thought oh God what can I do cause none of us wanted her to fall, and just then Fred gently slid up behind her, and he stood right in her blind spot, she never did see him, and he played softly, softly, each articulated note a strong support she could lean on and adjust her intonation, find her phrasing, keep her rhythm. He held her there and helped her move along through the song, and as she played her secret duet she gained more authority from his quiet, literal support and as she grew more relaxed and confident her bowing improved (gone was the dreaded skating) and she began to pick up the tempo and Fred shot a look at Greg alerting him of the shift and so Greg marked time with her and Fred gave him a short nod like yes, that's it, watch her, watch her, very good.... and Fred stayed right there with her, mother-henned her and the boys along, one of the few times I ever saw him play with his eyes open as he just bore his gaze into the back of her head forcing her to find first the right notes, the strong technique, the ABILITY to play, and then by sheer power of his will helping her fill her performance with the joy and love of music he knew was in her pounding heart.

It was one of the most intimate and unbelievably graceful and beautiful things I have ever witnessed. It was a sweet, delicate ballet, and only one partner knew there was a dance, for as soon as she found her musical center, the core of her playing, just as silently and surreptitiously as he had moved in behind her, Fred slowly worked his way back into the shadows, leaving her exultant and flushed with triumph alone in the middle of the stage.

To this day, I doubt she knows what he did, nor did most or any of the audience.

But that's just Fred's way.....

I was so moved I couldn't help myself and I feathered in a few long notes on my harmonica as she came near the end of the song and it so surprised her that she turned my way for a second and my efforts were rewarded with a radiant smile that conveyed thanks, wonder and astonishment all at the same time.

If I coulda found my voice, I woulda married her right then and there.

One time I did a shoot about the late Senator Sam Ervin and had the great pleasure of meeting and dining with his family over the course of about a week. At the end of that shoot, his sister gave me the best compliment I ever got or could ever give.

She told me I was a true Son of the South.

What Fred Minor did that night is just so typical of who he is, how he feels and thinks about life and music.

I've said it a million times: I wanna be Fred Minor when I grow up.

Bluegrass is my Second Language

He is a daddy, a grandfather, a teacher, a mentor, a virtuoso, a gentleman, a presence and a force. His generosity of spirit has taught me, not by words, but by example, SO MUCH about what music is and should be. There are people up at Julliard paying good money for a musical education who will never get what I have gotten from this loving, giving, caring man.

Ladies and gentlemen:
A true Son of the South:
I give you Fred Minor.

And THAT is what is in a name.

11

SACRAMENT

Well now I know what some of y'all are thinking: some of you folks are sayin to yerself, now this here fella CLAIMS to be a city boy and college educated and yet listen to the way he talks, look at the way he writes.

Well, let's just chew on that for just a second.

Bluegrass is my Second Language

Now it is true that musicians have a sorta natural knack for languages, can pick em up and do well with em, and speakin Southern, well that is a whole poetry into and of itself, and it is a pure symphony of rhythm and cadence and inflection.

They say form follows function, and I believe the dialect of the South is a perfect example of that. See, this language comes from a different tradition. It is the language of the fields; it is the parlance of WORK. In the old days, folks used to sing as they worked. Why did they sing? Well, yeah, it made the day go faster, made the load a little lighter, but really it was to keep everybody on the One. Only in this case, the One wasn't a matter of keeping all the players in time on the One beat (that came later), it was a matter of keeping all the WORKERS in time as they did the hauling, the fetching, the hoisting, the sawing, the whatever. The language of the South is a language of labor, of call and response from across the green tobacco fields, of give and take, of life and death. The language flowed into the music of the workday and then echoed through the music that was played in times of great joy like weddings and births, but also reverberated through the times of great sadness like death and loss and leaving. The form was rhythmic and the function was to keep everybody on the One, and the language became the music and the music became the language and form followed function and the FUNCTION was to keep everybody

TOGETHER. It linked the common experience of a hard struggle through life into a community often separated by distances greater than those folks who lived in town. This is not the language of the city with its jerky rhythms and rapid-fire mechanical cadences. This is not the clipped delivery and fast exchange of people passing on noisy city streets, no this is the poetry of long low notes called across acres of fields, of folks resting in the shade for a moment to share water and cool themselves from their labors in the brutal heat of the summer sun. These folks shared water, passed the time AND the bread and thus was born Southern Hospitality, the concept that there is time, we will MAKE the time, to make you feel welcome. Well come. See, the vernacular of the South has a true nobility to it, a majesty, and if you're a musician, if you're drawn to meter and intonation and time and enjoy the flight of a good melody line, if you spend any time at all around this fabled Southern Accent, if you open your heart to it and the people and the experience and the love, well, you're just gonna get it.

And I reckon that's what happened to me.

I AM from the city, and as much as I like to think I was life smart as well as book smart for most of the time I have spent on this here planet, I think I have told enough stories in this book to prove that I had myself a bit of learnin to do in the Life department.

Bluegrass is my Second Language

The definition of a Sacrament is an outward and visible sign of an inward and spiritual grace. Well, if we amend that definition a mite and look for an outward visible sign of an inward spiritual CHANGE, I think we can see what began to happen to me.

I was, and am, honored to receive this Sacrament, the Phraseology of the South. As I assimilated this music, met and began to appreciate this culture and love these people, their language began to appear in my every day conversation and I like to think their common sense wisdom emerged in my life as well. Form follows function. Wasn't long before I could draw on the whole patois as needed and when necessary and I believe I have become right fluent at it, if I do say so myself. I have tried in this book to bring those changes in my life and language to the reader gradually over several chapters, to simulate as much as possible my own transition from the percussion of crowded, busy intersections into the melody of the South and the culture of Bluegrass.

So for those of you for whom my accent posed no problem, I apologize for this intrusion. And for the rest of ya, well, I hope this answers some of your questions and problems and I hope you won't be offended if I say:

Y'all need to calm down and just not THINK so damn much.

Here endeth the lesson on Sacrament.

12

BILLY, B.J. AND SEVEN

Well it grieves me to tell you we are nearing the end of our journey. Though I have bounced around some, we are now just a month or two short of the end of my first year in Bluegrass. A few more songs to sing, tales to tell and then I will take my fare thee well.

It seems fitting that since this book started with Billy Yarborough, it should end with him. Along with his sister Jan and that fortuitous dinner invitation, he really was the key to this whole adventure. Without him asking me to come play in Burlington, I never would have met any of these good people, done any of these strange things, played any of this amazing music, never written a single word.

I try not to blame him too much....

So this part of the story takes place in the mountains of western North Carolina in Billy's hometown of Asheville. If you have stayed with me this far, you have undoubtedly come to know and expect that my idea of getting from point A to point B rarely if ever relies upon a straight line. I do tend to take the scenic route most times. No, it will likely be a long circuitous route but if I've learned one thing from these here Bluegrass boys in the past year, it is to enjoy the ride, enjoy the journey and I hope you picked up on some of that too.

Lord help me, it all started in July of 1992 with a dog.....

An English Setter who was all of seven months old.....

(See? I told you it was gonna be a ride....)

I told y'all earlier how I was producing records with a female a capella group from Duke University called Out Of The Blue and during the course of recording one of our albums (which often took, for musical and financial reasons over two years to make) my first English Setters, Watson and Peabody, had died. On the last night of our recording session, only a few short weeks after Watson had passed, the ladies of Out Of The Blue presented me with a little German Shepherd/Labrador Retriever mix and I called her Blue, after the group. Well that worked pretty well for a while, except for that little doggie needed a brother or something or someone other than me to chew on and play with, and I was kinda in a quandary about what to do. While part of me thought it was amazing that the ladies had given me this little puppy who was so small and cuddly she could fit cupped in my two hands, another part of me was horrified at the thought of going through the emotional distress should anything happen to this little one. Good ol Mac stepped up to the plate and made an executive decision on my behalf and as usual his wisdom won out. Basically, he had decided that a John without Setters was a John that just wasn't right so he began to ask around and jump on this relatively new fangled thing called the internet looking for breeders and making inquires as to what it would take to get a new English Setter for his friend John.

Mac musta talked to about a half zillion English Setter breeders, all of whom wanted big bucks for the dogs and none of whom seemed could care less where the dogs were placed or how they would be housed and treated. After trying to explain for the millionth time that he was looking for a pet, not a show dog or a hunting dog or a breeding dog, one guy finally said, oh you wanna call that Parsons lady up in the mountains, she's nuts.

Well, that got Mac's attention. I mean, we tend to do right well with folks who are a little to the left of normal: it's that whole kindred spirit thing, I think.

Whadaya mean she's nuts? he asks. Well, this fella says, she had a guy come all the way down from Ohio to buy one a her dogs, guy came all that way, drove down in his van, handed her the check (rumored to be in the five hundred dollar range) and when she passed over the leash the guy gave it a nasty tug and started dragging the poor dog off towards his car. BJ, it seems, just hustled around in front of the man, held up his check, tore it in half, handed it to him, snatched the leash right outa his hand and left him without a word, turning around and gently walking the dog back into the kennel, and that was how THAT song finished, end of discussion, the Ohio delegation was officially dismissed.

Now the breeder Mac was talking to just thought that was plain CRAZY.

Little did that fella know he had just made one of the best sales jobs anybody coulda done. Mac was now completely sold on this B. J. Parsons lady of

Bluegrass is my Second Language

Hendersonville, North Carolina as the sole source for my future dog and he began dig around and called and called till he found her, and he pleaded his case for me and damned if she didn't even flinch, it was all good to her. So they set up a meeting for us since it turned out she had a pup she felt didn't have good enough lines for showing. So Mac called me up and said we should go get a bite to eat and we did and then after dinner he kinda mentioned real casual like that this Saturday afternoon I needed to high tail it on down to the outskirts of Winston Salem and meet up with a lady what might just have a dog for me. My being used to Mac and all, this wasn't as unusual as it might sound to y'all, and so I just thanked him very much for his efforts on my behalf, took the directions he provided, and allowed as how I'd head on down there and let him know how it all turned out.

So I plowed the long furrow down to the western side of Winston, and met up with this here lady, Ms. Parsons, who it turned out was showing a bunch of her Setters at an outdoor dog show there. I wandered around with little Blue on a leash and eventually found her camper which was all tricked out with grooming tables and supplies and stuff for her dogs and Blue and I introduced ourselves. Her daughter brought up a sweet handsome boy, all of seven months old, and Blue and I pretty much instantly fell in love. BJ gave us the dog (who had no name that I recall) and said she had to prep some of her pups for a showing and that we should just wander around a bit and all get to know each other. Found out years later, that she HAD no dogs to prep: she just went inside that trailer and watched us like a hawk till she was satisfied that I was a fit owner for one of her fine animals. She was mighty sweet to me and Blue and watched us interact with her dog and waited almost an hour till she was convinced Blue and I were the right kinda people to have one of her dogs.

And that is how I came to own my third English Setter.

Driving back from Winston with Blue in the passenger seat (she only has her learner's permit) and my new dog in the well between the seats, I began to ask the dog to tell me his name. See I kinda believe an animal will tell you his or her name if you listen right and watch and learn, and a name is an important thing, a crucial thing. In talking to him I realized he was the seventh dog I ever owned, it was the seventh month of the year, he was seven months old and well, you can see where this is going. I was considering all this information when I popped the radio on and that little dog just freaked right on out. It occurred to me that he had likely never heard music, or at least that's how it seemed cause he just looked at me and Blue and the speakers and his ears would flinch up and he would look all puzzled and then pleased and so I hit the CD play button and there on the player was the latest CD from Out Of The Blue and the song those talented young ladies was singing was one by a feller name a Prince and it was called Seven and that puppy, well he liked this song a BUNCH. So much so that I had to pull off the road cause he was jumpin around and I was laughin so hard I thought we might just cause a wreck or something! We pulled over to the side of the road and my new dog settled in between those two front seats and looked back and forth from the speakers on each side of the car (we had done some very cool stereo tricks in that song) and he just smiled and smiled and when the song was done I gave him a hug and said well there ya go, yer name is Seven and that's sure nuff good enough for me if it suits you and he looked happy and so did Blue so I put on my left turn signal and got back on the highway and with my new dog Seven and his sister Blue, we played and sang his theme song all the way home.

We're now in June or so of 2002 and Seven is gone and my house and heart feel empty from the loss of that gentle, handsome boy. I got lots of emails from friends saying wonderful things about him and their relationship with my dogs and that helped more than I can say. One of the first people I contacted after Seven died was BJ. Parsons. I sent an email up to Hendersonville and she sent me back a sweet response expressing her sympathy and gratitude for the happy, loving years I had given one of her dogs and said she would stay in touch. A few weeks later, I got another email from her saying she had a Setter who really needed someone to love and was I interested? I wrote back that it was just too soon, and though I had the love for an animal in my heart, I didn't yet have the room, so I declined. About a month later she wrote me again, a sorta, hey how ya doin, sure could use some rain and, oh, in case you're wonderin, I still got this little pup up here who desperately needs somebody to love. He's seven years old and a good frisky boy. Let me know what you think.

Well I agonized over this one a while but finally sent an email off saying every English Setter I ever had, died at ten years old and the thought of getting this dog she called Scamp and having him and loving him for three years and then having to go through what I just went through with Seven all over again, well, I simply didn't think I could do it. OK, she wrote back, OK. And then, as if in an afterthought: Scamp's dad is our housedog and he's twelve and doin just fine. And oh, yeah, Seven was Scamp's uncle.

Hmmmmm......

Again I declined, but it was starting to get harder, take longer, and it sorta ate at me afterwards. And then a week or two later damned if she didn't send me ANOTHER email with general kinda chatty stuff in it and then a oh by the way, our house dog's dad (Scamp's GRANDFATHER) is fourteen and still goin strong.

Well I kinda mentioned this whole exchange to the Macs one Sunday afternoon at brunch. I went off as I am wont to do and when I finally got around to taken a breath the Macs were just sittin there lookin at me, just sorta blinkin and lookin puzzled. At last Mac Jr. said, Lets see here, the breeder you got your other dog from has called you up and told you she has a new dog and that dog is not only related to your old dog Seven, this new dog is SEVEN YEARS OLD.

He waited a beat and repeated: SEVEN years old.

When I just sat there Mac Sr. said John, I don't think God could send an invitation with any finer engraving on it than what we've got right here in front of us.

I kinda gulped and reached for my iced tea.

Later that afternoon I sent a frantic email to BJ asking if she still had that little dog and could I have him cause I sure did want him bad.

When I read her answer, I could hear her chuckling over the Internet.

Yep, she said with a smile, I've had some folks asking after him, but I've been saving him for you. Y'all come get your boy.

So like an idiot I set out on the 4th of July weekend to drive to Asheville and Billy Yarborough.

I did in fact promise you I would tie all this up and into the music and by God I will, y'all just be patient.

See, it's about a four-hour drive from my place to Asheville and then an hour on past that to Hendersonville. Goin up and gettin the pup and comin back to Chapel Hill in one day with a dog I had never traveled with before had very little appeal to me. Naw, WAY better for me and Blue to go up to Billy's and play some music over a long weekend and then pick up that boy on Sunday, subject Billy and his family to a freaked out dog in a brand new situation with people he'd never seen before and places he'd never been for a night and then head home on Monday.

And Billy and his wonderful family, God bless em, well, they all agreed to that plan.

Problem was, the first weekend everyone was where they all needed to be to pull this off was the July 4th weekend and we all know what a driving nightmare THAT can be. So I hit on the idea of coming up on Thursday and leaving Monday and avoiding the holiday traffic, and thus impose upon Billy, his wife Karen and daughters Kristen and Katelyn for an even longer, even more inconvenient period of time.

And he said, Sure, y'all come.

Well, I told y'all he was a great picker, I never said he was big on common sense....

Bluegrass is my Second Language

Got up there Thursday about four thirty or five and followed Billy up the mountain to his hilltop home where I was greeted by his lovely daughters and his beautiful wife and the mouth-waterin aroma of a big ol smoke cooker that I later learned contained our entire excellent dinner (minus the biscuits). We sat out on the back porch deck and talked and the girls loved on Blue (she was back in pity poor me mode and those otherwise intelligent girls just totally bought into it. It's amazing.....) and eventually some guitar or other came out and then there was music and laughing and then there was dinner and whoooeee was THAT some good eatin!

I haven't mentioned the girls much past those first chapters where Kristen mixed the music for Meg's party in Burlington, the gig that got this whole ball rollin. I'm not sure where Katelyn was while we were playing that day (remember I spent the greater part of that gig hiding behind the speaker bank) but I obviously saw and remember Kristen mixing the sound. Katelyn kinda showed up later at the end of the evening and helped break things down and I was really taken with how funny and bright she was and how well she and her older sister got along, which seems a rare thing these days. We teased each other and picked at each other the whole take down and that made all that work goin to and from the porch to the car carryin gear and cables feel like so much play. We laughed and joked and the time went by way too quick and then they were strappin themselves into their seat belts and I was saying good-bye. I remember thinkin as Billy drove them away: boy, those kids are great. If I ever have me some daughters I'd want them to be just like Katelyn and Kristen.

That Billy is a lucky son of a

......um..........

gun.

(Or words to that effect.)

Seeing those girls nearly a year later just shows how quick things change, how much we cling to the illusion that everything stays the same. Like it or not, life is change, my friends. While the girls had become even more charming and intelligent young ladies, Kristen had shot up and looked every bit the fifteen year old American teenager and her little sister wasn't so little any more but still had that brightness and twinkle in her eye. On Saturday afternoon I got to play some cello while Kristen played piano and that was a great pleasure on many fronts: it was terrific to see the musicality I had experienced as she mixed the band being channeled into her own pleasure at making music, AND she had figured out and learned to play piano entirely on her own and by ear. Billy had gotta be a proud daddy bout that, yessir, that's his girl all right. Not-so-little Katelyn was just beginning to play with singing and it'll be real interesting to see if any more of that manifests itself. But she has a clear love of and appreciation for music and she is obviously one of those people who just brighten a room when she walks in.

Got THAT from her mom, I'm sure.

I called BJ to let her know I was in town and we pretty much agreed that picking up Scamp (as her daughter had named him) on Sunday was the smartest idea, so we set that up: bout one o'clock on Sunday and I got directions to her farm.

In the meantime, I was getting settled in with the Yarborough family who clearly take the concept of Southern Hospitality WAY too seriously. Karen had cooked up a storm (she is a whiz with that smoker, I tell you what) and was a gracious and charming hostess and more importantly put up with Billy and I howlin at the moon till all hours and breakin out a guitar or banjo at the drop of a hat and singing and pickin instead of doin anything useful or helpful. I will always be grateful to her. Billy had built himself a two story structure just off from the main house, the bottom part a workshop, the top ostensibly a pickin parlor. Well, that lasted about thirteen and a half minutes till Kristen claimed that top story for herself and just moved on in. She graciously (I really don't think her parents made her do this, honest to God) gave up her privacy and willingly suffered the teenage humiliation of moving back into the house with the rest of her family, if only for a long holiday weekend, but still.... Thus I was relegated to the music room slash teenage girl bedroom with it's exceedingly odd mix of monitor speakers, mic stands and four poster bed with waterfalls of lace dripping down to meet the frilly bedspread. I think it was too much girl stuff even for Blue, but boy, what a gesture. I just think that was huge. Kristen giving up her privacy and room really touched me. Like I said: if I ever have daughters I'd want them to be as gracious and beautiful as Billy and Karen's daughters. (Maybe a little less with the lace, but hey, ya have to pick yer battles, right?)

So on Saturday night, Billy loaded the ladies into his car along with his guitar and I loaded my gear and Blue into mine and we set off to visit a friend of his to do some pickin. We drove awhile, enjoying the lush mountains and Carolina Blue sky that is Asheville, North Carolina. Drove on over to Swain County and pulled off the road and onto a fallow field near Bryson City where there was a huge stage at the end, and already cars pullin in and spread out in front like it was a drive in movie. We tooled around back and all hopped out.

Well, before I know what hits me, Billy is introducing me to this guy Jeff Darnell and saying, go on now, John, get yer gear outa the car and come on, ol Jeff wants us to come pick a few with him.

Bluegrass is my Second Language

We're standing behind this massive wooden structure:
all fresh beams and white plywood sheets, obviously
newly constructed and still unblemished by the sun
or weather. I nod and sorta stroll off toward my car
like I'm headin for my guitar, but instead I wander
around the bend and out front to take a gander at the
grassy field and the pick up trucks and cars spread
out before me. The girls squeal out a greeting from
the middle of the field and I wave self-consciously at
them gathered and giggling with their friends. There
are knots of folks sitting in lawn chairs and layin
on blankets and leanin up against the beds of their
trucks, all talkin and laughin and then BAM! A banjo
bursts out into the cool twilight mountain evening and
I look up and to my left and there on the stage a full
twelve feet above me is Jeff a pickin on his banjo and
another guy strummin a guitar and--- well you get the
picture. There is a BAND up there and they are being
amplified by some big ol speakers set up on the wings
of this stage, an enormous stage by most Bluegrass
club standards, a full fifty, sixty feet wide and a good
twenty feet deep. And speaking of deep, back behind
the usual band of suspects (guitar, bass etc.) is a white
haired lady who has seen a few evenings come and
go and she's poundin away on the keys of an electric
piano! Bout that time, ol Jeff leans out past the mic
to let a stream of tobaccy juice fly over the edge
of the stage (thankfully the opposite end of where
I'm standing) and leans back in and shouts over his

173

shoulder "Take It Ma!"

I shrug and nod a little, considering, reflecting a moment.

Not bad, not bad, I allow.

Not as cool as when MY Jeff hollered out "Take it Habib!" but as these things go, not bad a't'all......

I shift my gaze back out to the happy people stretched out before that tower of pressure treated lumber and piano tinged Bluegrass music and think to myself, choppin wood warms twice, but music, it warms about a million souls at a time or at least a couple hundred judging from the size of the crowd gathered here this evening. But still.........I believe I'll pass on this one.......just not big on walkin out on that enormous stage and facing all these good people. The mom roars out another piano break, then the guitar player screams one out, and yeah, it's tempting but...

Point is, there's not a chance in hell I'm going up on that stage to play with these fine lunatics. Not tonight. Just not gonna happen. I start easing my way back....

Not a snowballs chance in

And then the crowd erupts in laughter and applause and with a sinking feeling I look up and who is prancin on up to the edge of that stage, ears up and tail in the air, big ol happy ass smile on her face, than my dog Blue. She struts herself out to the center of the stage and just GRINS at all the people, clearly delighted that at last she has proved her point, she has FINALLY found the love she has sought all these years while living in a soulless canine relationship with the bald ex-con who is currently battling cancer. Regally, she looks out across the field, slowly turning from right to left, acknowledging her loyal subjects, her loving admirers......

You like me, you really LIKE me.....

Ohmigod.

My dog has become an applause slut.

An audience junkie.

A clap head.

She steps back a few feet as the applause dies down, looks around, finds a mic stand that is unattended and trots on over, circles a few times and lays down.

It appears I will be on stage tonight after all.

Sighing, I head on back, round the corner.

C'mon John, gitcher gear, Blue's awready out there, Billy hollers as I slump around the bend.

Really? I think. I had no idea....

I pop the hatch on the van and grab my overnight bag.

Gonna be real fun walkin out on stage with THAT tonight.

Moments later we're in the narrow hallway

behind the stage. My guitar is tuned and hanging by a brown leather strap across my back. I'm tuning my mandolin, the blue train case at my feet.

You almost ready? Billy asks.

Yep, I nod, all set. Where should I set up?

Billy looks confused, disappointed, almost disgusted. Just go over where Blue is, he says as if I am four years old and have no grasp of the obvious at all. She's picked out a spot for you. And giving me a 'what's yer problem?' kinda look he pushes out onto the stage. I walk out to some light applause (mostly for Billy) thinkin, this whole thing with the dog has gotta stop.... me and that little dog have got to have a SERIOUS talk, and I mean SOON.

She doesn't even look up, she's lyin on her belly, her face on her paws, big brown eyes gazing out at her adoring public as I approach the mic she has selected for us this evening.

I mean REALLY, this is gettin ridiculous.....

We pick a bunch a tunes with Jeff and his players then Jeff graciously introduces Billy and Blue and me and lets us have a turn on a few numbers by ourselves. We get a good response. Billy is such a fine singer, and a sweet picker that all I have to do is play a few easy notes on mandolin or harmonica and everyone thinks we're great. I sling that ol 35 of mine around and sing that cowboy song, Night Rider's Lament, and the crowd claps long and loud. It is an amazing thing to have your work acknowledged by that odd cultural habit of smacking your hands together. World would be a better place if, after we picked up the car with the new brakes, the mechanics stood around with an aw shucks look on their faces while we applauded their efforts. Bet the quality of work all over the world would go up substantially too. But even someone as generally clueless as I am has to be moved when standing in the bright lights of a cavernous stage as the last echo of a simple tune fades off into the dark mountain night and several hundred people hurt their hands and unleash a galvanizing collective smile.

Bunch of strangers throwing buckets of love at you. Not bad for a guy who comes on stage with a powder blue overnight case.

I keep telling y'all: music is a powerful thing, a humbling thing.

Jeff and the boys come back on and we send everyone home with some rousing stuff, big and strong and loud and fun. The lights dim and we break down mics and strike cables and move things backstage while the head lights from all those pick up trucks and cars weave their way up the mountain side, cutting a path out of the darkness, making their way home, hopefully a little happier, a little better, a little lighter for what we gave them tonight.

13

ASHEVILLE AND THE SCAMPER PUP

Naturally the evening didn't end there. Oh no, after all, it was only midnight or so, and Karen had driven the girls on home after we finished the show. No, we pulled some chairs on out to the side of that great stage and me and Billy and Jeff swapped tunes and stories and petted ol Blue till about three in the morning and then we headed on home.

Billy and I stood in the kitchen drinkin some iced tea and grinnin at each other, tryin not to wake the ladies. That was a great night, some great music, a great crowd. I kept tryin to thank him, and he kept tryin to thank me, so we just settled on a draw and called it a night and I headed out across the deck in the moonlight and through the cool dew stained grass and slid on in to my temporary home. I settled with a long sigh into that frilly bed, a little too short and narrow for a big guy used to his king size bed (I am, as I've said before, a blues player at heart) and laid my head down and closed my eyes to welcome some good ol mountain air induced sleep. There was a muffled gurgling sound from the floor and I looked down to see Blue looking very frustrated. That four poster was a bit higher than little Blue could jump, so I leaned over and pushed my suitcase against the bed and then snagged a chair with my foot and she hopped up the steps I made for her and jumped on the bed and snuggled in beside me, right in the bend of my knees, a bit cramped but welcome all the same.

Just as I was about to drift off, I felt her stand up and make her way back off the bed and across the floor to where she made the short hop onto the couch.

She always was the practical one in the relationship.

Sweet dreams, little one, I mumbled, tomorrow you get a brother.......

The smell of biscuits and bacon and coffee and the sounds of giggling and female-pitched voices greeted me around eleven or so the next bright morning. I laid in bed with my hands laced behind my head and listened to the sounds that women make, relishing this profound difference from the mornings in my usual life. I'm a big fan of women and am sort of continually fascinated and, in turn, delighted and appalled by em. But it was right nice hearing all those high voices and then hearing the low rumbles from somewhere in the house that was Billy and then the giggles and "da-ads" that only teenage girls can inflect in the correct two syllable way.

Like I said, that Billy Yarborough is a lucky feller.

Reckon I was just gonna have to press Jimmy Johnson even harder to introduce me to one a his daughters.

Maybe if I asked Martha really nice like.....

Over breakfast we rehashed the evening for the ladies who had left much earlier than we the night before and the girls asked a million questions about the dog I was going to go fetch in a few short hours. As I helped clear the dishes (my mama brought me up right) I asked Billy if he would ride with me and he said sure, so I took off to get a shower and get ready to go.

After calling BJ to let her know we were on our way, just a little behind schedule (musicians running late?? Imagine that....), we headed toward the door. By the way, I said casually to Billy, why don't you throw your guitar in the back of my car. What for? he asked. Ah, ya never know, just toss it on there, we might want to pick a few somewhere later on down the line. OK, he said picking it up as we headed out to the deck.

I clapped and Blue came running (she is only answering to applause now you see) and we loaded Billy's guitar in the back of my van (I was too tired last night to unload my instruments, plus it was cool --cold even--and I had parked in the shade so I knew all my gear was safe from the heat) and we made our way out to the highway for the hour long ride to Hendersonville and my new dog.

What were we thinking? Well fools that we were, clearly we weren't thinking at all. It's Sunday afternoon, the closing day of the holiday weekend and all the 4th of July traffic was backed up for miles of frustrating miles of hot asphalt and concrete. Luckily we had a cell phone so Billy could call in to the ladies and let them know we were goin to be home later than we thought and of course we called BJ back and told her about the traffic and how it was making us even later. (Once again: musicians running late, she dead panned, Imagine that....)

Lucky for me I had the good Mr. Yarborough to talk to and so we passed the slow moving miles with discussions of everything from guitars and song writing to teenagers and the eternal and blessed differences between men and women. Heard lots of funny, wonderful stories that only a man living with a truck load of estrogen could live to tell and once again I found myself thinking how lucky Billy was, and this time I got to tell him that out loud too.

In time, we exited off the highway and began to wind over the back roads that led to BJ's farm, talking and laughing and just enjoying the day. I began to tell Billy the story of how I had come to meet BJ and how she sold me Seven real cheap after I passed my parenting test and how we had stayed in touch over the years, me sending her album covers or copies of videos Blue and Seven appeared in or on. I told him how Seven had gotten his name, how tight he and Blue had been, how much she missed him.

At last we turned off the main highway and as the small iron English Setter figurines that guard the entrance way faded behind us and the dust rose from the long gravel access road they called a drive way, I said, you know Billy, BJ said she wouldn't take any money for this here dog we come to get. That so? he says. Yep, I reply, and she can charge right much for these dogs, too. I know he says, I know that.

Bluegrass is my Second Language

He nods and I say, So I'm thinkin you and me, well, we ain't gonna play for our supper this afternoon, we're gonna play for my doggie.

Billy looks straight ahead.

Whaddaya mean? he asks. Well, you and me are gonna pick for these kind folks and that is how I will pay for my dog today.

We road in silence as I slowly tooled up the bumpy drive, kinda proud of myself for this great idea I just had.

As the barns and kennels came into view Billy at last summoned the courage to ask the question that had been bothering him since I hatched this whole plan.

What makes you think they're gonna WANT to hear us play? he asks.

I didn't even take a beat. Right off I said

Well now, I don't know about me, but I've heard YOU sing and I've heard you play, and you're terrific, so I'm thinkin this is gonna go down just fine.

Before he could say anything, we pulled up to the big brown house.

This'll be great, I say as I put the car in park, switch off the ignition and hop out with a happy Blue following.

Billy looks unconvinced.

The recalcitrant Mr. Yarborough follows me and Blue as we make our way over to the kennels to find

B.J., who said she would be working on some drainage ditches down there. Ever the optimist, I am bopping along, whistling and feeling VERY positive about my plan for the afternoon, when B.J. looks up, sees us, waves and opens the door to a pen and a couple of English Setters, in a flash of white feathered fur and orange spots come skittering out. One of them, to my horror, looks EXACTLY like Seven, and my heart sinks as I am SURE this is the fabled dog Scamp and I know in my gut that this will not work, I will always see this dog as Seven, never as who he really is and I begin to think this is going to be bad. The dogs are running everywhere, jumping back and forth over the newly dug shallow trough, smelling at the fresh dirt and generally enjoying being out of their runs and free to galumph around the farm yard. I watch the dogs swirl around me and a sweaty B.J. comes up, puts down her shovel, mops her brow with a swipe of her gloved hand and, ignoring her protests that she is too dirty and sweaty, I give her a big hug. She points with her chin at one particularly bursting ball of energy who is just tearing up the track making circles and sharp turns, veering in and out of the mix of other dogs with a sheer exuberance of movement and the joy of being a dog. There's your boy she says with a smile, That's the Scamper pup.

My heart swells. This dog is a smaller version of Seven, a handsome English Setter to be sure, but other than the superficial breed resemblance, he in no way looks like his uncle. I am so relieved I can't help but smile. That smile turns into a laugh as B.J. and her daughter (and Billy and anyone else in the tri-state area) all try to get this little guy to slow down (STOPPING him seems out of the question) long enough to say hello to everyone. Well, I just told you he needed someone to love, I never said you wouldn't have your hands full doin it! an exasperated B.J. finally mutters as we give up and head for the house for some iced tea. Her daughter Kristen puts the dogs back in their runs except for Scamp who follows our lead (but at a safe distance) as we stroll across the sloping gravel drive and over the sparse lawn (the drought was very bad that year, even in the mountains) and start up the brown wooden stairs to the front porch of her large wood frame home. We're chattin and catchin up some and she asks if we'd like to come in, and I tell her I appreciate the offer, but I'd rather stay outside where we can keep an eye on Scamp and where I can talk to him and try to get to be friends. She says she's gonna go in and clean up a bit and will bring some tea out directly. I allow as how I'd be much obliged to some tea, and while she was straightenin up a bit ol Billy and I would break out some instruments to do some pickin. Seeing her raised eyebrow and the question in her eyes, I say, Well now, you are still adamant about not taking any money for this here doggie, correct? and she says, That is right. You just do him like you did Seven and that'll be pay enough. Well, I don't feel that is enough so Billy and I are gonna play some music for ya to pay for my dog. She looks a little bemused as she rolls that idea around a second and says well that will be fine.

Billy just looks uncomfortable.

B.J. heads inside and I lead Billy on down the stairs and over to the back of the van. Blue and Scamp are boltin around the yard playing and laughing, havin a big ol time. Well that is a good sign right there I say to no one in particular. Billy just nods his agreement as we pull the guitars, the mandolin, cello and of course the powder blue over night bag out of the van and trudge back up the stairs to the porch. Billy just sighs as he sits down in a wicker chair and tunes his Martin. This'll be great I say again, this is just a perfect day. Billy just shakes his head in acceptance, disgust, disbelief, or maybe all (or maybe none) of the above, I really don't know. It occurs to me he may harbor some skepticism as regards my plan for the afternoon and this whole playin for the dog thing.

B.J. comes out directly with some good Southern iced tea and that hits the spot and we strum a while and talk and I finally say well Billy my friend, whaddaya wanna sing for us today and damned if he doesn't just launch into a tune and I pick up my mandolin and strap on my harmonica holder and load in a D, and before long one tune has turned into two and then three and Billy is no longer a reluctant

participant in my egocentric plan, he is just a singer
and a picker who loves to play, he's just a Musician
with a capital M and I am just happy to be floating
down that lazy river with him and then just as we're
about to crank up tune number four, at the exact same
instant, as though by some psychic link, mother and
daughter leap to their feet with cries of hold it! and
hang on a sec, and we pause and look up and B.J.,
looking intently at her daughter says, I'll call and
Kristen says I'll email and they both turn to us at the
same time and say we'll be right back and run off into
the house.

Perplexed, Billy and I lean back in our chairs,
sip a little tea and look out at the dogs frolicking in
the yard. Blue finally comes up and lays down beside
me, panting. I go to the car and bring back her water
bowel and place it off to the side near the end of
the long porch. She trots over and drinks as I sit
back down. After a bit Scamp cautiously makes his
way up on the porch and, keeping an eye on the two
strangers, laps up some cool water and then slinks to
the far end of the porch and lays down.

I gotta be honest here, I say to Billy, I am just
not fond of the name Scamp for my dog.

I hear ya, Billy says as he checks his tuning.
His guitar being a Martin, it is absolutely in tune
of course, he's just bein cautious, it's just a nervous
habit. Daughter probably named him when she was
five years old or somethin.

I grunt in agreement.

Well I reckon he'll tell me his name if he needs a new one, I say. Billy, who understands dogs and what's in a name, nods while idly strumming a few chords. About that time the ladies come back out and B.J. resumes her seat, Kristen sits back down cross-legged on the floor. I start to strum a bit and then feel compelled to ask,

Um...what was that all about anyway?

Oh, B.J. says, Sorry, we were just callin the neighbors. Y'all boys are GOOD, we need to git some folks over to hear y'all!

I slowly turn to look at Billy and yes, I will admit it, I am only human after all, yes, I was feeling quite smug, my attitude was one of vindication and yes, I enjoyed the baleful look on his face. Yep, I allow, as I look straight at him, doin my level best to make my voice drip with the irony you always read about in novels, That Billy can flat pick can't he? and the ladies heartily concur, while Billy just looks contrite.

I didn't let him stew too long, just a beat or two, just a little "I told you so" moment there before I cranked up a blues tune and we started back playin again. After a song or two I noticed a plume of dust in the distance rising from the drive way as a car hurried on up and then a song was interrupted by the sputter of a tractor and B.J.'s husband rolled in from the fields. I got yer page he yells up at the porch, and then seeing the guitars, he switches off the tractor and says with a big smile, Well what have we got here? And as that car pulled up and another started in from down the road, he jumped off the tractor and moved toward the porch, taking off his work gloves and grinnin from ear to ear as we counted off another song.

God bless music.

At some point somebody mentioned the cello case, and I pulled out the cello and Billy thumped out a slow waltz and I played some sweet legato lines behind his high lonesome tenor and it was so purty it'd bout make you cry. Well them ladies was just effusin on me and that cello and I was bein all modest and thankful when ol Scamper Pup just walked right into the middle of us, lifted his leg and let go stream on a (thankfully unoccupied) wooden chair.

In the stunned silence that followed, B. J. looked at me and said,

You got to do something about your dog, boy.

And Billy said Yeah, apparently he's not much of a fan of yer cello playin!

And I guess that made it official for only a dog that you love and own can embarrass you, and he shore did and I turned red and everyone howled with laughter and I just shook my head in amazed wonder as my dog trotted back over to his side of the porch, apparently rather proud of hisself and his succinct musical commentary, and laid back down with a satisfied little grumble.

That boy's got some ISSUES, someone sang out and B. J. suggested I might want to spent some time house breakin my dog, or at the very least, PORCH breakin him.

Well, THAT got a big laugh and once again I just sat there lookin at that boy and shakin my head.

I wonder if he heard what I said about his name? I asked Billy who just shrugged.

Needless to say, I didn't play any more cello that afternoon. Pretty much stuck to guitar and mandolin for the rest of the session.

Well before it was done, we had about eight or ten people gathered over there and Billy and I picked for several hours until we felt we had paid our debt. We shook hands and said good byes to a bunch of fine folks who made us promise to come back and play some more. I am proud to say that I have kept that promise.

Every year, I go back to Hendersonville and Billy and I (and sometimes Greg, Jeff and Keith) set up on the porch and I pay the rent on my dog for another year. We get some right good turn outs some afternoons, but no matter if it's a small crowd, a big bunch of musicians, or just me pickin a guitar, I always enjoy that pilgrimage.

Bluegrass is my Second Language

It is a debt I relish paying.

And no, to this date the dog has not urinated on any one or thing during one of these subsequent performances.

Don't know if he's just gotten used to the cello or if I've just gotten better.

Believe me, I've asked him, but he ain't talkin.

Eventually we had to say good-by to B.J. and of course I was a mess of tears with a big ol lump in my throat that kept me from further embarrassin myself cause of all the things I wanted to say. I wanted to thank her for Seven and all those wonderful years and thank her for keepin this incredible doggie who jumped into the back of my car and settled on the floor without too much distress and who Blue just seemed to be nuts about. Giving me this dog was an incredibly generous gift, one that healed me and my dog in a time of pain and loss. It was and is my honor to play for him.

At last, I just gave B.J. a hug and hoped that she would know all these things in my head and heart, just feel it from me and Blue and so we packed up and pulled on out with waves and honks and hollers.

As we drove down the driveway, Billy said in a quiet voice,

John, I owe you an apology.

How's that, I ask.

You were sure right about singin for those folks.

That was just great.....it was amazing.

I figured I had my nyah nyah moment up there on the porch so I just kinda brushed it all off.

Yeah, that was pretty cool, I say.

No, he says, Really. Lissen....I asked around, that B.J., she's a VERY successful breeder, highly respected...

Oh, yeah, yeah...

How many dogs do you figure she's bred and sold over the years?

Lord Billy, I got no idea.... tons of em....

Well I will tell you something my friend, Billy intoned. She has probably sold hundreds of dogs and in that hundreds of dogs she may remember the sale of a few of em, but I guaran-damn-tee ya she will never forget THAT dog (he pointed with his thumb back over his shoulder to the Scamper Pup on the floor behind us) and she will never forget you and all that music we made and neither will her whole family. They will remember this day for the rest of their lives. John, you done a good thing here today. A real good thing.

I was stunned at his vehemence, the fervor in his voice. He was obviously genuinely touched and moved by what we had done today.

Well there, Doubting Thomas, I said, They'll remember YOU too, you're tied up in all of this now too, and well you should be.

He took a beat and then he said, sorta slow, as

if he hadn't thought of it
    I reckon that's true...
    And we drove a while in silence as we
considered that.

14

I'VE BEEN TO THE BEACH WITH A DOG WITH NO NAME

Having seen the wisdom of the whole play as you go thing, Billy pulled out his cell phone as we sped down the now almost deserted highway (at least in the west bound lanes) and began to call a hundred and fifty of his best and closest friends to see if they wanted a couple of traveling minstrel types to come and play for them. At last he found a taker in his daughters' youth group at church. We bombed on back to Asheville and headed over there in time to disrupt some organized sports (nothin says confusion like two high speed dogs, thirteen or fourteen teenagers and a volley ball) till finally we set up inside the rectory and sang a song or two for those kids and talked about music while they pet the dogs. Finally curiosity got the best of em, and they just HAD to ask about the cello.

One of the best things about owning a cello is saying to people (particularly kids), Here, play my cello. For some reason unknown to me, you just don't hear those words spoken much in real life, which seems a shame, cause other than ME playing the dang thing, there ain't nothin better than watching the sense of wonder, awe and achievement as you help a kid bow out that long, low first note. I always make em play a low C, the lowest note on a cello, and make sure they're holdin the cello real tight up against em so they can get that visceral feedback, FEEL that whole sweet wooden box vibrate and sing in the most elementary and tactile way.

It just feels cool as all get out.

Nothin better in the world than big, wide eyes and gasps of amazement from, as they say at the North Carolina State Fair, kids of all ages. So we passed the time letting the kids take turns holding, bowing or plucking that cello of mine, and I can't say for sure how it went for the kids, but I had a BALL.

Ol Billy was grinnin from ear to ear, just plain enjoyin the whole musicians on a mission thing and I felt good to be able to do for him what he had done for me. I keep tellin y'all what a wonderful thing music is, how strong, how powerful....... But I don't think I've told y'all it's never too late to pick up an instrument and play, never to late to begin that relationship with sound, God and the birds. Don't like to preach (much) but just wanna jump up on a soapbox here to tell y'all that if this book has touched you, then go get yerself an instrument of some kind and learn to play it.

Or not. Just make noise with it, it don't really matter as long as you have fun with it and the sounds you make please you.

Try to remember it's not about ACHIEVING it's about the DOING, it's the journey.

Just think of it as your own personal trip to Reidsville.

At some point we packed the dogs back in the car and headed for home. Poor ol Scamper Pup, he musta thought we was plumb crazy, what with all these people and all this noise called music and all this in-the-car, out-a-the-car stuff. But I gotta say, that boy sure did travel well, and that boded well for our friendship. I reckon after seven long years of being in that run and only out for shows and stud work (lucky dog) he musta thought the Big Bald Guy and that Cute Little Girl Dog were just the best thing since paper in the outhouse.

Well we returned home to find out that contrary to our worst fears, the girls had not been humiliated by our appearance at the youth group, and we had, in fact, been a big hit, to the point that a couple of teenage daughters could allow as how the whole thing was "pretty cool." We sat around on the back porch deck as the girls murmured and cooed over Scamp and loved on him to make him feel welcome and at home while we tried to come up with a new name for him in between the pickin and grinnin.

We were all in agreement that the name Scamp just wasn't working for anyone. Least of all the dog who kept wandering off in search of new things to smell and taste and do. He seemed to have no real concept of his name in that no matter what we yelled when we called him, he didn't come to any of it. I explained to the girls that we needed to be patient, that he really had no reason to come to us. It was just like if someone they didn't know hollered out their name from across the street. The girls wouldn't automatically just cross over to see who was calling (better not muttered Billy.) So I was stressing time and patience and hoping that Scamp would give up the details to his new name as soon as possible. You would think after ten years of walking through neighborhoods hollering Blue! Seven! at the top of my

197

lungs when calling my dogs I would be pretty immune to walking through mountain neighborhoods calling Scamp! and Scamper Pup, but no, I felt pretty silly nonetheless.

As far as a new name went, the girls were not much help as the thought of naming my dog after a boy band had little to no appeal.

God bless teenage girls.

After some struggle of which I thankfully have little knowledge, the decision was made that my no name pup would spend the night in the house and with Kristen in her old room. How that honor befell her and what price Katelyn paid, I do not know, but the older sister won out.

Next morning as we were cleaning up the crumbs from some corn bread Scamp had pulled off the stove during some nocturnal ramble or other and a bleary eyed Kristen was sharing the details of her night spent with a very restless dog in new and unfamiliar surroundings, I couldn't help but think maybe Katelyn had pulled a fast one and gotten the better end of that deal. But no, I think she would have given about anything to have snuggled up with that dog as much as she loved on him and doted on him. The girls were quite smitten with him, even Kristen after her mostly sleepless night.

We talked at breakfast about names some more. I was hoping for a musical name, was thinking Capo

or Monk or Thelonius after the famous jazz piano
player. But Scamp didn't LOOK like a keyboard
player and the whole Capo thing felt contrived. I was
pretty frustrated. Hurry up and tell me your name I
kept saying to him as he romped around the yard with
his new sister.

In spite of my best efforts to forestall it, the
time for leaving approached and I packed up my stuff
and Blue and I moved at last from Kristen's refuge
and I thanked her profusely for the inconvenience
I am sure I caused her. There were hugs and some
tears and little Katelyn gave me a good-bye card she
made on the computer and then decorated with a pink
magic marker that I still have up on the side of my
refrigerator in my house to this very day. I sure did
not want to leave these fine folks, I was in no hurry
there. But at last, Blue hopped up into the front seat
and the Scamper Pup jumped into the rear and finally
discovered the joys of the plush lined soft back seat
(as opposed to the floor.)

With some more hugs, I pushed off and began
to make my way down the mountain.

The next few months had to be rough on the
little Scamper Pup. First I picked him up from his
home of seven years and then took him to a house
and surrounded him with people and music and places
he'd never seen before. Then, after one sleepless
night, I packed him into the car, drove for three hours

and presented him with a NEW situation, a new place, people and sounds. Three weeks after THAT I packed him back into the car and drove for three hours to the beach for his first look at the Really-Big-Lake-That-Moves-A-Lot and yet another place to hang his leash. Two weeks later, it was back into the car, head back to Chapel Hill and then a week later the two hour drive to Fayetteville where my crazy friends Rick Allen and Cindy Burnam welcomed him into their home while I held my breath for the entire three day visit praying he was successfully house broken at last. (He was.) Then, back home to Chapel Hill once more where we actually stayed for a while. Point is, that poor dog musta thought the car was his only refuge from a cruel and eternally moving life. I guess it helped with the bonding process cause God knows the only constant in the little dog's life was the Big Bald Guy and the Cute Little Girl Dog.

I was glad to have him at the beach cause we got to spend a lot of time together, and I got to know him some. He would work the perimeter just like his uncle Seven did as I played banjo on the porch and watched the waves crash in from the Big Lake That Moves A Lot. Blue was happy and truly enjoyed his company and they had really taken to each other. It was like ten years came off her age. Only hard part was when we walked on the beach. See, I had taken Blue and Seven to the same beach at the same time each year for more than ten years. We had gotten to know a bunch of children over the years and seen little kids grow up in that time as even at the beach, kids would drop their shovels and water wings and run over to see the doggies. Some a them Yankee kids from the big cities had never seen a dog except on TV and so it was a big deal to come pet ol Blue and Seven. And now this year we would stroll along the beach and I would hear the squeals of delight as the little ones would holler out Blue! Seven! and come a runnin.

Now it is my personal philosophy that kids, particularly little kids, should believe that doggies live forever and so I just let those little ones think ol Scamper Pup was Seven while exchanging a knowing look with the parents. It was good, but it was hard, and a couple of hugs and pats on the back from the adults as we walked on helped a lot, more than they'll ever know.

Most of the adults knew if we were in town there would be music and often in the evening as we sat on the front porch, folks would stroll up and sit on the steps leading up to the cottage or bring lawn chairs and sit in the sand in front of the house and listen as we cranked out tunes late into the evening. I am always amazed at how the strumming of a chord will gather a crowd. We will get em all on any given evening of music at the beach: old folks, real little uns, disaffected youth, folks in their twenties and thirties, teenagers with spiked hair wearing black in the hot sun, we get em all. They all respond to the call of the music, all will come over and, looking up at the porch, call out, Hey d'y'all mind if we sit a spell and listen? Most times we'll invite em on up for some tea or a mint julep if they're old enough and the mint is growing out back. I don't suppose I will ever understand what it is that resonates inside us, that vibrates so hard against our chests that we throw away our hesitant social conventions and become friends, if only for a moment, all in the love of the music.

I reckon I don't need to understand it, I am just so proud and happy to be a part of it, glad that the bird song landed in me.

15

WHAT'S IN A NAME? PART TWO

A Minor Seven

So the weeks went by and everywhere I went I had to explain why my dog had no name. The exchange pretty much always went down like this: Well, his name WAS Scamp, but I don't think that's

REALLY his name, so we're just waitin for him to tell us what his name is.....OK, what I MEAN by that is....no, no I'm not crazy, well at least not in the TRADITIONAL sense....

That got old pretty fast. and so I spent a lot of time talkin to that boy askin him to tell me his name. I guess after seven long years, a dog gets attached to a name, even if it's the wrong one. I know y'all will think me unfair and unkind to say that, but it's not like the dog ever answered to Scamp to begin with. I think I'd get a twitch outa him once in a great while if I said Scamper Pup, which was what B.J. called him, but really, he never even remotely responded to his "name." It was DEFINITELY a problem and I was just about to give up when good ol Mac stepped up to the plate to save the day yet again.

I had really been grousin about the whole name thing, about how I'd originally wanted to give him a musical name (Piano, Forte, Springsteen, ANYTHING) but at this point I would settle for SPOT if that was what he told me his damn name was, I was so tired of not knowin and not calling him anything. I mean, he had been living and traveling with me with me now for six solid weeks, and STILL the dog had no name that he would answer to.

One Sunday a little after noon, I stumbled into a restaurant in Hillsborough, late for my brunch with the Macs cause we had played music till nearly three in the morning the night before so with drive

204

and unload time, I hadn't gotten to bed till nearly five. After greetings and gulping down some sweet Southern iced tea (the first caffeine and sugar of the day is always soooo wonderful) Mac Sr. spoke up.

So how're things progressing with the dog? he inquires.

He acclimating OK? You two getting along all right? It must be a daunting task to take a dog who's lived somewhere else with other people and try to forge a relationship. How's it going?

Things are progressing just fine, I told him, And as for forging a relationship, I am completely relying upon the Stockholm Syndrome for the successful integration of this dog into my life.

Well THAT got a laugh.

See the Stockholm Syndrome, for those of you who might not know, is what they call it when the kidnap victim falls in love with the kidnapper. And yes, that was my sole plan of attack: I intended to love on that boy and spend time with him and travel with him until he just plain fell in love with me. Cue the happy ending as we fade to black and roll the credits.

Mac Sr. allowed as how he thought that a sound plan, and one likely to work if past history (and Swedish psychiatry) was any judge.

How's it going with the name search? Mac Jr. innocently asks.

Man, don't get me started on that---

But of course, it DID get me started and so
I bored those two good friends of mine to tears
rehashing the whole problem yet again until FINALLY
Mac says

Well, he IS smaller than Seven.

I sorta blinked at him. Mac is usually good for
a zinger, never a non sequitur, so I pondered that
statement up and down, looking for it. Turned it
over, looked some more. Flipped it back on its front,
considered it a few additional seconds.

Didn't see it.

Uh-huh, I said.

He looked exasperated.

That little dog is, you might say, LESS than
Seven.

Took a beat. Stood the thing on its head, shook
it sideways, turned it inside out.

Still didn't see it.

Pass the salt, please, I said.

Mac leaned back in his chair, let out a long slow
breath of frustration.

I guess you could say he is a MINOR Seven....
A Minor Seven.....

!

Well I just about exploded!

Mac you have done it again, I exclaimed. A
minor seven is one of my favorite chords, A minor
is my favorite key to sing in, and damned if it don't

work to tie this pup to his uncle and honor Seven all at the same time! You are a genius!

And after all the congratulations and excitement died down a bit, I added

Uh, sorry you had to work so hard to get me to it...

Well John, he said, you can lead a guitar player to the music, but sometimes you just can't make him play the right song.

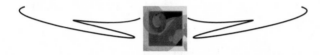

Well now I reckon if it was good enough to circle on back and pick up ol Billy Yarborough for the end of this book, I suppose it can't hurt if we revisit that true Son of the South, Mr. Fred Minor one more time before we part company.

Now many of you, my beloved readers, may well take umbrage with this statement, but I am here to tell you the name Am7 (again, pronounced A Minor Seven for you non-musical types) was plumb PERFECT for that dog, and lest you think, no John, that name is perfect for YOU, the dog could care less, let me just say that, Stockholm Syndrome or no, that dog responded to his new name IMMEDIATELY, and I am not lyin. He answered to it right off, come running around the bend when I first hollered it out and jumped into my arms as if to say well, what damn took you so long?

Point is, it wasn't too long after finally getting his proper name that we naturally began to shorten it and just call him Minor.

Thus it was one night after a particularly tasty evening of music up at Jimmy's Shop, that I sidled on up to Fred to ask him a very important question.

Fred, I solemnly intoned, You know I got this here new dog, and we're gonna call that boy Am7.

He chuckled a quiet laugh and shook his head at the sheer oddity of it.

So what I am inquirin of you is this: we are likely gonna call him Minor for short, and is it OK with you if we call him after you like that?

Now ol Fred had been pretty tight with Seven. Fred likes him some dogs in general and my pups I particular, and them dogs reciprocated in kind. They always had a lick and rub for ol Fred, but particularly Seven.

Well, Fred's eyes kinda welled up a bit and he put down his bow and stuck out his hand and said John, I would be honored. I shook that fine gentleman's talented hand and the deal was struck.

Word spread pretty quick cause I'd get people up at Haleyland sayin, That was a nice thing you did for Fred with yer dog, or I would be at Brown's and someone would make a joke about Fred's namesake being outside barkin at the musicians who showed up late. (For a while there Minor would bark and harass the latecomers and not let them come in the backstage area cause he thought they were gonna sneak up on me and my friends inside.)

Like his uncle before him, the boy's got my back.

I met with Keith, Jeff and Greg this past weekend to rehearse the music we're gonna play for a wedding at the end of the month. I broke it to the boys that the first part of my book was almost finished, and would they like to read it and oh yeah by the way: Y'ALL ARE IN IT.

Well THAT sure got their attention and after the initial disbelief they began to ask about who else might be joining their class action suit against me. I mentioned Fred and we began to reminisce about that first gig in Burlington. Big ol moosh that I am, I went to my ever present overnight case (or train case, never COULD get a consensus as to what the durn thing is called) and pulled out the guitar string wrapper that all those boys wrote their names and numbers on a little under two years ago. Naturally the boys found great comfort and humor in this. I passed out a copy of this book yer readin right now to each of them great players and said a thank you for all I had learned and experienced with em, thanked them for their time and generosity of spirit and said I hoped I had done right by em in my book.

The boys were thumbing through the pages and

reading here and there (drove me crazy standing there watching them skim through and read like that) and Greg finally looked up and said, well John, if I am even mentioned in a book with the likes of these here fellers ---he looked around at the assembled company--- and Fred Minor and the Queen Of Bluegrass, well I am just flat honored.

And Jeff said hear hear and Keith nodded gravely and I just held that moment for a second in my hand, just to make it shine a little longer.

Then everybody stashed their copies and we went back to playin music, cause that's what this is really all about.

So now my new dog's name not only honors and commemorates Seven, but also honors and acknowledges a great musician, mentor and friend, Fred Minor, and really, that's as good a way to end this book as any, I reckon.

So there's no big fan fare, no riding off into the sunset (unless you count a few of those later night rides home after playin all night, and really, that was more like sun UP than sun SET.)

Whatever point was to be made better have been made, whatever things touched and changed me did so and then we all moved on.

It was John Lennon, I think, who said

Life is what happens while you're waiting for the light to change.

Bluegrass is my Second Language

If that's true, and I think it is, then the book will end, unlike a movie or a REAL novel, rather quietly and hopefully with a little smile.

We still play music, funny things still happen, but the light has changed and so now it's time to cross the street.

16

LAST WORD
(SORT OF...)

As I write this, it is the fourth of March 2003. This past weekend, I went down to Brown's on Saturday night to get some relief from (yet another) ice storm.

This winter of 2003 has been particularly brutal

it seems, with snow early in the season and then an ice storm in December 2002 that left thousands in North Carolina without power for many cold days and nights. I had no electricity for nine days and when the forecasts called for a near repeat of that December storm here at the end of February, I, like most folks in central North Carolina, just cringed. Dreading this storm and the inevitable aftermath made its coming all the slower and more nerve racking. I watched with growing apprehension as the ice gathered and grew around tree limbs and power lines until by my measure we now had an inch of ice completely surrounding the vegetation. My heart went out to the groaning trees and the bitter, hard winter the forest and wildlife had endured. I also was extremely thankful for every hour my power stayed on cause that meant I had heat, light and, since I am on a well, water.

Somehow, miraculously, I made it through the storm and the subsequent re-freeze with only flickers of power loss, moments of holding your breath and thinking oh boy here we go. But then the power would come back on and I would let that breath out slowly and figure I'd dodged the bullet for another hour or so.

To the west of me, Winston Salem and the Piedmont were not so lucky. For them it was a complete repeat of the December storm with major power outages, tree damage and accidents and now

I had souls other than trees and squirrels to worry about during the bitterly cold, dark nights.

But by the time Saturday rolled around, reports were that life was getting back to normal in the Triangle and so I assumed in the Piedmont as well and thus set out with Blue and Minor and Tony Rice and Norman Blake playing on CD to make my way down to Brown's. Only one week earlier I left Chapel Hill about six o'clock in the evening wearing shorts in celebration of impending spring (I am, in case you haven't figured it out by now, the eternal optimist) and because it was a lovely seventy degrees.

I think I've mentioned a few times that I am topographically challenged, and while most folks would likely not have been surprised, I was quite astounded to watch in mute horror as the sun went down and the outdoor temperature gauge in my car fell from seventy to sixty five, to sixty, to fifty seven, to fifty two and finally, as I had driven as far west as I was gonna go, to a mind numbing forty nine degrees when I at last pulled around back to the musicians' entrance of Brown's, one hour and fifty-some miles west later.

I got razzed by the players AND the crowd pretty good when, with goose bumpy legs visible below my shorts, I announced the official beginning of spring, and even though I was vindicated when the front I left at six in Chapel Hill finally made it to McLeansville so that we emerged for the load out at eleven to find a balmy sixty eight degrees, I was warned to not put up my long pants just yet.

Of course they were right. Five days later the second ice storm came through and we were pitched back into winter with a vengeance. But by March first, the sun was out, all the ice was melted and things were getting back to normal up in Chapel Hill and Hillsborough where I live.

So I set off to shake out the last of the winter doldrums with an evening of fellowship and Bluegrass down at Brown's. I had talked to Greg on Friday and though he was getting over a bout with the very nasty flu bug that was making the rounds, he thought he would make it down Saturday and there was a rumor Keith and Jeff might show as well. So I was pretty pumped for a good evening of energetic and challenging music.

When I pulled in about seven ten, there wasn't a car in the lot. It was, in fact, a very raw night, not unlike the night when I first came here. I was so struck by the similarity that I stood for a moment in the slow cold rain and looked at the sign on the back door that had so intimidated me that first night: MUSICIANS ONLY. It's so odd and yet perfectly natural somehow that I don't even notice that sign now, or if I do I think yup, that's me.

The pups wanted nothing to do with outside (I raised em up smart) so they were more than willing to come with me and get out of the weather as I climbed the three cement steps to get inside.

John and Daniel Brown were seated where they always are, in the back sort of by the door where they can meet and greet. Daniel asked if I could help re-set the time on the white plastic wall clock as the power had just been turned on fifteen minutes before I arrived. I set the clock and the Brown Brothers pet the puppies while I brought in my gear and got set up. The Browns hadn't even had time to turn on the PA or put out the mic stands yet, so I did that and got myself set up in my traditional spot, the spot I take every time I play at Brown's Ole Opry, the spot where I stood the very first night I played, right by the piano, facing across the stage looking over to where ol Jimmy Johnson sits.

By seven thirty, a few folks had wandered in, some coming from homes with no power, happy to get to some heat and hot coffee the Browns had cooked up. The dogs had the rare luxury of stretching out on the stage without fear of being stepped on, and I asked the Browns if we should pack it up or wait a bit. They too had heard maybe Jeff and Keith would come, and I confirmed Greg, so they said let's wait and when I started to put up my guitar the folks all yelled out, Come on Chapel Hill, play us a few.

So as the dogs scratched and yawned, I did a couple of numbers, mostly slow ones, things that I wouldn't normally have a chance to play at Brown's. Not necessarily Bluegrass tunes, but good songs that told stories and were pretty to listen to and God bless them good Southern folk cause even though there were only five or six of 'em, and it wasn't what they came to hear, they clapped anyway. Then I played a couple songs that Shepp and I wrote cause I knew he'd like that and in another month we'd be coming up on the anniversary of his death, and that felt good and they clapped for those too.

I played an old hobo song by Jimmy Rogers called "Hobo's Meditation" and then "Nightrider's Lament" by Michael Burton. The guys always tease me that I can't sing a song unless it's got some weird, long title. I reckon that's true cause then I sang a song my buddy Ray St. Clair always sings called "Propinquity" written by Mike Nesmith. I was flippin through my notebook, just picking out songs and playing them. It was kinda fun, though I felt like I was lettin these folks down cause I don't ever SING the Bluegrass tunes I know, I just PLAY em, so I didn't think I was giving them a very good show.

I was floundering in the middle of a Johnny Cash song that Martin Brown usually sings ("I Still Miss Someone") when the lights flickered for a second, came back on, flickered off for a long second or two and then came back. In the silence that followed one of the old timers in back hollered out, That's God's way of telling ya not to do Johnny Cash songs ya haven't rehearsed, and we all laughed.

Got that right.

It was eight thirty and sure wasn't lookin like anyone else was likely gonna show up to play. I asked the Browns if they wanted me to pack it in, and they said you come a long way to play so short a time and I took that as permission to carry on. (Ya gotta keep in mind that when I open my refrigerator and the light comes on, I'll stand there and do ten minutes: thank you, thank you very much, want to thank you all for coming, enjoy the lettuce....)

I got a good round of applause when I played "You Are My Sunshine" and attempted a little break in there, trying my best to play what I thought Greg might play.

A couple of other folks showed up in the audience so we had about eight people there on an evening in March that seemed to enjoy pretending it was really an evening in February: cold, damp, raw and blustery. One last defiant swagger of winter before the soft ladies of spring with their sweet perfume would arrive. I will be glad to see this braggart go. (I've always had an eye for the ladies.)

I'd been playing about an hour and a half when it struck me this little crowd of people and I were stuck in some kinda weird Southern politeness loop. I said, Folks, y'all just need to tell me when to stop, cause we're all being real polite to each other. I don't wanna stop playing cause y'all braved this weather and took the time to come out after a real hard week and y'all don't want to tell me to stop cause I came so far and you don't want to hurt my feelings, but I know y'all are sitting here thinking, "Hey, I'll bet that power surge a while back means the power's on at home!" I know y'all wanna go, and I promise it's OK, just tell me...

And they all were laughing and so I played a few more and then I told em how ironic it was that here I am, a guy who played for the first time in this famous and historic place for all these wonderful and gracious people such a short sweet time ago, and now I am on this stage playing all by myself helping to keep the tradition of Brown's alive. To be honest, I'm not sure they cared about all that nearly as much as I do and did (hell I get all misty just thinkin about it) but still, it was pretty special and pretty damn wonderful.

While I was gettin all mushy up there, somebody hollered out that it was John's birthday today. And Daniel's had been yesterday. Daniel was seventy-nine. John was eighty and as of that moment he had been opening this old tobacco barn to his friends and musicians from all over North Carolina for literally half of his life.

Just take a second and taste that...

Literally half of his life.

And in all that time, they had never charged or taken a dime in donation for their troubles.

The boys just love the music.

I played "Happy Birthday" in C and everybody

sang to our hosts with laughter and gusto.

I did a couple more and then played guitar and harmonica on a blues song that Shepp and I wrote called "Lord Lord Lord" that uses rain as a metaphor, which seemed apropos given the weather and all, and then I pulled the plug and said Y'all go home now, go home to electricity and warmth and we'll do this again real soon only with more and better players and they all laughed and clapped and I thought as soon as my guitar was in my case that Shepp woulda liked that 'cept he woulda liked it more if I had done "Will The Circle Be Unbroken" for the last song cause he liked bookends in life, and by that I mean the fact of my circle of starting and finishing my year, and John Brown and all but I guess you get that and I reckon you would agree with Shepp but hey it's too late now the PA is off and those folks are pettin the dogs good-by and hoofin it through the rain for their cars and oh well...

The Brown Brothers came up and shook my hand and thanked me for coming and I told them (as I always do) that it was my honor and thanked them for letting me play. I packed up the gear and the dogs

and the Browns shut down and locked up and soon
the place was dark and I sat there a minute in my car
just thinking what a sweet and glorious journey it has
been.

Brown's Old Opry has had music playing almost
every Friday and Saturday night for forty years, and
I just helped keep that record straight. All by myself,
the kid who couldn't even find the place when he was
fifteen and who was too intimidated to play on stage,
the fella who didn't even know the names of the songs
he was playing up here. I am part of this now, and
it is part of me. My molecules are on this stage, my
sweat, my laughter, my DNA is in this place the way
those Bluegrass tunes got into my head and my heart.

I know there are young folks out there starting
new traditions, gathering players and friends together.
But boy this place has a history, a tradition that when
it's gone we'll likely never see again. A direct line
back to the origins, the true beginnings of this music
and culture. You'll never have music that came out of
the fields and the barns and into homes all over the
world like this again.

For a guy who keeps his strings and harmonicas
in his mother's powder blue overnight case, I am a
lucky, lucky man.

I cranked up the car, got the windshield wipers
clappin time and started out of the parking lot driving
slow down the sandy road out toward the highway.

I pass the Port-O-Lets (God bless em) and the

Brown's Old Opry sign up high on my right and a few farmhouses and fields, always the fields.

In the middle of nowhere has become a home for me.

I go halfway down the road when there's a big blue flash from above that illuminates the world, and then the skyline does a slow fade to black, and everyone is plunged back into night as the power fails again and I drive for miles in darkness thinking

I hope that's not an omen.

The End

ACKNOWLEDGMENTS
BOOK ONE

All of the wonderful people and players mentioned in this book deserve my thanks and admiration for their time, talent and generosity.

The author wishes to thank Leslie Alexander and Barry Hester who were the first to read this manuscript. Leslie is a fine violinist playing a variety of styles and her then fiancée Barry was just starting out on banjo and thus they were the perfect test audience when I approached them to read this. Their kind words got ten more pages written that Sunday night after they (finally) called to say they liked it. (I had been pacing for hours.)

Thanks also must go out to Mark and Lisa Clifford and their wonderful family who provided literal and metaphorical shelter from the storm and without whom this book likely would not have been written, at least not now.

Bob Langford deserves praise for cautioning me against re-inventing the wheel while urging me to further truthfulness and vulnerability in the writing. He has been a good coach and sounding board, the first professional with whom I trusted my story.

Other early readers were Lewis and Meredith Binkowski, and Judy Brown. Very special thanks to Suzanne Harris for her early and continued support and enthusiasm. She was one of my first real fans and she has been a staunch believer in this book for several years now, always with an encouraging word and smile and the firm belief that I had written A Really Good Book.

It meant a lot back then....

It STILL means a lot today....

Martin Brown insisted that I not give him a copy of the novel until late May of 2003 when he flew to Africa for a shoot. The thought of reading about North Carolina Bluegrass Music on a plane bound for Africa appealed greatly to him. (Me too.) I did read Chapter Ten to him as we rode up Interstate 95 on our way back from a shoot in Lumberton, North Carolina. When I got to the line about me having cabin fever, he laughed longer and louder than I had ever heard him laugh in the over ten years I've known him. As we nearly drove into a ditch it occurred to me that, as ways to die go, this one is not too bad: making one of your best friends laugh so hard he drives off the road. Luckily he got control of the car and thus got the chance to read more on the airplane.

Whenever I told one of these stories (during a lull on a shoot or when we were traveling to a location) to Jen DeMik, she would just shake her head and say, You gotta write this stuff down, John. Jen deserves thanks for planting and encouraging the idea first. She read an early copy of the manuscript seated on the floor of her new house in San Diego, California while awaiting delivery of her furniture, a little bit of North Carolina there to comfort her in her new home. She left a stunning message on my answering machine that afternoon, her voice full of laughter but also echoing through her new but empty home, when she got about 40 pages in, calling to tell me how funny it was.

That evening I read the entire novel (at that time just shy of one hundred pages) to Barbara Haight and Elizabeth Goodale at their home in downtown Durham. We ate some spectacular lasagna that Jen made for me before she left.

That was a great night.

I will always be very proud of the fact that the novel was Jen's first house warming gift and I helped to fill her new home with laughter, one of the sweetest kinds of music there is.

226

Bluegrass is my Second Language

Most of all, this book is dedicated to my parents and sister for all they have given me in my life. If I am lucky enough to have children and am one-sixteenth the parent my parents were to me, my children will be the luckiest kids on the planet.

Thanks also must go out to Ms. Grace Christopher, my sixth grade teacher who encouraged my writing even back then.

Ms. Gertrude Chewning, my high school English teacher who nurtured and led my classmates and I in ways we will never be able to thank her for, and of course, Doris Betts, my teacher, friend and mentor from the University of North Carolina, Chapel Hill, who, along with my mother, wants to know what took me so long.

Doris Betts is a great writer and an even more astonishing teacher. The number of lives she has touched through her writing and teaching is astronomical.

I am honored to have known her and call her a friend.

I have never wanted to be anything more than a storyteller, whether it was with a guitar and a song, a movie and a script, or just a simple tale to tell over coffee.

In my life I have been able to dedicate an album and a book to my parents.

No one is more surprised than me....

BOOK TWO

BLUEGRASS IS MY SECOND LANGUAGE

BOOK TWO

Grace Notes

When I'm reading a book I really like, I don't want it to end.

As I get closer and closer to finishing the book, as the number of pages left to turn dwindles, I find myself reading slower and slower...

I am quite sure I got my love of reading from my mom and dad. As a child, I vividly remember my parents getting up from the sofa, walking over to the console television set, turning it off -this is in the days BEFORE remote controls (a collective gasp from a certain -young- segment of the readers), and returning to the couch where one or both of them would open a book and begin to read.

When you grow up like that, it's only natural you develop a love of books and reading.

So this is my plan for my first book: if you liked

the Bluegrass story and have gotten enough, well,
I reckon you're done; you can put the book down
and stop now. If however, you enjoyed the story and
want to read and know more, well then, here is your
chance.

I felt some obligation to the reader to tell my
story, the year in the life of a Bluegrass musician, in
a concise and musically directed way. But as always,
there were things that happened, past and present,
that shaped my reactions to people, places, and
things. I felt that digressing to tell this, what we call
in the film biz, "back story," took away from the flow
and promise of the subtitle of the book. It was a bit
of a dilemma for me for a while until I hit upon the
idea of the grace note.

In music a grace note is an embellishment to
the existing musical phrase.

So, if you liked the song I sang in Book One,
and it felt like a complete melody to you, then you
may opt to skip Book Two. If on the other hand, you
enjoyed Book One and want to know more, want to
hear some variations on the theme, then Book Two
will give you the context and background I felt might
hurt the flow of the Bluegrass story but add to the
completeness of the year and my vow to tell the truth.

In some ways, it is my gift to those who, like
me, hate a good book to end.

What I will do is try to flesh out certain plot
points or tales germane to the story that were not

"necessary" for you to understand or enjoy Book One.

Elizabeth Goodale says it's kinda like a DVD where you have the deleted scenes that didn't make into the movie. That wasn't my intent, but I see her point. Bob Langford says any good editor will just meld the two books into one novel. But he also thinks I should lie and tell you I was reunited with that cute violin player in the Carolina blue sweater in Chapter Ten and we all lived happily ever after. Wish I could, but as of this writing, we haven't seen her back at Brown's again.

So see, it'll be that sort of stuff, just a little extra like when we play and finish the night, and then as folks are putting up their guitars, we start one up again, just one more, a little more music cause we're not quite done.

Like that.

I think it'll work, but for the record Barbara Haight says I should just combine the two and Bob says I'm trying to reinvent the wheel.

You know, if I had even the vaguest sense of control over this thing, I would do what people tell me.

But honestly, the book just writes itself.

Like you, I'm kinda just along for the ride....

PROLOGUE

Well now, see, after all that build up, here comes the let down. I really don't have too much to say about the Book One Prologue. The back-story for Brown's is, I reckon, thoroughly told in the course of the novel, but I loved starting there, love starting in that cramped, sweaty room with people and place left deliberately vague and unfocused. It conveys pretty convincingly how I felt to be there that first night, and I love when I get to tell the story later in Chapter Five and fill in the blanks of the faces and names. I guess the best back-story I can tell you about the Prologue was that it was originally called Chapter

Bluegrass is my Second Language

One. I wrote Chapter One and then leaned back in my chair and stared at the computer screen for a good five minutes before I began to type anything else. See, once you type in "Chapter One," there is a pretty clear implication there will, in fact, be a "Chapter Two," and then a "Chapter Three" and on and on. Once you knock that first domino over, there's a whole bunch of em what's gonna fall before you're done. It's a reasonably daunting thing. Held me up for a few long minutes before I just held my breath and jumped off the cliff.

You might also get a kick out of the fact that the main reason I called it a Prologue was because when I finished writing it, I realized it was only four pages long. That just did not seem to me to be enough to earn the title of Chapter, so it got demoted to Prologue. After a while, once I got used to the novel writing itself, I stopped that kind of judgment stuff: a chapter can be two pages or fifty, I no longer care.

Lo es que lo es.

It is what it is.

(There is a story behind this catch phrase involving a film crew, a small shuttle plane in Arlen, Texas and an incurably flamboyant flight attendant, but that is likely a tale for another book.)

1

THE PITTSBURGH KID
MEETS THE DELTA
BLUES

Those Bluegrass folks apparently just do not work hard enough in their every day lives and jobs. I know this for a fact because of their determined propensity toward standing up when they play music.

234

Bluegrass is my Second Language

Seems after a long hard day, you'd want
to rest your weary bones a bit and just drop into a
comfortable chair and take a break, sip a little tea,
maybe play some music. But no, those Bluegrass folks
seem to feel compelled to haul their butts back up
outa their seats and stand up and play music all night.

It is a mystery to me.

But then again, my roots are in the Blues....

I musta been ten or eleven. I lived in
Pittsburgh, Pennsylvania (to my eternal regret, I am
not a native Southerner) in a part of town called
East Liberty, but pronounced E. Sliberty, or more
accurately, Esliberty. I walked over to my friend Bob
Schmidt's house one sunny Saturday morning, climbed
the wooden stairs up to the second floor where he and
his family lived, said hi to his mom and she sent me
to his room to find him. When I walked into his messy
bedroom there was this marvelous MUSIC playing.

Like a moth to the flame I was drawn to the
record player and I stood and watched the vinyl
spin and inhaled the trebly twang of a guitar, half
strummed, half picked, sparking the pulse of some
hypnotic music, a music I had heard before, but never
quite like this. I listened for a moment to the deep,
powerful, regal tones of the man singing, and I was
captivated in the way only the very young can be
when confronted with honesty and passion. It didn't
matter that the recording was a re-issue (Hi-Fi!) and

of very poor quality, nor was that quality enhanced by Bob Schmidt's record player and its dime store needle gouging through the vinyl at thirty three and a third revolutions per minute with a quarter taped on its back. Through the static and pops and hiss was the clear, clean bolt of fabulous electricity that only strikes when a human being tells the truth and sings and plays straight from the heart.

"What's THAT??" I inquired anxiously.

Now, I have always been careful in my life to surround myself with people for whom the gift of stating the obvious has been lifted to high art. Bob Schmidt, two years my senior and no exception, rolled his eyes.

"That's the Blues, stupid," he said.

"I know it's the Blues, but what is that SOUND, what is that? WHO is that??"

"Oh," he says, " That's Leadbelly, he plays twelve string guitar. Here." And he handed me the album cover.

The sound of that twelve-string guitar was the most intoxicating potion I'd ever heard. I was completely enthralled. Leadbelly's gravel pit voice and that sweet, treble octave twelve string were about more than my pre-teen self could handle. I took the album cover and to this day I remember starting at the bottom and doing a slow tilt up, taking in the sepia tone photograph, the old fashioned suit from the early nineteen hundreds, the gnarled hands and then the guitar came into view and there were strings, more strings than I'd ever seen on an instrument, than I ever knew could BE on an instrument and the camera (my eyes) traveled slowly up seeing the round fret markers on the neck, until finally I reached the top of the guitar with its twelve tuning pegs and coils of wire (strings) hanging off the sides. I held my breath.

I'd seen guitars before, but never one like this. I'd heard some blues before, but never sung like this. In a show of respect, the whole world stopped turning, put to shame by the revolutions of a flat vinyl disc and the music of a distinguished black man who had cornered the market on truth in advertising. The medium was the message, and the message was Truth with a capitol T and he was by God the medium with all his might.

I held that photograph, that album cover, gently, reverently, in my hands like it was the Holy Grail cause in many ways it was. I bowed my head and peered into the stern eyes and grizzled visage of ol Huddy Ledbetter, better known to the rest of the world as Leadbelly, and I made a promise to that wonderful old gentleman and myself too.

"I'm gonna play twelve string guitar." I said in a hushed whisper to no one in particular.

"HAH!" sneered Schmidt, " You can't even play a SIX string guitar!! You'll NEVER play twelve string--they're really really hard to play! No way."

John Santa

I just remember looking at him and thinking, I am gonna get me one of those things and I am gonna play it just like this old Leadbelly fella.

So that was my introduction to the Blues, and by that I mean REAL Blues, the Blues of Robert Johnson and guys like Leadbelly. And, oh, yeah, I saved my money and my parents (once they were convinced I was serious) kicked in some and we bought my first guitar.

From Sears.

Seriously.

A Sears Silvertone guitar made of wood so cheap it barely qualified as wood and strung with strings so thick and with action so high it may as well been strung with telephone wire.

It hurt so much to play, I promptly lost interest and my sister picked it up. It wasn't till a few years later when we moved down to Durham, North Carolina, in that summer where I didn't know anyone, had no friends and nothing but the long, hot, bright days of childhood on my hands, that I turned to what would become a life long friend for the first time, and made the commitment and began to play to pass the time and teenage angst.

I got my first twelve string two years later.

That old Silvertone with its heavy gauge strings and all its flaws made my fingers so strong, I had no trouble at all making the transition to twelve string.

Many years later I was jamming with some

musicians on my carport one hot summer day. I was playing a resophonic guitar in a drop D tuning and my compatriots were playing Koto (a Japanese zither-like stringed instrument) and Shakuhatsi, a Japanese bamboo flute. During a break in the music, as we sipped some mint tea I had made, I couldn't resist and asked the Shakuhatsi player about his last name: Ledbetter. He shook his head with a kinda rueful laugh, and said, yeah, it's him, he was my great great great grandfather and went on back to his tea.

I of course was stunned.

That was quite a journey for an eleven-year-old kid from Pittsburgh, Pennsylvania to make based on a promise made to a man long dead at the time the vow was taken. And yet here I was, sitting in the sweet summer heat of Chapel Hill, North Carolina, playing music (in Japanese modes no less!!) with one of the descendants of my hero. I SHOULDA gone inside right then and there and got my twelve string, a beautiful thousand dollar instrument, and brought it right on out there and played a bunch for ol Huddy, the man himself. But then I figured, nah, right now he's smilin pretty big, no sense in pissin him off, and I let it pass.

Now I have never been one for restraint, and I am certainly not known for my gift of understatement, but at that time, at that moment, well, I just figured the six string was plenty good enough.

Well now, I also mention Sonny Terry in the Prologue and I am proud to say I've got a great story about him too. A lot of folks don't know it, but he had a strong Durham, North Carolina connection, not that I needed that to hook me into his great Blues harmonica, but I always thought it was pretty cool. Sonny blew harp and teamed up with a guitar player named Brownie McKee and their music opened doors and touched the hearts of millions of people as they toured the world. Over in England, where the Blues and Jazz are revered as distinctly original American art forms, the arrival of Sonny and Brownie at Heathrow airport was like the arrival of the Beatles here in the US. Thousands of people would line up to meet them and yell and scream and there were limousines and plush hotel rooms and royalty and respect.

Sad to say, here in the States, they were just another Blues act. They were playing at St. Joseph's, an old church in Durham, NC that had been refurbished to be a small venue concert hall, seating maybe two, three hundred people. It was there I managed to sneak backstage and get to meet the Master himself one cold winter evening.

At this point, there was little love lost between Brownie and Sonny, in fact theirs was a marriage of convenience and necessity, for the world wanted to hear that steel string guitar and that chunkin harmonica play together as they had for so many years. The animosity was so apparent it sometimes adversely affected their show, and was so bad off stage they had long since stipulated separate dressing rooms.

I don't really remember how I got backstage. I remember there was some stealth involved and also the help of a lighting tech who owed me a favor. (Apparently a BIG favor.) I do remember being shocked and disappointed when I finally managed to slip into Sonny's dressing room, or what passed for his dressing room. He was seated in a wooden chair that was about as creaky as he was in the middle of long rectangular room, with an old dirty gray linoleum floor reflecting the garish neon lights. The room was bare, with only an ornate scarred oak church door at the far end.

The place was just UGLY, hugely depressing and, I thought, demeaning for a Man and Player of Sonny's stature.

Not that it mattered to Sonny.

Blind or nearly blind since his teens, he could care less what the place looked like I reckon, but STILL....

As I snuck on in, he turned to look in my direction, and raised an eyebrow behind his black-framed glasses. Before he could speak, I jumped right on in.

"Mr. Terry, I was wondering if I could have a minute of your time, sir..."

THAT was my opening gambit.

Sometimes I am flat STUNNED at my creativity and originality.

"Who is that? How'd you get back here son?" he asked, more annoyed then alarmed.

I was frantically looking over my shoulder, sure that at any moment some burly security guard was gonna come cart me off and throw me into the alley out back.

"I..... well, I sorta snuck on in here to see you, sir." I stammered.

Sonny chuckled a low throaty laugh and sorta sighed and said, "Well, you gone to a heap a trouble to get on back here, let's hear whacha have to say," and gestured me forward.

I was sorta walkin in slow motion, just amazed that this was happening as I reverently advanced towards him across the room. There was no other chair, in fact no other furniture at all in the room, and so I sank to my knees in front of him.

"Now what's on yer mind, son, what you wanna talk to ol Sonny about, heah?"

I took a beat. I wasn't quite sure how to say this.

"Well. Mr. Terry, I....I didn't actually come here to TALK to you sir...." I managed to squeak out.

"Well why'd you come here then boy, what's on your mind?"

I gulped.

"I came to PLAY, sir. I snuck on back here to play some harmonica with you."

Two beats of silence.

"If that's all right..." I faltered.

Suddenly Sonny leaned back and laughed a good loud laugh. "You snuck back here to PLAY with me??" He hooted.

"Yessir, I sure did."

Over the laughter he was muttering things like "Son, you must be crazy" and "Boy come sneakin back her to play with--- that's just..." and he would laugh some more and shake his head.

I guess at some point he must've sensed my silence and seriousness cause he looked down at me, and said, "Well, now boy, I respect that, I really do, but you got to figure, ol Sonny, he play a Bb harmonica, and that's an odd key for harp, and I ain't got no spare..."

Now I don't know when this was, I mean what year, but maybe you'll be able to figure it out by the coat I was wearing. Remember those big brown winter coats that were lined in a yellow white fleece, and edged around the big square front pockets with that same fleece? Kinda cowboy lookin coats? Well, that's what I was wearing. And when he said, Well, now you would need a Bb harmonica, I dipped my hands into the over sized pockets on both sides off my big fleece lined coat and spilled every single damn harmonica I owned out onto that cold linoleum floor. They clattered in a heap at the famous Sonny Terry's feet and the echo died away as Sonny sat stunned in front of me, a look of astonishment on his face.

"Mr. Terry," I said, "I don't care what key harmonica you got on you. I have one in the same key right here."

And Mr. Sonny Terry said

"Well now I reckon you do." And laughed a pure clean laugh of joy as he fished around in his pocket and pulled out his Hohner Golden Melody.

He was chuckling away as he said, "All right son, I'm a playin a Bb here, let's see what you got."

And as God is my witness, he started to play.

Sonny started slow and took it easy on me: he wasn't sure how good I was and he was gentleman enough not to want to embarrass me by blowing me out of the water right off the bat. He inhaled and exhaled through the low bass reeds of the harmonica and set up a nice steam engine train sound and I, a huge fan of his records and technique, climbed on board with him. He laughed through the harmonica as I met his train and upped the ante with a little riff and he responded in kind and off we went.

I was in heaven.

Can't describe what this was like. I was playing harmonica with Mr. Sonny Terry. It was a pure Zen moment. I was completely in the music and completely alive, every synapse singing and every sense tingling as Sonny blew a longer, faster riff back at me. I returned the volley and chunked the train along and added some wood to the fire. The long empty room was a perfect echo chamber to bounce our low-end train sounds off the walls.

Sonny began to blow like he would on stage, and I was a sounding board to bounce his lines back with a twist and a turn and a fingerprint of my own. We were riffing fast and furious now, out of the bass and into the high notes, just tossing lines back and forth, a harmonica duet of call and response in the key of Southern Railways. We were thundering down the track now both of us huffing and puffing and Sonny leaned into one of his patented Sonny Terry licks from which there IS no response, nothing better and so I did the only thing I could. I played part of his riff back at him and triple tongued a high long note the way my friend David Draper, a flute player back at my dorm at Carolina had taught me the flutists do, and then bent that note with every bit of strength and wind I had. Having both played our aces, there was nowhere else to go and so we both stopped and began laughing together.

I have no idea how long we played. Coulda been thirty seconds, coulda been thirty minutes, I honestly don't know. Miraculously, there was a small crowd of people at the door I'd come in through, and they began to clap and, breathless and shocked, I turned toward them, the spell broken, and when I looked back to the other end of the room, I saw Brownie half

inside, peering around the oaken wood door at the
far end of the hall, and he shot me a look and with a
stern smile nodded once in my direction and stepped
back out and quietly closed the door.

"Son, you gonna tell me how you played that
last riff you pulled?" Mr. Terry laughed as he rocked
in his chair and I gathered up my harmonicas from
the floor.

I thought for a minute.

"Mr. Terry," I said, "I will tell you how I played
mine if you tell me how you played yours."

Sonny took a beat and considered and said,
"Well I reckon it's time for you to go." and then there
was laughter and hands behind me helping me up, a
large knot of black men, handlers and promoters of
the show I suppose, and as they moved me through the
crowd there were murmurs and pats on the back and
suddenly I was outside in the alley and I looked up
to the heavens and said, Lord, you can take me right
now cause it don't get no better than this.

Course I was wrong.

But I was young and stupid and flushed with
success so I guess I can't be blamed for saying that,
though I do want to acknowledge God here for not
taking me up on my words. See, I didn't know there
was even more wonderful stuff comin down the pike.

But I reckon God did, so I got to stay a while
longer.

2

THE PITTSBURGH KID
GOES TO NASHVILLE

Somewhere along in here, I guess it was when I was in my mid or late twenties, I, like many a musician before me, made the pilgrimage out to Nashville, Tennessee, to seek I'm not sure what.

Don't think it was really fame or fortune per se, though that woulda been fine by me. No, it was more a sense that some of the songs I was writing with Shepp seemed to have grown up over time and like all kids everywhere were beginning to ask for the car keys, beginning to want and need a life beyond mine. I really didn't want to go out to Nashville to be honest, but after a while the songs began to experience these awkward growing pains and began to tell me they needed to exist, not just when I was present and playing a guitar and singing them, but they needed to be OUT there somehow, on their own, in people's lives, doing what songs do. For a while, like any parent, I was loath to let them go, but like any teenager, they wanted what they wanted and they were pretty relentless about letting me know until they finally wore me down and so off Nashville I went.

Now I won't bore you with tales of my Nashville days as there were only two things that occurred of any note. One was that I realized Nashville was not the place I needed to be, though I learned a lot about the craft of songwriting, pitching my tunes down on Music Row. That was a vital lesson and likely the most important thing I learned out there. The second most important (and most humiliating) thing that happened to me while I was in Nashville, Tennessee, was that I met my hero, Charlie McCoy.

Now Mr. McCoy's name is littered throughout this book, mostly cause when the Bluegrass folks want to compliment my harmonica playing, they compare me to Charlie McCoy, and while I am flattered to hear my name mentioned in the same sentence as his, I have to tell y'all in no uncertain terms that Mr. McCoy could flat PLAY the harmonica. Me, I just play AT the harmonica, and trust me there's a big difference. Still, I can't deny he was a huge musical influence along with Sonny Terry, Toots Theilmans and to a lesser extent, Stevie Wonder. It is my hope if I ever get this book published to include a discography of some of the people mentioned here, just so y'all can go check out some fine music if you're of a mind to do so.

But this chance meeting with my hero Charlie McCoy, I offer up as a cautionary tale of sorts, cause the reader needs to know it don't always go down like it did with Mr. Terry and some of the other generous ladies and gentlemen mentioned herein.

Out in Nashville, I was told that EVERYBODY in the music biz hangs out at a couple of clubs and I should DEFINITELY go there if I wanted to meet people and blah blah blah. So I went to this here club, mighta been called the Exit Inn, but really I don't remember anymore. Only went once, never went back.

This club was a biggun with lots of people and music. It was loud and crowded and smokey and although I was young and shoulda been into that scene, even by then after all the years of being on the road and playing bars and such, I had pretty much had my fill of the club scene. There was a long dark wooden bar that ran the length of the room sorta stepped up from the rest of the tables with a brass railing along it that kept people from tripping but also made the bar area right crowded.

Well I was milling around with a drink in my hand and probably paying more attention to the ladies present than any of the music big shots I was supposed to be meeting and schmoozing, stuck in that tight area between bar and railing when a thin sorta smallish fella, head down, avoiding any eye contact was trying to make his way through the crowd. I dodged left and so did he, so I moved right and of course so did he. If we'd a been cloggin, we coulda won a contest we were so in sync. We did the hustle a few more times and finally he looked up.

"Omigod," I said, "You're Charlie McCoy."

Poor guy looked trapped.

Kinda did an Aw jeez... thing with his eyes.

I was too star struck to notice.

Never one for understatement and with a true gift and love for stating the obvious, I said, once again, "You're Charlie McCoy."

Now to this talented gentleman's credit, he said something along the lines of, "I am aware of that." when the look on his face was more like, "No shit, Sherlock."

Once again, ignoring his discomfort and his unstated plea to be anonymous, I said

"You're God."

Bluegrass is my Second Language

Well, THAT got a reaction.

He looked at me, rolled his eyes and muttered something under his breath about hating this while I rambled on about his album work and unreleased session tapes I had managed to acquire. By this point he was glancing left and right, frantic for a way out, but of course he was pretty well blocked in so he turned his gaze heavenward as if praying for deliverance in the form of some sort of divine intervention that may have involved me burning for eternity in a place of great discomfort.

Finally, someone moved behind him and an opening appeared and he vanished into the crowd with me left standing saying to no one in particular, "That's Charlie McCoy. He's God on the harmonica."

No one seemed to notice or care, and to the best of my knowledge, Mr. McCoy never did get that drink he wanted.

I am pretty sure I ruined his night.

That really is awful, and I am really sorry, and more embarrassed than I can tell you. I met my hero and in return for all the wonderful music he had given me and the world, all the inspiration he had provided me on that great harmonica he played, I ruined his night.

It was a terrible way to learn it, but I learnt me a valuable lesson there in that noisy crowded bar.

Most guys don't want to be God. Most of the really good, really talented ones, just don't wanna be

God.

Well, maybe if there's a beautiful woman around they wouldn't mind being God for an evening, but most of these great players just wanna play, just do the work and let the work speak for itself and live pretty much as normal a life as they can.

That knowledge served me well later on as I met other famous people with the possible exception of Ms. Etta James cause I just couldn't resist the opportunity to inform her that based on the quality of her subtle, gorgeous and incredibly sexy Jazz vocal stylings, it was my sincere desire to carry her love child.

Can't win em all I reckon.

3

TWISTED HALLMARK MOMENTS

OR:
A RIVER RUNS THROUGH IT

I have always had the ability to forget the bad and remember the good. Don't know where this came from exactly and calling it an ability isn't really fair, cause it implies some effort or input on my part when none exists. For good or ill, I have a selective memory. Mac Sr. often says he goes to our music gatherings and enjoys himself immensely, has a great time. A few days later he'll read a post session email I wrote and say to himself, "Now that sounds like a great party. I wish I had gone to THAT party." So it's obvious this editing inclination I have is not time related: it kicks in just about right away. So I don't mean to trivialize in any way the bad times my sister and I went through with our parents back in the fall of 2001, the bad bout with Parkinson's my dad experienced or the double hip replacement surgery my mom went through. I just have a knack for finding the silver lining which I am sure comes from a mom who told me (tells me to this day) a zillion clichés that, God help me, I find myself believing (and quoting) the older I get. I am sure had my mother grown up in another time, when life handed her lemons she would have opened up a retail lemon shop and become the Donald Trump of the citrus world with franchises as pervasive as any Gap or Starbucks. As it is, for women of the "Ozzie and Harriet" generation, she was and is extremely independent, and pretty darn feminist well before those words were so easily applied to women in this country.

Thus it was pretty tough to see her beaten down by the pain caused by the grinding of her hipbones. Unfortunately, as it became more and more difficult for her to get around, my father's Parkinson's disease

also began to kick up. It is hard for a child to see
the aging of their parents. All parents are super
heroes. Mothers all wise, fathers all powerful. Well
at least until you get to be a teenager and then it
is astonishing how much they have forgotten and
how little they know compared to an agile teenage
brain. But thank God, if things go right, there's a
point where you as a child get your perspective back,
and begin to appreciate your Mom and Dad both as
parents and as people, human beings who have chosen
to throw in their lot together and make a go of it on
this wonderful little planet we all share.

In October of 2001 I moved back into my
parent's home: the house of my high school years,
my home, my safety net. Back into my old bedroom
that of course had no trace of my passing in it after
all these years except my memories of the bed being
over here, my dresser here. My mom checked into
the hospital for her surgery, and I moved back home
to tend to my father who was so feeble he couldn't
take care of himself. If my father needed to go to the
bathroom in the middle of the night, he could not get
himself up because the Parkinson's had so paralyzed
and weakened him. So Blue and Seven and I moved
back into the house and slept lightly and listlessly,
waiting for the call for help to go give pills or help
him roll over, or deal with a cramp in the middle of
the night or help with chores and such during the day.
I don't know if it was just me, but I imagine it would

be any son looking at his father struggling to do the most basic things that just broke my heart.

When I was a kid I was a voracious reader of comic books and my folks not only allowed this but encouraged it as if knowing that it would lead to a lifetime relationship with words and reading and now even writing. I remember I was very young, must have been ten or so and was up at the neighborhood drugstore, a place called Manny's in Pittsburgh, Pennsylvania where the comics were displayed on a low wooden rack, just at kid eye level and kind old Manny would allow me to kneel reverently in front of that rack of bright exciting comic book covers with their stories of super deeds and far off planets and powers beyond those of mere mortal men. Looking back, Manny probably let me read three comics there in the store for every one that I bought, something I only now realize as an adult, and I mourn my inability to thank him for his kindness and generosity. All the day's newspapers would be laid out on a wooden shelf about six inches off the floor and my knees would wrinkle the fresh copies of the Pittsburgh Post Gazette or the Wall Street Journal as I furiously devoured the latest chapters in the adventures of Superman and Batman and The Justice League of America, sure that at any moment Manny would harrumph and tell me this is not a library, young man, and ask me if I was going to actually purchase anything today. I was lost in that world, racing along with the Flash, moving at the speed of light, when I felt something at my collar and suddenly I was levitated into the air and turned to look into the eyes of my father, who with one hand had lifted me from the alter of my reading and back into the real world. Instead of chastising or berating me, he hugged me into his arms and asked that I gather up all the comics I had been reading and I did and we moved to the high chrome and black counter where my strong, tall father helped me up on one of the rotating diner stools and placed a dollar on the counter for the comics (TEN COMIC BOOKS!! MY dad just bought me TEN comic books!!) and one more as he asked kind old Manny to whip up a couple of egg creams--one for him and one for his boy here.

I will never forget that moment of flight and delight to discover it was my dad, my super hero who lifts me with ONE hand and then buys EVERY new issue of my favorite comics and flips through the pages with me as we sit at the counter (like the big kids) and sip our sodas and talk like men do about nothing at all and yet everything that means anything to a small boy and his dad.

So I do not mean to diminish the pain of looking at my father's wracked sleep, his shame and embarrassment as his body failed him. But my mom taught me to make lemonade from lemons and my father, God bless him, somehow kept his sense of humor through this all, and thus you are gifted with my collection of Twisted Hallmark Moments.

As I talked about in Book One, water became an issue during this time of tribulation. We were in a very severe drought and I was living at my parents who kept the mean temperature in the house at an even 1,000 degrees whether they were warm enough or not. Even the dogs had changed into shorts and a tee shirt, if you catch my drift. You hear a lot how doctors treat the disease, not the patient. I never fully understood that till I moved back home. I remember looking at my dad and being stunned because he had a terrible case of dandruff. My father never had dandruff a day in his life. That sorta clicked something over in my brain, so I kept it close, not sure how to process it, but I had some sense it was important information. A few days later we went to the doctors and I again noticed my dad's dandruff and also the pallor of his skin. I sat through the exam waiting for the doc to say something about the way my dad looked, but of course, he did not, why should he? He doesn't know my dad never had dandruff, he doesn't know the house is an oven, he doesn't know my dad's skin never looked like that. What the doc DOES know is that my dad has Parkinson's and today's complaint is that my dad is constipated. INCREDIBLY constipated. Because of my father's obvious decline, changes are made in the Parkinson's meds and laxatives are prescribed for the constipation. During the drive back, all the data finally adds up and when we get home we sit down in the living room and I tell him my theory.

Pop, I say, I'm not a doc, but I do a lot of medical video, and I keep my eyes and my ears open and I think I've learned a few things over the years, and I think you're dehydrated.

Now to be fair to my dad, if you're not getting around well, the last thing you wanna be doin is drinkin a whole bunch of water what is gonna make you want to get up and pee a bunch, so you cut back, consciously or unconsciously. You get older, you get colder so you keep the furnace on more often, so there's this continuous flow of warm, dry (and DRYING) air in the house. You don't drink water, you get dandruff, your skin gets pasty and oily looking, and of course the plumbing gets clogged up because there's no water to um.......soften things up.

(Sorry.)

Pop, I say, I think these here Parkinson's drugs are based on a certain body chemistry to work well, a sorta statistical average of how a body will respond to them, and I think that statistical average is based upon a fairly well hydrated body chemistry which you do not currently have. So while there does seems to be a part of Parkinson's that responds to the emotional well being of the patient, thus you are not doing well because you're worried about Mom, there is also a physical element, and I don't think the meds are working so well because your body can't process them correctly cause you're just too dried up. I also think that's why you're so constipated, you're just too dried up. So instead of takin all these laxatives and stuff, I wanna try a little experiment and get you drinking a bunch of water.

He looked at me, looked at all the meds spread out before him on the coffee table and struggled for a moment (one of the symptomologies of Parkinson's is difficulty talking) and finally got out, Can't get much worse, lets give it a shot.

So we began The Great Experiment.

Because of all those medical videos I've worked on, I was not only familiar with, but had my very own copy of the Physicians Desk Reference which lists all the currently used drugs and the directions for their use, among other things. So I looked up my dad's Parkinson's meds and come to find out that the drugs were to be taken eight hours apart. My folks had somehow drifted into a three times a day regime of taking the meds which gradually (and quite logically) became breakfast, lunch and dinner. Thus there were times when my father was getting twice as much dopamine (basically fuel for his brain, what the Parkinson's somehow interferes with) as he should have been getting and there were other times (mostly when he slept) when he was getting no fuel at all. So along with the water we changed up his meds, following a strict eight-hour dosage.

The Parkinson's makes it difficult to swallow

so I would stand beside my father in the kitchen and cajole, browbeat, and tease him into drinking a full glass of water every time he took any of his meds. Being boys, I don't think we ever cooked a meal the entire time my mom was in the hospital, we basically went out or got take out. Whenever we went to a fast food drive through, my dad would order a small drink and I would make it a large, in restaurants I would keep getting his glass refilled, both tea and water. Changing up his meds showed almost instant results, and his condition began to improve, as it should being that his brain is now getting the fuel it needs a full twenty four hours a day. It becomes a bit easier for him to move around, get up and down. He still needs help, but it's easier, I can feel him helping me help him. We're both pleased by this. We have a talk about Parkinson's. I tell him he's got to fight this thing every day, fight like mom is doing at the hospital. Parental care duties sorta fell along gender lines it seems. My sister naturally gravitated to my mother, me to my father, though there was certainly overlap. My sister informed me that immediately after Mom's surgery, so determined is our mother to get back home that she doubles everything the nurses, doctors and therapists tell her to do. Post surgery, they asked my mother to sit up for an hour. She sat up for two. The next day they ask her to walk to the end of the hall. She walks to the end of the hall and forgoes the waiting wheel chair and walks BACK to her room on her own. Pop,

I say, you gotta fight like that everyday. We make a deal. If he wants to, he can tell me he's tired, and we'll take the day off from fighting Parkinson's. I know it's a drag to have to fight every day, I say, And everybody deserves a day off once in a while, so all you have to do is tell me and you can take a day off, but not too many or too often cause you have to fight this cause I need you here, I am pretty stupid and sorta just bumblin my way through life and I need my father and advisor here to help me, so you gotta fight, for me and sis and mom.

He never asks for a day off (still hasn't) and for that day, at least, doesn't give me a hard time about drinking the damn water.

I secretly turn the heat down some and frequently boil water on the stove to get the humidity up in the house. One afternoon a few days later we're sitting in the living room watching something mindless on the tube. My father sorta stirs in his seat.

You OK? I inquire.

Yeah, he says, Just........ something....

A minute later he's squirming around again. I look over. He shrugs. He's watchin the tube, I'm reading the paper when he says, You gotta help me up and I say OK and sorta finish my paragraph and start to fold the paper up and then he says, No, you gotta help me up NOW so I jump up and help him outa his chair and he starts toward the bathroom undoing his belt as he goes. We've had a few false alarms the past couple of days, so I don't put much into it, but he's gone a good long while.

I hear the toilet flush.

He doesn't holler for me to help him so I wait.

At last he comes back in the living room, stands in the hallway swaying a little bit and says,

That was......

Well, that was just... religious.

And I say,

Congratulations, and help him into his chair.

Part of the physical symptoms of Parkinson's is a difficulty swallowing and speaking. It's as if the automatic part of the brain forgets to tell the mouth how to do the simplest things. My father was and is a very social man, and he always enjoyed people and contact with people, a trait I am proud to share with him. As the Parkinson's progressed he became aware of his shaking and then when the brain forgot to send the messages to the mouth: he would drool on himself. For a proud man with an active and alert mind trapped inside a failing body this was an outrage, a source of frustration and embarrassment. My sister read on a web site somewhere that there had been some success with re-programming the brain to remember the previously automatic functions by switching the functions to "manual" mode. Apparently folks found that if you remind the Parkinson's sufferer to swallow and are patient with speech, you can re-groove these processes back to some extent. My sister and I decided we were going to try this with my dad, and to a large extent it really worked. The problem was finding a way to remind him to swallow or not drift off to sleep that was not humiliating or made us nags, or worse, the villains.

As my father's condition continued to improve, we began to go back into restaurants and be out in society, which was difficult for my father at first. I finally confronted him and he admitted to being ashamed. He said, I think people see us and say, "Look at that old man slobbering on himself and tottering along, it's so sad, and I don't want their pity."

I thought about it a minute and said, Pop, I am never ashamed to be seen with you. You're my father and I am and always will be very, very proud of you. He kinda took that in for a second, and I could see he was touched but unconvinced and so I said, I would like to suggest to you that when people see us out together instead of saying wow, look at that old guy, they are saying, wow, look at that father and son out together. Look how they interact, how much love is between them and those people might just in fact be a little bit envious of us and our relationship. They just might be a tad jealous. He kinda tasted that for a second and said, Well I have never considered that. But I think you might be right. Whether I'm right or wrong, I said, you and Mom never raised us to care all that much what other people thought of us if we knew what we were doing was right, so I don't really see that it matters much what anybody else but us thinks, and I am proud to be with you, sorry for the circumstances that bring us together but very happy with the time I get to spend with you. And he said, So am I, so am I...

About an hour later he allowed as how he was gettin hungry so I better go get some shoes on cause we were gonna go out for pizza and I knew we would not have the discussion about going out in public again.

Later as we were about to go into the restaurant, I saw some saliva gathering on his lower lip and said Pop, I have looked in the window of this here restaurant and there are some mighty good lookin wimmen in here and I know you don't want to kill my chances to give you grandchildren so you better--

And before I could finish the sentence, he swallowed hard on that saliva and pulled a handkerchief from his back pocket and dabbed at his lip.

I won't let you down, he said and winked at me. And he never did.

Well here's a weird one, and I apologize for those of you with gentler sensibilities, but you can skip this if you want to and if not, well, you were warned.

For some reason I'm not even sure of myself, it bothered me a bunch that my dad would sit down to pee.

(See? I warned y'all....)

I guess it had to do with that whole super hero thing, but it just rankled me that I would help my dad shuffle off to the bathroom and then he would set down just to pee, and I would admit that I hassled him about it on occasion.

Now one of my father's favorite things to tease me about was the fact that his son had gone to Carolina instead of a Good School like Duke. This would come up every time there was a Duke/Carolina basketball game or if I would ask some question, usually some stupid question, and the family would laugh at me and tell me the (obvious) answer and then my dad would throw the topper line, the slam dunk:

You'd'a known that if you'd'a gone to Duke, he would comment dryly.

So I am helping my dad once again down toward the bathroom, we're pre the Religious Experience, so the frequent trips to the bathroom have yet to yield any positive results and are thus a point of contention between us. He shuffles on in, I rebelliously lift the toilet seat, and he patiently puts it down, and turns and unbuckles his belt and settles on down and I leave to give him privacy. When the toilet flushes I come on back from the living room and

help him up and am hiking up his drawers and I say,
Any luck? referring to his Constipation, and he shakes
his head no as it is still difficult for him to talk and
so I start in on him sitting down to pee and he finally
sighs a long frustrated sigh and holds up a trembling
hand about head high to silence me. Making very
strong eye contact, he looks toward the once sure
and steady hand the Parkinson's has left shaking
like a leaf in the wind and slowly, very deliberately
moves it down to his crotch and simulates the act of
holding his penis to urinate. Hypnotized, I watch as
in my minds eye his trembling hand causes urine to
fly everywhere BUT the toilet bowl. I meekly shift
my gaze up to his eyes and manage to squeak out an
apologetic

Oh.

And he takes the precise two beats any good
comic knows is crucial for the delivery of a great
punch line and, though still struggling with the act of
speech, says:

If you'd'a gone to Duke you'd'a known that.

My father and I are standing by the sink in
the kitchen looking out the window at the gathering
clouds. Still in the middle of a terrible long running
drought, the threat of even a drizzle is a big deal.
Though it is October, it is a warm, almost spring
like day, Indian summer and thick and humid with
the promise of rain. It is morning and time to take

the first meds of the day. Because of the shaking of his unsteady hands, lifting a glass to drink from is difficult, so we use a straw, but even swallowing is hard. Finally we get the pills down and I harass him into drinking another glass of water. At last he says, If it rains, I'll drink two glasses, if it doesn't, I get to skip it and you can't give me a hard time about it. I simmer in frustration but have learned the value of picking my battles and, knowing that I will order a Big Gulp sized mug of tea at lunch for him, I agree. We gaze out the window and sure enough a slow gentle rain begins to fall. Damn my father mutters as I place a glass of water in front of him. The arguing over water is just a game for us now. The water is working its sweet miracles: he has had several more Religious Experiences, enough that the laxatives and prescription aids lie unused to the side of the batch of "working" meds. Yesterday I stood outside the shower as my father let water run over his body for the first time in over a year. He no longer has dandruff and his complexion is back to normal, he looks like he did when I was a kid. As we hydrated his body, his vocal chords, which depend upon moisture for elasticity--hey I'm a singer, remember?--have regained their flexibility and it is now easier for him to talk again. He's a believer in the power of water, but the game is just too much fun to give up and so he continues to give me a hard time about it. We watch the gentle rain come down and he says, Boy it's been a long time since we've seen that and I nod in agreement.

Hey, I say, When's the last time you stood out in the rain?

He thinks for a minute, looks out the window, then back over at me, then back out.

Jeez, I can't remember, he says. And then he says, 'Course, coming from me that doesn't mean much, it could'a been a week ago for all I know.

I like it a lot when he can laugh at the Parkinson's and so I have a good chuckle with him and then I say, Whaddaya say we go on out there and stand in that rain a little while and he looks at me like I'm nuts and then a smile slowly spreads across his face and he says, Sure, why not, the neighbors already think we're crazy and we go out the front door to the white cement walkway in the middle of the tortured brown grass and we stand in the rain and we look up into the sky and open our mouths like kids do and talk and laugh and just stand there and wave to the neighbors looking out their windows and yell greetings to the few crazy enough to join us outside standing in the warm October rain.

When it slows down we head inside and my dad says, Boy that was great and I allow as how, yeah it was, wasn't it?

My father, like so many of his generation, defined himself by what he DID. Work was who you were. I am quite content to sit on the couch and drink beer and watch Star Trek reruns until the end of time. I believe I do indeed deserve a break today. My father will have none of that. The Parkinson's has taken his ability to work from him, but not his DESIRE to work or his drive to DO something. At least once or twice a day he will become so restless that we go to the car and drive aimlessly, far out into the country, down side streets and on major roads. The feeling of moving, the tires humming beneath him, of going somewhere and having somewhere to go seems to help him, seems to calm him. Very social, but embarrassed at his current physical condition, being in the car means being OUT, out among people, out in the world, still having some meaning, some PURPOSE and so we drive.

At some point in the care of my father, I became aware of the silence in the house and became determined to fill my parent's home with music and sound again. When we're in the car, I play CDs that my father listened to when I was a kid. I have tracked these CDs down on the Internet and bought them to play for him. Although they are for him, I am staggered at the memories they evoke in me as we drive for hours out into the sunny afternoons. My father is often immobile as we drive, his eyes closed. I believe him to be sleeping through most of this but

Bluegrass is my Second Language

I continue to play the CDs and try for conversation, though I know it is difficult for him to talk. One day we're driving and listening to the Four Freshmen, songs he used to sing to my mom when I was little and suddenly he begins to sing along with a love song he used to sing to her, and I glance over at him, slumped down in his seat, mostly held up by the seatbelt, eyes clamped shut and I shake my head once again at the power and wonder of music and let the tears slide quietly out, glad to have given him a memory, happy to have helped him go somewhere else where he doesn't have to fight so hard every day.

As the water and pills begin to work their magic, our rides become shorter, our interaction more compelling. One afternoon as we wheel into the countryside I am playing some bluegrass CDs and my father says, Wow, that guy can sure play the mandolin and I turn to tell my father it is no wonder that guy can play the mandolin, that guy is none other than Bill Monroe and am stunned to see my dad buckled into his seat belt to be sure, but sitting upright still with his eyes closed yes, but playing AIR MANDOLIN with all his might and I can't stop myself, I laugh right out loud and he opens his eyes and says, Hey, I can't help it, that guy is GOOD and he closes his eyes and goes back to his miming and I say a silent prayer of thanks to modern medicine, water and music in general and Mr. Bill Monroe in particular.

Shortly after the air mandolin incident, I am helping my dad dry off after his morning shower. He now loves taking a shower and will often get impatient waiting for me to wake up and will start the shower on his own and go on in. The first time this happened I was terrified he might fall or get hurt, but am now delighted when he bursts into the bedroom to announce, I'm gonna go get in the shower---you gettin up soon or what?

So I am helping him dry off and get dressed and I work the towel into his ear to dry off and the towel comes away with a smear of earwax. I grab a Q Tip and swab a bit and come away with something the size of an engine block.

Damn Pop, when's the last time you cleaned out your ears? I ask and he shrugs. We proceed to put the makers of Q Tips' children and their grandchildren through college and into trust funds we use so many Q Tips in pursuit of clean, dry ears. I make a mental note.

The next day, I take my dad in to the General Practitioner's office for a check up. This doctor is beside himself at how good my father looks, how much he has improved, how much he has fought back from the edge. He repeatedly asks my father what brought about this change and my father points at me and says, Ask him, he did it.

So I begin to tell the doc my theory and our

plan for The Great Experiment and the miracle of water and body chemistry and he gets excited and says Wait, wait, and runs out and comes back with another doc and a physician's assistant and says, You have to listen to this, and makes me tell my story again as my father sits on the exam table smiling proudly.

After things calm down and we're almost done with the general exam, I ask the doc to check my dad's ears cause my mom keeps saying he's hard of hearing, but when we're in the car, he hears the music just fine. Secretly, I suspect my father might be suffering from the same amount of hearing loss any man who has been married to the same woman since the Pleistocene Era might, and by that I mean a certain degree of shall we say, self preservational selective hearing, and believe me that is said with all due respect and reverence to what it takes to make a relationship work over so many years. That plus the fact we used ten thousand two hundred thirty three Q Tips yesterday make me think we might have a problem. The doc takes an otoscope and looks in my dad's left ear and kinda lets out a yelp like Yikes and calls for a nurse. After the exam, the effusive doctor pumps my hand and honors me by thanking me for my help with his patient, slaps my dad on the back and congratulates him on his astonishing improvement and says to the nurse, You've got your work cut out for you, so call if you need me and heads on out of the exam room.

My father sits on the exam table as the nurse holds a curved plastic bowl up to the side of his head and rinses his ear out with warm water from a small syringe. We are both stunned as a Volkswagen Beetle and a small battleship come surging from his ear canal. It is simply inconceivable the amount of earwax contained in there. We are talking to him through the whole procedure when he suddenly sits up straight and says Hey wait a minute. And the nurse stops and we urgently ask What's wrong? What's wrong?? and he calmly says Jeez, why are you both talking so loud? and the nurse looks at me and I look at my father and say Because that's how loud we have to talk for you to hear us and he looks to the nurse as if questioning the veracity of what I just said and she nods meekly and he looks back at me and says, Well, that's ridiculous.

The right ear is not so bad and I begin thinking on this interesting puzzle and soon come upon a solution. My father sleeps on his right side, thus the LEFT side is up, and due to the Parkinson's he doesn't move much during the night so for all these months the ear wax that normally gets loosened by hot showers had no where to go but down, down further and further into the ear canal as every night my father turned on his right side and gave the left ear eight hours to compact even more wax down into the ear canal.

Bluegrass is my Second Language

Now I KNOW a lot of y'all are sayin, John SOME of this stuff is funny, but this whole earwax thing is just plain GROSS, why in the world are you tellin us about this? Well, I will tell you why: because we family members treat the disease not the patient too! If I misplace my car keys, nobody makes a big deal of it, I just forgot where they are. If my DAD misplaces the car keys, everybody gets all quiet cause it's THE PARKINSON'S. If my dad can't hear, it's either the Parkinson's or it's cause he's gettin old. Folks, we gotta look at the PATIENT, the PERSON and stop blamin EVERYTHING on the disease.

I was fortunate in my video career to become good friends with a geriatric physician name of Mark Williams. Mark would take me on rounds with him upon occasion, and I was amazed how he could diagnose a patient who WASN'T EVEN IN THE ROOM based solely on the clues he found around the patients bed, without ever looking at the patient's chart. I used to beg him to let me make a video series called "Doctor Sherlock Holmes" so he could teach other docs how to do this, and I am proud to say I learned a thing or two on those early morning rounds. (And yes, I generally stayed up all night playin music and then rolled on in about five-ish and made the rounds with Mark and then went on home and crashed out hard.)

Point is, not everything is the Parkinson's and that is real real hard to hold onto for EVERY

275

caregiver involved. We've ALL gotta become Doctor Sherlock Holmes, every minute of every day. My dad was having a hard time walking, said the floor felt uneven. One day my mom happened to pick up the tennis shoes he'd been wearing for probably seven or eight years, and lo and behold the heel on his right foot was worn down to an almost forty five degree angle. Well no wonder the floor felt uneven. We all thought it was THE PARKINSON'S, even ME and I pride myself on seeing the person, not the disease. Got him a new pair of tennis shoes and dang if he didn't walk better right outa the store! Later at a routine eye exam, we discovered he was also getting a CATARACT in his right eye which would also account for his unsteadiness along with the shoe. See, it WASN'T the Parkinson's at least not all of it, but we all thought it was, and all of us are ashamed because of it. So I'm tellin the ear wax story cause it's a cool bit of detective work and it's just disgusting enough that it'll maybe stick in folks' minds and the next time someone they love is havin difficulty and has a major illness, maybe they won't be so quick to GIVE UP on tryin to make it better by seeing PAST the disease and INTO the one they love. See, it's not just the person WITH Parkinson's that has to fight hard every day; it's everyone AROUND the person with Parkinson's too.

Later that night we're home and watching TV.

Bluegrass is my Second Language

My dad says, How loud did the TV have to be before? And I punch up the volume with the remote to where we had to run it for him to hear it and he just shakes his head in wonder. I pull the volume back down and we watch together in silence a while. A commercial comes up and he turns to me and says, This is a good show. The dialogue is extremely well written, it's very clever.

Smiling broadly I say, You know Pop, I could not agree with you more. Glad you're enjoying it!

And my old man and I settled in to watch the rest of the show together, just two guys at home eatin popcorn sittin in front of the tube on a Wednesday night watchin "Buffy The Vampire Slayer"

Well, as is my wont to do, I have saved the most twisted of my Twisted Hallmark Moments for last. Once again I apologize if it's a bit rough for some of y'all, but hey life is rough sometimes and God knows the tears will find you easy enough so you gotta take the laughter when and where you can.

I am proud and extremely happy to report that both my mom and my dad are doin just fine now. My father is back to coaching Little League and works part time at the offices of the Durham Herald (journalism is in the blood it seems) where he is well loved and well received by everybody there, as is my mother who works the reception desk a few days a week. Parkinson's is a degenerative disease, so I do not kid myself that we have a happy ending here, but I do take pride in having been witness to my father's brave fight back from the brink, and my mother's near miraculously rapid recovery from double hip surgery. I like to tease my dad that my mom handled her hip surgery MUCH better than Coach K. (The Duke basketball coach for any of you unfortunate non-ACC-ers living on Mars or Pluto.) My mother, as I have mentioned before, is a smart woman. She knows the last place you want to be when you're sick is a hospital. The docs all said they had never seen anyone more determined to get back home to her husband and family, so I reckon no matter what the age, Love can and will conquer all. Last year when we went to the beach, for the first time in many years both my parents were able to walk down to the shore completely under their own power, something my sister and I thought they would likely never do again, so life is pretty good right now and I am proud of the part I played in helping my parents, particularly my father. I am also forever in the debt of my sister for her astonishing work with both my parents, but with special emphasis on my mother. It helps a lot when you have a team...

One Sunday many years ago my sister and I were over to my parents house for dinner and we were sitting around the table eating and talking as we had done on so many wonderful occasions before and my sister and my mom were waxing eloquent on love and what love means and is and we boys had been silent for quite a while when my mother looks at my dad and says, Honey, what do you think love is? and without missing a beat my father said:

Love is holding the bucket when they've got the flu and gotta puke.

THAT'S love.

Now, as you might imagine, my sister and mother were horrified and immediately rejected that definition of love out of hand, but you know what? I've always kinda liked that definition of love and in my heart of hearts while I believe in all the other glossy, frilly stuff, I think it's a right good definition of love in action, in thought, word and deed. Way I see it, if love is an outward spiritual sign of an inward spiritual grace, well, heck, I reckon nothin says that better than holdin the bucket when the one you love has gotta puke.

But once again, I digress....

See, there was a period there just after the water and the new med schedule began to work that my father still lingered in that twilight of feebleness and I had to help him with the simplest of every day tasks. Not so hard at first but after The Great Experiment had proved successful, there came a call one day from the bathroom. Sometimes the Parkinson's ravaged my father so badly that it was not unusual for me to have to come in and help him up from a chair or, in this case the commode. Only the

Miracle Of The Water had added a new wrinkle to our adventure together.

Sheepishly he looked up at me, red faced with embarrassment. You're gonna have to wipe me, he said, I can't do it, I've tried, I'm sorry but I just can't...

Inwardly I was horrified. Rose-colored glasses kinda guy that I am, I had not quite extrapolated the success of The Great Water Experiment out far enough to foresee this in my future. Trying to remain upbeat, I said cheerily, Hey, no problemo Pop, I got ya covered and proceeded to attend to him.

When we were done and he was standing up and I was fastening his pants and getting his belt buckled he again began to apologize, struggling with his speech.

Look, I said, Up to now it's been easy for me to call myself your son. Now I get the chance to earn that right and I am proud to do it.

It was an odd place for such a profound statement of love, respect, and gratitude standing there in the bathroom and all, but life'll do that do ya sometimes, and I reckon you just gotta be ready for it when it comes. All that said, it WAS a solemn moment but still awkward, so trying to break the ice a little, I grinned at him and added,

So........I do that a couple a million more times and you and I will be square for all the times you did it for me, right?

Bluegrass is my Second Language

And he once again took that perfect comedic two beat pause and looked me dead in the eye and completely straight faced said,

"At least."

Here endeth the Twisted Hallmark Moments.

4

SHEPP WASDELL

There's a name that keeps coming up in this book a lot and that name is Shepp Wasdell. He keeps coming up because he had such a profound effect on my life and when he died at the age of 51 it was as if I had lost my brother. Y'all didn't need to get all bummed out in Book One, so I just kinda bumped up against him, let y'all know a bit about him and what we did and who we were together, and it's not my intention to bum y'all out here in Book Two either.

Bluegrass is my Second Language

Suffice it to say that when he died, I kinda fell off the planet awhile. To the best of my knowledge, I wasn't mad or depressed, I just became Extremely Existential. Though there are professional grief counselors and such who might debate my state of mind with me, I was really in a kind of fog where, since the delicacy and fleeting nature of life was so dramatically brought home to me, nothing really mattered much, because it could all be over in the blink of an eye and ultimately everything, every THING you strived for, worked for, simply became someone else's obligation. Interestingly enough, I give credit (no pun intended) to the credit card companies for helpin me outa my little funk there cause if you ever wanna be reminded of what matters in life, well you just set on down and chat awhile with an authorized credit card company customer service representative what is owed a back payment or two and by God they will set you right about what is important in this world and the nature of obligation in the twenty first century. So I do owe them a debt of sorts cause, believe it or not, they were the first to waken me from my Existential Slumber, so passionate were they about what they do for a living.

I mean, you just gotta plumb admire dedication like that.

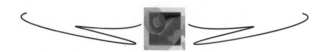

One of the things that was cool about the friendship Shepp and I shared was the multi-generational aspect of it, something I still enjoy to this day through my relationship with Edward, Shepp and Anna's son. See, my dad and Shepp's dad were best friends. Course, bein teenagers and thus contrary by nature and hormones, when we first met, Shepp and I hated each other instantly and passionately. When we got about fourteen or fifteen, we both ran for offices in the Episcopal Young Churchmen, or EYC as it was known. I don't remember what I ran for or why really, but I won and so did Shepp and so he was President of the EYC and I was whatever I was and we limited our interaction as much as possible given we were often stuck in the same room together and, because of our respective offices, had to interact on some level.

At some point, somebody came up with the idea that the EYC should take a trip to the beach, this being the South and the Beach a highly desirable destination for all right thinking young people, Episcopal or otherwise. That motion was heartily seconded by the assembled teenagers with nary a dissenting vote. At subsequent meetings the concept of how to PAY for the beach trip came up and thus it was we hit upon the plan to mow the lawn and trim the hedges and generally take care of the maintenance of the church grounds in return for the money usually paid out to the local adult contractors.

Bluegrass is my Second Language

We would tend to the needs of the church grounds
for the summer, take the cash we earned and in
late September head off as a group to the beach to
revel in the joys of sea and sand for a long weekend.
This plan was again unanimously approved to much
cheering and backslapping.

Now I will admit that time has passed and so my
memory might be a bit clouded as to these details, but
it seems to me that at first, there were a fair amount
of EYC members showing up to do the assigned
chores. Not ALL the EYC members mind you, but a
fair showing, a fair showing. Didn't take long for word
to get out that the actual WORK of caring for the
church grounds was pretty substantial, and though the
church DID supply the lawn mower and tools, there
was A LOT of lawn and the mower was not a RIDING
mower and did I mention there was A LOT of lawn
to be pushed over and raked over and hedges--HIGH
hedges--to be trimmed and raked and wheelbarrowed
and well, while the first Saturday was kinda a fun
party, the review we got from the folks in charge was
that we would likely have to do a bit less partying and
a lot more working if this deal was to continue.

So week after week, every Saturday from late
March to September, the work of caring for the
church grounds continued as I would pull myself from
my bed and drive to the church, half asleep to begin
the days toil, for as fewer and fewer EYC members
showed up, the work took longer and longer for the

285

ones who DID show up to complete. So yeah, I might be remembering it all wrong, but the point is, it didn't take TOO long till it was just Shepp and me showing up every Saturday, glaring at each other and sullenly stomping off in separate directions disgusted but committed to completing the task at hand. One week he mowed and I raked and trimmed. The next I mowed and he trimmed and raked and on and on. I don't know what Shepp was doing on his Friday nights, but I was out playing music with my high school rock n roll band and climbing outa that bed on a Saturday--a SATURDAY--morning was killing me! I'd roll in at two or three in the morning and damned if that alarm clock didn't go off fifteen minutes later CLAIMING to be accurate at eight AM and I would curse and moan and stumble out of bed into some old clothes and head to the church by way of a Hardees for a biscuit and a couple glasses of iced tea to get me through the hot summer days.

Seems like Shepp showed up in about the same condition as I did. We would minimize our conversation as much as possible, limiting it to the bare essentials of what needed to be done and who would do it and whether either of us had been able to brow beat anyone else in the EYC to show up to help. Most often it was just the two of us. We hated the work, we hated each other and we hated the whole situation.

Then an amazing thing happened.

Bluegrass is my Second Language

As it so often can and will do, work brought us together. As the weeks passed and then months passed I began to have a grudging respect for this guy who, like me, just kept showing up. Eventually I had to concede he was showing up for the same reason that I showed up:

We had given our word.

No coincidence our fathers were best friends, they had taught their sons at least one crucial thing: your word is your bond. And so our word had meaning to us, was, yes, sacred to us. I don't know if our fathers ever discussed it, or took pride in the fact that their sons continued to do the work more than a dozen had promised to do, but I hope they did and I hope they were proud.

One morning I brought Shepp a biscuit.

The next Saturday I was resting in the shade of a big elm tree for our lunch break when suddenly Shepp slides in beside me. Now I know we had talked before this, had, in fact, many conversations, however brief they may have been, but for me, these were always the first words Shepp ever uttered to me.

You know, he said, You're a pretty good guy. It's a real drag you're such an asshole most of the time.

I looked at him.

Lessee, I says, You're what? Fifteen, sixteen years old? Yer smokin a cigarette and

I nodded at the red, white and blue Budweiser beer can clutched in his hand.

Yer drinkin a beer on church property. So lets get this straight, I'M the asshole here??

Shepp took a pull on his Bud.

What's yer point? he says with a grin.

Jesus, I muttered and shook my head in feigned disgust.

A beautiful and literally life long friendship was born that day.

During the summer of my junior year at Carolina, I lived with Shepp in a sprawling wood frame house off Franklin Street (the main drag) in Chapel Hill on a little side street fittingly named Carolina Avenue. By this point Shepp, who went on to get a BA in English with a minor in Philosophy, was an incredibly gifted mechanic and the various rooms of this gray one level frame house were filled with engines and/or various engine parts as Shepp worked on cars for the fun of learning or for the profit (such as it was) of working on cars for his friends. His specialty was Volkswagen beetles, or bugs as we called them. The house was strewn with pistons and oil pans and transmission parts and as crazy as it sounds, all I can say is

1.) we were college students and

2.) it all seemed perfectly normal to me.

There was a great porch on that house and we sat for hours out there drinking beers (short Buds in cans, never talls or bottles) and talking and me strumming a guitar and playing some new song or other. There was a cute girl from Connor dorm Shepp had taken up with, named Anna Johnson and she was around a bunch as well, as you might imagine. There were dinners and conversations and sweet Anna not only tolerated Shepp's shall we say, peculiar home decor, she also tolerated his less than normal friends and all of us loved her for that and were happy for the two of them as they seemed extraordinarily well matched, and Shepp at long last seemed both at peace and incredibly happy.

People would ask us how long we'd known each other, how long we'd been friends, and Shepp was always proud to say he'd known me since before I could play the guitar, and not many people could say that for, just as Shepp was famous for the ubiquitous short Bud clutched in one hand, cigarette in the other, I was fairly well known for having sprouted a guitar at some point in my young life, and it was always being strummed or was close by at the very least. One day I played an instrumental for Shepp, a rather intricate piece on my twelve string that encompassed the use of a slide (bottleneck) Blues technique made famous by, among others, my original inspiration, Leadbelly. (In my case the bottle neck in question was a literal one: it was the neck cut off a bottle of Taylor Lake Country Red Wine, and then dragged or moved in a sliding motion over the strings of the guitar.) Shepp watched the performance, gave me some feedback for

things to change or play up a bit and then begged
off further discussion as he had to get back to work
on our friend Michael's VW bug. I stayed around to
watch him work (I enjoy watching an artist create)
and eventually he needed an extra pair of hands and
so he asked me to help out. Although he was always
a patient and dedicated teacher, my ineptness soon
left him exasperated and virtually speechless until he
finally stood up from under the hood and, wiping his
hands on an oily orange rag, said

I just don't understand how somebody who is so
good with his fingers can be so lousy with his hands!

And with that, he snagged the screwdriver out
of my delicate musician's hand and dived back under
the hood and said

Go sit on the porch and play me some music
while I work.

That line, that wonderful line, great with yer
fingers, lousy with yer hands, haunted me for almost
half my life, and I admit to some degree of shame
and disappointment in it but also some degree of
pride. Shepp was good at delineating what he called
"book smart" from "life smart." After graduating
from Carolina, he immediately enrolled at Holden
Tech to get certified as a Mechanic. (I'm certainly
never gonna make a living with a degree in English
and a minor in Philosophy, he would say. I gotta have
SOMETHIN that'll let me earn a decent wage.)

My fingers were a conundrum to him. A source

of pride and amazement as he watched them move across the fretboard and make my instrument speak, but also a source of befuddlement because he could never teach those same agile fingers a good trade.

To be honest with you, I think he worried about me making a living.

Years later when he was dying of lung cancer and I was helping out around the house, helping do chores for him that he hadn't had time to get to and that he wanted done so Anna wouldn't have to worry over them, he wanted the screen door taken off the outside porch so that Edward, his now college age son, could move some things into the house later in the evening. Shepp had a very particular way of wanting the door removed--the RIGHT way, by his reckoning--but I had been working in the film biz a good while by this point, and I had seen my share of doors come off hinges so we could get our gear inside, so I heard him out and then promptly ignored him and did it the way I had seen a dozen or so Key Grips do it. He sorta bitched and moaned at me a while and then when he saw where what I was doing would lead, he shut up and watched me, appraising as I went with grunts and nods.

Having finished the job, I moved the door to the side, leaned it against the wall and turned to face him.

He nodded affirmation at me.

Good to see your hands finally catchin up to

your fingers, he groused.

And then he smiled at me.

Need to talk a minute about that cute gal over in Conner Dorm, that Anna Johnson. I'm not really sure how she and Shepp met, probably through the music sessions we held on the front steps of Alexander Dorm at Carolina. Shepp and I lived in Alexander and would pass the time working on songs out front of the dorm sitting on the red brick stairs by a big ol magnolia tree. Wasn't too long before other musicians appeared and not too long after that we had a whole bunch of pickers sitting out there almost around the clock. Weren't too may times you could walk by our dorm that there wasn't at least one person out there with a guitar or a cello. It was pretty cool and I guess that's where they met, hangin around, horsin around on the front steps of the dorm cause Anna lived right across the way in Connor.

Amazing how such big things can start in such mundane ways.

I don't remember how long it took, but once it took, they were pretty tight, and the fit seemed right. Shepp needed a smart, good, strong woman to keep his interest and respect, and Anna was all that and more. They dated throughout college and where many couples split up after college, they stayed tight together then too.

But the road was sometimes a bumpy one.

One hot summer day of my senior year I went over to the house on Carolina Avenue and Shepp was nowhere to be seen. Usually he'd be outside workin on a VW bug or sittin on the porch drnkin a beer and listening to music, but when I pulled in, there was no Shepp, no music, no nothin.

Most importantly, there was no Anna.

The yard, as always was full of the carcasses of VWs, most with hoods and trunks open, jacked up on one side or the other, tires off, brake shoes revealed, plastic tubs underneath to catch the thick black brown oil.

As I approached the wooden porch, I could see the front door was open and, having lived there myself on occasion, I pulled open the screen door and walked in. There were car parts everywhere. It looked like there had been an explosion in a car shop and parts had just rained down at random: transmissions, pistons, valves, engines, oil pans, a chrome bumper. A dejected Shepp Wasdell was seated in the middle of this chaos, on the Thrift Shop couch, completely deflated, completely defeated; looking the worst I had ever seen him. He clearly hadn't bathed or shaved or possibly even moved in several days. Stunned I cautiously made my way in and, sitting down, I asked him what the heck happened.

After a moment where it seemed like it finally registered to him that I was there and had spoken, he said,

Anna's gone. We got in a fight, and I let her leave.

He sat for a moment in silence and looked hard at me with an intensity I had never seen before

I have made the biggest mistake of my life, he muttered, close to tears.

Well, we gotta get her back, I said, C'mon let's go!!

Man, he said, shaking my head, I been TRYING to do that, I have cannibalized all the VWs I've got trying to make ONE damn car that will run, one I can use to go get her.

C'mon man, I said, standing and pulling at his arm, I've got a car, let's go, let's go...

But he just mournfully shook his head.

Won't work, he said, can't do it...

Why not?? I demanded, Just where the hell is she?

And he looked up at me

Vermont, he said.

Well, I got him propped up the best I could, got him to eat something and take a shower and I promised him that I would work something out, find some way to help him fix this and then I had to head home. It was summer and I was staying at my folks' house to save money for school, driving my dad's brand new Datsun 1200 on the weekends to go out and hit some music jams and parties. I was despondent all the way from Chapel Hill to Durham, desperate to find a way to help, and could come up with only one slim, faint glimmer of hope and I was still pretty low when I slumped into my house and plopped into a chair with a frustrated sigh.

My dad looked up from the paper he was reading and said, What's wrong, you OK? And I said, Yeah, it's not me, it's Shepp, and I told him the whole sad story.

Now you gotta remember that Shepp's dad and my dad were best friends right up until Shepp's dad died, so obviously my parents knew and loved Shepp, and Shepp and Anna had been to my folks' house for plenty of Sunday dinners and my parents had come to love Anna too, so my old man was flat devastated by this news. What's he gonna do? he asked when I told him of Shepp's unsuccessful attempt to make one usable, travel worthy VW out of the husks of the dozen or so littered around the Carolina Avenue house.

My dad mulled this over, cogitated a while and said, Well, he's gotta do something, he HAS to go get her, work this out, those two are made for each other. What are you guys going to do?

And I took a deep breath and said, Pop, you know that Shepp is an excellent mechanic...

Yeah, he said tentatively.

Well, I am thinkin how maybe Shepp and I should borrow the Datsun and go up to Vermont and find Anna and bring her back.

He just looked at me and blinked.

My new car?

Pop, I said, I guarantee you two things: one is that Shepp'll make that car run better than it did BEFORE the trip once we get back, and KEEP it runnin for years in exchange for the use of it and two is I guarantee you they will end up gettin married if we can just get her back here.

And to my ever-lasting astonishment and delight, my old man said

OK.

And then he ruffled the newspaper back up to eye level and asked from behind the evening edition,

When will you guys be leaving?

Now I get a lotta grief about being Mister Romantic, Mister Rose Colored Glasses, but if this doesn't prove that I come by it naturally, I don't know what does.

I was dumbfounded.

I dunno, right away I guess, I gotta go call Shepp, I said and ran for the phone in a kinda daze.

Don't forget you need to call work and clear the time off, he hollered after me.

Yessir, I yelled back from the kitchen. And then I had a thought, and I went back to the living room and stuck my head in.

Pop, I said

The corner of the newspaper came down.

Thanks, I said, Thanks a lot.

He nodded at me from behind the Durham Sun.

You boys go get Anna, he said, And make it right.

He gave me a terse nod for punctuation and flipped the paper back up with a tight rattle, and I went off to start my journey.

Now the story of our trip to Vermont and finding Anna will have to wait for another time. Suffice it to say, we got on up there and we did finally find Anna and she and Shepp did finally make it right between them and while we returned to North Carolina without her, we were confident she would follow, and in fact she did.

Wasn't too long after that, those two went and got hitched, much to my eternal delight, and as these things go, seems like it wasn't too many years later that Edward Sheppard Wasdell the Third arrived and I will admit I have been right proud of my small role in setting all those wonderful events in motion.

I told my old man Shepp and Anna had gotten married by calling up over to the house and announcing that the second part of my Vermont Guarantee had at last come true, for over the years

Shepp was as good as his word and tended to that
Datsun like it was his own and even continued to keep
it running after my father had decided it was time for
a new car and had passed the 1200 along to me.

Edward was sixteen or seventeen, I don't
recall which, but I do remember it was the chilly late
evening of my annual New Year's Eve Party when
I asked him to accompany me outside. He dutifully
ambled along beside me and we wandered over to
a spot on the lawn where an old Datsun 1200 sat,
unused and undisturbed, it's flat tires visible proof it
had not been moved or driven in many many years.

As we stood there talking about nothing, just
looking at the car, I handed him an envelope.

What's this? he asked.

I have been saving that for you for about twenty
years, I answered.

And he opened the envelope and took out the
owner's certificate for a 1979 Datsun 1200.

I have been saving this car for you since before
you were born, since before there was a you to save
this car for, I was saving this car for you, I said. And
now, my friend, I'm going to tell you a glorious story
of two young people in love.

And I did.

Right then and there, out in the late December
cold, with frost on our breath and hands shoved
deep in our pockets, shifting our weight from side

to side to keep warm, I told Edward a story of great love lost, and great love re-gained, and I presented to him the very car his father and I had used to go and fetch his Mom-To-Be, and to that young man's credit he accepted my gift and my story with grace, understanding and generosity.

Now I say generosity cause, caught up in the moment as I was, it never occurred to me till a few days later when I walked outta my house into the noon day sun and looked over at that old beat up rusted out dry rotted covered in dirt little boxy foreign car, that no sixteen year old Red Blooded American Boy (let alone the son of a MECHANIC fer Gawdsakes) would want to have anything to do with that car, let alone (shudder) DRIVE it somewheres where people he knew might could actually see him!

I remember standing there in the bright sunshine, shaking my head in disgust thinking, Well, that was a cool idea, very romantic and all, but really John, WHAT WERE YA THINKIN????

But Edward was such a gentleman about it. He was able to look past the appearance of the gift to see to the heart of it, and he totally got it. We even talked about moving it over to his Dad's shop in Apex and the three of us working on it and fixing it up and getting it running and going for a spin in it.

Course we never did.

You think you have time, and then time runs out.

But it was a great plan and it brought smiles to our faces to think of it, to talk about it, to plan for it....

After Shepp died and Edward and I talked it over, I had the car towed away to a junkyard.

But before those boys hauled that car up on the bed of that big ol loud diesel trailer and left, I pried off the small plastic disc with Datsun printed on it in black and silver and blue and then I unscrewed the chrome 1200 off the left rear side of that car and I have those things to this very day should Anna or Edward, or myself...

...ever need them.

There was a time when the good people of North Carolina were subjected to an ad campaign promoting tourism within the state. Not to disparage the work of the talented folks who put this promotion together, but there was a particularly obnoxious aspect of the television and radio spots that quickly gained a kind of infamy among the residents here. Over pictures of landmarks and mountain vistas, with a sound track of a muzak-y kinda folk tune, some nice gentleman sang the following words with as much gusto as he could summon:

Lord, it's just like living in a poem
I like calling North Carolina home!

Bluegrass is my Second Language

Needless to say the English majors in the state were appalled, no one more so than Mr. Shepp Wasdell. The rhyming of "home" with "poem" never ceased to amaze, confound and annoy him, and the more the spots played, the more righteous his indignation became. That line of copy became a catch phrase that stayed with us North Carolinians for years and years after the ads were off the air, so to that extent, I guess you could say the campaign was a success, except for the way we came to use the slogan.

Went something like this:

You'd walk into a Seven Eleven and the guy behind the counter would say somethin like, Beautiful day isn't it? and you would respond, Why, it's just like livin in a poem, and some woman waiting in line would say, Ya know, I like calling North Carolina ho-em, and we'd all stand there and shake our heads in dismay fer a minute with a kinda rueful smile playin at the corners of our mouths.

And then we'd all go on with our business as if the whole exchange never happened.

Well, the point of this is that when we were driving back from Vermont to get Anna, we were hell bent for leather on the road, just completely burnt out from our endeavor which of course, being successful, we'd stretched out as long as possible so now we had to complete a two day drive in one day, tops. We left Vermont tired and disheveled, unshaven and, as I recall from the open windows in the car, unbathed as well, and of course all of that got worse the further we drove and the more road dust we picked up and the hotter the day got. (The Datsun, God bless it, did not have air conditioning.) So the long miles melted away and at some point after we got south a DC, Shepp, clearly the superior driver, caved in to fatigue and relinquished the wheel and left it to me to make the last leg of the long journey and take us in to home. Exhausted, he collapsed in the reclined passenger seat and was soon deeply and enthusiastically asleep.

I drove in silence having turned off the radio to make it easier for him to slip off into dreamland, as it had been a wrenching trip and I knew though he was triumphant he was profoundly weary; physically, mentally, and emotionally. So I motored down the interstate, doing what Shepp called "push and steer" driving while feeling really pretty good about myself and sorta marveling over the generosity and romanticism of my parents who had not only freely given over their brand new car, but their blessings as well (and a little on the side cash slipped into pockets and hands with the whispered admonition not to tell my mother/father.)

I'm pretty good company for myself (it's all the voices inside my head what keep me amused, I reckon...) and enjoy patting myself on the back and have gotten pretty durn good at it over the years, so the hours and miles kinda flew by and I knew we were approaching the North Carolina border, and I was plum READY, just couldn't wait to cross that line.

Now to this day I don't know if I let out a big sigh, or a little cheer, or said somethin or what, but to the best of my knowledge I made no sound a'tall when I at long last I saw that big green sign with the state flag on it that said Welcome To North Carolina appear on the horizon.

Just as we were about to come right up on that magic demarcation point between away and home, ol Shepp suddenly stirred out of his fitful sleep and, raising his head just enough off the rolled up blue denim jacket he'd been using as a pillow to see out the window and take in that blur of a sign, he muttered with a voice trembling with emotion:

Looord, it's just like livin in a poem....

And his head fell back and he was out like a light.

This became, beyond a doubt, my favorite Shepp Wasdell story, and I musta laughed for the next sixty miles that day.

I could tell you ten million really great stories about Shepp and Anna, what a great team they were, how much they loved each other, loved Edward. I could tell you about the evenings I would go over to Shepp and Anna's and we would have dinner together and then work on songs, work on lyrics, all of us trying to find the exact right words, and how Anna would eventually fall asleep and every time Shepp and I would get stuck--when we needed the elusive Magic Line, we would hesitate and then finally break down and wake her and somehow as she rubbed the sleep from her eyes and stretched and we brought her up to speed as to where we were in the song, what we wanted, what the song needed, she would invariably yawn and then just GIVE us the line, somehow she just HAD it right there and then she would take the blanket and, laying back down and curling up on the couch, pull it around her and go back to sleep as if it was nothin at all, and I would look at Shepp and say, How does she DO that? and he would shake his head in wonder and look at her with love and admiration and say, Damned if I know, John....

I could tell you how brave and strong and true Shepp was in his final days and what an honor it was to be there with him and for him, for Anna and Edward. I never once heard him say anything but, Hey, I went to college, I can read. I know what was printed on the side of those cigarette packages....

Accepting responsibility was a big part of who Shepp was, and what and how he taught, and he was true to that till the end.

I still miss him, still think of him every day, he still writes with me and I still run my songs by him to make sure they're OK.

He is still a tough taskmaster, but he taught me well.

Bluegrass is my Second Language

I think he is proud of me.
He was a great man.

And I reckon that's about all you need to know
about Shepp Wasdell.

5

WRITING A BOOK

THE GOOD, THE BAD, AND (SO FAR), THERE IS NO UGLY

OR
AND Y'ALL ARE IN IT

I've never written a book before, so this whole experience is new to me and I appreciate your patience those of you who've stayed with me this far. I know I have complained about some of this stuff, the writing and re-writing, the complete lack of any control over the book, the fact that it takes on a life and personality of its own and goes where it will whenever it wants. But there's other aspects of book writin that are just fabulous, and I'll get to those in a second, cause unfortunately there's sides of it that are just plain, well...odd, and there's just no preparing for em, they just kinda come up and whomp on ya when yer least expectin it.

There was a point where virtually all the principal characters in Book One had either read or had a copy of the book and a bunch of em felt compelled to quote me to me, and I suddenly found myself a character in my own damn book. I'd be at a jam somewhere and we'd be playin and singin and laughin and then we'd go to start up another song and one of the other mandolin players would yell out, Hold On! Hold on! I gotta get in tune! and Greg or somebody would lean over and whisper conspiratorially, Someone's ALWAYS tunin a mandolin, or quote some other line I had written and well, that gets a little disturbin after a while is what I mean.

Or I would walk into Jimmy's shop and feel like I was on a movie set or somethin, cause now this place was, at least in my own mind and in my own book, sorta famous, and here I was, and I would be seein it like I had always seen it, but also be remembering my descriptions of it and comparing and contrasting to the point where I was kinda stuck in the pages of a book I wrote! A VERY surreal experience heightened by the fact that I would be sittin there in between songs and sometimes the guys would look at me, and then sorta smile and patiently wait and then look at the pictures of the pin-ups on the walls and then look back at me expectantly and nod encouragingly and I found myself torn between tellin the joke I liked to tell about Jimmy's daughters and feelin like I HAD to ask to be introduced to his daughters, cause I said I ALWAYS asked about them girls in the book, and well, cause people were WAITIN for me to ask about em.

Now I can not tell a lie, it WAS flattering at first, and I know them good folks meant well, but after about the tenth time, you gotta understand, it's just plumb unnatural, and I am glad that phase didn't last too long because all those pickers up there knew me sorta BEFORE the book, and so we settled back into our friendship and music pretty soon, but it was right creepy there for a while.

See, the thing is, I LOVE teasin Jimmy about those pinups, love askin Martha when her daughters might be comin back home for a visit and would she mind if I just happened to drop on by when they were in town, it's a great game, a great tradition, it just kinda got all twisted up there for a time is all,

but now I am pleased to report, as we move on to
the Good Things that can happen when you write a
book, that folks and the music and the jokin are pretty
much back to normal at Jimmy's shop, meaning that
he teases me unmercifully and calls me by my myriad
onion related nicknames, and I wait, and when the
time is right, I ask him about the pictures of his
daughters up on the wall, and the boys just howl.

It's great.

So yeah, there were bad, well, maybe not
BAD per se, let's just say PERPLEXING things that
happened when I gave out copies of my book. But on
the other hand, there were great things that happened
too, things that showed me how the book had gone off
and made a path for itself in the lives of these people
I love and respect so much, that it had been, in fact,
welcomed into their lives.

One time I was down at the marina at Hagen
Stone Park helpin get a High Lonesome Strings
meeting set up, out of sight of anyone back behind
Pammy's big ol van, puttin a string on my guitar
and getting ready to play and I heard Greg and Jeff
teasin Pammy Davis about how she forgot the lyrics
to a song the night before and how the Queen Of
Bluegrass ought not to be droppin lyrics, and just
generally razzin her a bit and she finally stood up and
said, Well, boys, I guess I did forget the lyrics to that
song, but at least I have a whole chapter to myself

in a book that lists me by name, and lesseee....you guys, nope...no, I believe ya'll were sorta just lumped together in one little old chapter now weren't ya?

From behind the van I sorta gasped with both surprise and laughter but also with trepidation as I waited to see what the response would be to the Queen's tirade. Well, I shouldn't a worried cause after a second there was just this explosion of laughter as everybody started hootin and ooh-in as if she had just put them boys in their place real good.

Now, I'm sure they didn't know I was back there, so I'm pretty dang positive that exchange wasn't said for my benefit, it was just a bunch of friends playin and teasin at each other and the vehicle they were usin was a book I wrote and if you've ever sung a song or told a story, well, that'll flat make you shake your head at the sheer joy and wonder of it all cause you start to think, Lord have mercy, I musta got at least some of it down right, and it just about makes you wanna cry.

I am not gonna use names or correct places in this story, cause it gets a little personal, and I don't want to intrude.

Y'all stick with me a minute and you'll see what I mean.

I sent an early version of the book off to a friend of mine, and it wasn't but a week or so later when I got an email saying how much she liked it, and pledging to mail the copy back to me and thanking me for my efforts.

Needless to say, I was thrilled! Not only did she LIKE it, but at long last SOMEONE was actually returning my book to me and I sent her an email to tell her thank you for the kind words and constructive input and also for offering to return the book.

The next day when I checked my email, there was a letter saying:

John:
I know I told you I would return the book to you, but I just got off the phone with my daughter and she has had a miscarriage and I am wondering if it would be all right to send my copy down to her cause I think it might cheer her up.

Well friends, they don't tell you about stuff like that in writing classes.

My response was swift:

Of course you can send it!!!
Heck that's me knocking on your door right now!
Give me the book and I'll drive to Greenville and DELIVER it to her myself!!

Might seem like a small thing, but boy it sure was a big thing to me. To think that something I had written could help in a time of need and pain was pretty overwhelming. I guess it's not a particularly compelling or moving story, but it's just one of a dozen or so little moments that sure makes me glad I wrote this stuff down.

I didn't know where Fred Minor lived, so when I got the invite to come play at his seventy sixth birthday party I worked it out to meet up at Jimmy Johnson's place and then follow Jimmy and Martha on to Fred's, cause he only lived a short bit away, but as I am universally known for being geographically challenged, the greater wisdom was that I should follow someone over. My buddy Martin Brown got wind of the celebration and I invited him along with me, cept he had to drive himself so he could leave a bit earlier than the rest of us. After following me west on I 40 and north in to Brown's Summit, we pulled on in to Jimmy's place and up to the big white wood two story farm house with its welcoming old shade trees and stood by the car chatting awhile, and I let Blue and Minor take a little run with Jake while we waited for Jimmy and Martha to come on out.

I was parked beside Jimmy's white truck when Martha came on around the front with a rough draft copy of. my book. Now y'all need to know I never figured on all these folks actually KEEPIN the copies I gave em, it just kinda went that way, and well, how do ya ask the very people the book is about to give their copies back, so there ya go. My intention was to let the principals in the book read what I had written and decide whether or not they were comfortable bein part of this thing or not. Never occurred to me they would not only KEEP the dang things (which by the end cost me about thirty five bucks a piece to print up) but also PASS em around to the rest of their friends and family. So anyway, Martha comes around that truck with her tattered and worn copy and hands it back to me and I am about to thank her for returning it when she hands me a pen and says

Would you mind autographing this for me?

Well I believe I have mentioned to y'all I am new to this here writin game, so her sayin that not only caught me by surprise it took the wind right outa my sails because I was, and by now y'all will be able to attest to the rarity of this event, rendered completely and utterly speechless.

As I stood there gaping at her trying to find some right words to say, stuttering and fumbling and feeling alternately hugely flattered and totally undeserving, Martin Brown began to laugh his butt off while Jimmy just stood there watchin it all go down and shakin his head in disgust and lettin loose with the occasional spit of juice from the perpetual chaw tucked up there between his cheek and gum.

Flabbergasted as I was, I managed to get out, Martha, I just don't know what to say, what to write, and she said Well, just anything will do and I said, But I have to say the right thing, this is important, this is my first autographed book ever and besides, I owe y'all so much....

So while Martin laughed I thought about it a minute and handed the manuscript back to her and said:

I tell you what, give me some time to think about it, and I promise I'll sign yer copy, I swear I will, just let me do it right, OK?

And ol Jimmy Johnson took off his ball cap to run his hand through his silver hair, sighed in frustration and said

You'd think someone who could write a hundred page book could sign his damn name.

With that, he let go a flow of brown tabaccy juice and climbed into the cab of his truck and fired it up.

He rolled the window down as Martha got in on the other side and he looked at me with sympathetic eyes, as if he genuinely regretted how complicated I made my life on a daily basis.

He nodded my way.

You better saddle up if yer gonna follow me to Fred's, Vidalia, he said and, laughing, he drove away.

Martin and I jumped in our vehicles and sped off after Jimmy Johnson, and I enjoyed as I always do, the lush green pastures and huge canopies of the tall old trees of Brown's Summit, North Carolina. I DO love calling North Carolina home and coulda driven

with the window down just breathin in the clean fresh
air all day!

I admired the Carolina Blue sky and was happy
to be at the party, but sad it was such a short trip
when I saw Jimmy pull into a driveway. There was a
big tent set up in the back yard and grills smokin and
lots of people milling around.

Martin parked on the street, and being that I
had so much stuff, I pulled on up the side of Fred's
driveway and parked as close to the house as I could.
Blue and Minor hopped out and put on their best
"Please Sir or Madam, please help us, for we do
not get enough food or love from our Master" looks
and tore off to start working the crowd. I waited for
Martin and then we tooled around back to see who
was there. I didn't really see any one I knew, but there
was a small knot of folks gathering and tuning up
on the far side of the yard under the shade of a big
oak tree and Martin decided he was gonna go get his
guitar and headed off. Through the open windows, I
heard voices and laughter from inside and looked up
and saw Fred, so I decided to go on in and pay my
respects. Now at this point I had been playin with
these fellers a good while and Fred, having taken
me under his wing was (I hope) beginning to see
some rewards for his efforts on my behalf, so I was
tremendously flattered to be invited and wanted to
tell him so. I had given Fred his early copy of what
would later become Book One and was anxious to

see what he thought of it, a little apprehensive, but mostly just excited. I went up the wooden steps and went through the open back porch screen door and nodded some greetings to the folks seated there and pushed the sliding glass door aside and wandered on into the house. There was food in the kitchen just off the living room, and where there's food, there's bound to be plenty of people so I walked into a big crowd of folks gathered in a circle around the birthday boy himself, my friend and mentor, Mr. Fred Minor.

Now what happened next would have been more than enough for me cause when Fred looked back and saw me, he stopped talkin about what he was talkin about and said, Hey y'all...I want you to meet a friend of mine...this here's John Santa....

And he drew back towards me and put his arm around my shoulder and strolled me into the circle.

Now I tell you true, that was enough of an honor, compliment, whatever you want to call it, for as you know by now, I have a great deal of respect for this True Son Of The South, and to be introduced as his friend in such a grand style was pretty darn wonderful. But just then a woman in her thirties let out a little yelp and detached herself from the crowd and ran over to me and threw her arms around me as she burst into tears and started murmuring, Thank you for the wonderful things you wrote about my daddy, thank you for the wonderful things you wrote about my daddy over and over again.

Bluegrass is my Second Language

I was so shocked I didn't know what to do, and then I slowly closed my arms around Fred Minor's daughter and just kinda gently held her as she softly whispered her thanks into my chest and her tears wet my shirt.

Well I'll tell you what, if this book don't sell, if nothing else ever happens with it, it kinda don't matter cause when I think of that incredible moment, all the hours and frustration and work melt away into what really counts. A daughter got to read about her dad, and was touched by what I wrote.

Don't get much better than that.

There's a lot about getting older that is pretty cool, but one of the things that is a bit hard to take is how fast time goes by. When you're a kid the summers last forever and a day can last a week. It's an aspect I like about making movies and music: you can get so far in the moment that sometimes the time goes by like it did when you were little. Yep, those Zen fellers had it right, the way to do IS to be, and I enjoy wrestling with time a little. In fact I think that our perception of time, bein as relative as it is, well, it occurs to me sometimes that maybe we age a lot more like dogs do than we like to think. Just like how we say a dog year is seven human years, I think a childhood year is three, maybe four years long, which is good, particularly these days when kids seem to be growin up so much faster and harder. I like the idea they can stay kids longer than we think. We adults assess the time and add up the birthdays, and throw the parties but time only matters to the one EXPERIENCING it, so, as they say in Quantum Physics, it's all relative, y'know? You see the passage of years go by, and we add them up and say our age, but I have yet to talk to any adult ever who didn't agree that time moved differently when they were young. But bein that God likes to keep the ledger books balanced, we pay for those languid childhood years, and the bill comes due in adulthood when sadly the years just fly by.

So, like it or not, the days DO go by, dog days or human days, and I found myself coming up on the anniversary of having Minor join our little family here in Chapel Hill. So I called the ever patient, ever accommodating Billy Yarborough and asked if I could come visit, and would he accompany me back down to Hendersonville to play the rent on my little doggie one more time, and Billy, good soul that he is, said, C'mon up and we'll see to it, and we sorta planned on another Fourth of July visit.

Turned out instead of the beginning of July, we went up at the end of May cause Leslie Alexander and Barry Hester were gonna get married and they had asked me to come play at their wedding, and I let them listen to some CDs of Greg, Jeff, Keith and I, and they ended up hiring us to provide the music for their outside wedding to be held in Asheville on May 31st, 2003.

Bluegrass is my Second Language

Now Billy is generous to a fault, but he ain't stupid, so try as I might to get him to let me come on up there for another one of my (in)famous five day weekends, he was pretty firm on me comin in on Friday and leavin on Sunday cause a work and life and well, experience too, I reckon, cause as y'all know by now, a little bit a John can go a LONG damn way, so I packed up the instruments and stuff we'd need for the wedding, loaded in the pups, and off we went, one more wonderful time for the long haul up to Asheville. I was kinda bummed cause, unbeknownst to Billy, I had a reason for wanting the extra time with him and his family, and I was worried our wedding duties might keep me from completing my mission, but I had faith and got more determined to see it through the closer I got to Asheville.

Can't tell you how wonderful it was to see them Yarborough ladies, the girls even more grown up and gracious and beautiful than the last time I saw em, bein they were swimmin more on Karen's side of the gene pool and all. Kristen once again offered me her room, but gone was the young girl lace and frills to be replaced by a room that if I thought about for even a half second, looked for all the world to be a college dorm, and well, I couldn't face that cause it meant them girls was growin up and I just don't see how you parents out there can stand that, cause it just plumb tears me up to see it, and heck, those little ones aren't even mine!

I guess I shoulda been prepared for how much the girls had changed cause Billy sent Kristen out to guide me up the mountainside to the house and of course when she pulled up, though I was terribly flattered, I had no idea who this attractive young lady was who was wavin at me from behind the wheel and once I was able to wrap my head around the fact that Kristen was drivin (!), well, I reckon that shoulda set the tone, cause gorgeous Katelyn was taller and funnier and faster and the only thing that stayed the same was wise, beautiful Karen and the sumptuous table she set and her eternal Southern Hospitality and of course the fact ol Billy Yarborough could just flat burn up a guitar and a song, and I couldn't wait for Barry and Leslie to see my wedding surprise: the talented Mr. Yarborough was gonna join me and the boys and sing that girl down the aisle on Saturday afternoon and I was pretty sure we could get the folks what wasn't cryin to smilin once they heard THIS band start up a wedding march!

So the details of this visit will have to wait for another time, but finally, after dinner and a few songs and catchin up with this wonderful family who had come to symbolize Asheville for me, I finally got them to sit down with me in the living room, and there I was able to say the phrase I had been so nervous about all this time up here:

I have written a book, I said.

And they all smiled and gushed and then I said,

Bluegrass is my Second Language

And y'all are in it.

And, with their kind permission, I began to read to them from Book One and the girls would giggle and Karen cried and then I cried and the girls cried and every once in a while the ladies would look at Billy, and he'd say, Yep, that's just how it happened, or, Yeah, I said that! and the girls would laugh and shake their heads and I tell you what:

There is no writing class, no life experience anywhere, anytime to prepare you for reading to your protagonists and having them come hug you with tears in their eyes when you finish, and tell you how proud they are to be in yer book and how good it is, and, as if that is not MORE than enough than God could possibly give you, then they settled back down on the floor and in their seats and said,

Read us some more.

So I sat there in their living room with Blue at my feet and Minor up beside me on the couch and I read to them from this very book you are holding in your hands right now, and though I appreciate your presence here, I tell you there is not much in life that can possibly be much better than that sweet, sweet moment in time and somehow, now that you've lived through it all with me in Book One, I just couldn't stop there, and I wanted you all to know what happened next, and how moving it was and is so here we are.

It's unfortunate, but in the year since their wedding, we've lost touch with Leslie and Barry, and I kinda don't feel right talking about their wedding ceremony without their permission, but it sure was great and we sure do miss her fiddle playin and wonder how Barry's doin on the banjo now, and if any of you know em, tell to get in touch, tell em to come join us in a song or two like old times.

We played at the service, and then headed on inside for the meet and greet and though Barry and Leslie had booked in another bunch of musician friends to play the reception, (and of course Billy knew all of em), we had to leave early cause it was Kristen's sixteenth birthday and I had promised her a present and so, though it about tore us up to leave all that good music, good company and good food, we packed up our gear and we followed Billy back to his house.

We all drove up the mountain and parked and after we introduced Keith, Jeff and Greg to the ladies up in the main house, we tooled outside and pulled our instruments out of our cars and snuck on down the little hill that led to Billy's pickin parlor that had so quickly become Kristen's commandeered bedroom, and went up the wooden steps of the small deck porch and into the home away from home that Kristen's generosity had afforded me, and set up to play some music. We had arranged for Billy and Karen to keep their daughters busy up at the house till we were

ready to spring our little surprise on Ms. Kristen.
When we were ready, Billy brought her on down,
accompanied by Karen and Katelyn and from the look
of surprised wonder on her face as she took in the
banjo, mandolin, cello, guitars and Keith's acoustic
bass that had invaded her mountainside cabin, and
as I announced our musical birthday present to her,
I can say fer a fact that, as much as we hated to do
it, we had done a good thing leavin the reception
early. I believe it is the rare sixteen year old girl
who could say she had a Kick Butt Bluegrass Band
set up in her bedroom and play any song she asked
for (and many she didn't) until even a sixteen year
old with boundless energy and a smile of gratitude
big as an Asheville mountain range finally gave in to
the sandman and birthday fatigue and began to fall
asleep, curled up on a small sofa with her mom, her
sister and the family dog, while seated across from
her was her devoted daddy, his crazy ass friends and
two more dogs who were clearly delighted to see her
so happy. Smiling, we played a couple of ballads soft
and low to send her off to dreamland right.

When she finally surrendered and mom said it
was time to stop, there were hugs for all the pickers
as the boys packed up and drove off to stay at Keith's
sister's place and I got a big ol hug from Kristen
and a look from her mom that told me I had done
real good and I finally felt like I had begun to repay
Kristen for the kindness she had shown me in letting

me stay in her room all these times.

I think we all slept good that night, I know I did.

Sunday morning we awoke to another beautiful mountain day of bright sunshine, crystal clear blue skies and crisp, clean, cool breezes and I was sad as I packed my things away in preparation for leaving. We ate some breakfast and then I said my good-byes as Karen and Kristen were off to other endeavors (most likely involving more of K's birthday festivities) while Katelyn had agreed to come along with Billy and I down to B.J. Parson's place and help play the rent on my puppy for another year. Jeff had to head on back home to Reidsville, but we were gonna meet Greg and Keith at the Farmer's Market outside a town and they were gonna follow us on down to B.J.'s place. Because I was headin home from there, Billy drove his own car as well, but Katelyn agreed to ride with me since I promised to teach her how to play the harmonica on the way down. So we rode the highway towards Hendersonville with Katelyn strapped in the passenger seat next to me awkwardly holding a harmonica I gave her while I wore my harmonica holder around my neck which certainly elicited some strange looks from the people who passed us by as I was chunkin away tryin to teach little Katelyn how to play "Oh Christmas Tree."

(Hey--what else would a guy named Santa teach

fer a first song?? I mean, think about it...)

We eased into the Farmer's Market parking lot and I tooled around until I spotted Keith's van and pulled up along side him and rolled my window down.

Hey, he says, We just saw a couple a yer relatives over at the stand!

What are you talkin about?? I exclaim, My folks are back home in Durham!

And he says,

Naw they ain't! We done saw a peck of em right over there!

And with Greg nodding vigorously beside him, he gestures with his chin in the direction of the Market.

Seeing the consternation and confusion on my face, they both crack up laughin and then Keith says

Yeah, we saw a whole PECK a your people: Vidalias and RED onions and WHITE onions and yer cousins the Scallions....

And they both convulsed into spasms of laughter.

Katelyn shoots me a quizzical look.

What's THAT about? she asks as only a teenager can.

You don't even wanna know.... I say as I shake my head in feigned disgust and wave at those two crazy boys to follow my lead and I push on out of the parking lot and hook up with Katelyn's dad and off we go with Blue in the well between me and Katelyn supervisin our efforts at the harmonica playin and Minor sound asleep stretched out across the bench back seat, snorin up a storm of harmony.

Well we didn't get Katelyn to the point where she was ready to play solo in front of anyone, but it was an hour and a half of fun and gigglin and a good first lesson on playin the harmonica, and Katelyn thought so too. Wasn't too long though till we were turnin left into the long dirt driveway and goin past those stone English Setter statues that guard the entrance to B.J.'s place, and ol Minor jumped up from the back seat and started to sniffin at the air right hard, which pleased me greatly. See, my intention was to bring this boy back here, a year later and show him that all his brothers and sisters were still here and OK, and all the folks who loved him were still here and OK too.

Our little caravan of minivans (hey--we're musicians---ya gotta have AT LEAST a minivan to carry all yer gear!) pulled up to the house in a small cloud of dust and I marveled that there were tables and chairs set up and B.J. and Kristen were bringin food from the house to put out and Katelyn jumped from the car to go fetch her dad cause there were a BUNCH of lean, mottled English Setters announcing our presence with a chorus of barking and HORSES, majestic brown horses, to be fawned over and fed apples, and I reckon she was rarin to go. I undid my seat belt and looked back at Minor and said, Well, here ya are, Big Guy, home again, as I opened the door and got out to stretch my legs and take a good, long look at this place I was so glad to return to. Blue hopped on out and started makin the rounds and sayin hello and I slid the side panel door open for Minor and he just sat there in the back seat frozen and tense with a distinctly unpleasant look upon his white English Setter face.

I turned to walk over to show Greg and Keith where to set up and say hi to everyone and when Minor hadn't joined me, I went back to the van and looked inside and he was STILL sittin up in the back seat, STILL lookin perturbed about somethin and then it hit me.

I had been so intent on making sure that he knew his friends and kin and humans were okay, it never in a million years occurred to me that he might think I was bringin him back up here to drop him off and LEAVE him, but judging from the look on his face, that is EXACTLY what he thought was happenin.

I climbed in the back seat there with him and put my arms around him and gave him a big ol bear hug and said, Puppy boy, we are just visitin and you can take THAT to the bank! You are my dog now, and you will be comin home with me when it's time to go, unless YOU decide you wanna stay, I promise!

I got back out and he looked a little bit better,

he was lyin down at least, so I took him by the collar
and eased him on out. Little Blue wandered up, and
that helped cause she was givin him the C'mon man
there's FOOD and a lot of people we can scam for
attention and chow! Let's git goin! We got WORK
to do! and so off they went together, with a few of
the folks from his past callin Scamp! Here Scamp!
which set him off in the other direction. (I TOLD
y'all he never answered to that name!) I watched
him for a while as he wandered around the grounds,
watched while I opened the rear hatch and got out
my instruments as he eventually made his way back
down to the chain link fence runs where he and his
siblings had lived for so long, down by where B.J. was
diggin a year ago when I saw Minor for the very first
time. At one point I called for him and his head shot
up and he started trottin my way with his tail waggin,
and Blue ran out to meet him, and I waved him off
knowin that he was fine now and actually startin to
enjoy himself, and so I turned my attention to takin
care of the debt I had come so far to pay.

B.J. and her daughter Kristen had decided not
to waste any time this year, there were folks already
waitin on us and more pullin in as I introduced Keith
and Greg and re-introduced Billy, who of course,
needed no introduction, and true to my prediction
that he had become part of the history of Minor's
story, he got hugs instead of handshakes from the
Parson's family and smiles from those who had met

and heard him play last year.

Having already eaten, we commenced to tunin up and it wasn't too long till the music was wafting out over that porch and those good folks were clappin and singin along and dancin a few steps as they made their way down the food line. I will always be grateful to Billy especially for comin that day, but Keith and Greg really made the day special, cause what two could do well, four could do so much better and we played ourselves into a stupor that day and I am proud to say that even though I played the cello, Minor at no time urinated on anything other than trees across the way. Needless to say, this omission did not escape comment from Kristen and B.J. who allowed as how either my playin had improved in the past year or Minor had developed some taste for the finer things in musical life. I assured the assembled crowd it was nothing more than the fact that in three hundred and sixty five days I had plumb wore him down! They laughed and teased me about how fat he'd gotten and I teased THEM sayin they didn't have dogs up here, their dogs were so unnaturally skinny they had MODELS, and started callin their pups Tyra Banks and Elle McPherson and Cindy Crawford and any other model's names I could think of just to keep the banter going, and we laughed and picked and I had a big ol time, I tell you what.

It was great fun having those boys there to help me with my task of playin the rent and I was honored to be there, and particularly honored to be there with them, and I hope we get to do it again next year, cause it's a great tradition if I do say so myself. Before too long though, Keith and Greg were lookin at their watches and I knew it was gettin close to time to go, so we did a few more and then I helped those boys pack up, and hugged Katelyn a good by hug and then hugged her daddy too, and thanked them for their hospitality and comin with me to B.J.'s and stood there with tears in my eyes as they drove off to cheers and waves from these people who, for the most part, were strangers just a short while ago, but now through the grace and power of music, had become friends.

And that is the true blessing of the strings.

I keep tellin y'all in this book, don't just read about this stuff, git out there and FIND it, go listen to some of these old timers pick and grin and by all means, get yerself an instrument and lift it up and make a joyful noise.

It'll change yer life, I promise.

We all need to play longer, sing louder, y'know?

I wiped my eyes and headed over toward the food where B.J. was sittin in a lawn chair and there was Minor with his head on her lap just lookin up at her with big ol doe eyes full of love and she was just chattin to her friends and absentmindedly scratchin his ears and pettin him as he just pushed further and further up her lap, and as I approached she looked up at me and smiled and, gesturing to the crowd and the dog she was lovin on said, I reckon you work here is done.

And I said,

Not quite.

So I went on through the food line and grabbed a little chow, it bein close to four in the afternoon by now, and sat on a cooler and ate my grub and laughed and caught up with B.J. and Kristen and some of the folks from last year and got to know some of these new folks who had come to witness the playing of the rent for year two. Minor alternately was nuzzlin B.J. for a little more sugar and comin over to me to tell me how much fun this was and how cool it was to be back, and well, I just could not have agreed with him more and after a little while, after some folks had left, I strolled over to my car with Blue followin close behind me lest I decide to leave her here, and pulled out a big stack of papers and wandered back over to where all those good folks had congregated and I sat down in a comfortable lawn chair and I said,

B.J. I have written a book.....

And y'all are in it.

I don't know how other folks announce the birth of a book to the world or how those words are met, but as strange as it was for me to say back then (I have grown more accustomed to it now) the reaction was always the same: a sorta overwhelming wave of love followed by the audible gasp and then oohhing and aahhing and then lots of hugging. Truth be told, it's so powerful wonderful, feelin it kinda makes ya wanna write one more often. And then it sinks in what exactly I said, and the realization that they are in my book begins to dawn on em, and their expressions go quizzical and shy, as if, what could I have possibly done that would warrant bein written about in an actual honest to God book?? Course, those are EXACTLY the kinda folks you would WANNA write about right there, and I say so. When everyone settles down a bit, I allow as how, if they'd let me, I'd like to read the part where they show up to em, and this is met with hasty affirmations and nervous giggles and looks of amazement and wonder from the folks who had no idea this was part of the deal.

So I flipped the pages to later in the book where I first met B.J. and Kristen and Seven and commence to readin and the sun moves slowly across the sky to almost sunset, and the hollow there at the house is quiet, broken only by the occasional ripple of laughter or, in all modesty, the occasional sniffle at the sad parts, and I will tell you once again, there is no class, no words, that prepare you for the power of reading to twenty or so people and having them laugh in the places they're supposed to laugh and cry where they're supposed to cry and, when you are done, have them ask you to read some more. I have spoken

with y'all at great length about the power of music
and I reckon we have learned together the power of
words, cause I sure didn't know it could be like this.
To finish and have the people in the book in tears
and the sounds of laughter and applause echoing off
the weathered brown wooden walls and rolling on
out into the green tree covered mountain sides as the
friends of the people in the book clap and cheer their
affirmation that yes indeed, these people here are in
fact worthy of bein in a book cause they are good,
strong, loyal people of integrity and so full of love
why, they ought to be in seventeen books at least! And
so with Minor just about all the way up on B.J.'s lap,
and Blue curled up and settled in at my feet, I just sat
there and drank in their applause and love and let the
tears come on out cause sometimes they just gotta do
that, cause sometimes it's just too much and you just
have to let it out.

I hope this isn't too self indulgent, telling you
all this. In for a penny, in for a pound I reckon. If
you came with me this far, you must think it's worth
somethin of value. I just wanted you to know what
happened to the people you met when this thing got
handed to em is all. I mean, I can't conceive of it
really: guy walks up to you and says, I have written
a book and oh, by the way, you're in it. I'm kinda
stunned nobody's slugged me to be honest with you.
But I shoulda known it would be like this, I mean,

y'all know these folks now too, and what else would
you expect but this kind of response? I have said it
before and I am sure I will say it again: for a guy who
totes around his mother's overnight case, I am one
lucky sonnuva gun.

So the sun went down and twilight crept in
and after a bit I guess there was nothin left to say
as I had tried my damnedest to put it all in the book
and say it all the right way, with the right words and
meaning, so I packed my instruments back into the
car with the help of many many volunteers, and with
literal and metaphorical pats on the back, I finally
put Blue and Minor's food and water dish in the car,
the Santa family universal sign for Road Trip, and
Blue jumped in the driver's seat and I had to remind
her once again in front of all those nice folks in
Hendersonville that she only had her Learner's Permit
and that I would likely be drivin home that night
and she blinked at me once and huffed a little and
hopped over to the passenger seat and settled in with
a disgruntled sigh.

We were all gathered by the car, and I looked
at Minor and he looked up at B.J. and then over at
me and then he kinda backed up all nervous and
confused.

I knelt down and looked him in the eye and
said, Little Boy, if you want to stay here, you can, it's
your choice but if you want to go home with me and
Blue

Bluegrass is my Second Language

And before I could finish what I was sayin he flew past all of us at about two hundred twenty two miles an hour and jumped into the back seat and lay down across the bench and put his head on his paws and yawned.

Guess that settles THAT, B.J. said with a smile and everyone kinda laughed and I started the long process of shakin hands and huggin these new friends I just had the privilege to make, and lovin on the old ones and of course when I got to B.J. and Kristen, well them tears just came back out again and I was speechless.

I wanted so much to thank em for all of it: Seven, and Minor and food and support and just bein who they are, and of course I was struck plumb mute. Frustrated, I just hugged and cried and got in the car and cranked up the engine and rolled down the window.

B.J. put her hand on the side mirror and leaned in a bit.

Don't you wait a year to come back and see us now, she said.

And I managed to choke out a Yes, m'am.

And sobbing I drove away.

EPILOGUE

Well I reckon it is well past time for me to go.

I am the kinda person who has to have the wait staff bring the house lights up and start puttin the chairs on the tables before I get the hint and pack it in for the evening. I hope I haven't overstayed my welcome with y'all, it's just been such a good time tellin and relivin these stories of these wonderful good folks and this amazing music.

So let me leave you with this one:

It is Saturday, March 6 of 2004 and I have just returned from a long day of music. Jimmy Johnson asked Greg and Jeff to come play for a charity fund raiser pig pickin so of course they told me and Keith and so we showed up with a bunch of other players including my mentor the talented Fred Minor and we proceeded to play the day away. Minor and Blue were havin a big ol time wanderin in and outa the hut, chewin on rib bones and scraps the folks would toss to em and gettin pats and hugs and lots of attention from all the good folks who showed up to help out. I really don't know what the charity was, I think it was a fundraiser for a school or somethin, really didn't matter, I hear charity and music and generally I'm there. Plus this would be the first pig of the season, and it always tasted good! Later this year people will invite us to play at a pig pickin and we'll groan and accept and then secretly order a pizza to be delivered or something, but for now, the first one of the year, well it sounded just right and the day was fine, a clear blue sky after a rainy morning, but balmy now and sunny with the promise of spring in the air. We gathered in a circle in the hut and we played for the folks and it was great fun. After about an hour and a half of pickin Jimmy said, Boys, follow me on this, and he started into Happy Birthday To You in G and we jumped on in and played and sang till the point where the name came up and there was a some confusion until Jimmy hollered out, It's John and Daniel Brown's birthday!

And then it struck me.

John Santa

Unlike a year ago when the weather was so cold and winter so hard that power was out and I sang Happy Birthday sittin all by myself up on the stage at Brown's and Daniel turned seventy nine and his brother John eighty, this year I would sing in their birthdays in a different key and a different place and I was stunned that a year had gone by so quickly.

It's taken me a year to tell the story of my first year in bluegrass, and I have jumped around through time enough to make Kurt Vonnegut proud. I guess technically this book should a been subtitled "TWO Years In The Life Of A Bluegrass Musician," but I did the best I could. A book is an unwieldy thing, a stubborn thing, got a mind of its own and will tell its story any old way it wants. Most nights I feel like things would run a lot smoother if I would just do the typing and keep my opinions to myself, so there ya go.

But I have to say, I like it a lot that the book is finishing up almost exactly a year after I wrote the ending to Book One. Shepp woulda loved that, he was always into literary and musical bookends, no pun intended. (Well, maybe just a little bit intended.)

So we played the gig and then packed up and headed over to Brown's Ole Opry where, once again I got to play and sing for the Brown Brothers birthday with a whole NEW pack of well wishers, and that felt good and right and made me swell up with pride. We played a good set of music that night, warmed up as we were from three or four hours pickin that afternoon. We started at seven thirty at Brown's and ended about eleven and I was thrilled as I always am when John Brown came up to shake my hand and brushed off my birthday wishes by sayin,

Now you come back and play for us real soon, Chapel Hill, you hear?

A year may have gone by, but nothin in me has changed:

I am STILL proud when he asks me back, and it sure does make me smile.

I assured him I would in fact be honored to return.

I reckon I'll see y'all down at Brown's.

John Santa

The End

Oh, and by the way...

It took me a little while, and oh yeah, Martin Brown helped me with it, but I did finally sign my first autograph on Martha's manuscript, just in case you were wonderin.

What I finally wrote to her on that original copy was this:

Thanks for sharing your stories with me.
With love and respect,
John Santa
Blue and Minor

And then I thought for a minute and added, strictly for Jimmy's benefit:

PS
I sure would like to meet one a your daughters....

GLOSSARY

Of Terms and Characters

(Wherein I get to define some musical terms for the Civilian Reader and tell some stories about People and Places that didn't quite fit in the book but are worth the telling and thus delay the ending of the book just a little bit longer. PLEASE NOTE: Never in the history of Bluegrass Literature has an author toiled so Diligently on the behalf of his Loyal Readers.)

A A common key for bluegrass songs. If yer classically trained it means there's a certain amount of sharps and flats involved, but for street musicians, it just puts us in the neighborhood of what's gonna be comin at us in the song about to be played. For instance, a bluegrass song in the key of A will likely have a D as its second chord and an E will mosey on in at some time or t'other too. It basically lets us recall other tunes we know in the same key so we have a certain level of expectation of what twists the song will take based on what our past experience has taught us.
(SEE ALSO: G, Gear AND Harp.)

A MINOR SEVEN (AKA Am7) The name the Macs suggested for the dog I play the rent on every summer in Hendersonville, North Carolina. Once we got his name straight, the relationship between this dog and I flourished. He has become VERY protective of me and extremely affectionate to the point that I suspect I will never be able to have kids because the dog is sometimes so overcome with emotion and love that he will leap from across the room directly into my lap just to give me a big ol slurp.

This would be fine if he were a lap dog, like say, a Chihuahua.

But he is not.

He is a seventy-five pound English Setter.

The good news is I can sing the high harmony parts a lot easier now.

ALAN JACKSON Still guarding the door up at Haleyland, still (apparently) REALLY pissed off.

ASHEVILLE Home of the Yarborough family. Also the town where Leslie Alexander and Barry Hester got married. They foolishly invited us up to play at their wedding. I wrote a song for Leslie as a wedding gift called "Fiddle Playing Lady" that we sang as she walked down the aisle, the aisle in this case being a path under the verdant canopy of some huge gorgeous oak trees on the side of a beautiful Carolina mountain. At the rehearsal, I pulled Barry aside and played the song for him and he agreed it would be a good surprise for her since it is from his perspective about falling in love with this fiddle playing gal and how he would marry her one day, so Leslie never heard it before she walked down the aisle. When I sang the last line that changes the "we would get married one day" to " we WILL be married TODAY" she cried like a baby.

   We really got her.

   It was great.

(SEE ALSO: Leslie Alexander and Barry Hester.)

BANJO MUTE Can someone please explain to me just what the heck is wrong with these people??

BENDING A technique used to augment notes played on the harmonica. Sounds really really cool but the real reason we do it is cause chicks dig it. Can also refer to the Blues (and Bluegrass) technique of pulling up (or pushing down) on the string of your instrument to create a rise in pitch, a slur of the note. Something easy to do on an unfretted instrument like a fiddle, but harder to do with fretted instruments like guitars, banjos and

mandolins.
(SEE ALSO: HARMONICA AND HARP.)

BILL AND JOANNE BARBRE These are the

good folks who own the place I rent at the beach every
year. By beach I am, of course, referring to Emerald Isle,
North Carolina. I've been going there for over twenty
years and somehow Bill and Joanne allowed themselves
to get all caught up in the comings and goings of the
crazy folks who come to visit while I'm down there
relaxin. (Ya gotta keep in mind that Mac says my idea of a
vacation is to move everything I do and everyone I know
to another location and pretty much do what I do every
day, only do it at a different place. According to him, that
is my idea of a great vacation and God help me, I think
he's right....)

So over the years the Barbre's have met and
supported everyone from an Atlanta based dance
company called Moving In The Spirit that I write music
for, to the usual assortment of players who pass through
every year. We sit on the porch and drink mint juleps
(Joanne usually brings herself some white wine in a nice
goblet wine glass---she's a classy lady) and pick and grin
and the Barbre's just enjoy the hell out of it and I flat
love havin them. They take me out to dinner and make a
big fuss and I think my parents feel better knowin that
my Beach Parents are down there lookin after me.

God bless em they love them some dogs too. Little
Blue can always look forward to lots of pets and belly
rubs and Minor is gettin to know the Beach Parental
Units more and more too each time we're there. Ol Bill
took it pretty hard when Seven died and I think he was
happy to see Minor and I KNOW he loved the name that
honors both his favorite English Setter and a brilliant
fiddle player.

One time when we were down there I had a

Musicians Retreat where I invited all the players who could get away to join me on the porch for mint juleps and some songs. Well, we had over twenty musicians show up so the house was full of music almost twenty four hours a day and we had HUGE crowds out on the lawn and parking lot in front of the house as people came to listen, particularly at night. One evening we were playin along and somebody called for a John Denver tune and we cranked it up and were toolin along right well till I happened to look over at Bill and there were tears streaming down his face he was so overcome with emotion. We of course stopped as Joanne stood beside him, rubbing his shoulder and back and murmuring to him. She looked up and said Bill was good friends with John Denver. Needless to say our jaws dropped and we began to apologize cause God knows my friends and I have done horrible renditions of really good songs in the past and we just assumed we had done so once again. No, no, Bill said when he had gathered himself up some, it's just that...well, Johnny would've LOVED this, I woulda told him about you all and he woulda shown up just to be able to play with you guys. He woulda just LOVED this, I'm so thankful...I can't thank you enough for playing his songs and keeping him alive through his music.... thank you....thank you....

Needless to say, I pick me a Johnny Denver tune every once in a while out there on the porch at three or four in the morning when it's middle of the night quiet and the crickets chirp and the waves roll in and the breeze is warm and easy.

I play it soft and low and send one up there to him....when it's just me and Mr. Denver out there on the porch thankin the good Lord for people like Bill and Joanne Barbre.

BILLY YARBOROUGH Sometimes it takes creating

a Glossary to make you realize how truly rich you are. Seems I just wrote this sweet sad story about Bill and Joanne and here I am at yet another wonderful human being I am privileged to know and call friend. When I was in college, I used to take all my misfit friends over to my parents house for Sunday dinner. Many of them looked (and probably acted) pretty strange and many were alienated from their parents for political or visual reasons. When we were growing up my Mom always used to say there's always enough food, there's always enough love and so all the neighborhood kids ended up at my house and I continued that tradition till, well, this very day. But anyway, I had a bunch of those longhaired hippie freaks over to the house one time and I was helpin my Mom get dinner ready in the kitchen (always enough food...). She shot me a look as we scrubbed away at the sink and said, I don't know what you'll do with your life, and being a musician I worry you'll always be poor, but I will tell you right now that when it comes to friends, and I mean GOOD friends, good, honorable folks, you are one of the richest people I know.

   I'm richer for people like Billy, that's for sure.
billyar@bellsouth.net

B. J. PARSONS And B. J.

BLUE And of course little Blue.

BLUES My musical roots. Blues and Bluegrass really have much more in common than first meets the eye. The progressions run like this: I, IV, V. (Or for you civilians out there the first --tonic or NAME of the scale--determines the first chord of the song. Then you run up to the fourth note of the scale, make that a chord and then to the fifth note and make THAT a chord and there

you have your progression. Hope that makes SOME
sense to y'all normal folks....)

ANYway....

Blues and Bluegrass have the progressions and
often the lyric/melody in common. I have been surprised
many a time to hear the Bluegrass folks doing a song by
Delta Blues genius Robert Johnson and I have heard
many a Blues jam end the night with a soulful bluesy
rendition "Will The Circle Be Unbroken" or "Amazing
Grace." Biggest difference I can see in the mechanical
fundamentals is tempo and the fact that most Blues
is traditionally played in the key of E or A, and most
bluegrass is in either G or A.

While pulling out a Bluegrass tune at a Blues jam
will likely get you looked at funny (at least), I have to say
when I've done a couple of Blues numbers at Bluegrass
sessions the response is always very enthusiastic. One of
the things I want to do in my documentary is explore the
commonalties of these two distinctly and wonderfully
American musical art forms.

BLUEGRASS WIDOWS They also serve who sit
and listen.

BOB HALEY Warm, welcoming, wonderful Bob
Haley, the creator and host of Haleyland. Took him four
wives and a lot of years to get it right, but now it is. God
bless him and Linda and all them crazy folks down there
on Penny Lane.

BOB STANFIELD The bass player at that first gig
in Burlington and a bunch of sessions since then and
the one who spoke that incredible line: "Welp, we all
finished together and nobody got hurt. I reckon we're a
success." God bless him for that. We quote him all the

time.

BROWN'S (AKA Brown's Ole Opry) This place is really an old tobacco barn that was gutted (?) inside. At some point somebody brought in some movie theater seats when one was torn down in Burlington or Graham, but mostly it's just those old beige folding chairs you see everywhere. The inside is raw as you might expect but the dance floor is a real work of art. It is always way too hot in the summer and way too cold in the winter though the Brown's do their best with an army of space heaters that run at full blast till closing. I am truly honored to be a part of the tradition of this incredible North Carolina state treasure.
(SEE ALSO: Musician's Only)

CABIN FEVER God, that was embarrassing. I'm such an idiot sometimes.

CATHERINE HACKETT Artist and friend who drew the map for this here book. She has a company called Darkstar Design and you can see her work if you go to her website, www.darkstardesign.com. While you're there be sure to check out her watercolor painting of Blue and Seven.

CARLIE COATS My lawyer's husband, the gourmet cook. And yeah, as if THAT ain't enough to make ya just a tad bit envious of the guy, get this: the man can DANCE. And I mean DANCE. You ought to see him move sweet Jan across the floor in a Tango. That is some kinda wonderful. Looks GREAT in tux, too. Good thing he's such a good guy, cause you could just flat learn to HATE a feller what has all that damn talent like that. (SEE ALSO: Jan Yarborough.)

CAROLINA The University of North Carolina at Chapel Hill where I was "imprisoned" for four years. Was lucky as hell to meet Doris Betts there. Here's how we met:

It was the start of the second semester of my Freshman year and I was late as I walked into my first English class in Greenlaw Building one Tuesday morning (I am a musician, after all) and, even though the class was fully in session, strolled to the middle aisle and, seeing there were no seats available, ambled to the back (as Doris lectured on with out missing a beat) and took a seat in one of the large bay windows in the rear of the classroom.

Now to be fair, I kinda sorta HAD to go down the middle aisle cause I couldn't go down the sides cause, even though I didn't know it at the time, this was a DORIS BETTS class and thus not only were all the seats taken but so were the side aisles: standing room only if you catch my drift (Now Doris disputes this fact, but that's my story and I'm stickin to it.)

It was a long rectangular classroom, with high ceilings and equally high slotted rear windows, each equipped with a sill about three feet deep: perfect for the late arrivals to make themselves comfortable in. So I sat in the recessed window ledge and (again according to Doris, not me) made hangmen's nooses out of the long thin chords dangling from the blinds. (Now I will politely dispute THAT little tidbit if I may. I did no such thing. I sat back there and listened carefully. That, again, is my story and I am stickin to it.) When class was over I patiently waited till everyone else was gone and hopped off the ledge and strode up to the big oak desk in the front where she was standing, packing up her notes and said, If you don't mind my asking, just who the hell ARE you?? And she said I am Doris Betts. And I said What do you? And she said I am a writer and so I said What have you written and she began to tell me so I said, because I had come to class without a pen, I'm sorry to interrupt you, but may I borrow a pen? And she said Sure and she gave me a fountain pen. And then, because I had come to class without any paper, I said Can I borrow a piece of paper? And she said, Sure and gave me a piece of paper and I said Could you start over again?

And so she told me again her name and what she had written and I wrote it all down and when she was done I gave her back her pen and, clutching that scrap of paper in my hand, said thank you and quickly made my way out of the classroom. Eschewing the elevator (the first time in my life I had ever eschewed ANYTHING to the best of my knowledge) I pushed through the door marked "STAIRS" and my rapid footsteps echoed in the empty white painted stairwell as I hurried down two steps at a time and burst out the exit and went right across the red brick walkway to the Little Kids Library (the Undergraduate Library) and checked out every single damn book she ever wrote and cut my classes for the rest of the day and went back to the dorm and read EVERYTHING.

She was just so amazing.

I mean I had been blessed with some great teachers in my life, Mrs. Chewning being one of the best, but this woman was just ASTONISHINGLY good, and contrary to the old maxim "those who can't do teach," she was also an incredible writer. I was young and stoopid as I have told y'all before, but I was smart enough to know I had struck gold by the grace of God, the blessed randomness of the computer, and the luck of the draw that placed me there with her when all I had signed up for was an English Lit class!

When I was done reading some of em, I took them books downstairs to Shepp's room and dumped 'em all on his bed and said You need to read this and left. Bout midnight he stuck his head in my room and said Jesus. And I said Yeah boy. And he said I gotta get in that class and I said Damn right.

By the time I graduated from Carolina I had taken every single class she taught, some by enrolling, some by cutting the classes I was signed up for and auditing hers instead and some by design (independent study.) AND I had audited classes she taught at Dook (that's Duke University for the uninitiated.) Like I said, I mighta been young and stoopid, but I was smart enough to know pure gold when I saw it.

AND

I was never late for another class again.

(Now, if y'all ever get to talk to DB about this, she may very well dispute that last statement. But y'all need to know, as wonderful as she is, and she really is extraordinary, well, she can be quite contrary. She does have a mean, vindictive streak, and she will likely insist that I was, in fact, frequently late, but I tell you what: this is MY story.......MY book.

Let her write her own version if she wants to is the way I figure it.

And as far as y'all are concerned, from that day forward, I was on time dammit.)

CELLO The instrument I play so I can fly like Jen DeMik and Virginia Ward.
(SEE ALSO: Groove.)

CHAPEL HILL Where I live and what the Brown Brothers called me for the longest time back when they thought I had cancer. (Still call me Chapel Hill every once in a while. Probably still think I got the cancer too, now that I think on it....)

CHET ATKINS Ohmigod was he ever good. Got to see him play before he died. Made the pilgrimage, as every guitar player should. What a night. He was a real gentleman. Watched his hands through binoculars till I'd picked his pocket and learned a couple of his licks and then just sat back and enjoyed the show.
A class act.

CHARLIE MCCOY Well he was one of the best harp players out there and that's a fact. I have always been honored to be compared to him though I think it is a foolish comparison.

CIVILIANS Non musicians.
(SEE ALSO: Normal.)

CLAP HEAD That girl LOVES her some applause.
(SEE ALSO: Blue.)

CLASSICALLY TRAINED Players who have vast amounts of training on their instruments, who went to school to learn to play and can read and write musical notation. I have a tremendous amount of respect for classically trained players and work (and play) with them often. But I also get classically trained players who come to me desperate to learn how to improvise, to be able to speak with their own voice and not just recite the thoughts and feelings of others who wrote things down long ago. Doesn't lessen the value of those fine players who wrote things down long ago, doesn't challenge the validity of what they felt and wrote, in fact you COULD say the power of their recorded thoughts helped inspire these new players to want to talk on their own. But so often there are loud voices in the heads of these new inspired players from years and years of teachers and professors saying no no no, just play what's on the page. Sometimes the noise in their heads is so loud I wonder how they can hear the music at all. Martin Brown once warned me off a young lady who was a classically trained pianist I was lusting after by saying, You know John, you just can't throw a kid in a twelve by eight room with a piano four or five hours a day for most of their adolescent years and expect a fully functioning adult to emerge on the other end. Might play a heckuva piano and be fun to hear, but you're just lookin for trouble if you're fixin to hook up with that.

Interestingly enough, he was right as rain on that one....

So I now pre-screen all my dates with at least a drive by through Martin's radar to make sure they're gonna be OK.

(Kidding...I'm kidding.....)

(SEE ALSO: Street Musicians.)

CLEARLY LABELED I just want to go on record and say I think life would be a whole lot better and easier if everything was clearly labeled like up at Haleyland.

CLYDE DAVIS Clyde is married to Pammy Davis and I don't know if that makes him the King Of Bluegrass or not, but I DO know it makes him one lucky fella! He is a GREAT guy, a great picker and a terrific person to go to when yer instruments get sick, cause he does some FINE repair work, yes he does. I take all my gear down there including my Martin and my Deering and y'all know how much I love those things!

Back before I knew Clyde did repairs, I had

my grandfather's fiddle restored by a classical repair
fella in Raleigh and after about six weeks or so the
sound post kept slippin and fallin over! Now for you
Civilians, the sound post is INSIDE the fiddle and
underneath the bridge and is what transmits the sound
from the string to the wood of the instrument and into
the sound chamber. Without that post, you can't play
cause the pressure from the strings across the bridge
is too much for the thin wood surface of the top of the
violin (it could crack) and yer volume and tone is cut
substantially! Took that thing back to that Classical guy
in Raleigh and he said, Yes sir...your sound post is one
sixteenth of an inch too short and I said Well you need
to make me another one cause you restored the violin
and how come you made that dang post too short and
he said, Well the sound post fit when it left the shop
but because of humidity and just how wood is, it has
shrunk so if I make you a new one it will take me about
a month to get to it and cost about two hundred dollars.
TWO HUNDRED DOLLARS!!! Well. I said, I am a poor
musician and I don't have that right now cause I just
PAID you a buncha money to fix this thing and besides I
think you ought to make it right cause it's YOUR work.
Needless to say he didn't see it my way, so my poor violin
languished awaiting some influx of funds so I could get
her back up to speed. A frustrating month or so later I
happened to be talking to the Queen about stuff and my
fiddle came up and she said, Oh, give it to me and I'll
take it to Clyde, he can make you a new sound post, and
so I did cause I knew I had a big check coming in soon
and violin repairs ALWAYS take AT LEAST a month or
two. Next weekend I see Pammy and she hands me the
violin and says, Clyde says play it a while and let him
know what you think. Says the old sound post was one
sixteenth of an inch too short and I thought well, we're
all in agreement on that, so I took that fiddle and played

it and traveled with it and tossed it in the back of my
car and darned if that sound post sat up and behaved
and never has fallen down to this very day, and it's been
almost a year and a half since Clyde did that work! So
after a week or two, I called Pammy up and said, This
here sound post is PERFECT! I'm so happy! What do
I owe Clyde? And she said, Oh I don't know, I think he
stuck a bill in the pocket of the fiddle case. So I hung
up and went to the fiddle case and sure enough there
was a bill in there and I opened and read it and my jaw
plum hit the floor! Called the phone number on the top
of the invoice and Clyde answered. Hello he says. Clyde,
says I, This here is John Santa and I am callin about my
fiddle. And he says, Yeah, how's she doin? And I said,
GREAT! But I am callin about this invoice! It CAN'T
be right! And he said Why not? And I said, Well the
guy who restored my violin told me it would cost two
hundred dollars and take at least a month for him to
make me a sound post one sixteenth of an inch longer
out of seasoned maple and YOU made me a sound post
out of seasoned maple in less than a week and you only
charged me twenty damn dollars!

And ol Clyde he took a minute and finally said,
Well John, you know how people are always askin
Bluegrass folks what the difference between a fiddle and
violin is? And I said, Yeah....and he said, Well, a sound
post for a VIOLIN costs two hundred dollars and the
sound post for a FIDDLE cost twenty.

And a big ol smile broke out on my face and I
said, Clyde, I appreciate your good work and I will put
a check in the mail to ya, and he said, You can just give
it to Pammy the next time you see her. I'm glad you're
pleased with my work, and he hung up.

The difference between a Fiddle and a Violin...
Now THAT is a great Bluegrass story,,,
AND a great Clyde Davis story!

Bluegrass is my Second Language

(SEE ALSO: The Queen Of Bluegrass.)

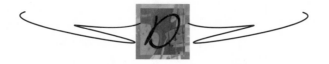

D 35 GUITAR I taught guitar to Martin Brown for quite a few years (still do in fact). During those beginning years he played him a perfectly serviceable Yamaha guitar. It's what we call a five year guitar, meaning that you get it, play it five years and about that time if you're still playin then you're good enough to know you're gonna KEEP playin and also good enough to know a guitar that sells for a couple hundred bucks is just not gonna cut it for a lifetime of playing, it's time to move on up to a better (read: more expensive) guitar. Now bein that I am a teacher of superior quality and consummate ability and Martin was a motivated student with a true love of music, he kinda burned through his five-year guitar in about three. So he began to get the itch and started lookin around to see what might suit him. Martin is not one to rush into a new purchase, particularly when that purchase involves a high end, big ticket item and I reckon I didn't help things much by tellin him to take his time, do it right cause he was lookin to get married to that new guitar, and just like with his wife Judy, it was important you get it right the first time. So he tried this guitar and that, including some higher end models of the Yamahas that sounded pretty darn good but he found he just kept driftin on back to the Martin guitars, and a D 28 model in particular that had kinda winked at him and caught his eye and ear. Now in my opinion, there are just certain

things that are true and meant to be: Martin playing a
Martin just seemed like a natural to me, call me crazy. So
it turns out that I had been playin some Martins down at
the Music Loft and lookin and listenin on his behalf at
the same time he was out a courtin this here 28. Gets to
the point where things are comin to a head and Martin
is pretty hot to pledge his trough to that little 28 what
had his fingers twitchin from the sweet feel of her. Never
one to muddy the waters, I held my piece for about as
long as I could, which in this case was about two and a
half seconds fore I dragged him off to play this here 35
I had found that I thought had a right good sound and
feel. In fact, the tone and color of that 35 was pretty darn
close to the tone and color of MY 35 which was a good
20 years older and more mellowed. For you civilians,
really good guitars--and Martins certainly qualify under
that definition---actually get better as they age. Their
tone gets warmer, darker, richer as the woods marry
and blend and the player shapes the sound. A 35 that
sounded as sweet as the guitar what stole my heart and
caused ME to marry her, well, I just had to intercede and
play matchmaker here. So poor Martin went back and
forth, back and forth, playin one, then the other, and
was still leanin toward that 28, a fine instrument, don't
dare get me wrong on that. A 28 is made to have what
we call "cut:" the ability to push on through the sound
of the other guitars and ride on top, a great guitar for
leads, a well-spoken guitar. The model D35 is acclaimed
for two things: its three-piece back (most guitars are one
or two pieces) and a rich, distinctive signature Martin
bass boom. In other words, a very rich bottom (bass)
end (sound). I understood Martin's dilemma, but was
increasingly frustrated as I could not make him see the
wisdom of my musical judgment. Back and forth we
go, back and forth: 28, 35, 28, 35 until finally I grab the
35 from him and say Play the 28. And he does. Then I

Now play the 35 and make it sound like the 28. And he struggles a bit, and then finds by changing his attack, and where he strums and how, and he can make that ol 35 do a pretty darn close impersonation of that 28. Then I take the 35 from him and hand him back the 28. Now make the 28 sound like the 35 I implore and as hard he tried, he could not do that. You see, you can attack an instrument with bass in such a way as to minimize the sound of the bass, but you can't take an instrument without that distinctive low end and make it somehow more bass-y. You just can't. After a bit, Martin looked up at me and smiled and said,

So...two for the price of one, huh?

And I said

Exactly

And he said I reckon I will be buying this here D 35 and I said Excellent choice sir.

And THAT is how Martin come to play a Martin. (Which is what God clearly intended all along.) (SEE ALSO: Left Handed, Martin.)

DEERING An American banjo manufacturer, some would say THE American banjo manufacturer. Gibson traditionally made the most sought after banjos for Bluegrass, but the Deering banjos are becoming a staple on the market and are really fine instruments with great tone and power. The Deerings are such superb instruments that even the most diehard Gibson devotee cannot deny their impact on the market and the music. American made, they are fast creating a name and tradition in Bluegrass all their own. Under the guidance of my good friend Jay Miller, the creator and former owner of the North Carolina based music store franchise The Music Loft, I had purchased a Deering banjo about six months before I met banjo genius Jeff Wiseman. Needless to say, I was delighted to see he played a

Needless to say, I was delighted to see he played a Deering.

DOCUMENTARY I set out to make a documentary about these wonderful people and places but events conspired against me. After September 11, the recession the country was experiencing worsened and the hope of getting some civic (or music) minded sponsor to donate some money to help me tell these marvelous stories did not seem too likely, so I took to writin all this stuff down, afraid that I would lose or forget it. Started out with the one page treatment and just grew from there. Now that things are getting better, I am ever more hopeful I will be able to let the world hear and see these great players and the music they make.

DOGHOUSE BASS What the classical world calls a double, acoustic or upright bass, the Bluegrass world calls a doghouse bass. Like the difference between a violin and a fiddle, it's all in the eye of the beholder I reckon.
(SEE ALSO: Keith Carroll, Down beat.)

DONNIE EVANS One of the best dobro players I've ever had the pleasure to play with. Unfortunately we have lost touch with him in recent years. We still look for him to show up though and figure one of these Saturday nights he'll just come strollin on in and sit down at one of the RDU session Players gatherings and blow us all away like he always did.

Here's the kind of guy Donnie is, and why we miss him so much:

One afternoon we were over at Phil Boysen's farm playing for his wife Burta's birthday party. We gathered at Phil and Burta's around noon and played for a solid eight hours that day till almost nine o'clock, with some time off for some real good eatin. Now playin for that long isn't really a problem, cause we all carry big thick ol notebooks full of chord charts and lyrics for about a half zillion songs. So we just sit there and leaf through the book until one strikes our fancy and then we play it. It's a lot of fun. We had some new players joining us and they tend to gather round the books so they can see what's going on and keep up. At one point one of these new fellers noticed that we have the songwriter's names prominently displayed in our books and frequently talk about them before and after a tune, and this struck them as a little odd. Now point of fact, a lot of the RDU Session Players and the Bluegrass Folks write their own stuff, so that's a factor in why we care about who wrote what, but only a small piece of it. Donnie summed it up best after that newbie had gone on about it a while. Well, ol Donnie said, You know, I don't think the folks who actually WRITE the songs care very much if we talk about em or not, but I know for a fact their moms do. I like to think that whenever we mention a songwriters name or praise their work, the author's mom gets a little warm feeling in her heart, and that suits me just fine.

What a great guy.

I love that story.

We sure do miss Donnie.

(SEE ALSO: Will The Circle Be Unbroken, Honor and The Marathon Jam.)

DORIS BETTS What Fred Minor is to the fiddle, Doris is to words. A superb writer, teacher, friend and mentor.

(SEE ALSO: Carolina as Doris Betts will forever be linked with this august institution ---and they are damn lucky to have had her.)

DOWNBEAT All God's children got to know where one is. Really good bass players and really good drummers just flat LIVE for knowin where one is, for the downbeat. I worked at the Music Loft in Durham for a while when I was just starting out and there was a drummer there, name a Carlton Miles. Now, if I don't get to be Fred Minor when I grow up, I wanna be Carlton Miles. Carlton is an extraordinary drummer, singer, studio wizard, teacher and just all around great guy. At the time, he was just startin out too, so while we both worked at the Loft (our real job and main source of income), we supplemented our meager musicians wages by teaching lessons: I taught guitar and Carlton taught drums. I will never forget, will remember till the day I die how every time I followed one of my students off to the practice rooms, Carlton, eternally perched behind the counter practicing paradiddles and flams, would stop mid roll and holler

SANTA.

And I'd turn to him and say Yo.

And he'd raise up a drumstick to his eye level and point that thing at me and sternly and earnestly say

You teach them little white boys where One is now, hear?

And I'd smile and nod and say

Yessir.

And as I would be walking out of the room I'd hear him trailing off, Don't make it the drummers job, we're all tired of teaching them guitar players where one is, we're all countin on you John, all the drummers out there, not just me, we're ALL countin on ya! You hear? You hear?

I heard.

EASTER SUNDAY I am writing this on April 11, 2004, Easter Sunday, because last night as I was standing in the shower before I made my way up to Brown's to play an evening of superb music with all those great players, it suddenly hit me just WHY taking you back to Billy Yarborough's family and B.J. and HER family was so important to me. I mean, you'd think I would be the one to know WHY I wrote what I wrote, and why I wanted so much to tell you what happened when I started passing Book One around and got all those wonderful responses and little stories, but that would imply I was actually in charge of this expedition, and we all know that definitely ain't the case!

See, we hear a lot about how the world reacts to the artist, but we don't hear about how the ARTIST reacts to the world reacting to his or her art. Right there in the shower it hit me what I wanted y'all to know is that art is a DIALOGUE and creation doesn't happen in a vacuum. I started to write down all these stories cause of the amazing people and places I encountered, and created a book out of that experience. The book went out into the world, and then--and this is the cool part, cause I wasn't expecting this at all-- the book came back to give me a little kiss on the cheek periodically, a little thank you for putting me out there in the form of the astonishing reactions people had to reading it, and I got to see and feel how this book intersected their lives and touched their hearts and I think that's important for us to talk about: how the REACTION to art effects the artist, cause it's big and it's powerful and while I am not currently too much interested in reading a book about how the world reacted to Picasso's art (I pretty much KNOW that), I would be VERY much interested in reading a book about how PICASSO reacted to the way

363

the world reacted to his art. You readers and art fans and music lovers need to know about this: YOU matter very much to the artist. Let me put it this way: when I first set up the RDU jam sessions, way before we were the RDU Session Players, back in the beginning, I based the jam on a simple precept, a maxim of the Jazz world: the best music is made at three in the morning BY musicians and FOR musicians. To that end, it was musicians only, no civilians, no LISTENERS, just players. One summer night after we'd been meeting sporadically for a few years, we were pickin out on the carport about one or two in the morning, when my neighbors Stacy and Eugene down the street drove by. Seeing the cars and all of us out on the carport, they went home and got Indy and Soli, their dogs, and walked up to say howdy and take a listen. They sorta slid in and sat down and truthfully, I didn't hardly know they were there, till after we finished a song they began to clap. Just the two of em sittin there on a bench with big smiles on their faces and clappin and grinning and we all turned to them like What the heck…and then we went back to playin, but I noticed something magnificent in the next song, and I learned a good lesson: the best music ISN'T made for musicians and by musicians alone in a room at three in the morning. The very best music is made by musicians in a room full of people who love and appreciate what the musicians are doing, and THAT'S what makes the music turn into magic. In Quantum Physics it's called the observers affecting the observation, and all of us who play and paint and write and sing, we all owe you our thanks, and I'm proud to say there's twice as many Civilians on our email music invitation list now as there are players!

    And, by the way: I got to sit beside the talented Mr. Jeff Wiseman up at Brown's for the WHOLE night last night! Man, what a treat that was hearin that boy

up close! I reckon I was observin him so darn much, he
nearly broke a string or two tryin to keep up with my
observations!

So the next time you hear somebody say
something about supporting the arts, do me a favor and
take it literally, OK?

EIGHTWENTYTHREE You would think that a bunch
a fellers who play so well together, have such a natural
rapport and make some plain ol magic when they sit
down to play could come up with a damn name fer
themselves. Well, me and Jeff and Keith and Greg, we
have struggled and struggled with tryin to find a name
for our band and Greg's wife Cindy finally came up with
this after several disastrous attempts on our part. You
would, in fact, think that guys who write songs and are
otherwise intelligent could come up with something, but
no....

Took Cindy to do it for us, God bless her! The
name refers to the first time we all played together
(except Greg) at that job in Burlington on August 23rd,
2001, and I have to say, I think its pretty cool.
And just so you know, my own personal favorite was
"The Jeff Wiseman Trio," which I STILL think is a great
name for a band!

(And yeah, I know there are FOUR of us.... that's
what makes it so cool....)

ETHICS The cause of all my problems in life can
be traced directly back to my father who, for reasons
unknown to my sister and me, instilled in us from a very
young age the concept of right and wrong and a strong
sense of moral obligation and capacity for acceptance
of those different from us. Now why he (and my mother,
clearly a willing participant in all this) would instill these
values in their children in an age of disposable values

365

and graying guidelines, of "oh poor pitiful me" self help books, is absolutely beyond us. He has certainly done us no favors as we are constantly confronted with the clash of our upbringing and the reality in which we must live on a daily basis.

I often wonder if he somehow knew I would one day meet these people, make these life long (and life changing) friends and just wanted me to be ready. Nah... couldn't be.....

FEAR You know, there ought not be so much fear in the world, let alone in the music people play.

FRANK GORDON Frank is a member of the North Carolina All Star Band but our history goes way back before that. There was this really great production facility over in Raleigh where Ray St. Clair worked as an audio engineer called Videofonics and they had a party one Saturday and I wandered over and, like I do at most parties and particularly after I have a little sip a somethin, I started to get the itch to pick a little music out. I went lookin fer Ray but he was out of town on a shoot or somethin so I just wandered around till I ran into my old buddy Sabine French. I knew Sabine from the old days in video, and it seems she had up and married this good lookin feller she had with her and he and I got to talkin music and he sorta mentioned how he wouldn't mind scratchin out a tune or two either and Sabine said Well, I know where there's a guitar and started off towards the office and then stopped and looked back at me and said, Oh, but you're left handed... we don't have any left handed guitars here and I just

smiled me a big broad smile and said, No problem. I
just happen to have my Martin in the car and looked at
Frank and he said, Don't leave home without it and I
said Nosirree Bob boy, so off we went to find us a vacant
room where we could play. Ended up in the middle of
one of the big sound stages Videofonics had and we
pulled a couple of chairs out and Sabine came in from
Ray's studio with one of his spare acoustic guitars and
we started playin and it was just like we had been playin
together for twenty or thirty years. I knew where he was
goin, when he would stop and when he would go. It was
like we had rehearsed those songs for days or weeks
they came off so smooth and so good. I was astonished
to find myself thinkin, and I know Ray won't be hurt
by this--in fact I know he'll be honored--Wow, this is
just like playin with Ray St. Clair who, of course, I HAD
been playing with for over twenty years. Ol Frank would
whip out a John Prine song and then a good ol Jerry
Jeff Walker tune and then a Steve Earle and then a Lyle
Lovitt and then---well, I reckon you take my point. He
was all over the place but in a journey that made great
musical sense and like puttin one foot in front of the
other and walkin on down the road, he just put one song
out after the other and I began to sit back and enjoy the
ride, smilin at the view. He was, in my humble opinion,
just what this party needed, at least for me, cause before
you know it, I was sayin, Hold on here, just hang on
a second, I'll be right back and I'm sure y'all can tell,
knowin me as well as y'all do by now, that when I came
back in on that sound stage I had my sweet cello right
there with me. Well we played some John Hiatt and
some Rolling Stones and then he started a slow, easy
acoustic guitar version of Bruce Springsteen's famous
rock anthem, "Born To Run" and I was holdin my 35
and I started to play and then I thought better of it and
switched on over to the cello and bowed in nice and

low and let the cello just underline his soulful singin of those lyrics full of angst and rock n' roll pain. Well some folks had gathered in that big ol sound stage and someone had dropped the lights down low and there was a bunch of folks talkin and socializin but we got a ways into that song and everything stopped cause we all knew we were experiencing something very special, a version of the song we all needed to hear but didn't know it and two good players who would go on to become real good friends but didn't know that yet either and there wasn't a sound in that room but Frank's gentle tellin of the song and that steel string guitar and my lonely cello that wrapped itself around the golden rims of that song and strapped itself to the engines. As we played I began to move through the octaves of the cello, leaving the low notes behind to augment the wistful tone of those yearning lyrics and we finished up with a sweet vibrato and a final strum of a chord and that whole sound stage just held that thought, cupped that instant in its hands and gently blew on it to keep the spark glowing for just a moment longer to breath in the smoke of it and then those kind folks began to clap and cheer and I looked at Frank and said, We need to play together and he said, I believe we do.

I really love when Frank comes and jams with the RDU Session Players and I DEFINITELY love it when he joins in with the All Stars. But in my heart of hearts, I have to say my favorite times with Frank Gordon are when it's just him and me and an audience that wants to hear some great vocals and some very unique arrangements of tunes they have already been friends with for years. Frank can take those songs and make em shiny and new, keeping the best of what we knew and bringing in a whole new interpretation and feel for what was there in that song that we didn't even know about. He loves to throw new songs at me in performances,

songs I have never heard before and have me play on
them and react to them and I have to admit, while it IS
a little nerve wracking sometimes (it IS a performance
after all) I really enjoy comin through to the other end
of a brand new song and have Frank look over at me and
shake his head in amazement and approval and say, Nice
job Buddy.
Don't get a whole lot better than that.
www.mgsattorneys.net

FRED MINOR A true Son of the South and my
friend and mentor. It would be no great surprise I
suppose, to inform you that Fred's niece, Deborah,
is also a great fiddle player. We all sorta take that for
granted, I mean look at the gene pool she swims in.
But that really diminishes her own achievement on the
instrument, an achievement that can best be summed up
as follows:
    One evening at a rehearsal for a Christmas party
gig the North Carolina All Stars were going to play,
we got to talking about female vocalists, and Debbie's
name came up. (And see, this is where we take her for
granted cause the girl can flat SING and to the best of
my knowledge Fred can sing about as well as he can fly
a helicopter which is to say crash and burn.) Anyway,
Keith gets a bit of a furrow in his brow as he slowly
shakes his head and conjures up a strong mental image
and he's says, John, you ever heard Debbie and Fred play
fiddle together? And I allow as how No, I have never had
that pleasure and Keith says with awestruck vehemence
in his voice,
    Well then you ain't never heard nothin.
    !
    This from a stunning musician who's heard
himself (and played himself) some fine music in his time.
What a great thing to say and what a great compliment.

FUNERALS As soon as they start getting good, I tell all my guitar students to prepare for the day they are asked to play a funeral. I have played more of 'em than I care to think about frankly. Most, thankfully, were not for really close friends and family, but for friends of friends and very often, complete strangers. I've played maybe three or four times for departed folks I love, maybe twenty-three, twenty-five for acquaintances or people I didn't even know. Now that might seem odd to you, but it makes perfect sense to me. See, the music is there for all the happy times: the falling in love, the weddings, the parties, the births, the graduations, and so it is only natural that we be there to share the times of sorrow too. Music means so much to us players, but in a very real sense it means, I think, even more to the Civilians. So inevitably a friend of a friend asks for a singer, or some musicians to come play at the service and help ease the pain...and so you get The Call.

In some inchoate, chromosomal way, when the hurt comes, we reach out for the things we know will comfort us, the things that will help express the inexpressible. I have been paid all kinds of money to play for folks, but it comes as no surprise to me that I have never, ever, been offered money to play a funeral, nor would I take it. Its just part of the job you see. If we get to share all those fine happy times, it is our duty to be there for the sad times as well.

A funeral is the hardest gig you'll ever play. Getting up in front of a couple thousand people is nothing, exactly NOTHING, compared to facing a small congregation full of grieving, angry human beings who are questioning just about everything right then and directing all that doubt and anger at YOU, the musician. I can tell you I have NEVER performed at a service where I wasn't just SHAKING before I got up to play or sing. But once the music starts, and that sweet balm begins to ease the anguish and soothe away the resentment and disappointment, well...there's just nothing like it in this whole great wonderful world. Stranger or family member, that explosion of release and resolution the music brings is always completely overwhelming.

Playing a funeral is absolutely the most rewarding and powerful experience you'll ever have as a musician.

I sincerely hope you never have to play one.

G A common key for bluegrass songs.
(SEE ALSO: A, Gear AND Harp.)

GEAR As in, What gear y'all in? A common phrase you hear called out when someone suggests a new song to play. It is the musical equivalent of what the diner wait staff did calling decaf "unleaded" and coffee "regular." It really means, What key are you doing that song in?

GINA NORMAN A singer and one of the RDU session players. Part of the backup group "The All Day Sucker Singers" for the way she and Megan Day sucked on lollipops all day long at the April first RDU/Bluegrass Gathering. Turned their tongues bright purple and red. It was disgusting.
(And funny as hell.)

GTCC Greensboro Technical Community College. This was the place I first met the Queen Of Bluegrass, Ms.

Pammy Davis. As I said in Book One, I did in fact join High Lonesome Strings, and it didn't take me too long before I decided HLS needed a theme song so I set out to write one for em. One nervous Saturday night at a jam session, early before most folks showed up, I played it for Pammy to see what she thought with Keith on the dog house bass and the wonderful Miss Virginia Ward singin back up vocals to flesh it out some. Well, I am proud to say Pammy just flipped out over that song and made me sing it to a couple hundred HLSers at a Christmas potluck the following Sunday afternoon. So there in the cafeteria at GTCC, a scant year and a half after meeting her, hearing her play and then getting to jam out with her for the very first time, I climbed on stage with the Queen Of Bluegrass on dobro and the talented Mr. Carroll on bass to show my homework to the class. The response from those great pickers was just amazing. I had no small amount of trepidation tryin to speak for so many different people with so many disparate views of what bluegrass music is and how it should be played, but over a dozen folks come up and asked for copies of the song and a bunch a those generous pickers slapped me on the back as I walked through the crowd after playin my brand new song and I tell you what, it was some kind a wonderful that day was. Because of their support and strong response, I have come to believe they do in fact, really like the song and I have to say I look forward to the day when I attend a High Lonesome String meeting and hear a couple hundred of my pickin buddies singin out about the sweet, soulful sounds of those High Lonesome Strings. Now THAT will be a great day....
(SEE ALSO: High Lonesome Strings.)

GREG ELDRED One of the most amazing guitarists I've ever seen, let alone having the pleasure to play and perform with him! A great singer, a great songwriter, a

great picker and a great husband and father.
His mama must be SO proud....
foureldreds@hotmail.com

GROOVE The whole groove thing is intimately tied
up and into the One (and I mean that in a Zen and
Rthymic way.) It never ceases to amaze me: you can get a
bunch of talented players together and whatever it is, "it"
is just not there. The groove can be elusive and, like all
good religions, is best caught, not taught.
Stevie Wonder said it best:
    "Just cause a record's got a groove, don't make it
IN the groove."
    But if you tell the truth and let the music come,
that ol groove thing will just sneak right on up and
snuggle on in there with you and make herself to home
and the next thing you know you're just flat out flyin.
    That's when the birds really start to sing....
    (SEE ALSO: Cello.)

HABIB Good ol Habib. We still holler out "Take it
Habib!" when we git goin good. Unfortunately, when
he went back to Lebanon I lost touch with him. I am
hoping the book might help to reestablish contact. A
VERY talented musician and a terrific fellow.

HALEYLAND Has to be seen to be believed. When
I get some money to do my documentary, it's the first
place I'm goin.
    (Gotta get pictures so folks will finally believe
me....)

373

(SEE ALSO: Bob and Linda Haley.)

HARMONICA The "traditional" name for what used to be called the Mouth Harp. A wind instrument played by blowing air out and drawing air in across reeds encased in a metal housing to produce a tone. I enjoy teaching harmonica because it is one of the rare occasions when you can say "blow" and "suck" in mixed company and not get slapped.
(SEE ALSO: Harp.)

HARP Harp is to harmonica as fiddle is to violin: they're both the same instrument only the harp is the bad boy brother to the harmonica. There are essentially two kinds of harmonica you can play: straight and cross. "Straight" harp refers to playing a harp in the same key as the song. For example, if a song is in the key of C, you play a C harp and thus have access to the notes necessary to play a faithful rendition of the melody. In "cross" harp, if the song is in C, you play across the key by playing an F harp, thus losing the ability to play the melody, the nouns and pronouns of the song, BUT you gain the use of all the verbs, adjectives and adverbs by accessing the sevenths, ninths, and sixths etc., of the scale. Add to that the technique of bending the note by a rapid aggressive inhale, and the color you can add to a song becomes virtually limitless.

In other words, a harp can take a good boppin song that you're tappin yer feet and enjoyin listenin to and just make ya go nuts till you and everybody else in the whole joint is dancin on the tables.

(NOTE: It is important to only use this power for the forces of good, never evil.)
(SEE ALSO: Harmonica and Bending.)

HARRY TEUTING A guitar player with the RDU
Session Players and owner of Harry's Guitar shop in
Raleigh, NC. Most famous in the group for his always
tasteful pickin and his stunning rendition of the song
"Tear Stained Letter" by Richard Thompson.
www.harrysguitarshop.com
888-974-4190
(SEE ALSO: RDU Session Players)

HIGH LONESOME STRINGS Name of a
Piedmont North Carolina based Bluegrass society and
the name of the song I wrote to honor all those great
folks and tell the story of those wonderful pickers.
Pammy Davis is founder and president.
www.highlonesomestrings.org

HONOR Rick Allen told me my book was not about
bluegrass. He said my book was about Bluegrass the
way steak was about ketchup. He told me my book was a
book about exceptional people and places so vivid and
extraordinary they were almost characters themselves.
He told me my book was about people the way they used
to be in some long ago time, where honor and integrity
were not just words, but a way of life. He told me my
book made him wish for friends like mine and made him
proud to live in a state where these people still lived
and worked and played music and made their homes
and raised their families. He said these people gave him
hope. He said he wanted to have every single one a these
folks in this here book over to his house for supper one
day, that's how much he admired them and enjoyed
reading about them.
　　　I reckon it takes an honorable man to feel and say
that.
　　　One of these days I'm gonna have to load up a bus

full a these wonderful, crazy pickers and head on down to Fayetteville and surprise ol Rick and Cindy with a little concert on their front lawn. I have to say, I would enjoy introducing Fred Minor to Rick Allen.

Always a pleasure to introduce men of honor to each other.

HUDDY LEDBETTER (AKA Leadbelly.) A master of the twelve-string guitar and a consummate blues man. A Blues icon.
(SEE ALSO: Leadbelly.)

HUDDLE HOUSE Ummmmm.......breakfast anytime......unnnhhhhh

INTEGRITY Well now, for some reason I always think of ol Donnie Evans when I think about integrity. I reckon it was how he sings "Wayfaring Stranger," "Will The Circle Be Unbroken" and "Amazing Grace" that did it. There is power and conviction and honesty in how he respects these songs. I used to kid Donnie that he was born in the wrong time, used to tell him he was an honorable man in an age of dishonor, a man of integrity in an age of lies. But then I met Billy Yarborough and he took me to Burlington to play music one day and my whole life changed. I used to think the RDU Session Players were sorta the last outpost of things like Honor and Truth and Integrity. But I found there was a whole universe of wonderful people out there, just waitin to be discovered by someone a little lost, lookin to be found.

(SEE ALSO: Honor, Truth, Ethics, Donnie Evans, and Will The Circle Be Unbroken.)

JAKE Martha and Jimmy Johnson's dog.
Fer God's sake. if anybody asks you, BE SURE to tell em
Jake is a CHOCOLATE LAB.
> Trust me, trouble like that, you don't want....
> (SEE ALSO: Jimmy Johnson, Martha Johnson.)

JAN YARBOROUGH The one who made this
whole thing happen. Without her, there's no book, no
Bluegrass, no nothin. How wonderfully odd that one
home cooked meal could so much change a life.
> Thanks Jan.
> (SEE ALSO: Carlie Coats)

JEFF DARNELL This is the guy that Billy
Yarborough and I went to meet up with over in Bryson
City to play music that weekend I got Minor. Poor ol Jeff
was drivin his wife nuts cause he set up a huge stage,
bought a PA system and lights and plopped em all down
in the middle of a field on the side of a mountain and
invited everyone to come on over to play and listen to
some music every Friday and Saturday night. Problem
was this was in the middle of a drought when the farm
was not exactly rakin in the money and of course Jeff
was pretty adamant about not chargin for the music,
cause, you know, it's not about the MONEY....
Bout drove his poor wife plumb crazy.

JEFF WISEMAN The best banjo player I've ever

picked with.

He's so good but he's also incredibly humble about it. Often when we go to a jam and another banjo player shows up, Jeff will just sort of melt away and let that other player slide on in. Next thing you know, Ol Jeff is gone. One time at Brown's he just quietly slipped on out and I happened to look backstage and there he was in the back, pickin along like mad and grinnin like crazy, he and Minor, just both backstage having a big old time while the rest of us were out front on the mics. I learn a lot about music, humility and class from hangin around Mr. Jeff Wiseman, the best banjo player I've ever picked with, and one of the best I've ever heard!

boogdoolus2@hotmail.com

JEN DEMIK Lord can this woman sing. Her love for music is incredibly powerful and she has that rarest of abilities to become transparent in the music, to BE the music, to BECOME the melody. Her absolute honesty and vulnerability when she sings are the keys to her talent. She is completely transported by the song, the act of singing, and so lifted up as to be in some kind of rapturous Zen state. The girl KNOWS where One is if ya know what I mean. Has a tremendous natural ability to lead and guide, to gently shape the dynamics through the subtlest of gestures and finely nuanced phrasing and intensity of her sweet sweet voice. It became a game to us players to make her smile with something we played, some lick or a fill or a vamp at the end of a song. A beautiful woman by anybody's standards, when the music really gets going she just glows, becomes stunning, radiant, and I tell you what, if you can play something that gets her to nod her head or do that little Mona Lisa smile as she sits there eyes closed, softly swaying in her chair to the beat, letting the music take her away, well then you know as how you are playin some damn fine music then by God.

One of the finest moments of my life came one Saturday night not long after Jen moved to San Diego. Virginia Ward was sittin in with the RDU Session Players for one of the first times and we were doin Bonnie Raitt's version of Del Shannon's great song, "Runaway." Now there is a place in that song, on the chorus, where one night years ago I hit this little blues rock lick and filled the space between the lyrics and Jen smiled and nodded and so bein that I ain't stupid and I am a boy and will flat do ANYTHING to make a beautiful talented woman smile in my direction, I never forgot that lick and I play it every time we do "Runaway" and Jen smiles the same smile every time. Well, Jen was gone and we did the tune and come up on that chorus and either out of habit or homage, I threw that lick and bent those strings and beautiful Virginia Ward grinned her a little Mona Lisa grin and beamed her encouragement at me and I thought to myself, Folks we have a winner. Just when we need a Singer with a capitol S this here girl has found herself a home with us, and us with her, and I am glad of it. We were lucky to have Jen for as long as we did. We're INCREDIBLY lucky to have Virginia with us and I will not rest until I somehow get these two together and get them singin.

The good Lord above would buy tickets to THAT show.

jmdemik@yahoo.com

(SEE ALSO: Out Of The Blue)

JIMMY JOHNSON One of the regulars down at Brown's, the one who dubbed me first Onion Head and then Vidalia. Most importantly, he's the father to them twelve purty gals what have their pictures up in the shop.

Never see em around the farm none though....it's right odd.....
(SEE ALSO: Martha Johnson.)

JIMMY'S SHOP A tractor....
Imagine my surprise.

JOHN PRINE Man wouldn't you love to be able write songs like that?
I really enjoy performing his stuff, particularly when Frank handles the singing chores.

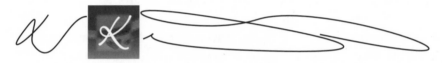

KAREN YARBOROUGH The woman who takes the concept of Southern Hospitality to a whole new level. This wonderful woman was kind enough to take pity on poor ol Billy Yarborough and marry him and raise up two of the finest daughters on the planet. She will surely go to heaven if for no other reason than being willing to put up with Billy and me playing music and being useless for long stretches of weekend at a time. God bless her.
(SEE ALSO: Billy, Katelyn, and Kristen Yarborough)

KATELYN YARBOROUGH Billy and Karen's youngest. I taught her some harmonica on the way down to B.J. Parson's place when we went down to play the rent on Minor that second year. We had a ball in my car laughin and makin a BUNCH of funny noises on that ol harp! I'm pretty much nuts about her....
(SEE ALSO: Billy, Karen, and Kristen Yarborough)

Bluegrass is my Second Language

KEITH CARROLL Well now, there was a time when
I thought if you were gonna be any good at playin this
here Bluegrass music, you had ta lose a least a finger
or two. Seemed to be a prerequisite. I mean, one night
we're up at Jeff's playin and Greg is strummin up a
storm, and I'm chunkin that mandolin and blowin on my
harp for all I'm worth, Jeff is plinkin that ol Deering of
his and I'm sittin across from Keith and I kinda notice
how the fingers on his chording hand seem, well, shorter
than they oughta be. I kinda shrugged it off to an optical
illusion--I mean the boy IS playin so fast he's practically
a blur so I am certainly mistaken. When we stop after a
bit to laugh and catch our breath I look again and, sure
nuff, his four fingers are a bit, well, truncated. Never
one to stand on formality, I said Keith what the hell
happened to yer fingers?? Seems there was an accident
at the mill and his left hand got caught in one of the
machines and slap, there went the ends of his fingers.
Now he tells this tale with no sadness or bitterness, or
edge at all, it's just a tale he's tellin and he's as matter
of fact as he can be while I'm curling my toes and
thankin the Lord for my fingers all the while marveling
at how in the world can this boy DO what he does
with fingers only half their size. He allows how at first
when it happened he was, needless to say, despondent
at what appeared to be the end of his musical life. But
after his hand had healed up some, he found the music
kept callin to him and even though he kept saying but I
CAN'T, it just kept callin and callin and so he picked up
his banjo one day and after a few tentative chords and
picking patterns, all that pent up music just started flyin
outa him. He said his wife came to the door of the room
he was in and said, Thank God. I thought you'd never
play again. And he looked at her kinda dumbfounded
and said, So did I and started playin and she winked at

him and went back to washin the dishes.

Well after that evening, seemed like everywhere I went all these great pickers I played with had fewer fingers than one would suppose would be necessary to play so incredibly well or had fingers of shall we say diminished stature like Keith's and yet they all were pickin up a hurricane and grinnin from ear to ear.

Scared me for a while as I thought I might have to offer one of mine to the Great Bluegrass Gods In The Sky till I noticed Jeff still had all his fingers and so did Greg. Course none a them boys were right in the head, so I figured I probably done paid my dues already bein a bit to the left of normal my own bad self.

Had me a little anxious there for a while though.

tkcarroll@bellsouth.net

(SEE ALSO: Dog house bass, Down beat.)

KRISTEN MOONEY B.J.'s daughter and the one who named Minor Scamp until I rescued him from the living hell of misnomenclature. She has subsequently redeemed herself by naming one of her new English Setters Music.

(Ya gotta love that...)

KRISTEN YARBOROUGH Billy and Karen's oldest daughter. Like her sister Katelyn, she takes after her mom in beauty and grace, and also in Southern Hospitality. She lets me stay in her room every time I go visit these fine folks and I just can't say how much I appreciate it.

(SEE ALSO: Billy, Karen, and Katelyn Yarborough)

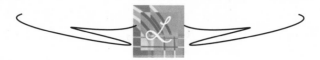

LEADBELLY (AKA HUDDY LEDBETTER) The man who started me on this journey.....
    (SEE ALSO: HUDDY LEDBETTER.)

LEFT HANDED Sometimes when I get a compliment on my playing I just brush it off by saying, Well, sir, I'm not really that good it's just that I'm left handed and since the music I play comes out upside down, y'all think it sounds good. It's supposed to be funny and most times gets a laugh, leastwise when I say it to musicians it does. When I say it to civilians, they just look at me funny.
    Being left handed has its advantages: nobody asks to play my guitar, or if they do they always give it back right quick. Out of all the folks in High Lonesome Strings, there's only one other fella what's left handed, so needless to say we bonded instantly. Down side used to be that getting a left handed instrument was often tough and always expensive. Nowadays most guitar shops routinely make instruments for lefties and tend to not make a big deal of it. When I got married to my D35 I had to go all the way to Wheaton, Maryland and the Washington Music Center and a good ol feller name a George Hauer to get me a left handed Martin. Went down in the basement (why would they waste valuable sales space putting a LEFT handed guitar out on display??) and had the pleasure of sorting through about twenty or so left handed models the Music Center had been forced to buy as part of their Martin contract. (Martin was ahead of their time on this as with most things guitar related.) Played two or three and set them aside for another look but when I put my hand on her neck and lifted her out of the case, I knew I had THE ONE right then and there. Kept playing and looking through the rest of em, but none of em felt as good as that 35 and so I got myself married to that guitar that

very same day. Can't say as how I haven't ever looked at another guitar since (I'm only human after all) but never bought another one after her and a decade or two have slipped on by so I reckon that says somethin. All these years, all the films I've scored, commercials, music and jam sessions, and that guitar has never said anything to me other than, Yeah, I can do that. What else ya got big guy? She's never let me down.

Now gettin a banjo was a horse of a different color all together. I been wanting to get me a banjo for YEARS but nobody was makin left handed models so I kept waitin and waitin for the revolution that swept through the world of guitars to make it on over to the Bluegrass world so I could get me a left handed banjo. Periodically I'd call my buddy Jay Miller up (at the time, he was the owner of the Music Loft stores throughout North Carolina) and say Jay, do me a favor and sniff around and see if you can get me a left handed banjo yet. Finally after several years of comin up dry, he said I think I just might have a lead on one for ya. Seems there was this relatively new company called Deering that was makin quite a name for itself with some kick ass all American made banjos and Jay sweet-talked somebody at Deering into making me a lefty. These days, gettin a lefty banjo from Deering is no biggie at all, but back a few years ago it took some finesse. I was pretty leery of ordering up an instrument and buying it sight (or more importantly SOUND) unseen, but Jay assured me that this banjo company was making great instruments and that I would not be disappointed, so I gave him a down payment and he ordered it up and I sat down to wait my four to six months. About three months later Jay told me to come on over and see my baby, and so I did and even though I didn't really know how to chord it or play it much at all, when I picked it up, it had that same feel like my 35, that same feel of quality and heft and when I brushed those strings and she sang out a few chords and notes, I knew I had a winner. I figure with any instrument of quality, you got to spend at least a grand, and so that's what I did, ordering their top of the line instrument without any inlay or decorative features that would drive the cost up figuring I was a studio musician, so who would ever see it anyway? Little did I know in just a few months I would be out playin with a bunch a Bluegrass boys, and I will admit, my little banjo is a bit of a Plain Jane, at least to look at. Now once she starts to singin, it's a whole other ball o wax, my Deering can stand with the prettiest banjos out there with her superb tone and clarity. Every once in a while I wish I had sprung for something a little more festive looking, sometimes I wish she looked as distinctive as she sounds, but we're pretty happy together.

Now if I can only get the left handed revolution to (finally) sweep into the world of mandolins......
(SEE ALSO: D 35, Deering, Martin.)

LEONARD COHEN Different than John Prine but man, I wouldn't mind being able to write songs like Leonard neither! Shepp turned me on to him when we were in college at Carolina. Been a fan ever since, and not just when I'm depressed....

LESLIE ALEXANDER AND BARRY HESTER
At the time I started writing this book, these two had just gotten engaged. We had the honor of playing at their May 31, 2003 wedding up in Asheville.
(SEE ALSO: Asheville, North Carolina)

LEWIS BINKOWSKI One of the RDU Session Players, Lew is a classically trained violinist who'd branched out into mandolin. A little over a year ago his wife Meredith signed him up with me for a month of mandolin lessons as a birthday present. Lew enjoyed the lessons and extended his stay. That's the GOOD news. The BAD news is, we digressed off the mandolin to guitar and it wasn't too long after that Lewis found himself the proud owner of a beautiful D17 mahogany Martin guitar. From there we branched out into bass (he didn't buy one of them--yet) and then tied it all up back into viola and violin and then finally mandolin. He carries about as many instruments around as I do these days I reckon.

     Good for him.

     I knew we were making progress when one night he looked up from his mandolin and said,
You know, John, I don't want you to take this the wrong way, but I think I'm starting to get it, and I'm starting to understand that it's really no big deal you play so many instruments.

     I just smiled at him.

lewisbinkowski@email.unc.edu

     (SEE ALSO: Meredith Nicholson)

LICKS Originally a blues term that made it's way into rock and now is pretty much universally used by musicians of any style to describe the lead (improvisational) phrase of a player. For example, Jeff Wiseman's got some of the most amazing licks I ever heard on a banjo while Ray St. Clair's got some of the tastiest I ever heard on guitar. Ol Greg is just a dang GATLING gun on HIS lead breaks, but that's a WHOLE other story all together!

LINDA HALEY Our tour guide up at Haleyland and a sweeter, more wonderful person you just won't find anywhere.

     Bob's a lucky guy.

LUCILLE PAYNE Blue and Minor's grandmother. She and her fella Stanley keep a five pound bag of dog bones in the trunk of their car and when we come into Brown's to set up, ol Blue will just strut across that stage and jump on down to the dance floor and sashay over to her Grandma with a big ol smile and her tail up high and lots of kisses to give. Minor usually stays outside or in back more than Blue (we all know how she is with an audience--don't get me started on her) so Lucille and Stanley will wander out back at some point in the night and make sure Minor gets his fair share of hugs and biscuits too, cause as y'all well know, my puppies just do NOT get nearly the attention and affection at home that they should and they will be more than happy to tell you so.

I always get a big hug and a howdy my own bad self from Lucille.

It's one of my favorite things about playing at Brown's.

(SEE ALSO: Stanley Cobb, Brown's)

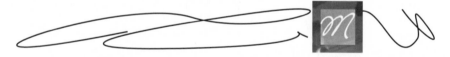

MAC MONROE My buddy Mac's dad and my parole officer.
(SEE ALSO: The Macs.)

MAC MONROE III Mac's son and my best friend.
(SEE ALSO: The Macs.)

MARATHON JAM (THE FIRST ANNUAL)
Jen came back to North Carolina for a wedding and said she's be able to sneak away for a few hours in the

afternoon and wanted to sing with all of us again as she missed us and deeply regretted moving away to California and ruining her life. (Not exactly sure about that last part, but that was my take on it...) Since some folks could make it in the afternoon, some not until evening I proposed we build on our eight hour session out at Phil and Burta Boysen's farm, and make it into the First Annual Marathon Jam, the goal being to keep the music going for at least twelve hours. Now it wasn't the Marathon Jam that drew Ray St. Clair back from DC, no, it was the thought of hearing sweet Jen DeMik sing again and so he drove on down to join us. We started playing at 12:34 PM on Saturday, November 8, 2003. We finished at 1:37 AM, Sunday, November 9 and we had a BALL. We had folks in and out all day and night and I am proud to say that Ray, Pammy Davis (The Queen Of Bluegrass), Whit Kenny and I played for a solid twelve and a half hours with only three five to ten minute breaks over the course of the day.

My only regret is that I didn't think till too late that we should have played for a charity. I mean if you're gonna play for twelve hours SOMEBODY oughta make some money, but it just didn't occur to me till after. So at the SECOND Annual Marathon Jam, we will seek sponsors (you know, like, get folks to pledge five bucks an hour for every hour each person plays or sings) and I figure we oughta be able to raise AT LEAST a thousand dollars for some worthy charity. And THAT will make the music even sweeter that day....

MARK WILLIAMS An internationally known geriatrician. Mark And I met when we were undergrads at Carolina. The story he tells is that he heard me perform somewhere and became a fan and one day decided to just show up on my door step, guitar in hand with a buncha questions about music and writing in mind. For once in my life I wasn't a complete jerk and welcomed him in my dorm room and we proceeded to talk music for a several hours and even worked on one of his songs where I fleshed out the progression he was using with some additional chords and relative minors for him. Now I am ashamed to admit I have no recollection of this meeting from all those years ago, but Mark reminded me of it years later when he hired me to produce some videos for him when he was Chairman of the Program On Aging at UNC. I returned the favor by using the exact same chord progression we worked on in my dorm that day as the basis for the theme music for a series of ten medical videos I produced with him.

MARTHA JOHNSON So Jimmy Johnson and Fred Minor are standing outside Brown's when me and the pups pull up in the van. I wave as I glide past and slip into a spot near the back steps. They don't wave back, they're just chatting, standing there, leaning against the whitewashed wooden side of the Ole Opry in the last warm glow of the fall sunset. I park, and the dogs hop out and I amble on over toward them as the pups strike off in search of new pee-mails to read. Howdy boys I say. Jimmy kinda looks down in disgust, Fred averts his eyes. What's up? I press on. Jimmy, body language closed, arms tight across his chest, ball cap pulled low over his eyes, lets go a stream of tabacccy juice and says Son you have bought yerself a whole world a pain. Fred just shakes his head and looks toward the pasture out back, watches the dogs romping around, says nothing, but his mouth is drawn tight, he looks upset. Hey, whadid I do? If I got you guys mad at me somehow, I'm REALLY sorry.

Parting with a little more tabacco juice Jimmy

says, Us? T'ain't got nothin t'do with US. And for the first time he looks me in the eye and says, Hell, if it was just US you pissed off, you'd be OK, you could FIX that. But you're in a heap a trouble boy, cause you done upset my wife, and I'll tell you what: there ain't no comin back from that!

Fred nodded in agreement and murmured That's right, that's right. WHAT I exclaim, what are you guys talkin about?? Fred just looks like he can't believe I am in such denial, and again looks off to the distance as Jimmy says, Man you screwed up bad this time.

WHAT??? WHAT DID I DO???

I'm frantically searching my brain and comin up with only one thing: I'M INNOCENT.

What?? I demand again, tell me. Jimmy pauses just a beat, blows the whole clump a chaw outa his mouth and says, deadly serious like, You called Jake a hound dog in yer book. He ain't a hound dog, he's a Chocolate Lab. You shoulda known that. She's never gonna forgive you for that.

Needless to say, I am flushed with relief, but seeing how important this is to them, I keep from showing it and say, Boys, I think I can fix this. Jimmy looks at Fred, Fred at Jimmy. An eyebrow goes up as if to say, think he can clear this? and they both reach the same conclusion, evident in the downturn at the corners of their mouths and the slight shake of their heads.

Naw, he's screwed.

Nonetheless, I venture inside. I'm actually pretty cool with the situation. Large and in charge, I am confident I can make this whole thing go away till I see Martha sitting in the front row just off the dance floor. As I cross the stage to approach, it's obvious there's only one place for me to sit if I'm going to talk to her and that is off to the left in a chair along the wall. As I get closer, she turns her body to face toward the right.

I sit down.

Martha. I say by way of greeting.

John. She says tersely.

Now normally I get a big smile and a hug from Martha so I have pretty clearly joined the pups in the doghouse over at the Johnson residence. Truth be told, I believe the dogs have pretty much moved into a hotel somewhere and left that big, empty dog house all for me.

I press on.

I understand you're kinda upset with me.

Martha busies herself picking lint and other random bits of invisible stuff off her pant leg.

Mmmm mmm, she says.

Plunging on in, I offer, Martha, if I change the hound dog to Chocolate Lab, do I need to SHOW it to you, or will you just BELIEVE me when I say I made it right?

She considers for a moment.

Well, I reckon it'd be OK if you just tell me it's fixed.

OK then, I push on merrily, happy to have this over with, Consider it fixed! I will fix that tomorrow, first thing, you have my word.

I am rewarded with a blinding smile as Martha turns back toward me.

So how're your folks? she asks pleasantly.

(SEE ALSO: Jimmy Johnson.)

MARTIN BROWN As great a guy and player as Martin is, as great a cinematographer and director as he is, the one thing that impresses me most about Martin Brown is what a great father he is to his two terrific kids, Jamie and Tyler. (A dancer and horn player respectively.) Great husband to wise, wonderful Judy too. For these things above all else, I truly admire and envy him.

www.treehouseproductions.tv
(SEE ALSO: D 35.)

MARTIN GUITARS This here book, like the history
of Bluegrass itself, is full of mentions of Martins and
Martin guitars. There are many popular models of these
fine instruments, but the most common are the D18,
the D28 and the D35. Now I am told that the names for
these guitars came from their actual cost way back in
the late 1800's, early 1900's. I do not know if this is a
true fact, but if it's not, well, it oughta be, cause it sure
feels right and makes a nice story. At any rate ol C. F.
Martin and his boys (and girls) have been makin these
here superior wooden boxes since 1833 based up there
in Nazareth, Pennsylvania. At this point, as is my wont, I
will digress and then get back to the point, what little of
that there is.

When I was a kid, as you might imagine, I got
teased right regular what with a last name like Santa
and all. I may have gotten teased, but one winter it was
a plain nightmare for my dad. He was the traffic and
distribution manager for an aluminum company here
in North Carolina. This is back in the days before cell
phones, way back even before CB radios. In those days,
if you needed to bring a long haul trucker in for an
emergency or something, you would call the Highway
Patrol in whatever state you thought the truck was in
at that point, and they'd put you through to the closest
city you thought the truck to be near, and hopefully
they could flag him down and stop him and deliver
the message: your wife had a baby, the shipment was
canceled, whatever. One December my father shipped
a big load off to upstate New York, with an add on pick
up in West Virginia, so by the time the driver left West
Virginia he was packed to the ceiling and running full

and heavy and haulin it on up to Rochester or wherever,
makin time so he could get on home for Christmas. Well,
it just so happened there was a big sudden snowstorm
what come in and swooped down from Canada and my
father wanted to reach this driver and tell him to turn
back. It was clear the driver would be trapped in the
blizzard either in a hotel room somewhere or in his rig
and be shut down for likely days. The shipment wasn't
crucial, so my dad wanted to bring the driver home
for Christmas and send him back up in the New Year
after the storm had passed and things had cleared up.
Needless to say, as he had done a million times before,
he called the Pennsylvania Highway Patrol office.

   Conversation went something like this:
   Highway Patrol
   Yeah, listen this is John Santa and I've got a truck
somewhere around Nazareth and we got to get a
   Who'd you say this is?
   John Santa.
   SANTA? NAZARETH??
   CLICK.
   Re-dial and do it again, get hung up on again.
   Now my father is tryin to handle other drivers in
similar situations up north so it's not like he is calling
back every ten seconds, but he IS trying to get a call
through to someone who will listen to him in a timely
manner, but in fact time does go by so that when he
gets to calling back, the truck has moved farther on
up the line, closer to the impending storm. So he calls
ANOTHER Highway Patrol Station, a little farther north.
Highway Patrol.
   OK, listen, DON'T HANG UP but my name is
John Santa and I've got a truck headed to Bethlehem, PA
and
(Sound of laughter and troopers voice, off the phone,
yelling to the room:)

Hey boys we got Santa here tryin to get to Bethlehem!!

Sounds of laughter cut off by an abrupt CLICK.

It is sometimes true that no good deed goes unpunished I fear.

OK, two things:

First off, why did my dad keep using his name? Well, like I said, in those days, the managers did this all the time, so he was hoping to get someone he had worked with before, someone he knew. (Keep in mind, the HP flagging down trucks was a courtesy, not a service they were required to perform.)

And yes, my dad finally DID get through to someone who knew him who teased him a time or two about Santa trying to get to Bethlehem and all, and then that kind officer sent a patrol car out and that trucker got turned around and ran his butt on home to his wife and kids and Christmas.

(When you're last name is Santa, that kinda stuff is important to ya.)

So, where were we? Oh yeah, Nazareth and those Martin guitars. Well I reckon they are some finely crafted machines and I am proud to play one and I guess if I'd'a said that up front y'all would be in the "N" or "O" section by now. I apologize for my digression, but hope you enjoyed the Christmas story bout my Old Man all the same.

MCLEANSVILLE Home of many things I am sure, but famous for just one: McLeansville is where you find Brown's Ole Opry.

MEGAN DAY A singer and one of the RDU session players. Part of the backup group "The All Day Sucker Singers" for the way she and Gina Norman sucked on lollipops all day long at the April first RDU/Bluegrass jam. Turned their tongues bright purple and red.

      It was disgusting.

      (And funny as hell.)

MEG SCOTT PHIPPS When I started writing this book, Ms. Phipps had just been elected Agriculture Commissioner for the state of North Carolina. By the time I finished it, she had been removed from office over campaign finance transgressions. All I can say is that she was mighty nice to us pickers that day in Burlington and I will always be grateful, and yeah, I voted for her too. I was sorry to see things go the way they did, and I wish her well.

MEREDITH NICHOLSON An attorney, sometimes singer with the RDU Session Players and wife of Lewis Binkowski. I call her The Judge all the time cause I'm trying to talk her into running for the bench over in Raleigh. We need good, smart, level headed, no BS kinda people wearin them black robes in North Carolina, and she'd be a great addition.

      THIS JUST IN!!

      And as we go to print with this book, Mer and Lewis have entered into God's Great Sleep Deprivation Experiment by giving birth to Xavier Ansel Binkowski, so now they are three.

      (SEE ALSO: Lewis Binkowski.)

www.KurtzandBlum.com

888-505-7780

MINOR AKA Scamp and the Scamper Pup. Can't tell
you all how good friends we have become. Like all good
things, it kinda snuck up on me. I hadn't had Minor but
a bit less than a year and one afternoon my buddy Lewis
Binkowski was over to the house to take a mandolin
lesson. (Well, it started out bein mandolin lessons, then
went to guitar and then a little bass and then back to
mandolin and violin and then back to guitar. At some
point in there, needless to say, he bought himself a
Martin D17 guitar.) We were finishing up after playing
outside for a couple of hours and Blue and Minor were
off lazin in the warm spring grass and last dyin embers
of a beautiful Carolina day. As we were walkin towards
his car I was joshin at Lew about his playin and just
ribbin him in a good natured way and ol Lewis was
teasin back and finally just gave me a playful shove at my
shoulder when outa nowhere there comes this blur flyin
at Lew's leg and I scream NO! as loud as I can and that
white blur veered off and stopped and became Minor
again, just standing there lookin at us, kinda poised
and ready to go again. I reached over real slow and
deliberate like and touched Lewis on the arm and said
See Minor, it's OK, he's a friend, it's OK and the dog
relaxed and laid down in the grass, pretty convinced but
still watchful. Man, I said to Lew, I am so sorry.... he's
NEVER done anything like that before....that was close!
And Lewis turned the back of his leg toward me and
said, You don't know how close and pointed at the wet
mark Minor's saliva had left on his khaki pants. Looks
like you and that dog have gotten pretty tight pretty
quick, he said.

    Kinda in shock I said,
    I reckon so.
    (SEE ALSO: Am7.)

MIXING The act of blending the different musical instruments and voices that come through a PA (short for Public Address) system. There is a real art to mixing music, and there are not many folks who do it really well. In front of you on the sound -or mixing- board are the individual volume controls for all the voices and instruments on stage. A good band that plays with good dynamics can make it real easy on the sound mixer to the point where the sound person just has to gently enhance the mix so the crowd can hear what the musicians intended. But a band that doesn't understand their own sound or dynamics can make being a sound person a nightmare job.

I am of the belief that you can educate a person to do a competent mix, but that you can't teach a person to have ears. The best compliment producers and recording engineers can give a fellow sound tech is that he or she has great "ears."

Imagine my delight that day in Burlington to find Billy Yarborough daughter had ears!

And at only fourteen years old!!

Thanks Kristen!

MRS. CHEWNING My High School English Teacher and a great educator. A huge influence on me along with Doris Betts. This bein a work of fiction and all, I'm gonna tell you a little story, all completely made up of course. Seems I was a Senior at the fabled University of North Carolina at Chapel Hill and I was pretty conflicted: desperate to get out of school, ready to be gone but also apprehensive about what the future would bring. Needless to say, the best way to deal with that kind of dichotomy is to play a bunch of music and go drinkin and carousin with yer friends and so I did my share of that just in a kinda medicinal way, to, you know, ease the pain of transition and all. Seems a paper I was assigned in one of my Journalism classes kinda sorta got away from me and suddenly it was due and was a major part of my grade for the semester, or at least it would be in this purely hypothetical situation I am presenting solely for your edification. Being in a real bind and DEFINITELY needing to not screw this up so I could graduate and all, I pulled out an English paper I wrote in my senior year of high school for my English teacher, Mrs. Chewning. Without changing a word, I re-typed that paper on which I had made an "A-" and handed it in to meet my deadline, or at least that's what happened in this fictional parallel universe of which I speak. Couple weeks later went to get my final grade and pick up my paper and there on the cover was a B+. Four years later, the exact same high school English term paper handed in to a major university and it went from an A- to a B+. Now friends, THAT is what happens when you have a Teacher who demands the best of you.

Wish there were more like her out there, the world would be a whole lot better place.

(SEE ALSO: Yo-Yo Ma.)

MUSIC I know you're sick of me telling you music is a powerful thing and you'd think by now I would be sick a sayin it, but of course I am not. One summer I was down at Emerald Isle, sitting on the front porch, the pups lounging in the lazy shade, all of us enjoying a light breeze off the ocean, me sawing away on my cello, just noodling around randomly, when a family of four starts up that little hot pavement dance we all do as they walk by on the street below on their way to the beach. Now, it's mid afternoon so everybody's in

shorts and swim suits and the two parents are wearing
sunglasses and hats and carrying all the towels and
drinks and toys and chairs they're gonna need for their
young son and daughter. I am sitting up in the shadows
of my porch, about twenty wooden steps and one story
up from street level when the brown haired little girl,
about eight or ten years old, carrying her bright yellow
pail and shovel, suddenly snaps her head up and stops
dead in the middle of the simmering pavement and
begins turning her head in small increments as if aurally
sniffing the air for something she caught a scent of a
second ago. This being Emerald Isle, there is not much
traffic to speak of, so mom is not alarmed and dad and
son just keep on trucking, their fishing rods carried
high and jittery in the air above their heads. I bow out
a few more notes and that little pre-teen girls' stereo
hearing locates me, and her head snaps in my direction
and up, and the next thing I know she is standing at the
top of the stairs as her mom gawks on in amazement
and (probably) horror. My pups, being the great and
conscientious guard dogs that they are, lift their heads
an inch or two in her direction as she stands on that top
step and limply thump the wooden deck a few feeble
times with their tails, drop their heads down with a
sigh, and immediately go back to sleep. I stop playing.
What's that? she says. That there's a dog, I allow cause,
well, you know how I can get. She shakes her head as
if I am sorely trying her patience, her dark brown hair
cascading around her face and points her shovel at me.
No, she says with exasperation, What's THAT?
That's a cello, I say. She considers for a moment.
Vaguely in the background I hear a faint female voice,
Rebekah?.....Rebekah??

    I play violin, she says.
    No you don't, I say.
    Do too.

Nuh uh, I say.

She drops her pail and shovel, turns and races down the rough wooden stairs, past her mom who is halfway up the walkway to the cottage, struggling with her clutter, and runs across the street and into her house. Her mom looks up at me and shrugs a little embarrassed shrug and starts back down the weathered plank walk. A moment later the child I assume to be Rebekah emerges from her house with a slam of the door and lo and behold, she is, in fact, carrying a violin case! She darts past her mom and back up the stairs and, breathless, stands before me and holds out her case and triumphantly says,

Do too.

And I say, Ok, kid, git that fiddle out and let's see whatcha got.

And over her shoulder, as her mother dropped all her tote bags at the bottom of the stairs, I hollered down and said, My name's John Santa. Let me get you some iced tea. I think we're gonna be awhile.

Well, I played music with little Rebekah for AT LEAST two hours every day of the week she was at the beach that year, which is pretty amazing when you consider she was so young and on vacation and all, but we really played well together and I enjoyed her musicality a lot. I got to know her folks, and shared many a glass of tea and a few meals with them as well. In fact, I am STILL friends with the Givens family, dad Thomas and young son Christopher, dogs Neyland and Yoda. AND mom Lori (who plays flute) and Rebekah have even come over and joined the RDU Session Players at a jam or two over the years!

So here is yet another example of why music is a powerful thing: it let me meet a buncha real fine folks and started a musical friendship I hope goes on for many, many more years!

Bluegrass is my Second Language

And lest any of you think ill of Rebekah OR Lori in these often disturbing times, I wanna go on record as saying that Lori and Thomas had walked by my porch on more than a few occasions over the years and tossed up a howdy to me while I was pickin my mandolin or dobro, and Rebekah was and is a sensible, intelligent young lady, and while the pull of that cello might have brung her up the stairs before she could stop herself, she was good about staying back and off the porch till she knew it was safe and her mom said it was ok. And if any of you don't think Lori woulda been up those steps seven times faster than Rebekah was had she thought her daughter was in any danger, well, you just don't know Lori. It is a sad commentary on the times we live in that I have to add this to my little tale, but in some ways, with all that is going wrong in the world every day, it's good for folks to know that even as cautious as we must be, music and goodness can still prevail.

Like I keep saying, we all need to strum harder and sing louder....

MUSICIANS ONLY Well I reckon it is time I fess up to one more inaccuracy. This one's right up there with callin ol Jake a hound dog instead of a Chocolate Lab, and y'all know how THAT turned out....
See the sign there on the wall of the backstage door of Brown's does not, in fact, say "MUSICIANS ONLY.

I lied.

The actual sign was just too long to recite when the point I needed to make there in the story was one of feeling excluded, bein an outsider and more than a little intimidated by the People and Place that Brown's Old Opry was and is.

In the interest of telling the Truth (which my Mama and Doris Betts always told me was the Best

Policy) and in the interest of Full Disclosure, I herewith reveal the actual wordage on the signage at Brown's.

The sign is metal, tin I think, about one foot by one foot, and in large white vinyl stick on letters on that fire engine red background it reads as follows:

DO NOT ENTER

UNLESS YOU ARE
PERFORMING

ON STAGE

This room is too small
for people to congregate

I hope y'all feel better about this now.
I know I do.
(SEE ALSO: Brown's.)

NORTH CAROLINA ALL STAR BAND The performance arm of the RDU jam sessions, the all Stars are a highbred of the best of the Bluegrass players and the best of the RDU players. This group evolved to some extent from Frank Gordon and I playing together. Sometimes Frank and I get paid, sometimes we donate our performance to charity or play for fund raising events. When people wanted a more fleshed out band, I just hand picked players to suit the occasion and it went on from there. The North Carolina All Star Band currently consists of (but is not limited to) the following: Keith Carroll, Pammy Davis, Jen DeMik, Greg Eldred,

Frank Gordon, John Santa, Ray St. Clair, Harry Teuting, Virginia Ward and Jeff Wiseman.

NC 87 The (pre-Bluegrass experience) long road up to Reidsville. I sing about it in "Bluegrass Widows." I have done a buncha soul searchin and contemplation on this road. It's now one of my favorite stretches of road in North Carolina to drive.

ONE All good musicians know where One is. (SEE ALSO: Downbeat.)

ONION HEAD Please don't encourage him.

OVERNIGHT CASE The place where I keep my extra strings, harmonicas, capos, rosin, picks, whatever. OK so it's powder blue and is also called a makeup case or a train case. All my stuff fits in there and its the only thing my mother had, so shoot me.
When she read the book and found out I had stolen it from her she asked for it back.
The nerve.

OUT OF THE BLUE A female a capella group at Duke University in Durham, North Carolina. I worked with this group for over eight years, producing four records with them in that time. I will always be in debt to these wonderful, talented women for a couple a three things (at least). During one of the last recording sessions for the CD "Legacy" (the only Out Of The Blue

CD to ever completely sell out) the ladies gave me a little puppy--a German Shepherd/Labrador Retriever mix that was so small I could hold her in the palms of my hands. I named that little pup Blue in their honor and have cared for her in proxy for all the Out Of The Blue moms from that and subsequent permutations of the group to this very day. Having that little pup led to getting ANOTHER dog, named Seven after the seven graduating seniors that year, the fact that he was the seventh dog I ever owned, he was seven months old and of course, for the Prince song "Seven" that had taken the group all the way to Carnegie Hall via a nation wide competition. So they set me down a road with wonderful dogs who have added greatly to the quality of my life, and they gave me the opportunity to go to Carnegie Hall with them which of course is every musicians dream.

One of the greatest things they gave me is a real love of melody. Before OOTB, I was primarily a rhythm guitar player. I mean I played my share of leads, don't get me wrong, but there is nothing like hanging out with a group of musicians who HAVE no instruments, who create their own rhythm for each song by voice and who are totally focused on the vocal qualities and potential of a song. I really credit Out Of The Blue for my obsession with and dedication to the cello. I knew I could never, ever sing like these gifted women, could never make my voice soar like they could, never achieve the flight of their pure vocals. But with the cello I could achieve the same rarefied atmosphere they knew so well, and it kept me trying and practicing and playing when I might have otherwise given up.

The ladies defied all conventional studio wisdom, which says if you don't get a good take in five or six tries, give up and move on, you're not going to get it that day. I have seen OOTB attempt a song after multiple false starts or errors and then not only achieve the song but really find the heart and the magic and yes, the truth of the piece and just flat nail it. I marvel that these women who went on to be scientists and lawyers and engineers never really understood how truly unique and special their studio experience was. Most of them are not in the music business today, but all of 'em have experiences and memories that many professional musicians will never have, most notably, capturing the pure essence of a song and standing in the studio and recording that song with your entire body tingling, every synapse firing and every neuron in your body KNOWING the song is RIGHT.

All this while sharing that experience with fourteen or fifteen other incredible singers, incredible MUSICIANS, INCREDIBLE FRIENDS.

The time I spent with them was and is some of the most valuable in my musical life. It was an honor to work with them and I am proud to say several of these amazing women have remained my friends over the passing of these many years. In fact, one of those talented women from Out Of The Blue was none other than our very own Jen DeMik.
(SEE ALSO: Jen DeMik, Cello)

PAMMY DAVIS The Queen Of Bluegrass, a fantastic bass player, an incredible dobro player and my good friend. I tease Pammy about how her face must surely hurt after a long night of pickin cause she just smiles this beautific little smile that just gets bigger and bigger as the music gets better and better. At the Marathon Jam she grinned for twelve straight hours! I reckon the only other thing that makes her smile bigger than that is her husband Clyde, but I tell you what: it's a close damn call!

pammydavis@juno.com
(SEE ALSO: Queen of Bluegrass and High
Lonesome Strings.)

PARKINSON'S I hate this disease.

PAUL CYR Ray St. Clair and I were working on a
project over at Videophonics in Raleigh one day several
years ago and when we came back from lunch we were
walking down this long empty hall when we heard some
INCREDIBLE guitar playing. Lots of leads flying around
and some nice chording and really just some VERY tasty
acoustic guitar playing. Naturally, we were wondering
who in the heck was MAKING all this great music
cause, to the best of our knowledge, there weren't any
other guitar players on staff! We snuck up on a closed
office door and peered in through the little rectangular
window and there was our own Paul Cyr strumming
away like a mad man! Soon as he saw us, he turned
bright red, put down that guitar, denied everything
and tried to run, but we cornered him and made him
promise to come over and pick with the RDU Session
Players. Took a while of leaning on him, but he finally
came on over, and now we have the pleasure of listening
to Paulie as he shyly peers over his bifocals and plays
some of the sweetest licks you'll ever hear!

PEABODY The second English Setter I ever owned. A
sweet little guy who is still missed.
(SEE ALSO: Watson.)

PENNY LANE A great song and the street in
Reidsville where Haleyland is located. Y'all need to visit
sometime.

Bluegrass is my Second Language

PIG PICKIN' Now it pains me greatly to have to define this term. I mean I really feel for you poor folks who have not had the great good luck to experience a pig pickin in your life and frankly, I am surprised I have to define it at all, but I do, and here's why:
My buddy Cathy Hackett (who made the wonderful map y'all saw when you first opened this here book) has a friend down in Austin, Texas name a Karen Butler. Cathy got to talking to Karen about my manuscript and drawing me a map and all, and Karen allowed as how she might like to read my little effort! And I thought, wow...this will be great! This woman has no allegiance to me, no reason to lie, nothing to gain and so I will get a completely unbiased reaction and opinion of my book from a totally unsuspecting reader! This will be GREAT!!

See, about this time I was trying to shop this book around and as you well know by now, this is not yer garden-variety kinda ordinary book. It is, in fact, a pretty darn WEIRD book and it was tough to get publishers interested in it and so I had begun to doubt myself. I mean, I thought it was a good book, I really liked it but I'm not sure that was the point. So the idea of testing it out seemed really, really good to me before I expended more time and energy on the darn thing. Consequently, I sent a manuscript down to Karen and waited and waited and finally one evening after a week or so, my phone rings and there on the caller ID it says "Austin, Texas," so I get all excited and worried and happy and I pick up the receiver.

Hello I say and Karen's first words ever to me are, "What's a pig pickin'?"

Now y'all got to remember this is from an area of the country that CLAIMS to be in the South and yet you will be hard pressed to find a glass of sweet iced tea ANYWHERE within the boundaries of the exceedingly large state of Texas!

(I know...I've tried....)

As much as it saddens me, I reckon I shouldn't be too surprised they are culturally deprived in other venues as well. So for all you folks who DON'T know what a pig pickin' is (and by that I mean, all you Yankees and you TEXANS) a pig pickin is a big ass party where a buncha good ol boys get themselves a pig, or a part of pig, but a least enough meat to feed anywhere from twenty five to a hundred folks, and they dress that pig and about three o'clock in the afternoon, they put it in a big black metal cylindrical smoker and then they settle down for the night to baby sit that pig and talk to it and tell it how much we appreciate what that pig gave up for us and what we're gonna eat tomorrow, and they will sit all night long and talk and maybe strum a few songs if so inclined and well, there MAY be some kinda alcohol involved, but that is certainly not required by any means, and them boys will stoke that fire and turn that pig and watch it and stay up all night, even in the cold and the rain, tending the coals and the meat for those of us lucky enough to be invited over the next day. After a good twelve to fifteen hours a cookin, that meat is RIGHT and tender and falling from the bone and thus the term PICKIN': cause you can just pinch you off a good ol hunk of some of the best damn pork you ever tasted in your natural born life. If my mouth wasn't waterin so much right now thinkin about the taste of that succulent hickory smoked pork, I would probably get all teary eyed thinkin about how turrible it must be for those of you who have never experienced a pig pickin in your poor pathetic lives.

PLAY THE RENT The annual gathering at B.J. Parsons where I go to play music for B. J. and Kristen's friends so I can keep my puppy for another year. I used to have to drag Billy Yarborough to it, but now he loves it and considers it as much a tradition and honor as I do. (SEE ALSO: A Minor Seven.)

PORT-O-LETS Someday someone will explain the connection between the coolest Bluegrass hangouts and these contraptions.

Right after they explain what's wrong with the banjo players.

(THE) QUEEN OF BLUEGRASS Pammy Davis is the Queen Of Bluegrass. I know this should technically be in the T section, but there's plenty of stuff in the T section and nothin in the Q section so here we are. pammydavis@juno.com

RAY ST. CLAIR Jeez, don't get me started.....
I mean we could seriously be here all day....
What a great guy, what an incredible friendship this has been. My buddy Ray and I played together for over two decades. He is a brilliant player, a second guitarist of consummate style and grace. What we call in the biz, a "tasty" player, meanin his licks are just so tasteful they make you shake your head in wonder and delight. A second guitarist is the one who pays the fills and runs in and around the vocals. It requires a deft touch and excellent timing, cause too many fills means you're obnoxious, too little means you screwed up and left the song empty. Ray is ALWAYS just right.

Habib once described his voice as a fine red wine--a good Merlot.... It's not the best voice you ever heard, but it's the best voice you ever heard singin the songs he likes to sing and that's a fact. After twenty plus years together we have a kind of shorthand and expectation that makes anticipating what's comin next in a song or a jam session a breeze. When he moved to DC it bout broke my heart thinkin of playin without him over there on my left like he'd been for so many wonderful years. Just makes the times I DO get to make music with him all the more special now.

Sure do miss him though....

grail30@yahoo.com

RDU SESSION PLAYERS This group started many years ago as an off shoot of my wanting to get some studio players together on a semi regular basis to play for fun. We gradually opened the festivities to non-pro players and then beginners and finally to civilians who just wanted to come hear some good music. It literally took years to grow the group, but we now have over a hundred names on our mailing list and are at the point where if everybody DOES in fact show up on the same night, we are in BIG trouble. The name sort of evolved as I guess we had to call ourselves something, or have some kinda name to refer to what it is we're doing. We generally meet the first Saturday of every month and most evenings there's twenty or thirty of us, occasionally there's over fifty and every once in a while there's only three or four. But we ALWAYS have a great time.

REIDSVILLE The epicenter of my spiritual musical journey. Whenever I sing Johnny Cash's "Folsom Prison Blues" I always change the famous "I shot a man in Reno just to watch him die" line to "I shot a Man in Reidsville...."

410

Always gets a laugh

RESONATOR GUITAR Unlike the dreadnought guitars that most Bluegrass players use that get tone and volume from the wood and bracing used in their construction, the resonator gets its tone from the spun metal cone set in its body, giving it a distinctive crisp sound and substantial volume. In the days before amps and PA systems, these were the guitars of choice to play with an orchestra or band. Also known generically -- though incorrectly--as dobros. The Dobrowski Brothers became so famous with their line of resonator guitars that, like Xerox and Kleenex, their brand name became synonymous with the instrument. Trust me, all resonator guitars are NOT Dobros.
    If you don't believe me, just check the price tag....
(SEE ALSO: Donnie Evans, Pammy Davis)

RICK ALLEN AND CINDY BURNHAM Rick is an underwater cinematographer in Fayetteville, North Carolina. He has produced many documentaries, and I've had the privilege to score and sound design quite a few of em. He is married to Cindy, an award winning photographer, who's work has appeared in many places, most notably the cover of "Newsweek" magazine. The only reason Rick hires me to come on down and do some video work or write some music for his documentaries is cause he and Cindy get to missin my dogs a heap and they have to have someone willing to drive them puppies down there so I win.
nautilusvideo@earthlink.net
www.nautilusproductions.com
(SEE ALSO: Honor)

RIFF A line of lead notes, a lick. Originally a blues

term, now used everywhere in street music.
(SEE ALSO: Lick, Street Musicians)

RUTH DISHMAN My blues buddy and soul mate up
at Haleyland. That girl can SING....man oh man.......
(SEE ALSO: Haleyland)

SCAMP OK, I admit it. I actually kinda got to like the
name (particularly Scamper Pup) but I swear to God he
never did respond to it.
(SEE ALSO: MINOR/Am7.)

SCORING Folks don't realize how much music
can effect a movie. The act of composing music to be
played under a particular scene of a film or video (or
commercial, or cartoon...) is called scoring.
I am proud to say I have written music that took films
that were a B average and made them into "A" movies.
Music can do that: it can lift the movie, it can heighten
the emotion and impact of a scene and the apparent
level of acting on the screen.

It can also screw up a movie pretty darn quick if
you're not careful.

It's tricky business, but it's really fun and I love
the challenge every time I do it.

I hardly ever put my projects in for awards, and
I'll tell you why. I scored an independent film called
"Pictures of Helen" by Matt Ferber and there was this
long montage scene toward the middle of the film and
everyone was advising Matt to edit it out, and I told him
to leave it in, let me take a crack at it, I thought I could
show folks how it worked in the movie by the music I

put over it. Well, I did a moody cello quartet over that montage and when Mr. Matt Ferber came to look at his movie he sat in my studio and when the montage came up he began to cry, just sobbed away sitting there in front of the mixing console, tears streaming down his face he loved it so much and was so moved by that scene cause NOW it worked the way he always wanted it to work.

The Writer/Producer of a film sat in my studio and cried over music I wrote.

I produced a recruitment video for the Anesthesiology Department at the University of North Carolina that tripled their enrollment, but more importantly helped bring new and highly skilled doctors to the UNC Hospital system.

If you get sick in Chapel Hill, you will receive better medical care because of a video I produced.

After that, I don't need someone to hand me a piece of metal or a plaque to tell me I done good.

I already know.

SHEPP WASDELL My best friend and my brother, my advisor and confidant, teacher and critic, co-writer and mechanic.

A great husband, father and teacher.

I still miss him and talk to him and need him around every day of my life.

He died in 2001.

SEVEN My second Out Of The Blue dog, my first from the great B. J. Parsons. Like Blue, this dog LOVED music and was at home in recording studios and video editing suites throughout his life.

(SEE ALSO: Blue, B. J. Parsons, Am7, Out of the Blue)

SINGLE (AKA SINGLE KINDA FELLER) Even I am appalled at this patently transparent device to get a damn date.

I am pathetic....

May not really be a factor if Minor continues to jump into my lap from across the room.

(To the best of my knowledge, eunuchs do not date.)

SITAR An eighteen-string instrument native to India that has a tremendous power of emotion because of the startling nuances available in its palette of sounds. My sitar guru is a wonderfully talented and patient woman in Durham, North Carolina named Sudha Iyer. She handles my ridiculous questions with equanimity and ease and guides and nurtures me in subtle, gentle ways that embody her love of music and life.

If y'all get the chance to hear her play, by all means go.

She's really quite amazing.

919-792-0679

sudhaIyer@aol.com

SONNY TERRY Ah, Mr. Terry...

Born Saunders Terrell in 1911 in Greensboro, North Carolina, he lost an eye at five and badly injured the other at sixteen. He picked up a harmonica and changed the world.

Sonny Terry and Brownie McGhee are legends of the Blues idiom.

You know, sometimes I think to myself, it sure is peculiar wonderful how so many talented black men inspired and influenced this little white kid from Pittsburgh, Pennsylvania.

Is this a great country or what?

(SEE ALSO: Leadbelly)

SOUND DESIGN The use and manipulation of sound effects to heighten the drama/impact of a film or video. I scored a documentary for Rick Allen on submarines off the coast of North Carolina in World War II and I matched the sound of bombs and explosions I was adding to archival battle (silent black and white) footage to the pitch of the kettledrums in my symphonic score. It really added to the tension of impending battles as those sounds began to blend through the course of the film. Sound design is like painting with sounds. Along with an effective musical score it can really enhance a project.

SPANKING What all the too loud banjo players need a good one of, but in this case referring to the way Keith Carroll smacks out a bass line when he plays, or what the Queen Of Bluegrass did to my cello when she took it to school one night at Jeff's house in Reidsville.

STANLEY COBB An extremely fortunate man, as he is a courting Miss Lucille Payne. Also a man of discriminating musical taste as he almost always gets me to sing a wonderful Jimmy Rogers song called "Hobo's Meditation" when I'm down at Brown's. He is the grandfather of my dogs. (SEE ALSO: Lucille Payne, Brown's)

STEVIE WONDER A truly gifted musician and composer and a chromatic harmonica player. An early harmonica influence, and a lasting lyrical/song writing influence. (SEE ALSO: TOOTS THIELEMANS.)

STING Usually happens at the end of a song. Everybody beats on the last chord and the lead players riff all over it while the singer thanks Cleveland or whatever town she's in.

Bluegrass players don't usually do this, they like to end things clean. Us city folks know life is never that simple and besides we ALWAYS have more to say.

(Gotta say though, I'm likin those clean endings more and more lately....)
(SEE ALSO: Vamp.)

STREET MUSICIANS The term I coined for non-classically trained musicians, especially the self-taught players. There's a little bit of a thing goin on between the classically trained folks and the street players. When I was comin up, the classical folks were always fairly condescending when we talked music. One of the things I always got was, "Oh, you're a GUITAR player...well, that's a FOLK instrument, you know, ANYONE can play a FOLK instrument..."

The implication being that the oboe or cello was not for the likes of us plain folks. When I got my first cello, I had to confront a lot of that attitude and my own fears and insecurities about music and the playing and attaining of music. I remember drivin home with that cello in the back of my van thinking, What have you done??? You need to have formal training and be able to sight-read music and know the bass clef and wear a tuxedo to play this thing!

But of course I was wrong.

Let me tell y'all something:

ALL instruments are FOLK instruments.

ALL instruments were made by human beings for other human beings to play.

At some point in the learning of the cello, as I stumbled along and laughed at how terrible I was, I had a thought and that thought was this:

I am at least as intelligent as medieval man.

And then I had another thought:

Before there were people in tuxedos telling folks HOW to play these things, how to hold em and bow em and tune em, someone had to first BUILD one and THEN screw around with the dang thing and figure out how to make it work!

And I figured I could do that, cause I figure the first cello construction, many, many years ago, went down somethin like this:

Guy looks at his wife one evening and says, Honey, you know that crate the peaches came in? The one what got smushed in on the sides so now it kinda has a shape just like yours? And you know the cat that died a few days ago? I am thinkin I am gonna take that there crate and I am gonna stretch the intestines of our poor ol dead cat over that crate and then, you know the switch we use on the youngins? Well, I am gonna take that switch and I am gonna chase our plow horse down and tear some hair offa his butt and I'm'a gonna stretch it over that there switch and I am gonna scrape that switch with the horse hair on it over those cat intestines strung up over that crate and it is gonna be so damn pretty it's gonna make you cry.

EVERY instrument is a folk instrument.

And y'know, the cello's not so intimidating when you think of it that way....

THE BEACH Now for you Yankees who might happen to be reading, y'all call it the shore, but we call it the beach, just so we're all on the same page here. (I always figured y'all Yankees call it the SHORE cause it's so crowded up there you barely get to see any actual SAND, you just kinda see the edge of the water as opposed to down here in the south where we call it the BEACH cause it's considered our birthright to feel the sand in your toes, the wind in yer hair (if ya got any) and the sun on yer face. Being of polite society, we keep a minimum of fifty feet between sunbathers unless of course you're family or lookin to cause trouble.)

THE BLUEGRASS BOYS What the RDU players called the pickers from the Piedmont area till some female players started coming up to sing and pick with us. I have to say, they kinda showed our ladies up, cause we don't have many who play an instrument, they mostly just sing. But them Piedmont gals, well they sing AND play. It's pretty cool. They have inspired a bunch of our ladies to take up instruments too.

And just so you know, we call em the Bluegrass FOLKS now....

THE GIRL IN THE CAROLINA BLUE SWEATER Still lookin for her....haven't finished her song yet either....
(SEE ALSO: Single.)

THE MACS: My standing brunch partners every Sunday. They come two to a booth. Like sitting across from the entire chorus of a Greek comedy. The Blue Plate Special: the Gurus over easy. Purveyors of wit, wisdom and wisecracks. The perfect combination over Eggs Benedict. Best enjoyed with some sweet Southern iced tea (with lemon for tartness.)

THE MEDICIS Not sure.....think they're a Bluegrass band outa Kentucky or somewhere.

Heard their records sold right well in Italy a while
back....
(SEE ALSO: Haleyland).

TOOTS THIELEMANS The chromatic harmonica
is different than the type I play. A chromatic has a
little push lever thingy on the side that allows you to
play all the steps and half steps (sharps and flats) of a
scale. Most people don't know what a chromatic harp
is, but they know the SOUND of the chromatic harp
from various records made popular by Stevie Wonder,
cause he played too, but TOOTS THIELEMANS was the
master of the chromatic harmonica. He was a Jazz Man,
and if you weren't listening close, you'd swear that was
a saxophone laying that lead down and dancing all over
the music there, but no, it was just Toots tap dancing his
way through a song like nobody before him and nobody
since.
A true Jazz innovator and genius.
(SEE ALSO: Stevie Wonder.)

TRUTH Seems like we don't see a lot of this much
these days, but you can still hear it and feel it in any of
the music you really love, the music that is played and
written without concern for sales and commerce, but
with dedication to heart and communication. When bad
things happen in the world, I always send out the same
email to the RDU Session Players and all my friends:
We need to sing longer, play louder.

YOU What's the plural of y'all?
All y'all.
God I love that....

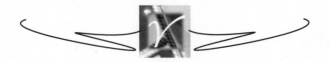

VAMP Often used interchangeably with "sting," it really means just take a few liberties with your lead break and stretch out a bit.
(SEE ALSO: Sting.)

VIDALLIA OK folks, let's move it along....nothin to see here......just move along....nothin to see.......

VIRGINIA WARD Jen DeMik's replacement.

VISIT Now truth be told, there is no real reference for VISIT in the book per se. See, I knew if I put that "Jen's replacement" line up there as the definition for Ms. Ward, well, Virginia would laugh her butt off and Jen would scream, and I mean literally scream right out loud when she sees it. In general I am an awfully nice guy and I can produce witnesses to substantiate that claim, but the idea of Virginia laughin out loud and Jen screechin away out there in California when she gets to readin this, well, it was just too much to pass up and I apologize for that bit of self indulgence though I could also produce witnesses who would say this whole damn book ain't nothin more than self indulgence but I reckon I digress. Ms. Ward was (and is) a singin buddy of Ray St. Clair's, so I'd heard her name (and heard recordings of her) a bunch over the years. When Ray moved to DC, well all us Ray St. Clair junkies were kinda in withdrawal and just mopin around. Virginia and I ended up talkin on the phone connivin a way to induce enough guilt in Ray to get him to move his ass back to North Carolina where, frankly, he belongs. We didn't have a heck of a lot of luck convincing a grown man that our selfish interests should come first and we knew best, so Ray has (thus far) remained in DC. But the cool thing is, from talkin and what not, Virginia and I ended up gettin together and one thing led to another and that thing sorta naturally led to a song and she's been a regular part of our RDU Session Players AND a North Carolina All Star ever since! And the even better news is, Ray KNOWS this and KNOWS he is missin some great music and Virginia and I (and the rest of the All Stars) are by no means done tryin to manipulate Ray to acknowledge our own musically self motivated needs. And I have to say, him knowin we're singin with the girl DOES tend to make him antsy to get on home and hear some of her sweet vocalizations. That said, Virginia is much like Jen in that she too has an angel in her throat and it sure is fun to hear the lovely Ms. Ward sing. Now bein a singer of some renown and excellence she sometimes suffers our, shall we say "extended" instrumental breaks with a sigh and a shrug. We're tryin to teach her what we taught Jen: her voice, her INSTRUMENT and talent INSPIRES us and the breaks are our way of talkin BACK to her, RESPONDING to her, in the language she speaks so well and in which we are surely and sadly lacking. Thus we have to pick up instruments to talk to her. Alas, there are no angels in our throats. The dialogue is so important to us, and I know it is to Virginia, but she's new to our arcane ways, but I tell you what: she is a fast learner and a good teacher. A bunch of us have been so inspired by her singing we've played stuff we never THOUGHT to play before. So we miss Jen, but damn, we're happy to have Ms. Ward lifting her voice with ours.

A truly welcome addition to the music.
Thanks Ray!

WATSON Watson was the first English Setter I
ever owned, though I didn't really own him cause my
girlfriend at the time Donna (we'll skip the last name
cause she might be embarrassed by this story) was the
assistant manager of the Animal Shelter in Chapel Hill
and this dog was due to be put down and Donna, well,
she really loved that boy, and so I agreed to adopt him.
The things you do for love are often the best things you
EVER do, and adopting him was definitely one of the
best things I ever did in my whole life cause Watson
was a great and good true friend and that dog just
WORSHIPPED Donna.

You know, you hear stories about rescued dogs
and how they somehow KNOW they where pulled from
the jaws of death they are so loyal and true. Well, Watson
was like that, both cause he KNEW he was saved by her
but also cause he was just the sweetest boy you'd ever
want to take a walk on the beach with, so full of life and
such a gentleman. He really loved him some Donna, and
that's a fact.

She used to like me to play her to sleep, liked me
to come sit on the edge of the bed and play some soft
guitar or sing an easy song to her to help her slide off to
dreamland with a smile and a good thought. One night I
was in there playin and Donna was long since gone, long
since fast and deeply asleep when Watson sorta strolled
into the bedroom. He looked up, saw me, saw Donna
and hopped, as he did every night, up on the bed to lay
down in the upper left hand corner to snuggle in to go
to sleep. I watched him jump up and land softly, and

422

then, rather than circle around a few times and lay down like he normally did, he stopped half way up the bed and looked at the sound asleep Donna, sprawled under the covers on her stomach, blanket up to her chin, and he stopped there and sat down and looked at me a second and then back at her and, I swear to God, very gently and quietly, so carefully it was obvious he was trying not to wake her, he moved up beside Donna and reached out with his right paw --I almost stopped him but caught myself in time-- and he slowly and ever so delicately lowered himself down beside her with his right arm draped across her back. It seemed like it took an eternity for him to do this, he was so deliberate and slow, so cautious of waking her, and in fact, she never stirred and when at last he was settled in, he looked up at me like, OK, I got her now, you can take a break, I'm on the job. My eyes welled up with tears and I reached out and gave him a gentle, loving pat on the head and caressed my Donna's long blond hair and with a nod to Watson, acknowledged the changing of the guard and took my guitar and went silently into the living room and sat on the couch and thanked God fer lettin me experience somethin like that and just marveled at the beauty and wonder of it all...
(SEE ALSO: Peabody.)

WES LAMBE All through this book I have complained about not being able to find a good left handed mandolin anywhere. After the good folks at Deering started making left handed banjos, I really thought the mandolin companies (or maybe even Deering!!) would follow, but they did not, which is a shame not only for me, but for them, as I think they are missing out on a big share of the market of left handed players out there. I kept looking at old Gibsons and was thinking about getting an "A" style and flipping it and

423

turning it into a left handed model. But for the money it sure seemed a shame to do that and, frankly, I hated the thought of performing surgery on a vintage instrument and I just wasn't happy. Finally I asked Wes Lambe of Wes Lambe Guitars if he would make me a mandolin and he just grinned and said, Sure, no problem. Which was, of course, EXACTLY what I needed and wanted to hear. See Jim Dennis, the owner of the Carrboro Music Loft and a good friend and great picker in his own right, occasionally comes to our RDU jam sessions. Frustrated after a night of trying to compete with all the Martins and Taylors and Deerings, he went to Wes Lamb and said, I want you to make me a cannon. Make me a guitar that can stand up in a big acoustic jam and be counted. And Wes sure did that and more. Made Jim a beautiful guitar that is, well, a damn cannon. Loud as can be with a clean, pure tone. So that's what I told Wes I wanted too: a cannon. A mandolin with a great rich full tone and strong bass, and ol Wes, he didn't even blink, just kept sayin, Uh huh, I can do that ...what else you want from it?

So now the mandolin is pretty much put together and I wish I could tell you how great it is except for one thing: I have no problem at all telling Wes how that mandolin of mine should FEEL in terms of action and the neck and playability. I got no problem telling him how it should SOUND. I just can't for the life of me tell him how it should LOOK, which I know probably sounds stupid (and yeah, well, it IS, kinda) but looks have never been important to me as long as the instrument I am playing SOUNDS great. But this is the first instrument I have ever owned that will be made exclusively for me, and well, I just can't resist the idea of getting me a mandolin that is kinda the equivalent of a beautiful girl in real high heels and a real short skirt drivin around in a red convertible sports car, and though

I can visualize THAT just fine, I shore am havin trouble
seein my damn mandolin! I am pretty frustrated by this
impasse and poor Wes is probably climbin the walls, but
I think I'm starting to see her and how she should look
so hopefully before TOO much longer I'll know what
to tell Wes and put the poor guy outa his misery and let
him (finally!) finish my mandolin for me!

WILL THE CIRCLE BE UNBROKEN The album
by the Nitty Gritty Dirt Band which for all these many
years has been my bible of Bluegrass music. A great work
that still stands up today because it does everything
right: great players all tellin the truth with all their
might. Don't know the subsequent volumes cause I've
always been afraid I'd be disappointed and let down, so
I've never listened, but I sure do love the original....

WILL THE CIRCLE BE UNBROKEN In many
Bluegrass circles, traditionally the last song of the night
and the song I played with Richard McDevvitt and
Ray St. Clair at the open and close of Shepp's funeral
service. (Shepp liked the concept of bookends.)
I never understood the wonder of this song, always
thought it was a cliché until I heard Donnie Evans sing
it one hot summer night on my carport at two thirty in
the morning as we closed out another wonderful session
of music with the RDU players. This was before I had
met Billy Yarborough or any of the Bluegrass folks.
I remember sitting there playing the cello and thinking,
      Oh.
      NOW I understand why this song is an American
Classic.
      I just never heard the right person who felt,
understood, knew and grew up in it, sing it. I had no
idea how much Donnie was preparing me for what was
to come in my life and sure hope to get the chance to

thank him one day. His powerful tenor, ol 1929 Martin D28 and his wonderful sparkling dobro lines were the prep courses I needed to help me feel and "get" the Bluegrass I would experience later.

We sure do miss Donnie.

WINTER Man I hate cold weather.
Y'all remember to feed the birds when it gets cold now, hear?

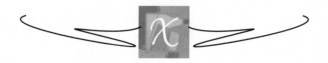

X Bluegrass music is pretty much the antithesis of ANYTHING X rated. In general it's pretty family oriented and its not unusual to see family members from eight or ten on up to eighty or ninety playing and enjoying the music together.

Yo-Yo Ma I got to meet Yo-Yo Ma one evening.
He had the most amazing hands I have ever seen.
My friend Nancy Bolish is the Assistant Director of the Student Union at UNC. One day she called me up and we chatted a while. You see where Yo-Yo Ma is coming to play for the Union Concert Series? she asked. I allowed as how Yes, I did in fact know that and as I am someone who claims to play the cello, I tried to get some tickets to go see him but they sold out in about thirteen and a

half seconds. (For a cellist I reckon goin to see Mr. Ma is like a guitar player goin to see Mr. Chet Atkins. Ya just kinda gotta make the pilgrimage at some point in your life.) Anyway, she says, yeah I figured you might come up short so I pulled two tickets out for you. Well when I finished screaming and hollerin and dancin around the room Nancy said, There's only one condition: I gotta go with you and I said Hell, girl, you're ON! Wouldn't have it any other way!

So we sat all sorta dressed up in the sweet heat of an early fall evening on the campus of the University of North Carolina at Chapel Hill in Memorial Auditorium and Mr. Ma came out on the stage to rousing applause. There was only a gray metal folding chair on the big bare stage and he wore a black tuxedo as he carried his cello and bow out and proceeded to sit down and play and I just melted into the evening and enjoyed the crickets chirping outside the huge auditorium open windows and the rustle of leaves as the too frugal breeze moved on through and though I think Bach might not have approved of the police siren that tried to horn in on one of his pieces, it was really quite exquisite having Mr. Ma play for us, or, as I imagined it pushed back in my padded chair with my eyes closed, my private concert in my back yard. After some mighty fancy bow work there was an intermission, and it was at this point as I was goin on and on about Mr. Ma's performance (y'all know how I can get) that Nancy announced that we MIGHT be able to get back stage and meet Mr. Ma as she had acquired two back stage passes for after the show. Well, after the EMT's had brought me back to life, Ms. Bolish asserted that, once again there were conditions: You must, Nancy explained, tell Yo-Yo Ma that YOU can do two things HE can't do on the cello. I was mute, horrified. One is you must tell him you play the cello essentially backwards as you are left handed and two is you must tell him you can play the harmonica and the cello at the same time. Now friends, there is mute horror and there is mute horror, and I reckon I was experiencing the second kind right then with about all my might. See, telling Mr. Ma that I can do something he can't is not only insane and suicidal in many ways it also virtually GUARANTEES that he will hand me a cello and say Oh yeah? Show me what ya got hot shot! and that would be the point where I would either wither up and die, curl into a fetal ball and whimper mommy mommy, or just jump through the nearest window. And of course, Ms. Bolish knew all this which is why she made the conditions, or pretended to make the conditions cause after letting me sweat (literally) for a few hilarious (in her eyes I'm sure) minutes, she conceded that maybe we could go back stage and just say hi and she might or might not throw down the gauntlet, she'd have to just see how the spirit moved her at the time and with a smug smile she hands me my back stage pass. At this point I am eighty to eighty-five per cent sure she is just kidding so I begin to allow myself to believe I might actually get to meet this guy without humiliating myself after all, and how cool is that providing of course, I don't screw it up by saying something stupid or Nancy can refrain from saying something like, Hey Yo, John here says he can do a few things on the cello you can't.

Dear God.

I decide I need air and hurry up the aisle in the last few moments of intermission to run outside and gulp a few times when who do I see sitting several rows back in the aisle seat over on the right but my High School English Teacher, Mrs. Chewning. I stop and we talk and she is simply over the moon at Mr. Ma's playing and is so in awe of him that I'm about to tell her of my incredible good fortune when the lights dim and

come back up again and so we head to our seats and
sit back down. As the murmuring and soft whispers
begin to abate, I have a thought, a really great thought,
a Wonderful Idea and I lean over to my right towards
Nancy and I mutter, I'm not going to go back stage with
you.

WHAT? she asks and people for several rows
around turn to look in our direction.

Yer gonna take my High School English Teacher
back stage with you instead I say proudly and the
crowd signals their approval of my Wonderful Idea with
tumultuous applause as Mr. Ma coincidentally happens
to come back on stage.

Nancy's face is the dictionary definition of an Oh
Really? look and I settle into my seat, the half time show
completed, eager for the second half to begin.

Well, the boy can play, what else can I say? I
tried to watch him and pick his pocket and learn a few
tricks but he was so fast and so distractingly good, that
I eventually just gave up and settled in to enjoy the
evening and once again closed my eyes and let the music
rinse me down. All too soon it was over and we clapped
and he came back out and played some more and then it
was done and I hustled my butt up the aisle frantically
trying to catch Mrs. Chewning before she could get away.
Wisely, she was waiting in her seat letting the crowd
thin and just drinking in the last few molecules of all
that exquisite music that lingered in the air. I wandered
on up, feeling VERY proud of myself and made some
light conversation about the concert and life in general
savoring the fact that in a minute I was gonna make Mrs.
Chewning just about delirious with joy. And finally as
the ushers began to scatter about the auditorium picking
up programs and the line to get back stage finally started
to move and Nancy gave me the raised eyebrow look

429

from across the hall, I casually asked Mrs. Chewning, my beloved High School English Teacher, the woman who had led me to "The Scarlet Letter" and e.e. cummings, the person who made her classroom a haven where my fellow students and I could be free to be ourselves and express ourselves in the all too conforming and demanding world of high school, I ever so casually asked her if she would like to meet Mr. Yo-Yo Ma and maybe shake his hand.

Now you read the phrase "her eyes got as big as saucers" in books but you rarely get to see it in real life. I got to see it that evening as she nearly keeled over with shock and delight and then as we made our way down toward the line to go back stage, trepidation and doubt that she was worthy to meet this gifted musician, this magnificent artist, began to set in. I assured her there was no one in this great hall more deserving of that singular honor, and so we made our way up to the stairs leading back stage and I introduced her to Nancy and they chatted and laughed and Mrs. Chewning was clearly, delightfully nervous and beside herself and it was too cute and wonderful for me to put into words and I was grinnin from ear to ear and I reckon that rhymes right well with those eyes as big as saucers, but I swear I was. Just as we're about to make the final steps, I hand Mrs. Chewning my pass and begin to back out when Nancy sidles up and hands me HER pass. B-but what about you?? I know you really wanted to meet him...? I plead with her, not wanting to take away her opportunity and more than willing to give mine away to this fine Educator who had such a powerful influence on my life, an all too small price to pay really, when Nancy stuffs her pass in my hand and says, Badges? I don't need no stinkin badges....I'm the Assistant Director! Who's gonna ask ME for a pass?

And in we walked.

Well as you might expect there was a HUGE
crowd of well wishers around this great man and Mrs.
Chewning, wonderfully modest creature that she is,
demurred immediately and allowed as how just gettin
back stage and sippin some champagne punch and
looking and listening to the great one talk in an informal
context was MORE than enough. Nancy shot me a look
that said, Oh no it ain't and we each took an elbow and
began to escort her over to confront The Great One. At
last we pushed our unwilling victim through the jovial
crowd and Mr. Ma looked us over and said Well, what
have we here? and I said, Mr. Ma, this is my High School
English Teacher Mrs. Chewning and I have brought
her back stage to meet you. And he shot me a quick
look like I TOTALLY get this, don't you worry, I got
your back on this one and took Mrs. Chewning's hand
in both of his and looked into her startled brown eyes
and smiled deeply and said, I am honored to meet you
and she bout fainted clear away. And as he was talking
to her about the concert and she was stammering out
her flustered answers I shot an elbow into Nancy's ribs
and whispered Look at his hands look at his hands. And
she looked and they were the most amazing hands I
have ever seen, and I've seen surgeons hands and great
players' hands up close but nobody I ever saw was even
in the neighborhood of how stunningly graceful and flat
MUSICAL his hands were: long, lean fingers that were
fluid and smooth and elegantly powerful. And Nancy
saw and smiled and nodded and then Mr. Ma said to
Mrs. Chewning, You must be very proud of your prize
student here, and Mrs. Chewning said the only complete,
unstuttered sentence she spoke to Mr. Ma when she said
with a gentle grin, Yes, I am, I have ALWAYS been very
proud of him, and my heart about burst.

People were tuggin at him and the handlers were lookin at their watches and the time was close for us to leave and so I asked him quickly if he would sign a program for Mrs. Chewning cause I knew she would NEVER think to ask that of him for herself and so he signed her program and handed it to her and she was effusive and the handlers moved in so I thrust my hand out and said Thank you so much.....for the music, the concert...----and with a glance at Mrs. Chewning----...for everything... and he shook my hand and winked at me as if to say Man I did right good with her didn't I and I smiled my approval and he gave me a big ol grin and then he vanished into the throng.

The crowd kinda moved with him and suddenly we were alone in the middle of the very space that Mr. Ma had given his concert from and we walked Mrs. Chewning back stage left towards the stairs to go on out while she just muttered over and over again, He thanked ME ...he said he was honored to meet ME...I never got to tell him I was honored to meet HIM.....he just said he was honored to meet ME....

I was feelin pretty good about things right then and yes indeed, all was right with the world. You don't often get to say thank you to one of those incredible teachers what gave you so much as a youngin, and I did what I did for me and for all of us lucky but mute students and for all a them teachers out there that might not be fortunate enough to be shown and told just how vitally important what they do is, and how powerful they are in a young life.

Damn, Nancy muttered, and I looked over Mrs. Chewning's brown hair and raised a questioning eyebrow at her.

I was just fixin to tell him about you playin the cello and the harmonica at the same time and they took him away!

A shudder went through me as she grinned at me and started to laugh.

You know, ol Yo is gettin in a heap a trouble fer acknowledging the virtuoso talents of many Bluegrass pickers. I have learned first hand just how true his statements are and can only shake my head in wonder and disappointment at the classical music community that is turning their backs on Yo-Yo Ma and their noses up at the thought that these "untrained" players can be any good.

Well they are.

Y'all git over yerselves.

You go Yo, keep on playin, testifyin and tellin the truth both in your music and in the classroom....
and dude:

I appreciate what you done for me.

I got nothin here; no Z's to speak of.

I hope y'all enjoyed the Glossary, I sure did.
If you got this far, and if you think my humble effort qualifies as a good book, well, the best advice I can give is, now that you got all the back-story, now that you know everything about everybody, go back to Book One and read it again.

Cause like I said, I hate to see a good book end...

ACKNOWLEDGMENTS

Book Two

Glossary

I was driving back from Kinston, NC with Michael Davey, a very talented painter and video editor in early February of 2004 when Michael began giving me some feedback on this book and he said one of the simplest and yet most brilliant things I've ever heard him say.

He said my book needed a map.

A map.

God, ya gotta love that.

A book with a map in it....

How cool is that??

I was so overwhelmed with the rightness of my

book needing and having a map in it, I completely disregarded the fact that Michael is an artist and perfectly capable of drawing a map (I assume, though in truth I have never actually SEEN any cartiological work has he has done), and resolved right then and there to contact my friend Catherine Hackett and ask her to create one for me and the book. Thankfully, Cathy was equal to the task and Michael was and is generous with both his friendship and forgiveness, and so my little book has a map in it to help all of you have some sense of where in the world I am going when I talk about going places and where that is relative to where I live and well, let me just say that one of the keys to being successful is surrounding yourself with really talented and creative people and then stealing their ideas like there is no tomorrow while always remembering to give credit where credit is due!

So thanks for the map idea, painter and freelance video editor Michael Davey of Durham, North Carolina (see map) available for hire.
mdavey00@nc.rr.com

J. J. Love did the cover photo and digitally manipulated the black and white photos Ken Hackney had taken of Blue and Minor at the back door (the famous Musicians' Entrance) down at Browns' Ole Opry that is now the back cover photograph of the book. She also digitally enhanced Cathy's map and, as if THAT were not enough, is responsible for the look and feel of this book as she did the formatting and layout, selecting the fonts and all graphic elements. AND she took all the instrument photos that appear throughout the book. I asked her to take a photo to create the cover for my book, and she (logically enough) said, send it on down to me, let me read it. She called back a few days later and

said, I have the cover of your book. Cynic that I am, I
said, Have you finished the book already? and she said,
No. I said, What page are you on? And she said Twenty
and I said, You don't have the cover of my book.

Yes I do.

No way.

Yes I do.

I said, If you've got the cover to my book in twenty
pages, I'll buy you a lobster dinner!

She said, Great, let's go eat.

Send it to me.

Ok, check your email, I'll send it up.

The next day I opened my email and there was her
fantastic photo of the Blue Mandolin and I sent her a
one line email that read:

When should I pick you up and where do you
want to go?
mwkdesigns@gmail.com
www.wmkdesigns.com

I wish I could credit somebody with the idea for
the Glossary, but I can't. It was mine and I am right
proud of it, though I guess Edward Wasdell can take
some inadvertent credit for it.

See, when I was at Carolina his dad Shepp gave
me this huge thick book called "Dune" by Frank Herbert
and said I needed to read it. I did and loved it, loved
the vivid detail of the world this man of great talent and
imagination created. Couple a decades later we're sittin
around on the porch at Emerald Isle, Shepp and Edward
and I, talkin about books and music and somehow
"Dune" came up and Edward allowed as how he had
never read it. Well, as you might imagine, the idea of
returning the favor his father had done for me so many
years ago greatly appealed to me, so I ran out later that
afternoon and bought the book and gave it to Edward

as a gift. That started a nice tradition because Frank Herbert's son Brian continued the science fiction series his father had created by writing sequels and prequels to the "Dune" saga along with his friend Kevin, and I was able to give one to Edward every Christmas for many years, including the one just past.

Point is, I finished reading the latest prequel and turned the page to find a glossary and began to read and suddenly was hit between the eyes with the thought that my book needed a glossary of its own, but being that this is MY book, it would be a twisted kinda glossary with definitions that went on for pages sometimes as I found it to be a wonderful repository for the tales that wouldn't fit into Book One OR Book Two.

I really like it and hope you do too, so thanks to Frank Herbert, Shepp and Edward Wasdell, and Brian Herbert and Kevin J. Anderson.

Poor Coke Arial.

We were comin back from Hampton, Virginia, after a week long shoot and Martin and I decided to pass the five hour drive with a little home made music, so as Coke drove and Martin and I contorted our bodies into shapes that would allow our instruments to fit inside the van, we picked and grinned and sang a bunch of songs and somewhere in there we allowed as how, yes, it was to help us pass the time and the monotony of the ride, but it was also our way of thankin him for the wonderful line he had given us while on the drive up to DC for the first leg of our shoot for the VA Hospitals. We were talkin about my book and music and the power a song has and Coke just said, Well, you know, that is the blessing of the strings isn't it? And I said Jeez Coke, that's just beautiful, I need to put that in my book or write a song with it or somethin, it's just so perfect. And Martin high fived him and Coke grinned as it sorta struck him that, yeah, it IS a great line, isn't it?

Sure is.

Thanks, Coke.

My eternal thanks and gratitude go to Theresa Sull, a Chapel Hill writer who not only encouraged me, but also sent me home with a sack full of articles, magazines and books on writing. Her encouragement and faith was overwhelming and I learned a lot from the advice and articles she gave me. Belief and guidance at the very beginning is crucially important, and she was there for me in a BIG way.

Pammy Davis, The Queen of Bluegrass, needs to be acknowledged here as well. She was so supportive of my feeble efforts, so positive in her attitude and feedback that I owe her a lot more than thanks. Over time she became my Bluegrass Fact Checker: corrector of misspelled names, places, distances (I'm topographically challenged as y'all know) and musical terms. She was (and is) an inspiration in the way she loves and plays music too, and when I talk about how honored I am to have her attend our RDU Session jams, and play with her in The North Carolina All Star Band, well, it's more than just words. She and Keith, Greg and Jeff have been my staunchest supporters, both of this book and my music and I'm proud to call them friends and humbled every time I take a stage with them.

Boy, God bless Carlean Moser! She volunteered to take an edit pencil to my book, and while I didn't always agree with her changes, I LOVED the way she made me justify any choice I made and the way she held me to such a high standard.

If you had problems with the writing in sections of this book it is undoubtedly where I chose to ignore Carlean's sage advice. This was a HARD book for an editor. I drove her NUTS. I ignore punctuation in favor of flow and convention in favor of feel, an editor's nightmare. Her work was excellent and the experience a great writing lesson, which is as it should be. Once again, the solid passages are hers, the weak ones mine.

If you see her, give her a pat on the back.

This may surprise you, but I am not always easy to work with.

carlean@blessyourheartmusic.com

www.blessyourheartmusic.com

I love to read this book out loud.

It being a book about music, I wanted it to have a rhythm and flow and I feel pretty good about capturing the tempos and dynamics of music in this bit of prose I have created, and I reckon I might shoulda told y'all to read it out loud a whole lot earlier than the almost end, but I DID leave you little clues lyin around. Throughout the book there are fragments of lines from various songs, Bluegrass or Otherwise. The most flagrant example was at the end of Book One on page 115 when I talk about my windshield wipers clappin time, an obvious (I hope) reference to Kris Kristofferson's famous song, "Bobby McGee." If these references tripped you up, well then I am sorry, for my idea was to pay homage to these compositions and their great lines and the talented writers who penned them, and also have them lend their inherent musicality to my feeble efforts. So I hope you caught them, hope they made you smile like sorta runnin across an old friend in an unexpected place, unless, of course, you're upset that I quoted your song in my book and you think you might like to sue me, in which case, I deny doing any of that stuff I mentioned above.

This is, you'll recall, a work of fiction after all...

One person who really needs to be thanked in this book is Doris Betts. Her name keeps coming up in these pages and there's a good reason for that:

She's a great teacher.

When I write, whether lyrics or prose (and even sometimes music) I hear the mantra from her writing classes:

DOES IT WORK, DO YOU NEED IT?

IS THERE FAT IN THE COPY?

and most importantly

SHOW, DON'T TELL

It gets crowded sometimes with her standing over one metaphorical shoulder asking those questions of my writing and Shepp looking over the other going, That's just lazy, you can do better than that, and Whoa, GOOD one! when I get it right.

Crowded but I wouldn't have it any other way, and if there IS fat in the copy, if I didn't show, if it didn't work, well it wasn't from any lacking on the part of Shepp and Doris, I assure you. The successes of this book (if any) are truly theirs, the failures solely mine.

I emailed Doris after I'd written about forty pages to say, Look, is this any good, should I keep on with this or am I just kidding myself? I felt I was too close to it and desperately wanted to send her what I had done and get her opinion.

She adamantly refused to look at anything.

Send it to me when it's done, she said, I am not in the habit of judging a baby's appearance based on one arm or leg.

Send it when it's done.

When I expressed some frustration at this, she asked,

If I told you to stop writing, would you?

Well, this here MIGHT be a case where having a tremendous amount of respect for a teacher and friend is a NOT so good thing cause, to be honest, my gut answer was,

Well, yeah...HELL yeah!

Course I didn't tell HER that, but yeah, I woulda stopped.

Well, maybe.

I think I would have wanted to know what about it DIDN'T work. Having learned that from her I guess it's a coin toss as to whether I would have pushed on or not. Always teaching, (the great ones always are) she taught me an important lesson: be yourself, trust yourself. The book was gonna sink or swim on my efforts, my voice, my structure, my stories told my way. In the long run, it didn't matter what anyone else thought, I either did it or not. Don't mean to sound like such a hero, cause believe me, there were plenty of days where her gentle emails of encouragement and support got me back to the computer to go at it again. And that I guess is the true talent and gift of Doris Betts. She has always made me feel special and important, always made me feel REMEMBERED from the literally thousands of students she's had over the years.

Now THAT is a gift.

And you know what?
I bet ALL her students feel like that.
A rare gift indeed....
So here's to you DB, squirming in your seat reading this and being embarrassed and trying to figure out how to get me to cut it from the book, here's to you my teacher, my friend, my mentor.

I sure am glad I walked into that Lit class in Greenlaw that day....

Bluegrass is my Second Language

THE GLOSSARY

is dedicated to all my Teachers, but especially:

Mrs. Gertrude Chewning

and

Ms. Doris Betts

BOOK TWO

is respectfully dedicated to the memory of

Shepp Wasdell

Clyde Alexander "Trey" Cheek, III

Daniel Brown

Jonathan Chilton

Ann Stanley Carpenter

J.R. Dennis

Andrew Kaplan, MD

Gillman Cyr

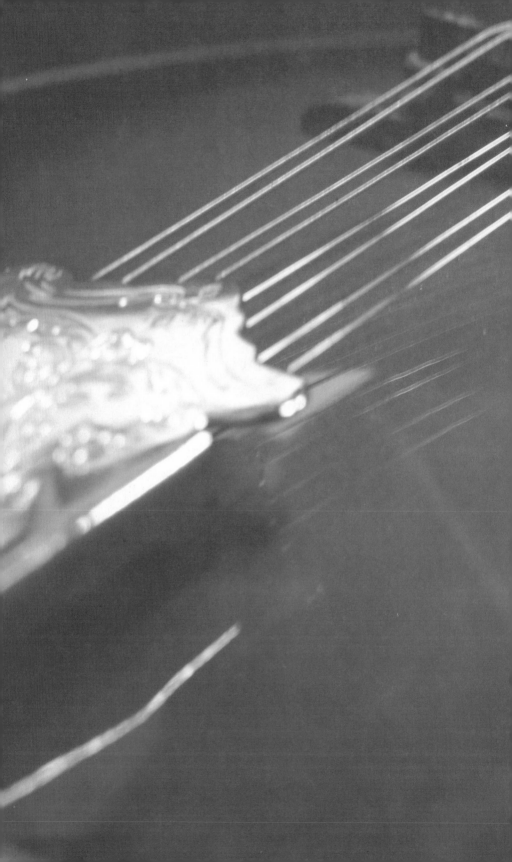

Shameless Plugs

SHAMELESS PLUGS

I have tried wherever possible to include a way for you to get in touch with some of these good people and places I have written about in this here little book of mine. On the following pages I have listed some contact info for people and places I just want to acknowledge as among the best in North Carolina in my humble opinion.

Allen and Son Bar-B-Que
5650 US 15-501, Pittsboro, NC
6203 Mill House Road
Chapel Hill, NC
Man, this place has the best damn BBQ in North Carolina, bar none. Two locations, one outside of Pittsboro and one on NC 86 just north of Chapel Hill. Seems like there's a bit of a competition between these two in that there ARE some local differences. For instance, I particularly like the slaw (little bit of oregano in there??) and the hush puppies at the north Chapel Hill location, but the meat seems to be a little leaner down in Pittsboro. Honestly, you can't lose at either place and I'd be hard pressed to pick a favorite.
On a personal note, just wanna say that as many years as I been coming here, I have yet to see any of the sons anywhere, but I reckon I enjoy looking at the DAUGHTERS that work there a whole lot more anyway.
Come hungry.
Pittsboro   919-542-2294
Chapel Hill 919-942-7576

446

Beauty Meets The Beast
112 West Main Street
Carrboro, NC

Now in the Interest of Full Disclosure, I need to warn you that if you go into this establishment you are liable to be accosted by Beth Johnston, the owner and head groomer, about buying a copy of this here book you are currently holding in yer hands. Just tell her I sent ya, and she'll calm down. (Be nice to her: she can't help it. She was a BIG fan of the book and read some of the first drafts early on.)

Beth is the ONLY groomer I have EVER trusted Minor to in the whole time he has been with me! That I guess is the best recommendation I can give other than to add the following for the guitar pickers out there: Beth's place is right beside the Music Loft in Carrboro, so come early for yer dog pick up and go over and strum a while with the guys at the Loft and then go over and see what a great job Beth did on yer pup! She is a very talented and dedicated Professional, VERY meticulous and caring, very loving with the animals and always does a stellar job!

That said, I really can't stop before I embarrass Beth a little bit.

See, when I first gave her a copy of my manuscript (she'd heard from the guys at Loft I was writing a book and bugged me till I brought her a copy) she read it and called me to come pick it up. I went in and said what did you think? And after a while of her saying she loved it and stuff I FINALLY got her to admit the following: "Well," she said, "It WAS a little bit slow at the beginning with all that music stuff and all, but once you got to the part about the DOGS... WOW! That book REALLY took off!"

Once a Groomer, always a Groomer I reckon.

447

yankeebikahchic@yahoo.com
919-967-7593

Calvander Crossroads Grill And Service Station
108 Dairyland Road, Chapel Hill, NC

For the best biscuits in North Carolina get there before 11 AM Monday through Saturday when Miz Thelma serves em up fresh. Plan to stay awhile cause the show is about as good as the food. Get you a drink (fountain, can, or bottle) and lean on the counter while Rhonda, Linda and Cheryl toss little one liners at the men who come in and pick at each other all day long as only truly good friends can.

Nickie is new but seems to be holding her own just fine. Grab a newspaper from the machines outside (my mom helps keep the Herald Sun in good supply there by buggin the delivery guys) and pretend to read while these great ladies cook up food and humor and serve it to a willing, respectful, hungry, and grateful crowd. Mr. Glenn keeps the lot outside cleaner than any gas station/food mart you ever drove onto and he'll tell you joke now and then too. Wednesday is spaghetti day and you can get a big ol plate of spaghetti just about as good as any you're gonna eat at half the price! If you head over there, do me a favor and do what I do when I leave: just before you step out the door holler out: "Thanks for the good food Ladies!"
They get a kick outa that.
919-942-8225

Coast Guard Station Elizabeth City, NC
The United States Coast Guard
Elizabeth City, NC

I'm putting the Coast Guard in my Shameless Plugs section for two reasons:
One because I have filmed at the station in

Elizabeth City and I have seen the kind of training
the dedicated men and women of the Coast Guard go
through and trust me, you don't wanna mess with the
Coast Guard!

But mostly I just wanna thank them cause while
most folks sat around in the aftermath of hurricane
Katrina with their thumbs up their butts waiting for
"orders," the United States Coast Guard went out and
did what they were supposed to do after the shores of
the United States had been attacked by a deadly menace:
They went out and RESCUED people.
They went out and SAVED LIVES.
They didn't wait for "orders."
They have standing orders:
RESCUE.
PROTECT.
SERVE.
The Men and Women of the United States Coast
Guard just plain KICK ASS.
Rock on Coasties, rock on…
And thanks…
252-335-6540

Dr. Philip G. Boysen
University of North Carolina
The former Chair of the Department of
Anesthesiology, he is now the Executive Associate Dean
for Graduate Medical Education for the Medical School
at UNC Chapel Hill. We've made quite a few videos
together, a lot of em pretty darn good, most notably the
award winning "Collateral Damage: Drug Abuse and
Anesthesiology."

He is a great man and a total class act and I am
proud to call him a friend. Our regular dinner sessions
together are a particular delight in my life and I look
forward to many more. A Florida import, his blood now

runs pure Carolina Blue and that's a fact.

If you need some medical advice, or a good Anesthesiologist, or if you're a doc with a substance abuse problem and don't know where to turn, this is the guy to call.
pboysen@aims.unc.edu
919-966-1586

Dr. Mark Stacey
Duke University Medical Center
932 Morreene Road, Durham, NC

I met Mark on a shoot a few years ago and he was so amazing I stepped out in front of the camera and asked him to be my dad's doctor. Well, like a lotta folks, he shoulda called security to have me removed, but God bless em, he didn't so all these many years later he is still stuck with me and more importantly my dad still has this gifted, humane, generous, funny and talented man as his primary Parkinson's physician.

Folks, if you or anyone you love has this terrible disease, I can think of no better person to treat your Parkinson's than Mark Stacy.

(And yes, not one to let a major neurological disease get in the way of a little college rivalry, my dad lords it over me that Mark is affiliated with Duke, NOT Carolina.)

PS

The Duke thing is, as near as I can tell, Mark's only character flaw.
mark.stacy@duke.edu
919-668-2493

Dr. Mark Williams
Box 466 Hospital Drive
Charlottesville, VA.

A talented physician who specializes in geriatric medicine. If you've got some aging parents, get a hold

450

of his book, "The American Geriatrics Society's Guide
To Aging And Health" which is, in fact, a great guide
to aging and health problems. (Heck…we're all gettin
older—grab a copy for yourself too!)
aging@virginia.edu
804-243-4851

East Franklin Car Care
1710 East Franklin Street, Chapel Hill
    Ok…. so I've told some pretty good stories in this
here little book, but let me tell you how my life REALLY
is. I am the guy you're behind in line at the supermarket
when the cash register tape runs out or when it's raining
and there's a long line and the ATM machine crashes.
I'm the guy that makes everyone wait at the dry cleaners
cause for reasons they just don't understand, while we
DO have a record of your laundry being left with us Mr.
Santa, we um…can't seem to FIND said laundry.
THIS is my true lot in life.
    One Saturday afternoon I'm loading my
instruments into the van cause EIGHTwentythree has
a gig that evening when I notice I have a flat front tire.
With a sigh and a few bad words (sorry ma) I go to work
there in the carport and jack the car up and change the
tire out and put on the spare and drive off to get the
tire fixed. I go to a place downtown and they find a nail,
pull it and plug the tire, take off the spare and put on
the repaired tire and with ANOTHER sigh (this one of
relief), off I go back home where I shower off the dirt
and bad attitude and finish preparing for the evening
gig.
Hour and a half later I emerge rested, freshly scrubbed
and ready for an evening of music with my talented
compatriots but when I begin to load the pups in the
van I see, much to my dismay and with a flurry of not so
nice words, (sorry again ma) that my REAR tire is almost

451

flat!!!

Grrrrrrr.

Not wanting to get all sweaty and stuff again, I break out an air compressor and, gambling that this is a SLOW leak, hook it up to the sagging tire in the hopes I can DRIVE the bad tire to a service station to get it fixed. While the dogs look on in amusement, I finally get the tire pressure back up and throw the pump in the back seat with Minor and hop in and quickly (but safely!) drive to downtown Chapel Hill. But this being MY life, this is the first May weekend after school at UNC Chapel Hill has let out, all the students are gone, summer school hasn't started yet and so
ALL THE SERVICE STATIONS ARE CLOSED!!!

In fact, at seven PM on a Saturday night, the impossible has happened: there is hardly a single place open ANYWHERE downtown, let ALONE a service station!

Fuming, I drive down Franklin Street and head east toward the edge of town and Durham frantically praying my tire is not going to go flat on me and also praying I can find somewhere to fix this tire so I can get to my evening gig. Station after station is closed until, at last, there, like a shining castle in the sky, a city of Hope, was East Franklin Car Care and THE GARAGE DOORS TO THE CASTLE ARE UP which means they're either open or being robbed and thank God they are in fact open! I pull in and explain my situation to two guys working on a car up on a lift in the bay. They say, sure, we can set you right up and then begin talking and tinkering again on the problem confronting them before I showed up.

I pace a little.

I try to be patient.

But the clock is ticking so I head back into the bay.

Bluegrass is my Second Language

"Fellers. " I say shyly," I don't mean to be ungrateful, I mean, I am REALLY happy y'all are here and can help me and all, but if you don't get that tire fixed so I can get to Greensboro, there's gonna be a Bluegrass band playing without a mandolin player tonight."

They both stop and regard me for a second and then one says, Man, we're sorry, I'll get right on that for ya, and the other says, Nah, I got it and as he wipes his hands on a little pink rag he walks out toward my car where I point out the offending tire and thank him profusely. He jacks my car up and proceeds to wet down the tire with soapy water to find the leak (on the rim to save time — good man!!) and as he's spinnin that shiny black tire and wettin it down, half out of curiousity and half outa just tryin to get me to stop apologizing he stuns me when he says to me:

"What's a mandolin?"

I just look at him.

"Yer kiddin," I say.

"Naw..." he answers as he finds the hissing spot and marks it with chalk, "Seriously.... what's a mandolin? Don't believe I've ever heard one."

So as he ambles over to the stack of greasy red drawers by the bay door to get a plug, I go to the rear of the van, pop the hatch and pull out my case, open it and strap on the Blue Mandolin.

And that is how I came to serenade my mechanic while he fixed the tire on my car so I could get to my gig in Greensboro. He liked my playing so much I even broke out a harmonica and played a harmonica and mandolin tune for those boys while they worked. At the end, when the tire was fixed, he smiled a big ol smile and said, "Wow...that was great. Thanks. I believe maybe I HAVE heard that instrument before but I sure never seen one, and certainly never seen one or heard one up close like this before, so thanks."

I paid up and went safely on my way on my newly repaired tire, but I musta run through a construction sight or had a string of REALLY bad luck or somethin cause I was back seeing them boys about five or six times in the next week or two getting my flat tires fixed and you know what?

They were ALWAYS open. ALWAYS friendly. ALWAYS prompt and ALWAYS did good work, God bless em!

So here's my thanks to Kelly Delosh, Chris Bassett and owner/manager Ronald Ragan.

Y'all boys are the best.

DAY: 919-942-4284   **Night: 919-942-7676**

Helen Spielman, M.A.
Performance Anxiety Counseling

Now I have not availed myself of this here service cause, as y'all can tell, I am not one to be shy or fearful when it comes to bein on stage! And if I was, well, old Blue would always be willin to go on out there first and break the ice for me and let me know where to set up. But I know a buncha folks what were excited to hear about Helen offering this counseling and I think it's a good thing and I urge any of you who struggle with public speaking or stage fright to check this out! Helen, by the way, is the wife of Dr. Fred Spielman, a REALLY good guy and the Vice Chair of Faculty Recruitment for the Anesthesiology Department at UNC. He has appeared in several videos I've produced as an expert, teacher, mentor AND an historian! He's got a GREAT slide show presentation on Anesthesia through the ages that I just LOVE (did y'all know the ancient Egyptians performed BRAIN SURGERY???) and I am constantly looking for funding to turn it into an hour-long PBS documentary, so if you got any connections, get in touch!

Bluegrass is my Second Language

(Come to think on it, we probably ought to do a video on performance anxiety TOO...)
hbs@email.unc.edu
www.unc.edu/~hbs

Jay Miller
Former owner of about a million Music Lofts all over the state of North Carolina, he sold his stores off to his managers and is now doing a lot of work giving back to the community. A truly great guy, largely unsung in his roll of supporting and assisting many struggling musicans in their careers (including mine.) His former employees have toured with Sting, been on the Tonight Show, played on Broadway, written music for commercials played during the Super Bowl, played on hundreds if not thousands of records, film scores and commercials, and one of em even wrote a damn book!

Back when he owned the Durham store, Jay and I used to drive his accountant crazy cause we never in all the years we did business together ever signed a single piece of paper, and believe me, I have bought me some EXPENSIVE equipment and instruments from this guy over the decades of our friendship! All our deals were always done with a handshake and a smile, and I never, EVER had a single problem or misunderstanding with him. Those ways of doing business are probably gone now, but it still amazes me we did all that work on a handshake only for all those years.
nonprofit@sharedvision.org
www.sharedvision.org

John and Margie Labadie
Dept. of Digital Media
University of North Carolina, Pembroke
There's some pretty cool stuff going on down there in eastern North Carolina and John and Margie as

455

well as the other Professors of Digital Media, Dr. Larry
Arnold and George Johnson, are behind a lot of it! One
of the Labadie's own graduates, J.J. Love, designed all
the visual elements of this very book you're holding!
Another former student, Gina Gibson, designed the
cover and inserts for "Collateral Damage," an award
winning video I produced. Lots of talent down there
and if you're into art and digital media, you should
check it out! Been my pleasure to teach a buncha film
seminars over the years down at Pembroke, something
I ALWAYS enjoy and look forward to immensely. It's
also been my honor to teach a few Master's Classes
there with Dr. Larry Arnold and we've spent more
than a few late nights making some mighty fine music
after those classes! I can certainly testify to his acumen
when it comes to Music in general and the upright bass
in specific. A nice feller name a James Thomas outa
Los Angeles has been a real patron to the Pembroke
Business School AND the Digital Media Department. His
support of the Digital Professors has meant more than
he'll ever know and you should keep an eye on UNC
Pembroke cause some exciting things are happening
there!
Labadie@uncp.edu

Kanoga Animal Clinic
704 Kanoga Road
Hendersonville, NC
        This is B.J. Parsons' veterinary clinic up there
in Western North Carolina. B.J. has given me a little
help with Blue over the years and of course, she is
responsible for me having Seven and Minor, and trust
me, I've seen how she cares for her pups and you could
not find a more caring or dedicated animal physician
anywhere! She is so good and generous, she has asked
that I publish the English Setter Rescue organization

she endorses, so if you want a loving dog with a gentle temperament that's great with kids and got a whole buncha love to give, do yerself a favor and go git you an English Setter!
www.kanogaanimalclinic.com
828-692-0941

Above and Beyond English Setter Rescue
www.esrescue.org

Kristen Mooney
I've talked a fair amount about B.J.'s daughter Kristen. She does a GREAT job showing Setters and has, as you would suspect, a real gift for animals. (Wonder who she got THAT from??) If you need some help showing or training your pup, give her a holler at
sportypoo@aol.com
And I would consider it a PERSONAL favor if you would give her some grief over that email address. Sportypoo???

Paula Shelton
Jostens Publishing
2505 Empire Drive
Winston Salem, NC
I need to start this off by acknowledging a guitar player named Ed Sullivan down in Greensboro, NC, cause he was the one who introduced me to Paula and boy did he do me a great favor THAT day!!
(Next time we go to lunch, order the lobster Ed, cause I owe ya!)
Paula has been MAGNIFICENT through this whole publishing process. She REALLY knows her stuff and is not only a topnotch publishing professional, but also a really genuine, caring, sweet person. She made

457

this whole task, which COULD have been painful and scary, a real pleasure.

Could not recommend this woman or this company more highly.
paula.shelton@jostens.com
336-774-7337
800-669-6783

Serv-U-Servicenter
227 Hwy 100 West
Gibsonville, NC
OK, here's the deal: you're gonna have to sit around for several hours while you get your car worked on, no matter what, right? So if that's the case, why not take your car someplace where you can sit and pick a few tunes with the other patrons while you wait?? Just don't be surprised if owner Mike Whittington doesn't stroll on in the "customer lounge" and pull out his guitar and pick a few WITH you while you wait!! (But you right handed folks take yer own guitar down there, don't think you can play his cause, like me, Mike is NORMAL and of course by that I mean LEFT HANDED and plays (like me) a LEFT HANDED Martin!)

First time I went down there, Mike changed the oil in my car, fixed a broken electric window in my van, rotated the tires and lubed the chassis. When presented with the bill, I asked him if he'd given me the musician's discount. Nope, he answered. Well a friend's discount? No again. Well how about a left-handed guitar player discount? Naw, he said, the price is the price. And I said, Well you did all that work and yet you're charging me what I would pay for just an OIL CHANGE up in Chapel Hill!

John, he said as he patted me on the shoulder, That's cause you live in Chapel Hill where a dollar buys a quarter, but now you're in Gibsonville where a dollar still buys a dollar.

There's some wisdom in that....

Y'all come gitcher car fixed and pick a few.

336-449-4515

Soldiers
All Across The United States

Regardless of your politics, you gotta acknowledge the debt we owe these men and women who are coming home or gonna come back home, many of whom, God bless em, are gonna be injured.

Injured or not, we have an obligation to provide for these brave folks who gave so much to care for them FOR THE REST OF THEIR LIVES. And that doesn't just mean Soldiers from the current conflicts, that's for Soldiers involved in EVERY war, every deployment.

They say all politics is local and I believe that, so this is the question I ask of every politician who wants my vote:

Would you vote for a bill that would designate money for Veteran facilities and Veteran care, even if it meant raising my taxes?

And if they say, "No," then I won't vote for em.

If higher taxes are what it takes, then paying taxes to care for all these Soldiers is MY patriotic duty.

It's that simple.

The Music Loft
116 West Main Street, Carrboro, NC

Jim Dennis is the owner of this eclectic little music shop, and if you're a player, you owe it to yourself to come visit. They have a really wonderful staff of VERY gifted musicians. Ask for Ted, Lance, Patrick or...wait...it doesn't matter! Ask for ANYONE...they're ALL great players and all know the merchandise from a "sales" AND "use" stand point since they are all performing musicians. A while back Jim and Darrell Young, owner of Reel Time electronic repair, merged and Darrell moved into the Carrboro location. Darrell does GREAT work and has fixed a BUNCHA my stuff, always fast, accurate and VERY fairly priced. He's a great addition down there. I highly recommend this store to anyone looking for an instrument or advice. A really friendly and knowledgeable staff and they get a lot of letters and feedback from the women who come in saying they feel particularly comfortable asking questions or buying here. Beginner or pro, y'all come!

Jim Dennis is also a great guitarist and a member of the RDU Session Players. When Jim took over the Loft several years ago, Jay Miller introduced him to me and we've gone on to become good friends and pickin buddies since then.

It was my great honor to be a pallbearer when Jim's dad, J. R. Dennis, died in 2006.

www.musicloft.com
919-968-4411

The Vet Center
Bereavement Counseling
1649 Old Louisburg Rd.
Raleigh, NC

One of the great things about my job is getting paid to learn about amazing places like the Vet Center in Raleigh. So many of our troops are coming home broken, or not coming home at all, and this Center and others like it around the country are there to try to help the families who lost their loved ones. There were a lot of truly caring people at the Center the day we filmed, but I spent most of that day with Dr. Greg Inman, the Team Leader in Raleigh, and I KNOW he's good cause I saw him work and I spent time with him. If you're in pain because of the loss of a soldier, no matter which branch of service, no matter which war, from WW II to the present conflicts, you can come and get help from docs who are actual veterans.

We spent a few days with Betsy and Randy Beard whose son, Spec. Bradley Scott Beard, was killed in action in Iraq in 2004. Theirs is a painful journey from which there is no recovery, only constant repair and it's important we let them know we have not forgotten them. To that end, I ask that you pickers out there dedicate a song to Brad every once in a while. Just send one out there for him, and for Betsy and Randy and their daughter Staci. And you non-pickers too, y'all raise a glass and honor this man, this son, and the brave parents who soldier on.

My support for the Vet Center means exactly NOTHING, but I can tell you Randy, Staci and Betsy hold the Center and Greg in high regard.

There can be no higher recommendation.
919-856-4616

UNC Department of Anesthesiology
University of North Carolina at Chapel Hill
Chapel Hill, NC

You've probably noticed there's a buncha docs in this section, and more than a few of 'em are Anesthesiologists! It's been my privilege to be associated with the Anesthesiology department at Chapel Hill since 1999, and as we go to press, I am currently producing a recruitment video for the department via Dr. Luke Lucas and Chapel Hill icon (and department Chairman) Dr. Ed Norfleet. I can tell you from first hand experience these are incredibly talented and dedicated physicians and I GUARANTEE you will receive extraordinarily compassionate and gifted care if you come to any of the UNC Hospitals. Also want to take a moment to thank all the attendings, the residents and the office staff support

461

team up there for making it so easy for MY team to do our jobs. All of us behind the camera are moved by what we see you do every day and it is an honor to capture that experience on tape.

As always, you inspire us....

919-966-5136

Victory Junction Gang
4500 Adam's Way
Randleman, NC

I first worked with Kyle Petty on a Kendall Oil commercial quite a while ago now.... I think he's moved on to Mountain Dew and other sponsors since, but I know for a fact one thing has remained the same: this guy is one of the NICEST celebrities you're ever gonna meet. He's a guy who is INCREDIBLY aware and appreciative of his fans. That day we shot the Kendall Oil spots, Kyle spent more time posing for pictures and signing autographs for the crew than he did on the commercial itself! He coulda (and most big shots WOULDA) left as soon as their part of the commercial was done, but not Kyle. He stayed to make sure he made everybody happy and signed and smiled and posed till even I thought, jeez, we need to let this poor guy GO HOME already! And then he saw some fans gathered in the parking lot and went outside and signed and posed some MORE. A really good guy.

The proof of that is in how he has used his celebrity status to help so many people and charities over the years. The latest and greatest achievement has to be the Victory Junction Gang. He and his wife Patty founded this place as a retreat or summer camp for kids with chronic illnesses and serious diseases in June of 2004 in memory and honor of their son, Adam. The best I can say is, Victory Junction is a lot like Haleyland in that you gotta SEE it to BELIEVE it! It'll just knock

462

your socks off! Completely tricked out in a Nascar/racing motif, the entire place (from buildings shaped like race cars to dorm lockers shaped liked old fashioned gas pumps) is a Dr, Suess-like explosion of color and humor designed to make critically ill children forget their troubles for a little while and just be kids again. And lest you think Kyle and Patty have forgotten the GIRLS, well, first off remember there are a LOT of female Nascar fans, AND you should know there are plenty of female touches down there too, including a racecar themed beauty salon! Check out their web site and see for yourself. You could do a lot of good for some kids and their moms and dads by sending some money or volunteering there!

It is a dream of mine to get EIGHTwentythree to go on down and play for Kyle and his kids one day. And on a personal note, I MUST go on record as saying Kyle Petty has looked me right in the eye and SAID he was a guitar player, though I have yet to get to pick with him, so maybe we'll get him on stage with us for a song or two!

www.victoryjunction.org
336-498-9055 (Office)
336-498-9090 (Fax)

Vin Rouge
2010 Hillsborough Road
Durham, NC

Wow what a restaurant! Not the place to go if you're on a budget, but if you wanna go spend some money on some food that is about as close to ART as you can get, you need to get on over to Durham and take a seat. I go there with the dazzling and delightful Barbara Haight as much as I can and though the company is always compelling, it's the amazing food that brings me back again and again. Add to that a down to earth, knowledgeable staff who can guide you to the best meal selections and the best wines to compliment the meal. Chef Mathew Kelly, Sous Chef Douglas Freeman and their staff are just plain GENIUSES with food. Not cheap, but worth every penny. VERY highly recommended.

www.ghgrestaurants.com
vinrougeinfo@ghgrestaurants.com
919-416-0466

Wes Lambe Guitars

Well I finally did get my act together and tell Wes exactly what I wanted in my mandolin and that boy went off and created the Blue Mandolin you see on the cover of this here book via an amazing photo by J.J. Love. As pretty as it is to look at, it is sure a pure pleasure to HEAR. And man, to PLAY that sweet thing, well, its just heaven. As I write this its about two years old and has really settled in and is aging and refining nicely with a clean, bold sound and a deep, rich timbre. When I first got it, it played like a dream but as the weeks went by, the intonation went off and the action got higher and I finally called Wes all freaked out and sweaty and agitated cause my perfect mandolin was going bad, or so I thought. Now, on one level, I KNEW that every hand made instrument needs a little settling in time, and, in truth, we won't know the true depth of the projection and tone for the Blue Mandolin for several more years now, and I know that, KNEW it then but I was just ALL discombobulated and pulling what little hair I got on my head out when I called poor Wes for some help. He very calmly reminded me how he had told me, WARNED me, this would likely happen, and very coolly and reassuringly murmured, "Just bring her over to the shop John, I'll take care of it, it's no big deal, we knew this was gonna happen, just bring her on over, I'll make it better..."

So I jumped in my car and flew over there and started out good, but by the time I got to his shop I was all bent outa shape again and just blusterin and frantic and a very serene Wes Lambe met me in the gravel driveway outside his shop and extended his hands toward me like a preacher at a baptism to accept my crippled baby.

"John," he said calmly, "A couple of months ago it was Tree. And now it's a Mandolin. It's got some issues, ok??"

And putting his arm around my shoulder, he walked me inside to get it taken care of.

Now that right there is the kinda guy you want makin yer instruments, I tell you what.

Great guy, great maker.

Highly recommended.

www.wlguitars.com

919-932-9729 Shop

919-302-5236 Cell

Songs of
Bluegrass is
My Second
Language

For Mark

THE SONGS OF

Bluegrass Is My Second Language

A Year In The Life Of An Accidental Bluegrass Musician

It is one of the great regrets of my life as a musician that I don't read or write music very well. My only defense is that if Bach or Mozart were alive today, I'm not sure they would either. In the age of instant and easy recording, notation is imprecise and slow at best. RE-CORDING (which I have been fortunate to have access to for most of my musical life), is EXACT and IMME-DIATE. Thus I turned to others more skilled than I to assist in getting these songs out to you, the reader. I hope you enjoy them.

Lisa Pepin, one of my best guitar students, did the first transcription work on these songs. She laid the groundwork for which Michael Capps, a music teacher and horn player, built the songs you see before you now. I beg your indulgence here for the nuances of a skilled vocalist (as Greg Eldred, the singer of both "Watching The Water Rise" and Jeff Wiseman's "A Little Melody" certainly is) are difficult to notate when working from a recording. I supervised and approved the songs in this book. Any error of transcription or omission is solely mine. Any offense to any of the songwriters is deeply regretted.

The idea of including the songs mentioned in the book was to give you a little added value, a little more bang for your buck. I try to be appreciative of your time and money.

Thanks to Tyler Brown, a gifted trumpet player

(and Martin Brown's son), for his help with the songs
and for leading me to Michael Capps.

By the time you read this, I hope to have this sheet
music in down loadable form and available to hear on my
website, www.bluegrassbook.com.

MIGHT be a CD on there too if you look around
a little...

CONTENTS

Wanted to put a Blues tune in so you would see
what Shepp and I could do. Love this song....

Jeff Wiseman is a really great composer. This one
is a semi-autobiographical song: Jeff's dad really did work
in the mines of West Virginia.

This is for Jeff's wife, Amy, since she liked it so
much the first time she heard it when I played it for the
guys in Jeff and Amy's living room up in Reidsville.

Before I bought the Blue Mandolin I was looking everywhere for a good mandolin. Jimmy Wren
brought an old Gibson in to the Music Loft and Jim
Dennis grabbed it for me to look at. While I was playing
it (upside down since I'm left handed) I stumbled on to
this melody. Decided not to buy the mandolin, but the
melody stuck and I ended up finishing the song on my old
Epiphone lefty mando. Seemed like the least I could do
was name the song after Jimmy Wren, so I did.

Fireman's Carry (for E. Miller)
I was carrying fragments of this tune around in my head for weeks and was humming it one afternoon while working in my studio. There is a big red fire truck sitting on top of my computer, a gift from a former Out Of The Blue director, Emily Miller.

(It's a long story.... I'll explain some other time....)

Looked up, saw the fire truck, thought of Emily, thought about carrying that tune around, smiled and gave her the song. Finished it a few days later.

High Lonesome Strings
The theme song for Pammy Davis and the High Lonesome Strings Bluegrass Association. Pammy partic- ularly likes the line "...I never met a stranger...who carried a guitar..."

Me too.

Sandy Yeggo (for Jen DeMik)
Was missing hearing Jen sing since she'd moved to San Diego and wrote a simple, sorta wistful melody. The first song I ever wrote on the Blue Mandolin.

Them Blues
Put this in as an example of a weird sorta crossover tune Shepp and I came up with. It starts real bluesy and then goes into a folky, rock kinda thing then ends back in the Blues (sorta). Weird song but VERY powerful when done with a good arrangement and dynamics.

Last Night..page 493
    First Bluegrass song Shepp and I ever wrote, and frankly, it's a still a KILLER! Both to play (it's FAST) and SING (long holds and cool harmonies!) and listen to!
    Note the reference to dogs in the lyrics. Wonder where THAT came from...

Jimmy Johnson's Shop.....................................page 496
    Tried to write this so it would stand alone as a good (and humorous) song but also have it mean more (sort of an inside joke) if you read my book. I like to sing it in a Steve Earle kinda vocal but I REALLY want Greg to sing it....

Watching The Water Rise...............................page 500
    One of the best examples of Greg Eldred's art: a seemingly basic song with great lyrical and musical hooks and what appears to be a simple melody line, but is in fact, in the hands of a gifted singer like Greg, a really intricate vocal. Incredibly well crafted, it is one of our bands most popular songs. (I love to sing it when Greg's not around but I can never do the vocal justice like he can. Still.... it's fun to try...)

Lord Lord Lord

John Santa and Shepp Wasdell

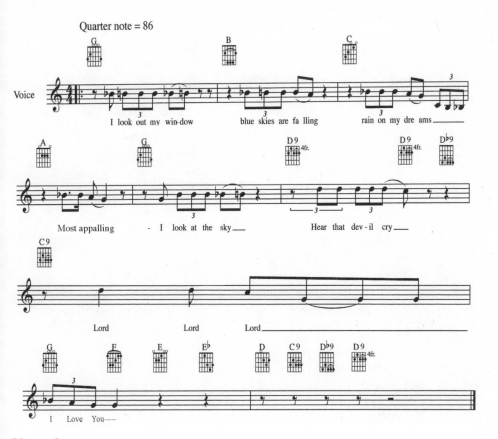

Verse 2

Lightning flashes across the sky, Thunder crashes and so do I, I look at the sky, Hear that devil cry, Lord, Lord, Lord, I love you

Verse 3

Rain on my window silently weeps, Pain in my heart bitterly sweet, Everytime I see you my heart skips a beat, Lord, Lord, Lord, I love you

Verse 4

Wet water colors hang from the trees, Rain touches everyone it heals the disease, Somewhere blue skies live, Give it all you can give, Lord, Lord, Lord, I love you

477

A Little Melody

Jeff Wiseman

478

A Little Melody

479

F   C   F   C   G

In time

Third verse

I came back from the city
with my boys to the old home place
on the front porch sat ol' daddy
with his fiddle he was ready to play

to chorus

Song Structure: verse, chorus, verse, chorus, bridge, verse, chorus, tag

* Stop time - allows lead singer show off while band strums on notated chords

Copyright Jeff Wiseman 2006

Bluegrass Widows

John Santa and Shepp Wasdell

Quarter note = 118

Voice

Well it's six o'-clo-ck on a Sat-ur-day eve-ning and I'm driv-ing out on highway eight-y
night aft-er night the wid - ows listen to that mus - ic so by now they know all the

sev - en North - west up to Reidsville I'll fly in-to the sun I'm gonna play me some music and have some
songs - And when the boys get rock-ing they all gather round the door___ to see what all___ the fuss is

fun When I get to the part - y I park un-load my gear and I go in-side and take___ a___
for And a part of them wond-ers just what is go-ing on how could their men be so tak-en by a

chair And all the boys say howd-y come on let's get in tune be-cause the mus-ic will be starting prett - y
song But they love that mus ic too and they know just what to do so they smile and___ soft-ly sing a-

soon And the blue - grass wid-ows sit in the oth-er room and they - tap their fe - et in
long And the blue - grass wid-ows sit in the oth-er room and they - tap their fe - et in

481

Bluegrass is my Second Language

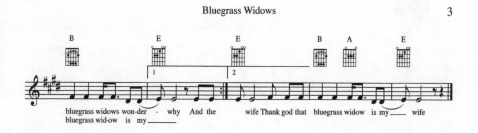

bluegrass widows won-der - why And the wife Thank god that bluegrass widow is my___ wife
bluegrass wid-ow is my___

The Mandolin in Jimmy Wren's Closet Rag

John Santa

Fireman's Carry
(for E. Miller)

John Santa

Fireman's Carry

High Lonesome Strings

Written for High Lonesome Strings Bluegrass Society

John Santa

487

High Lonesome Strings

high   lone - some   strings (High   lone - some   strings)   Go and get   your   fidd - le   out   and
high   lone - some   strings (High   lone - some   strings)   Go and get   your   guit - ar   we'll   play

ros - in   up   the   bow (High   lone - some   strings)   Break   out   the   fing - er   picks   and
ev' - ry   song   you   know (High   lone - some   strings)   Break   out   the   fing - er   picks   and

play   your   old   ban - jo (High   lone - some   strings)   Gath - er   in   a   circ - le   now   and
play   your   old   do - bro (High   lone - some   strings)   List - en   to   the   bass   play - er   just

let   your   voi - ces   ring   I need the   sweet soul-ful   sound __ of those   high   lone-some strings
thump ing   on that   thing   I love the   sweet soul-ful   sound __ of those

high   lone - some   strings   I   hear   the   sweet   soul - ful   sound __   of   those

high lonesome strings I need the   sweet soulful sound __ of those   hi - gh   lo - ne - some   strings

tenuto

Sandy Yeggo
(For Jen De Mik)

John Santa

Sandy Yeggo

Them Blues

John Santa and Shepp Wasdell

John Santa

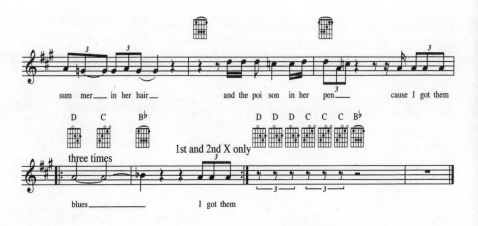

sum mer___ in her hair___   and the poi son in her pen___   cause I got them

three times   1st and 2nd X only

blues___   I got them

Bluegrass is my Second Language

Last Night

John Santa and Shepp Wasdell

Quarter Note = 130

Last night the thun-der and light-ning was call-ing me to bring you home
Well you said your love was mine and no one could take that love a - way

Last night the dogs - were barking and howl-ing cause I was all a -
Well you said then I said but those words are all dead just one more thing for you to

lone You must be some kind of girl if you can love like that you know how to drive me in-
say

sane But I'll tell you one thing, it's no lie that you're bringing me pain

The good Lord a-bove is gon-na see what you done, you know your day will come You

493

think it's al-right 'cause you ain't a - lone at night but I tell you it ain't the_ Same no it ain't the

Same Your at - ten tion was-pleas ing but you were just teas-ing a - bout the prom-ise that you

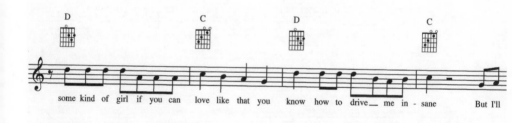

made But now in the cold light Right here in broad day - light I was be - trayed You must be

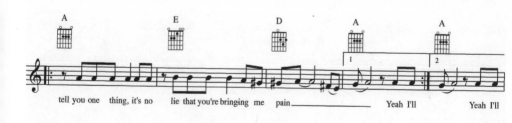

some kind of girl if you can love like that you know how to drive__ me in - sane But I'll

tell you one thing, it's no lie that you're bringing me pain_____ Yeah I'll Yeah I'll

494

Bluegrass is my Second Language

Last Night

tell you one thing, it's no lie that you're bring - ing me pa - in hey - y hey-een

Jimmy Johnson's Shop

John Santa

497

Jimmy Johnson's Shop

cards old Jake will stand guard and the mus - ic don't ev - er

stop   But them girls on the wa - lls just don't re - turn my

calls up at Jim - my John - son's sho— p   Up at

Jim - - - my____ John - - - son's   shop___

Watching the Water Rise

Greg Eldred

Bluegrass is my Second Language

Watching the Water Rise

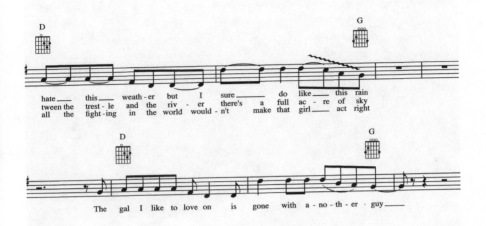

hate___ this___ weath - er but I sure___ do like___ this rain
tween the trest - le and the riv - er there's a full ac - re of sky
all the fight - ing in the world would - n't make that girl___ act right

The gal I like to love on is gone with a - no - th - er · guy___

The Final Word

(Finally...)

Well if you're still with me after all this time
and all these words, I reckon that means I did SOME-
THING right, and God Bless you for stickin with me
all this way. If you read this far, I am in your debt,
and if you PAID for this book and read this far, well
then I am DOUBLY in your debt and appreciate your
investments, both financial and intellectual.

I truly do.

My friends are currently pretty upset with me
because I am experiencing a kinda separation anxiety
and I can't seem to quite be able to finish this book
and they are wanting me to git the darn thing DONE
and get it on out and PUBLISHED already! See, I
have been working on this thing for several years now,
and as much as I complained about the process of
writing a book to you, I have grown quite accustomed
to it and frankly, I am gonna miss the damn thing and
I find I am in no particular hurry to be done with it!

But then stuff like THIS happens to me that
makes me know it's time:

I walk into the Calvander Crossroads Grill one
early morning to get me some eggs and biscuits and I
hear Rhonda's voice booming out from in back:

"John," she roars from the kitchen, "Where in
the hell is my damn book??"

I love it when God reaches down and just
thumps you behind the ear like that, just to get your
attention.

"Hmmm..." I said to myself, "Gettin on time to

git that book out I reckon...."

But I was still not in a hury to say goodbye to you wonderful readers, the folks who gathered around my computer at night, the ones I tried to make laugh and cry and share my stories with. And then about ten days ago, I finished writing the Shameless Plugs section and I leaned back in my chair and something caught my eye. See, for the past two, two and half years, the entire frame of my computer screen has been literally plastered with post-it notes. Notes to check the spelling of this, to make sure you tell that story, check the web address for so and so. And about one in the morning that fateful night, the pale yellow note caught my attention and I said to myself, Oh, I already DID that and reached up and pulled it off and threw it in the trash. But there was ANOTHER tab under that one, and lo and behold, I had already TOLD that story, so I tore the post-it off and trashed it and kept reading and pulling and trashing and finally, for the first time in two and a half years, my computer screen is empty of post-it notes.

Except for one.

And that one is for Paul Cyr's dad who passed away a little while ago. I needed to make sure to put Paulie's dad's name in the dedication section of the Glossary, and now I have done that and if you look on page 443 you will see Gillman Cyr listed there with the other good folks we all miss so very much. And so except to tell you that Martin Brown does a great old timey rendition of "You Are My Sunshine" and whenever we play it, we play it extra good because we send it on out to Mr. Gillman Cyr, Paulie's dad, since that was his favorite song, I can no longer deny the fact that I am done.

This book is finished.

My book is finished.

There's a saying in show biz:

Always leave em laughing.

So even though I am gonna miss being with you all, and I am sad at the thought of leaving you, I will honor that tradition to the best of my ability.

I sent a copy of my manuscript up to my friend Jody O'Brien in New York City to see how the book would play in the Big Apple.

In response, Jody sent me banjo jokes.

(BANJO jokes from New York City!!! Who'd a thought THAT could happen???)

Turns out Bluegrass is pretty big in New York City.

(Who knew??)

So here's the joke she sent that made me laugh the loudest, and with that, I'll say Bye.

Bluegrass is my Second Language

What's the difference between

a banjo and a chain saw?

A chain saw has dynamic range.

Bluegrass is my Second Language

THE END

JOHN SANTA

is an award winning
Producer and Musician.
He proudly lives in Chapel Hill, NC
with his dogs,
Blue and Minor.

"Some say the glass is half full...

Some say half empty...

John just drinks the water."

-Mac Monroe

I met John Santa almost two years ago and the first time I walked into his home my jaw dropped. He had more musical instruments in his living room than I had ever seen in any one place before. Ideas of photoshoots swam through my head and a few months later when I worked up the courage to ask him if he would let a non-musician use his instruments for a shoot, he agreed.

The day of the shoot John was working on a DVD that focused on Belize. So while working with fiddles, mandolins and 12 strings, I was entertained with salsa, rumba's and cha-cha's being created by John.

A few months later when John asked me to make his cover (I was not as cocky as he said) I used a photo from the collection that I was beginning to fear would never be used. When John came to me with the aspect of creating the book I was intrigued. It was a chance to use the series of photographs that I loved.

Inspired by the music surrounding me, I bought my own guitar and took pictures of it, but being a novice, I didn't realize that mine was a "Cheap" guitar. Upon seeing the series of photographs in the book for the first time, John was taken aback by the less than professional guitar.

I explained to him that there are many, many people who will read this book who are not professional or can not afford expensive guitars, between Paula Shelton and I, we convinced him and the guitar on page 115 is mine.

Really I just wanted that picture in the book.

-JJ Love

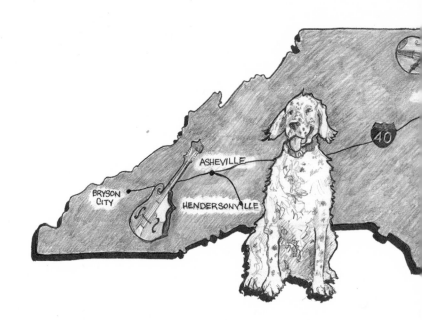

The Great State of
North Carolina